CHRONICLES OF

AGAMEMNON

ALEX KORNEYEV

PAGE PUBLISHING
Conneaut Lake, PA

First originally published by Page Publishing 2024

ISBN 979-8-89157-092-4 (pbk)
ISBN 979-8-89157-105-1 (digital)

Printed in the United States of America

CONTENTS

Part I.   Hesione
    Chapter 1:   Treaty with Laomedon 3
    Chapter 2:   Preparing the Assault on Troy..............................7
    Chapter 3:   Capture of Ilion 16
    Chapter 4:   Accession of Priam 33
    Chapter 5:   Exit from Ilion 40
    Chapter 6:   Departure from Troy 45

Part II.   Deianeira
    Chapter 1:   Meeting at the Gate...55
    Chapter 2:   Chat with the Priest 60
    Chapter 3:   Journey to Pisa 69
    Chapter 4:   King Broteas...72
    Chapter 5:   Escape from Pisa 78
    Chapter 6:   Dwelling in Calydon 91
    Chapter 7:   The Tale of Meleager 99
    Chapter 8:   Theseus Visits Calydon 106
    Chapter 9:   The Tale of Hercules 113

Part III.   Clytemnestra
    Chapter 1:   Return of the Atrides to Mycenae......................125
    Chapter 2:   Accession of Agamemnon...............................135
    Chapter 3:   Conversation with Diomedes 138
    Chapter 4:   Mission to Thesprotia.....................................146
    Chapter 5:   Vassals of Mycenae 149
    Chapter 6:   March on Sicyon 151
    Chapter 7:   Freeing of Theseus..155
    Chapter 8:   Theseus Comes Back to Athens........................159

Chapter 9:   The Plan for Attack on Tantalus Jr. 163
Chapter 10: Capture of Pisa..169
Chapter 11: Return to Mycenae...176
Chapter 12: Treaty with Sparta 180
Chapter 13: News from Calydon 182
Chapter 14: Visit of King Oeneus...188
Chapter 15: Birth of Orestes..194

Part IV.   Helen
Chapter 1:   Helen's Wedding 199
Chapter 2:   Birth of Hermione...206
Chapter 3:   Wars of Argos against Thebe.............................210
Chapter 4:   The Royal Scepter and Other Gifts of Gods 219
Chapter 5:   Trip to Crete 228
Chapter 6:   Kidnapping of Helen...237
Chapter 7:   Debate of Response 243
Chapter 8:   Tantalus's Kingdom Recovery Plan 250
Chapter 9:   Embassy of Menelaus in Ilion............................259

Part V.   Iphigenia
Chapter 1:   Menelaus Approves the Conquer of Mysia..........271
Chapter 2:   The Leaders Decide to Invite Achilles................282
Chapter 3:   Peleus's Requirement 288
Chapter 4:   Calchas Visits Phthia...298
Chapter 5:   Discussion of Peleus's Terms 307
Chapter 6:   Reply of Odysseus 310

Hypothetical Restoration of
Lion Gate Bas-Relief

Lion Gate Bas-Relief
Present Time

HESIONE

CHAPTER 1

TREATY WITH LAOMEDON

The king of Troy, Laomedon, summoned Hercules to defend Ilion from a monstrous threat and would not pay the promised reward for his labors. The risk of destroying the city had been so great that Laomedon had agreed to sacrifice his daughter, Hesione, to appease the gods.

Hercules's intervention had protected Ilion and saved Hesione. After the danger was left behind, a messenger went to the city to find out when to come for the reward. Hercules was waiting for an answer in the Achaean camp on the shore of the Hellespont. But the messenger returned with nothing. King Laomedon refused to see him.

The next morning, Hercules, accompanied by Telamon and several warriors, went to get an answer. After crossing the coastal hills and the Trojan plain, they waded across the Scamander River, flowing at the foot of the hill on which Ilion stayed. The travelers climbed the slope, walked along a well-worn road along a high stone wall, and stopped at the Scaean Gate, the main gate of the city, where, according to tradition, Laomedon received travelers. The gates were closed and guarded by warriors in bronze armor.

Seeing the Achaeans from the wall, the king's youngest son, teenage Podarces, shouted that Hercules had come to collect his reward. For the salvation of Ilion, the king had promised to give a couple of wonderful horses. They were much larger than ordinary ones and possessed great powers. Legend said that in the old days, the great king Tros, Laomedon's grandfather, sacrificed his son to the gods. The gods accepted the sacrifice. Among other rewards, Tros received several extraordinary horses capable of carrying a warrior with the speed of the wind.

Seeing the descendants of these horses at the royal stable in Ilion, Hercules had demanded a pair from Laomedon in payment for his service. However, the treacherous ruler of Troy did not keep his word. Instead of the promised ones, two regular, local horses harnessed to a chariot stood near the gate.

Telamon looked at the horses and at the warriors who were standing on the wall without tension and said, "It looks like Laomedon intends to breach the agreement. After all, King doesn't need anything else from you, and he's not afraid of your revenge. My father, Aeacus, complained more than once that just such a thing happened to him.

"I remember him telling me that many years ago he visited Troy. About that time, Laomedon hired builders from overseas countries to erect a new fortress wall around Ilion. My father admired their art, inherited from Poseidon himself. From the earthshaker, they learned to lay strong walls that are not afraid of earthquakes and did not pass their secrets to anyone.

"Look at the magnificent masonry. The entire southern and eastern walls of the city, as well as the towers at the Scaean Gate and to the east of them, were built by overseas craftsmen. As my father told me, vertical ledges every ten steps are the boundaries of the wall segments. You see how exactly they are laid out.

"The builders laid segment after segment and moved on to the next only after receiving a reward for the previous one. When they reached the western gate, the king did not pay for the last segment but demanded that they finish the entire western wall and tower, promising to pay for everything in its entirety. The builders rejected his offer and demanded he pay according to the contract—for each segment. They could not agree, and the builders left on their ships, calling on the lord of the sea, Poseidon, to punish the treacherous king.

"My father was one of those whom Laomedon hired to finish the western wall. Aeacus complained that a certain god had clouded his mind when he undertook to finish the work for which the previous masters had not been paid. The same thing happened to him. The king of Ilion did not pay either my father or his partners and threatened to cut off their ears and sell them into slavery if they did not get out of Troy. My father threatened more than once that if not himself, then his descendants would return to Troy to collect the debt.

"I heard from him that it is possible to storm Ilion from sunset. There is no more suitable place to find. And who better than him would know about it? Because he himself built the western wall. But Father's advice will not help us. Even if we had ten times as many warriors, they wouldn't even be enough to storm the western wall. The siege is also not worth thinking about, because the rulers of Dardania and other surrounding cities are always ready to help. The king of Troy has many Phrygian leaders as allies. They say he is also favored by the rulers of the great Hittite empire. Therefore, Laomedon does not doubt his impunity—"

"This time, he was fatally mistaken," Hercules interrupted.

Laomedon went up to the high tower crowning the Scaean Gate for negotiations. He rejected the demands for a just reckoning and ordered them to leave the borders of the Trojan kingdom. In response, Hercules vowed to return on his own and punish the king, calling the lord of Olympus, Zeus the Thunderer, to witness.

Resentment and rage demanded that he immediately rush to the assault, and ten years ago, he would have done so. Hercules saw that the western wall was damaged by recent earthquakes, and it would not be difficult to overcome it. However, the experience of many past battles suggested that Telamon was right. With forty warriors, he could not overthrow the defenders of Ilion. The insidious king had decided to disregard the contract and had probably prepared fighters at the gate in case of a possible conflict during the conversation.

There were not so many soldiers on the walls, Hercules thought, and if he had brought the whole squad with him, he could have risked a sudden, lightning assault. Of course, you couldn't take the city. But you could climb the wall, capture the king, and demand a ransom.

Suddenly, a suspicion came to mind. What if the treacherous king was counting on this? He knew that Hercules was returning from the campaign in Pontus, and his ship was loaded with rich booty. Attacking the famous hero who had just saved the city was very risky. But what if you provoked a confrontation, destroyed Hercules's squad, and seized the treasures?

This plan was quite feasible. Laomedon, as they said, managed to deceive even the gods. What if two dozen chariots were waiting behind the closed gates, ready to rush at the Achaeans at the first sign of the king? The way to the ship was not close, and it would be impossible to hide from rushing chariots on the flat plain that gently descended to the sea. The understanding of the reality of the threat cooled his rage.

Telamon saw that Hercules was considering immediate retaliation. Trying to sway him against the attack, he said, "My father once told me that revenge is like wine. The longer it ages, the more pleasant it is to taste."

"But if you wait too long, the wine can get spoiled, or there will be no wine left to enjoy," replied Hercules.

He hesitated briefly, waved his hand, and headed away from the city to the ship. After persuading Telamon to swear to take revenge on Laomedon, Hercules sailed to Peloponnese.

CHAPTER 2

PREPARING THE ASSAULT ON TROY

Many years passed before Hercules returned to Ilion to fulfill his oath. First, he had to complete his years of service with the king of Mycenae, Eurystheus. This service was both punishment and treatment for the murder of children he committed in a state of mental confusion.

Then there was an unsuccessful attempt to marry the daughter of King Eurytus and the murder of his son. As a punishment, Hercules had to serve three years in Asia with Queen Omphale. She ruled in a large city located at the foot of Mount Tmolus, about five days' journey southeast of Troy.

Shortly before the end of his service, Hercules heard that a large detachment of Trojan warriors had gone far to the east to participate in the military campaigns of the Hittite empire. Hercules knew about the enormous military power of the Hittite rulers, and not by hearsay. He had witnessed and participated in the grand encounters of the Hittite and Egyptian armies. Hercules could compare these battles only with the titanic fights of the gods. However, that was in the past, and now it was time to return to Peloponnese.

Hercules arrived in Smyrna with a modest reward for the years of service and boarded the ship sailing for Nafplion. Leaving the port early next morning, the ship moved by oars to the exit of the bay. Looking at the rocky coast, Hercules recalled the legends about Tantalus, who in ancient years was the lord of these territories.

Tantalus, like Hercules, considered himself the son of the almighty Zeus. He ruled a rich kingdom spread out between the rivers Kaikos and Meander with the capital at Mount Sipylus on the southern bank of the river Hermus. According to storytellers, less than a century had passed since Tantalus started a war with the ruler of Dardania and Troy, King Tros.

Some said that Tros was the first to seize the lands of Tantalus in the valley of Kaikos. According to others, Tantalus himself attacked neighboring rulers, trying to expand the limits of his kingdom. The war was long and went on with varying success. Before the decisive battle, Tros received a prophecy that the one who sacrificed the most precious to the gods would win. Inferior in military strength to Tantalus, he was ready to do anything and gave to the gods his eldest son. The sacrifice was accepted, and Tros won a decisive victory.

Tantalus perished in the battle, and his son, Pelops, retreated south, beyond the river Hermus. From there, he continued the war with Tros and, later, with Tros's son, King Il. Il enlisted the support of his brother, the famous warrior Assarakos, and of other neighboring rulers. At the head of the united army, he crossed the river Hermus and attacked the last stronghold of Pelops at Mount Sipylus.

Pelops defended stubbornly but was defeated. He was forced to leave Phrygia and sail to Peloponnese, and his kingdom was divided by Il and his allies. Later, Pelops managed to conquer the Pisan kingdom in Elis and became an influential ruler in Peloponnese. However, in his old age, he quarreled with his wife and sons and was forced to hand over the throne to his younger brother, Broteas, a cripple devoid of ambitious aspirations.

The children of Pelops dispersed throughout Peloponnese. Two of them, Atreus and Thyestes, went to Argolis. Hercules met the grandsons of King Tantalus in Mycenae several times. When the influence of Pelops came to naught, Mycenae rose and became the most powerful city in Peloponnese. The current ruler of Mycenae, Eurystheus, fortified the city and expanded its possessions.

Hercules served the king of Mycenae for many years. But despite his faithful service and kinship, Eurystheus became increasingly hostile to him over time. When Hercules's term of service came to an end, Eurystheus expelled him from Mycenae, setting aside Tiryns for the residence. Hercules no longer appeared in Mycenae. At about the same time, the sons of Pelops, Atreus and Thyestes, came into power at the court of Eurystheus.

After leaving the bay, the ship turned to the west. Hercules frowned at the sea, covered with morning haze. On the right, the coast of the blessed Lesbos was approaching; and at the end of the strait separating the island from Asia, there was Mount Ida. Beyond it lay the Trojan kingdom. Il had ruled there in the old days, and now Il's son, Laomedon, reigned. Hercules recalled the grave insult inflicted years ago by Laomedon. The feeling of anger that he experienced then woke up in him with the same force, inspiring him to action.

Thinking the situation over, Hercules found more and more arguments in favor of going after King Laomedon. The raid will not only be a reckoning with the perjurer, but it will also help improve his financial situation, which was much to be desired after many years of service and numerous family troubles.

By the time he arrived in his native Tiryns, he was sure that the day had come for a march to Troy. However, it was not easy to assemble a detachment sufficient to capture a large and well-fortified city. Ilion was long known in Peloponnese for his wealth and power. The city controlled the vicinity of Mount Ida and the Hellespont, through which trade between Hellas and the coastal cities of Pontus Euxinus passed. King Laomedon had strengthened and expanded his possessions in the many years of his reign. He could attract numerous allies from Phrygia, Thrace, and other surrounding lands to his side.

Hercules, admittedly, was the strongest fighter of his time. He was invincible in hand-to-hand combat and was a successful leader of several military campaigns. But apart from the modest wage he received for three years of service in Asia, Hercules did not have the means to recruit and maintain any significant army until the booty from the campaign began to cover the costs.

In densely populated Tiryns and neighboring Nafplion, where Hercules enjoyed well-deserved fame, it was possible to recruit hundreds of fighters. However, Tiryns was part of the Mycenaean sphere of influence, and the king's dislike for Hercules was widely known. Hercules believed that the fear of trouble from Eurystheus would prevent the recruitment of soldiers in Tiryns, Mycenae, and other cities of Argolis.

He sent a messenger to Mycenae to Atreus with an offer to join the campaign against Troy and to avenge his father's defeat but received no response. The powerful rulers of Peloponnese, such as the king of Sparta, Hippocoon; the king of Elis, Augeas; and the king of Pylos, Neleus, also did not have warm feelings for Hercules, which meant it was not realistic to count on their help.

Trying to find the opportunities for recruiting troops, Hercules thought hopefully about Telamon, together with whom he once carried out a couple of risky campaigns. At that time, Telamon, a young warrior exiled from his native island of Aegina for murder, was ready to risk everything to achieve fame and fortune. Now he was a wealthy ruler of a small island state, Salamis, and married to the daughter of an influential king.

Telamon's participation was not only important, but it would also help attract his brother Peleus, an unsurpassed swordsman, and other famous warriors and leaders. However, would Telamon remember the promise he once made and go on a risky undertaking? It was possible to learn only at a personal meeting.

The journey from Tiryns to Megara, where the nearest ferry to Salamis was located, would take two days. Already sailing to the island, Hercules learned that Telamon's wife was about to give birth, and the king's friends had gathered to celebrate the joyful event.

"Long live the valiant lord of Salamis, and might luck be with him in all matters," Hercules shouted as he entered the banquet hall.

Telamon rose to meet him, and having filled a cup with wine, he handed it to Hercules.

"I greet you, godlike Hercules. Ballads about your exploits are heard in all parts of Peloponnese. Take a place of honor at our table and share a meal with us."

It will not be easy to convince Telamon to go to Ilion, Hercules thought, looking at the tables filled with delicious food and at the happy faces of the numerous guests and servants hurrying around.

Having refreshed himself after a long journey, he sat down closer to Telamon.

"Let me congratulate you again, Telamon. A bountiful island and a lovely wife—a worthy reward for your exploits and valor. What is life like in your kingdom?"

Telamon looked intently at Hercules.

"Everything is calm on Salamis. The gardens and vineyards are full of fruits, and fishing nets bring plenty of fish. Friends are feasting with us, and enemies are far away. I am glad to see you, great Hercules. After you went to Asia, there was no news about you for a long time. I only recently found out that you have returned from your voyages, having performed great deeds and with worthy rewards. We want to hear about your exploits, because travel stories are not only enjoyable but also broaden your horizons."

Hercules had a lot to tell, but he didn't want to get stuck in a long conversation and miss the purpose of his visit.

"King of Salamis, I have seen and experienced lots of truly amazing things, which I will tell you with pleasure. You know that in the east of Asia is the great Hittite empire, to which all the neighboring states and many rulers of the Syrian lands pay tribute. The Hittite kings do not worship our gods and are so powerful and invincible that they are called titans.

"Beyond Syria, if you move along the sea, you will meet the cities of the Phoenicians, whose ships often come to our shores. If then you turn westward following the seashore, you will come to the great Nile River in the Egyptian kingdom, of which you have certainly heard. Egyptians worship the same gods as we do, only they call them by different names and believe that the country is ruled by a god in the appearance of a pharaoh.

"The pharaohs of Egypt have long been at war with the Hittite kings. In one of the battles of this war, which surpassed in scale anything I have ever seen or could imagine, I happened to participate. I will be glad to tell you about this terrible battle and many other things, but first, I have a question. Do you remember how many years ago, during our joint wanderings, we happened to visit Ilion, one of the richest cities on the Asian coast of the Hellespont?"

"It was a long time ago, but I have kept in my memory the exploits that you performed in the Trojan lands," Telamon replied.

"Do you recall the task we have accomplished on the request of Laomedon and his promise of cumbersome reward? But when the work was finished, he paid nothing. The ruler of Troy deceived me, just as he deceived your father, the godly Aeacus, many years ago. Now it's time to punish a scoundrel. If it pleases the gods, I intend to call Laomedon to account. Ilion is a rich town. The king has accumulated huge treasures by taking tribute from the ships passing through the Hellespont. Those who help me punish the perjurer will receive a worthy reward.

"Tell, Telamon, can I count on you to march on to Troy? After all, Laomedon deceived your father, the favorite of gods, Aeacus. Remember, you told me how Aeacus predicted that his descendants would collect the debt from the king. We are going to do the right thing and become famous among the Achaeans as unbeatable warriors. You know, Telamon, that I have crushed all my enemies, and the king of Troy is no exception. Remember, you took an oath to come back with me to Ilion. It's time to keep this vow."

After a short silence, Telamon spoke.

"Truly, you have suggested a glorious venture, valiant Hercules. The campaign to Troy has worthy goals—to punish the perjurer and get the reward that belongs to you by right. The restoration of justice will please the gods. Indeed, my father said that what was not paid to him by the ruler of Ilion would be recovered by his descendants. I do not dare to judge whether it was a prediction or a wish.

"However, you know that my wife is expecting offspring, and I cannot leave her without making sure that everything is in order. Therefore, I suggest you stay with me in Salamis and discuss this enterprise in detail with a fresh head soon. I would like to hear how you plan to sail, how many ships and warriors you intend to take, and how to carry out the siege and capture of Ilion.

"I remember that the city was well-fortified and had a standing army already in the years when we happened to visit there. King Laomedon has many influential allies. Invincible Hercules, we must have a plan that leaves no doubt of success. We'll talk about this later, and now let's indulge in fun and relaxation."

Days passed by, but Telamon was in no rush to commit to take part in the campaign. He listened with interest to the news that a large detachment of Trojan warriors had recently gone to the east and supported the intention of Hercules to hurry with the raid before the Trojans returned. He nodded in agreement to the proposal to carry out an assault immediately after landing since the siege of a fortified city would require much more manpower, effort, and time.

Hercules revealed his tactical plan to go to Troy from the north and not from the south, as merchants usually did. After all, Ilion itself and the royal coastal outposts were located on the southern shore of the strait. In order not to be noticed, Hercules decided to ascend to the Hellespont along the shores of Thrace and approach Imbros from the north. The invaders would rest, waiting for the tide, hiding behind Cape Chersoneses, and would cross the Hellespont from north to south.

Hercules knew well that ships usually kept to the southern shore because the current coming from the Hellespont was especially strong near the northern shore. Therefore, all the outposts of Trojans, like Ilion itself, were located on the southern shore. However, he hoped that the mighty rowers would be able to row against the current and land on the shore above the mouth of the Scamander, at the shortest distance from Ilion. After that, using the knowledge of the terrain, they would immediately move to the town and storm the walls without wasting time on setting up a camp.

"Yes, that is a good plan," said Telamon. "This is what sea robbers do, counting on the reluctance of the townspeople to immediately take up arms. On the other hand, Ilion is built at a sufficient distance from the sea to have time to prepare for an assault when attacked by pirates.

"In addition, the town of Laomedon is surrounded by a high wall. Even the wall damaged by an earthquake on the eve of our previous visit presented a significant obstacle. Enough years have passed since then, and Laomedon most likely repaired and strengthened the wall.

"I remember my father saying that the walls of Ilion are nearly impregnable. Only some sections of the western wall need strong protection, but one can quickly gather warriors from the city there. Moreover, soon after the alarm signal, detachments from the suburbs and surrounding villages will begin to approach the town."

Hercules understood that the habit of a quiet life and doubts about the success of the raid on the powerful Trojan city compelled Telamon to search for evidences of the difficulty of the undertaking. The ruler of Salamis did not want to offend the guest. He tried to show how small the chances were of taking the city, hoping that Hercules himself, after thinking it over, would abandon the campaign. Of course, the risk was inevitable, but it was outweighed by the chances of surprise attack and the size of the expected trophy.

Hercules did not have time to start talking. A cry came from the women's quarters, and a moment later, a maid came running to report that the queen had successfully delivered a boy from the burden. The guests were scattered in congratulations, and Telamon ordered to take the baby to the show. Hercules was glad for Telamon and for the fact that the forced waiting had come to an end.

If Telamon's answer was negative, it would not be easy to assemble a squad.

It is a pity that Theseus is not in Athens now. He would certainly join the campaign, so thought Hercules while looking at the strait and the coast of Attica lying behind it.

Thanks to his keen eyesight, even at this distance, he could see the figures of fishermen on the shore and wondered what the catch was. If seagulls were hovering over fishermen when fishermen were cleaning their prey, then the catch should be good. However, at this distance, you needed the vision of Apollo to see a bird soaring in the sky.

He tried to focus his eyes on the far shore and suddenly saw a point floating in the sky. There was only one dot, so it was not a seagull. Besides, she was much closer, already over the strait. After a minute, he began to distinguish the movements of the wings and was almost sure whom they belonged to judging by the frequency and rhythm of the flaps.

At that moment, the newborn was brought into the gallery, and Hercules suddenly realized that the gods were giving him a decisive chance to convince Telamon. He suddenly walked to the front and took the baby from the nurse's arms.

"Courageous Telamon," said Hercules, "you have become a father. By the grace of Zeus the Thunderer, your firstborn will be as invincible a warrior and as loyal a friend as his father. I ask the lord of heaven to give a sign that my prayer will be heard, and I name your son Ajax."

Telamon got up from the bench and stared at Hercules in amazement. He knew that Hercules considered himself the son of Zeus. Moreover, even the earthly father of Hercules, Amphitryon, believed in this. But for the first time, Telamon witnessed his direct appeal to the god, and he watched as Hercules, carefully giving the baby to the nurse, turned and stretched his hand out to the sea, where a distant point turned into an eagle approaching on slow flaps of the wings, a sure sign that Zeus had heard and approved the prayer.

C H A P T E R   3

CAPTURE OF ILION

Hercules sailed to Troy, leading a fleet of eighteen ships. Six of them were under his command. The other vessels carried the warriors of Telamon, Peleus, Dimachus, Oikles, and other leaders. The chosen path led north along the coasts of Thessaly and Macedonia, skirting Cape Athos and turning east past Thasos to Samothrace.

The builders of Ilion had positioned the city far enough from the coast so the citizens had time to take up defense when enemy ships appeared. Hercules knew that Laomedon had an observation post on Tenedos. If the ships were spotted from there, the king of Troy would have time to prepare for an assault. An attack with such a small detachment could be successful only if unexpected.

Hercules had decided that having bypassed Samothrace from the north, the ships would turn south and approach Imbros, remaining invisible from the Trojan coast and Tenedos. At the northern shore of Imbros, he would give the rowers a rest and, leaving in the afternoon, would go around Cape Chersoneses and cross the Hellespont with a powerful push.

If the attackers were lucky, they would land and would be on the way to Ilion by the time the costal guards gave the signal and defensive forces began to assemble in the town. Hercules, Telamon, and several other warriors had already been to the Trojan coast and could find the route to the town at dusk. The darkness and surprise should help to climb the walls.

Before sailing from Samothrace, where the detachment had stopped for a day's rest, Hercules ordered sacrifices to the gods and reminded the helmsmen that as soon as they rounded the Chersoneses, they should start raking hard against the current, striving to land as far as possible at sunrise. Despite the confidence in victory, which he tirelessly demonstrated in conversations, Hercules understood that he would have a chance of success only with a lightning assault on the walls of Ilion.

As soon as Laomedon realized that the threat to the town was real, he would call for help. Within a few days, he would be able to assemble an army in Troy and Dardania that would far exceed the incomplete thousand fighters that Hercules had brought. Then the capture of the city and even the preservation of one's own life would become very doubtful. Therefore, he decided to risk everything, including the ships, in the hope of outrunning fate and climbing the walls of Ilion ahead of the soldiers of Laomedon.

He knew from previous visits that coastguards were more often on the shore west of the mouth of the Scamander. There, from the coastal hills, they looked out for ships coming from the south and kept in touch with Trojan outposts on Tenedos. Of course, the guards would see the ships crossing the Hellespont. But most likely, they would not have time to reach the landing site or get the support of sufficient forces to attack. If the Achaeans landed east of the river mouth, they could avoid a fight during the landing, as well as the need to cross the Scamander in the night. This might be enough to tip the scales of fortune.

The sacrifices to the gods were not in vain. A fair northern wind was blowing into the sails when the ships crossed the Hellespont, and the rowers could make every effort to row to the east. Having found a convenient place with a gentle, sandy shore, the ships landed without meeting anyone.

Watching the fighters disembark, Hercules wondered how much time had passed since the messenger sent to the town by the guards had set off.

"If the captain of the guard thinks that the pirates will not act until next morning," he told his companions, "the messenger to Ilion will not be in a hurry. Then we have a chance to reach the walls of the city not much later than him."

However, hopes for the sluggishness of the enemy did not come true. When Hercules, accompanied by several warriors, climbed one of the coastal hills to inspect the surroundings and plan a route to Ilion, signs that the town had been notified were evident. In the last glimmer of the passing day, he saw the walls of the city on the opposite side of the coastal plain, saw the roads coming out of the gates.

Hercules noticed the lights motionless at the gates and wavering from the flickering torches on the towers. But most of all, he was looking at a group of lights slowly gliding from the western gate toward the Hellespont, where his ships landed. He assumed that this was a group of scouts and that their goal was to find out about the intentions and delay the aliens until the approach of the main forces, which would be formed overnight from the townspeople and surrounding farmers.

"The expectation of surprise did not come true," Hercules wanted to say but did not, stopped by the ringing feeling of a new chance in a dangerous game. Perhaps, he thought, Laomedon was sure that the pirates would remain in the camp by the ships until morning and sent most of the city guards to intercept or even went himself. After all, he was a proud, impatient king who always preferred attack to defense.

He was also an experienced and cunning strategist and understood that the aliens would not abandon the ships, the only means of escape from the hostile Trojan land. If so, then the walls of Ilion were left almost unprotected, at least until reinforcements from the surrounding areas arrived. A swift charge in the coming darkness to bypass the detachment approaching from the city and an immediate assault on the walls of Ilion could bring success despite unfulfilled hopes for a surprise.

Ordering the soldiers to stay on the hill and immediately report any changes on the plain, Hercules hurried down to the shore, where the unloading from the ships continued. The leaders of the detachments had already gathered and congratulated one another on a successful landing.

"Noble warriors," Hercules began, "you know why we came to this shore. We hoped that the surprise and unpreparedness of the enemy would help decide the fate of the battle in our favor. However, I have just learned that Laomedon is aware of our landing and has already sent soldiers from the city to the shore. We must now decide what to do—whether to wait here on the shore, ready for defense, go ahead and meet Trojan warriors on the way, or try to avoid a fight and aim our strike directly at Ilion.

"I believe that our main forces should evade the battle with the approaching detachment and immediately move to storm the city. After all, regardless of the outcome of the battle on the shore, if we join it, we will certainly lose. The time spent will be used by Laomedon to gather troops and strengthen the defense of the city. Our main ally, surprise, will be gone. We will lose soldiers and time and end up storming the walls of a well-fortified town, a town that can withstand a long-term siege, for which we are not ready."

"You're saying reasonable things, invincible Hercules," Oikles said, joining the conversation. "If the gods and surprise are on our side, we will take Ilion and seize great trophies. But how do you propose to return to Peloponnese if warriors of Laomedon capture and burn our fleet? Without ships, we will remain in a hostile country.

"And even if we manage to cross the Hellespont, the journey by land through Thrace and Macedonia is far and dangerous for a detachment loaded with rich loot. Rumors of the plundering of Ilion will reach local tribes on the wings of birds, and they will fight among themselves for the right to engage in a battle with us."

"You are right, noble Oikles," Hercules replied. "I have been to those parts more than once. Thracian tribes are warlike and will never miss easy prey. An overland trip to Peloponnese is not in our plans. We will leave several warriors from each ship to defend the camp. I believe the detachment sent by Laomedon to the shore is not very large. As soon as Trojan warriors realize that our fighters are already storming the walls of Ilion, they will immediately return to the city.

"In the meantime, I suggest that you, Oikles, lead a defensive squad and do everything to save the ships. Try to keep the Trojans

19

away from the ships as long as possible. As soon as the battle breaks out on the walls of Ilion, they will not stay on the shore. I ordered not to pull the ships ashore. The warriors need to be ready to take them away from the shore if the Trojans begin to crowd our defenses, and there is a real threat of destruction.

"However, we should not delay the departure to Ilion any longer. Every flying moment takes away our chances of success. Noble leaders, lead your troops after mine. Order the soldiers to go without noise. Do not light torches and do not rattle weapons until they approach the town by two flights of arrows. Let those who have reached the walls immediately begin the assault, and do not wait for idlers. The biggest prize is for the first to climb the wall. Remember, the glory of victory, great booty, and the rescue of the ships are waiting on the walls of Ilion."

The rapid march of hundreds of soldiers in full armor at a distance of twenty stadiums was not easy, especially when the movement took place at night on a hilly terrain crossed by ravines. Hercules and some of his companions had previously visited Troy and remembered the landscape on the way from the coast of the Hellespont to Ilion. If you took to the left, you got into the Kallikolon hills; to the right lay a swampy lowland dotted with ravines and streams flowing into the Scamander.

Hercules knew that there was a road along the river and decided at the beginning to deviate to the east. Hiding behind the tops of gentle hills, he wanted to leave aside the detachment of Trojan warriors. When more than half of the way was left behind, he signaled a stop and, ordering to cut down a couple of trees to use as a battering ram, climbed the nearest hill.

In the coming darkness, Ilion was visible ahead. The way to it lay along the lowland, framing the Simois riverbed, at the confluence of which in the Scamander the ancient builders located the town. Few torches were burning on the fortress wall, suggesting that almost no troops were left in the city. Laomedon apparently decided to put all his strength into the detachment sent ashore to intercept the pirates. Hercules did not see the Trojan troops themselves and assumed that they most likely had already passed the valley of the Simois and were now hidden by the hills.

Returning to his army, Hercules made sure that everything was ready for the last throw. He called the leaders and turned to Telamon and Peleus.

"Your father, god-wise Aeacus, told you about the western wall of Ilion as the weakest point of the city's defense. Follow my squad and begin the assault on the western wall without delay. May the wisdom of your father, which the gods themselves recognized, make your task easier. My unit will move forward and check whether all the gates of the city are firmly locked. If we fail to find an accessible gate, we will try to crack the gate on the western wall or climb the wall next to it.

"I assume that the king, with the best warriors, rushed to the shore of the Hellespont, hoping to intercept and destroy us at the landing site. If when he returns he finds us by the wall, our situation will be unenviable. I will say more, most likely, with dawn, reinforcements of Trojans from the neighborhood will begin to approach. Our best chance to win is to meet the enemy from the walls of the city. May the gods help us punish the perjurer Laomedon, and the riches of Ilion reward us for our armed labors."

Father of Hercules, Amphitryon, who spent most of his life in battles, frequently said to his sons that a true leader did not look back on the battlefield; he watched the enemy and was sure that the fighters followed his lead. After leaving the hills, Achaean soldiers ran across the shallow riverbed of the Simois and found themselves on a small plain dissected by small ravines. On the opposite side of the plain, Ilion stood on a hill, illuminated by the rare lights on the towers. Everything indicated that a sudden assault was not expected in the city.

The warriors rushed forward, skirting the city on the right, aiming for the western wall. Once near the walls of the city, Hercules felt a surge of strength. The long-awaited moment had come. He sent out detachments to all the gates, and himself, hoping for quick luck, rushed to the Scaean Gate, located in the center of the southern wall. After all, most likely, a detachment of Trojans came out of here, and the guards could leave the doors partly open while waiting for their return.

However, the heavy oak doors did not move, even when the battering ram hit, and deadly arrows and rocks were already flying from the walls and the adjacent tower. When another huge stone killed the warrior and broke the ram, Hercules realized that he could not take the gate by a quick assault. At this time, Iolaus, sent to the Dardanian gate, arrived with the same news. And soon, the messengers sent confirmed that the other gates were firmly locked. It remained to use their best chance to overcome the western wall.

Walking away from the Scaean Gate, Hercules slowed down in front of the tall stone obelisks installed along the wall of the tower next to the gate. After all, the trunks of trees cut down in the forest had not been massive enough as a ram. If only one of these obelisks could be dragged to the gate without a protective tower. Such a mass would be enough to knock out the sash.

Deciding not to miss such a chance, Hercules called on the warriors to tilt and put one of the obelisks on the shafts of the spears. Twelve of the strongest warriors, together with Hercules, dragged the stone column along the southern wall to the nearest gate at the beginning of the western wall. There, using the obelisk as a battering ram, they managed to knock out the gates together with the hinges on the second attempt under a hail of arrows.

Drawing his sword, Hercules called Zeus and Athena to help and rushed into the gate opening. He barely remembered the details of the fight; the intensity of the action did not give time to capture what was happening. The defenders of Ilion were skilled warriors and fought desperately.

When there were no opponents left in the small square adjacent to the gate, Hercules sent soldiers to the wall with an order to capture the southern and eastern sections but to not open the gates. The noise of the battle on the fortress walls came from both sides. New groups of Achaeans were entering the broken gates. Hercules and a group of fighters headed for the city citadel, Pergamum, located on the opposite northeastern side of the city. Rounding the massive wall of the building adjacent to the area beside the gates, Hercules saw the gleam of armor and the flickering of shadows ahead in the gap between the buildings.

Someone was able to break through the defense before me, and the glory of victory will go to him.

This flash of thought caused a burning resentment. The fury of the recent fight was pounding in his temples again. He rushed in that direction and, in a few moments, found himself in the town square. Round Trojan shields flashed on the right; a detachment of guards of about thirty people left in reserve was waiting for a signal from the defenders. Hercules pointed them out to Iolaus, and he rushed into attack, followed by the soldiers.

Hercules himself, sword in hand, ran across the square and dived into the passage between the buildings leading to Pergamum. As he approached, he saw bodies and armor on the ground, evidence of a recent brutal fight. Several Achaean warriors were smashing the front door of the citadel with axes. Hercules recognized Telamon a few steps away. He was dragging a rock to a pile of stones stacked against the wall.

"What are you doing here?" Hercules roared, advancing with a growing fury that washed away fatigue and made the sword weight-less in his hand.

Telamon looked at him quickly and, without making the slightest attempt to defend himself, replied, "I am setting up an altar to the glory of the abominator of evil, godlike Hercules, the conqueror of Troy. Let everyone know that only a hero born of the great Zeus and endowed with divine power is capable of such an unheard-of accomplishment."

Seeing the anger burning in Hercules's eyes begin to subside, Telamon continued.

"Legend has it that King Tros, the grandfather of Laomedon, gave his son, the beautiful Ganymede, to the gods in exchange for the victory over the enemy. In addition, he received the ancestors of those horses that the king of Troy pledged to you for saving Ilion. Laomedon has violated his oath and must be punished."

"And the reckoning for his crime is already at hand," exclaimed Hercules.

The outburst of rage passed, and he suddenly realized that a minute ago, he could have ended the life of his closest companion. Hercules did not forget how a few years ago in Tiryns, an attack of sudden anger had led to the death of the son of King Eurytus, Iphitus. Memories of the murder of Iphitus and other similar cases tormented Hercules from time to time. He felt a wish to immediately make amends to Telamon.

"Son of the god-wise Aeacus, you have earned great fame for your exploits at the walls of Ilion. I give you as a reward the daughter of the king of Troy, Hesione, and her dowry in excess of your share in the spoils. Now you must capture the citadel. When the defenders' resistance is broken and the loot is collected, immediately prepare to leave Ilion. I'll meet you at the Scaean Gate, from where we will send wagons with trophies to the shore."

Hercules headed to the town square, where the battle with the defenders of Ilion had already ended. He found Iolaus and told him to send messengers around with a call to collect loot on the town square. Soon, the first wagons loaded with trophies began to arrive. The warriors gathered at the square let out shouts of joy at the abundance of gold jewelry and armor of skillful overseas work.

Peleus came up with the news that Laomedon and his sons were not found in the town. He confirmed that there were no Trojan fighters left within the walls, and Achaean warriors controlled all the gates. Hercules asked him to prepare the loot for shipment to the shore and continued to inspect the trophies. He saw that the captured goods were sufficient for the rewards of the participants and also for the preparation of future campaigns.

Suddenly, Hercules heard a summoning cry. He rushed to the sound and met Dimakh, who reported that a detachment of warriors was seen advancing toward Ilion from the Hellespont. This news made the surrounding fighters grab their weapons and filled the soul of Hercules with joy. The gods had answered his prayers and overshadowed the mind of Laomedon.

Most of all, Hercules feared that Laomedon would try to detain the Achaeans in Ilion. He assumed that the cunning king would not try to storm the city but would camp at the Achaean ship docking place and begin to gather reinforcements among the surrounding vassals and allies. The lord of Troy could also summon warships from nearby ports and attack the Achaean vessels.

If the king managed to hold the Achaeans for a few days and gather enough forces, their situation would become critical. There would be almost no chance to get away with the loot. They would have only the chance of negotiations on the exchange of the lives of the members of the royal family and the captured trophies for permission to leave unhindered.

But Hercules knew from his own experience how treacherous and dishonest Laomedon could be and had no doubt that he would break any contract. Therefore, the leader of the Achaeans planned to force a withdrawal to the ships. He expected to meet and defeat Laomedon's detachment on the way or on the shore in order to have time to set off with the loot before the approach of the king's allies. However, events unfolded in a different direction.

In his many years of military campaigns, Hercules had never had a chance to defend the walls of the town. Now he saw what advantages were present in this position. Hercules looked around the square. At the coming dawn, it was filled with Achaean warriors and wagons with loot.

"Achaeans, unbeatable warriors," Hercules exclaimed, "you have accomplished a great deed. Ilion lies at your feet. Now Laomedon, the perjurer and villain, is coming here to share the fate of his city. He wants to take away our loot and to stop us from leaving for our homeland. But the lord of heaven, the great Zeus, always punishes perjures. With the help of the gods of Olympus, we will give the king a worthy welcoming. All on the walls."

A friendly, multivoiced shout sounded in response, confirming that the fighting spirit had not dried up after the night battle.

"Truly, your words have been inspired by Athena herself, invincible Hercules," said Iolaus, who just came up. "They and of course the sight of rich booty, which is impossible to part with, will help our fighters meet Laomedon with dignity."

"Iolaus, son of the noble Iphicles, and you, illustrious leaders of the Achaean warriors, listen to me," Hercules replied. "We should not try to repel or drive away Laomedon's detachment from the town. On the contrary, we need this detachment and, above all, Laomedon himself to remain by the walls of Ilion. Only then will it be possible to get to the ships with the trophies without hindrance and sail to Peloponnese.

"The great gods of Olympus favor us by encouraging Laomedon to attack the city. I did not expect such a gift from the insidious and experienced king. In fact, I was afraid that he would try to gather reinforcements and wait for us at the ships or attack us on the plain with superior forces. I don't know for what reason he decided on such a risky attack.

"But now is not the time to wonder which deity inspired him with such a disastrous thought. We must take advantage of his mistake and, being under the protection of the walls, open our way to our homeland. To this end, let each leader occupy one gate of the city with the wall adjacent to the right until the next gate.

"To you, noble Dimakh, I entrust the western gate, which we destroyed during the assault. Go there with your warriors immediately and try to fill up the breach with stones and logs. You don't have to worry about opening the passage, because we will exit through another gate.

"Peleus, son of Aeacus, dismiss your deputy and few soldiers to complete the preparation of trophies, and yourself, at the head of your squad, occupy the Dardanian gate with the adjacent wall. Hold the defense, and don't open the gate until you get a signal from me."

Hercules saw an approaching messenger.

"Invincible Hercules," he shouted, "a detachment of Trojans will soon be at the walls! There are several hundred warriors in armor and about two dozen chariots. Siege tools are not visible. What will be the orders?"

"Noble leaders, let everyone choose for themselves a gate for defense and go there without delay. Keep the gate closed until my signal. Iolaus and I are going to the Scaean Gate to set a trap for the Trojans. We will open the doors a little so that they will try to break into the city. As soon as the punishment befalls the perjurer Laomedon, the signal for a general offensive will be given. Wait for the signal, and may the gods grant victory to the Achaean warriors."

Having climbed the tower crowning the Scaean Gate, Hercules and his escorting squires found themselves on a vast square platform surrounded by a high stone balustrade with loopholes. From here, there was a beautiful view of the surrounding area; the entire Trojan plain lay at the feet. Behind the plain, one might see the Hellespont rolling its waves into the Aegean Sea. The rising sun lit the opposite shore of the Hellespont formed by Cape Chersoneses.

Turning your head to the left, you could see the peaks of Mount Ida illuminated by the first rays of the sun. To the right, to the north-east, lay Dardania, from where the Trojans could expect the first rein-forcements. However, Hercules did not take his eyes off the squad of chariots, accompanied by foot soldiers, who were approaching Ilion.

Hercules carefully examined the chariots, richly decorated with metal, which were carried by beautiful, mighty horses, drivers, and warriors standing in chariots. Laomedon must be among them. He ordered the gates to be slightly opened to make it easier for the attackers to choose the place of attack.

The vanguard stopped at a distance of three or four spear throws from the walls, and the soldiers began to prepare for the assault. Soon, the attackers donned shiny bronze armor decorated with gold trim, which was rarely seen in Hellas, and began to climb the wide road leading along the hillside to the Scaean Gate.

The warrior standing next to Hercules, who was in Ilion about a year ago, pointed to the front group.

"Here are the sons of the king. The eldest, Prince Tithonus, heir to the throne, is in the front. He is followed by the princes Lampos and Clytios, experienced leaders of the warriors, each at the head of his squad."

Hiding behind shields from arrows flying from the walls, Trojans reached the gate and engaged in battle with the Achaean fighters who came out to meet them. Following the vanguard, more fighters were reaching the walls to engage in combat. A large group of soldiers, before reaching the walls, began to turn left, toward the western gate.

"They saw that the gate has been destroyed and decided to take advantage of this opportunity," Hercules said. "I wonder whether Dimachus has managed to erect a barricade."

More and more attackers joined the assault. The battle was going on at the very gates, and it seemed that the Trojans were about to smash the resistance and break into the city.

"Great Hercules," the voice of the messenger, who had risen from below, sounded, "Iolaus asks if it's time to lock the gates, because if Trojans will manage to break into the city, our losses may be significant. Or are you going to counterattack?"

"Wait for my signal," Hercules replied. "Send a messenger to Peleus, Dimachus, and other leaders with a call to be ready for a general attack at my signal."

He continued to carefully study the Trojan warriors, who were climbing in groups along the road to the walls of Ilion. Finally, his gaze settled on a tall warrior in gilded armor, wearing a helmet burning in the sun. His proud bearing and the attention paid to him by others betrayed the leader. With the help of two squires, the warrior completed putting on his gear and, accompanied by a large group of fighters in bronze armor, slowly headed up the road to the Scaean Gate.

"Look over there, at the group of warriors that just started climbing up the road. Do you recognize King Laomedon, the tall one in the shiny helmet, leaning on a heavy spear? Behind him, the squires carry a shield."

"Yes, you are right, invincible Hercules, this is undoubtedly Laomedon. He holds a scepter, a spear that he received from his father, King Il. Look how hard he leans on it climbing up the slope. The king is no longer young and should be tired after a night march to the shore of the Hellespont and the battle with Achaeans by the ships. I hope the gods have heard our prayers and helped save the ships.

"Look. To the right of the king comes his son Hicetaon, a skilled charioteer and javelin thrower. It was said that Hicetaon was the favorite son of the king and could become a competitor of Tithonus for the throne of the ruler of Troy, but he does not yet have a family and heirs."

"King Laomedon probably does not know that I am waiting for him here at the Scaean Gate, where years ago I swore to take revenge on him for a broken oath," Hercules said. "Otherwise, he would not have performed so proudly and fearlessly. The gods of Olympus themselves brought me here to take revenge on Laomedon, the son of Il. May the great Zeus the Thunderer witness the punishment of the perjurer. Valiant squire, stand to the right and keep your arrows ready."

Without taking his eyes off the approaching king, Hercules picked up a bow, checked the string, took a few deep breaths, and approached the parapet of the tower. A fierce battle was going on below at the gate. The clang of weapons thundered from all sides, and screams of rage and pain could be heard. Pulling the bowstring, he suddenly changed his plan, and the first arrow hit Hicetaon. The king froze for a moment when he saw how life was leaving the body of his beloved son. Then he turned to the squire to take his shield and at that moment was hit by a second arrow.

Seeing Laomedon slowly lean on his spear, settling to the ground, Hercules moved away from the parapet and shouted to the squire, "Hurry to Iolaus! Let him give the signal for a general attack."

The Trojans fought fiercely and did not retreat when the gates opened wide, letting Achaean fighters out of the city. They abandoned their attempts to break through in other places and concentrated on the wide-open Scaean Gate, striving to break into Ilion at all costs. Only when Hercules managed to hit the sons of Laomedon—Tithonus, Lampos, and then Clytios—with arrows from the tower did the attackers flee and scatter across the plain.

Hercules ordered the pursuit to be curtailed and to prepare for the departure to the ships. A small detachment on captured chariots was immediately sent ashore to assess the condition of the fleet. After making sure that there were no enemy troops on the plain and leaving observers on the tower with an order to immediately report any changes, Hercules, accompanied by Iolaus, descended from the wall and headed for the town square, where soldiers, prisoners, and trophies were gathering.

He approached a group of captured Trojans who were waiting for their fate near the walls of a stone temple adjacent to the square. All of them were already without armor, which had become the prey of the victors. However, the richly embroidered tunic and sandals with elaborately intertwined straps and silver buckles gave away the leader in the gray-haired warrior who, despite the wounds on his head and thigh, watched what was happening with lively eyes full of energy.

Hercules slowed down and pointed him out to Iolaus.

"I don't think this warrior will want to tell us where Laomedon sent for reinforcements and when they should be expected even if he knows about it. However, he can answer one question truthfully or at least offer his guess."

"Valiant warrior, you fought bravely, but the time of battle is over. I, Hercules, have come here to punish King Laomedon for breaking an oath made years ago when, at his request, I saved Ilion from destruction. The gods wanted the retribution to happen, and the criminal was punished. However, I was very surprised when Laomedon, with a small detachment, went to storm the city walls. After all, he could take the city under siege and gather reinforcements to accumulate a large advantage in strength. Then our situation would have become very difficult.

"Laomedon has always been a treacherous, deceitful, and cruel ruler. But no one could call him a fool. Tell me, brave warrior, did the gods muddle the mind of the unworthy, or was there some other reason? Answer truthfully, because Laomedon is dead, and by lying, you will bring my wrath on your head."

"Noble Hercules, the invincible leader of the warriors, I recognized you. However, when we went to storm the town, we did not know that you were at the head of the attackers on Ilion, just as the king himself did not know. Let me tell you that many Trojans, including myself, believed that Laomedon did wrong and broke his word when he refused to give you a well-deserved reward. I was on the wall of the town when you promised to return and punish the king. You have fulfilled your promise. I ask you for mercy to the people of Ilion, who have always been grateful to you for their salvation.

"Now, noble Hercules, let me answer your question as truthfully as I can. Laomedon thought that Ilion had been raided by a pirate fleet. Initially, he expected that the pirates were going to spend the night on the shore. And in the morning, they would go to the city to lay siege to it and demand a ransom. That's how pirates usually act. That's why he wanted to get ahead of them and, attacking by surprise at night, capture or burn the ships. The king was very angry that the pirates had managed to deceive him by bypassing his army.

"He engaged in a skirmish with a small detachment left on the shore, but the ships moved away from the shore at our approach. When we arrived on the shore and tried to capture the ships, we estimated that there were about a dozen fifty-oared vessels that could carry up to a thousand fighters. Laomedon believed that the pirates' forces were significant but not overwhelming.

"Having lost a lot of precious time in the battle on the shore, Laomedon learned that the enemy was already storming the walls of Ilion. We rushed back, and when we came out from behind the hills onto the plain, we realized that the city was already in the hands of the attackers. Laomedon did not want to attack Ilion. I heard from him that the pirates were trapped, and the question was whether they would come out voluntarily, or they would have to be smoked out.

"He sent messengers to the surrounding towns and was going to encircle the city from all sides and wait for reinforcements. However, at the council of war, the sons of Laomedon—Tithonus, Lampos, and Clytios—spoke in favor of an immediate assault.

"Tithonus was the most impatient. He reproached Laomedon with the decision to leave the city for the sake of a surprise attack on the pirates while he himself offered to defend the walls and send for help. He repeated that Laomedon could not wait, because his family, wives, and children of his sons are in the hands of pirates. He was supported by Lampos. He also believed that it was necessary to immediately go to the assault.

"At that moment, Clytios, who was scouting around the town, returned and reported that the Scaean Gate was partially open, and there were no doors visible at the western gate. The military commanders were under impression that pirates, carried away by the robbery, forgot about the danger, and the moment for the attack is the most appropriate.

"Seeing the general mood, Hicetaon, a skilled warrior, also spoke in favor of the assault. After listening to his sons, Laomedon reluctantly agreed and gave the order to attack with all his might. However, noble Hercules, I am sure that if Laomedon had known

31

that you were at the head of the warriors who captured the city, he would never have taken such a risk."

Hercules was satisfied with the answer and ordered to call a healer to take care of the wounds of the prisoners. Preparations were being completed on the square for sending the trophies to the ships. Telamon, Peleus, and other leaders were there, watching the loading of the loot.

"Has anyone seen Dimachus?" Hercules inquired. "He fulfilled the difficult task of defending the gate without shutters and deserves special thanks."

One of the warriors stepped forward and said, "Invincible Hercules, I have brought you sad news. Noble Dimachus perished defending the western gate. We were slow in dragging stones to the gate opening, as we had to first free it from the bodies of the defenders of the city and our glorious fighters.

"When a squad of the Trojan warriors headed to our gate, Dimachus, with a group of fighters, came out of the gate and repelled their attacks from the outside, giving us time to fill up the passage with stones. They lasted long enough for us to close the gap, but only two warriors were able to get inside. The rest of the warriors, including the fearless Dimachus, lay down at the gate."

"This is a heavy loss for us and for his native Boeotia," Hercules replied. "Let's make sure that the brave Dimachus and the rest of the Achaeans who fell at the walls of Ilion receive a decent burial. I know that Dimachus had a girlfriend who is expecting a child. Iolaus, let her be provided with everything she needs. It is our duty to make sure that noble Dimachus's family does not cease."

CHAPTER 4

ACCESSION OF PRIAM

Looking around the city square, Hercules noticed that Telamon had left the group of soldiers loading the wagons and was heading toward him. Along with him came a tall, slender girl in a richly embroidered tunic and a cover shimmering with gold thread. It was the daughter of the king, Hesione.

"Fearless Telamon," said Hercules, "I told you that this visit to Troy will be much more successful than our previous one, on the way back from the country of the Amazons. You have witnessed the insult inflicted and my oath of vengeance. Today, that vow has been fulfilled.

"You and your brother Peleus can be proud that you have paid justly for the insults that Laomedon inflicted on your father, Aeacus, the favorite of the gods. You have fulfilled his prediction. May your satisfaction be supplemented by the joy of rich trophies. May the glory of the conquerors of Ilion accompany you.

"Telamon, I remember my word given at the height of the battle. Hesione, the beautiful daughter of Laomedon, is henceforth your wife. Her property and the bride's dowry are at your disposal. All other captives and trophies will be distributed among the participants of the campaign on the shore. Our business here is over. It's time to leave Ilion. Let us not delay and retreat to the ships."

"You are right, godlike Hercules, the conqueror of Ilion," answered Telamon. "We are finishing the collection of trophies and will soon be able to go ashore. Almost all wagons are loaded. The forefront detachment, under the command of Peleus, is already moving out of the city to take a place at the head of the column.

"Noble Hercules, your generosity is comparable only to your fearlessness, which all Achaeans never tire of admiring. You yielded to me Hesione, who is ready to follow me to Salamis. She pleads with you for a great favor—to grant her the life of one of the captive Trojans. This is her brother, young Prince Podarces, the only surviving man from the royal family. He did not take part in the battle and was always with Hesione and his mother, Strimo, in the citadel.

"Do you remember the last time we came to the gates of Ilion to demand the promised reward? Podarces was the one who acknowledged your claim to it. However, he was still a child then, and his word was worth nothing. Now he is a handsome young man with a calm, peaceful temperament. If you generously grant life and freedom to Podarces, he, being the only heir of Laomedon, can take the empty throne and peacefully rule the Trojan kingdom."

"Let's go, noble Telamon. Let's consult with Iolaus about this matter," said Hercules, taking Telamon to the opposite corner of the square, where Iolaus conferred with a group of soldiers.

After briefing Iolaus on Hesione's request, he turned to Telamon.

"Tell me, son of Aeacus, whether it would be wise to punish the father and give the Trojan kingdom to his son."

"Let me, great Hercules, share my thoughts with you and Iolaus," replied Telamon.

"From captured Trojan warriors, I learned that if there is no heir to the throne in Ilion, the cousin of Laomedon, the ruler of Dardania, Capys, will ascend the throne. This is an experienced warrior and leader who fought in many battles. He and his son, the young but skillful javelin thrower Anchises, were in the city and took part in Laomedon's crusade ashore. After the death of the king, they may have managed to escape.

"I sent soldiers with a Trojan prisoner to examine the dead at the walls and those taken prisoner. They were not found. Most likely, they survived and went to Dardania for help. If, returning with reinforcements, Capys takes the throne, he will be able to organize a pursuit and summon ships from Dardania and other ports of the Hellespont, as well as from Smyrna and Lesbos. Therefore, the accession of Capys to the throne of Ilion may greatly complicate our return home.

"However, if you decide to put Podarces on the throne, then we will have much less to be afraid of. I think there will be no chase. Podarces himself, due to his youth, most likely will not take such a step and will be busy in the near future strengthening his power. Nor would he entrust the organization of the chase to Capys or anyone else for fear that if they returned victorious, they would be a threat to his precarious rule.

"Noble Hercules, Hesione begs you to preserve the life and freedom of her only brother. Maybe we want the same."

Hercules thought for a moment.

"What do you say, Iolaus? Should I, contrary to common sense and the experience of ancestors, give the kingdom to the son of the enemy I killed?"

"Under other circumstances, I would not give a dry leaf for Podarces's life," answered Iolaus. "But there is truth in the words of the worthy son of Aeacus. That Trojan warrior with whom you recently spoke told me that the ruler of Dardania, Capys, was in the group of soldiers who accompanied Laomedon, and after his death, he managed to escape in the chariot. He may have been wounded, but the warrior couldn't tell for sure. The son of Capys, Anchises was also in the detachment, but he was sent to Dardania even earlier to assemble the militia.

"After questioning the soldiers, I learned that Capys was not only the cousin of Laomedon but also the husband of his sister Themiste. He is the closest adviser to the king, an experienced military leader who has been on long campaigns more than once. During the battle at the walls of Ilion, he could estimate the number of Achaean soldiers. He has seen our ships, so he knows enough about our detachment. Most likely, he went to Dardania for reinforcements and will return as soon as he has gathered enough forces.

"I think after becoming the ruler of the Trojan kingdom, Capys will leave his son Anchises in Ilion, and he himself will lead the pursuit. Then the situation will turn into a serious threat. If it can be avoided by enthroning Podarces, then so be it. Maybe that's what the gods want."

Hercules, who had been listening to the leaders with intense attention, raised his head and looked around the area. Seeing a fountain nearby, he went up to it, rinsed his face, and got a drink.

"Telamon, call on Hesione. And you, Iolaus, find a herald and let him wait nearby, along with Podarces. Also, send a warrior to find the scepter of Laomedon among the trophies."

Hesione approached and knelt, begging for mercy.

"Hesione, noble Telamon conveyed your request and urged me to agree. Do you remember how I saved you from death on the shores of the Hellespont? And now I am ready to do for you even more than you ask. Your brother will receive not only freedom, but I will also give Podarces a symbol of royal power, the scepter of Laomedon, and make him the king of Troy. Get up from your knees, beautiful Hesione, and tell me if you are satisfied with my decision."

"Invincible Hercules, there are no words to express my gratitude. I will forever pray to the gods for your well-being. Last time, you saved my life, and now you give life and freedom to my beloved brother. A wonderful gift, the young man will always be grateful to you.

"However, fearless Hercules, placing Podarces on the throne can be a risky step, above all for himself. Indeed, he was the youngest son of the king and did not prepare for official duties. He has no experience either in military affairs or in public administration. By nature, he is soft-spoken and tends to avoid conflict, rarely participating in military exercises. Podarces never had a chance or, it seems to me, a desire to become king.

"Laomedon had four more sons, all experienced warriors who participated in the campaigns. The eldest son, Tithonus, a skilled military leader, was the official heir, recognized by the Trojan people and warriors. Tithonus's wife, the beautiful princess Eos, bore him two sons, Emathion and Memnon, supporting his already undeniable claim to the throne. They are not in the city now. Together with their mother, they are in the east, within the Hittite empire. After all,

Princess Eos is the daughter of a relative of the Hittite emperor. The marriage of the king's son to a Hittite princess strengthened ties with the mighty empire.

"Tithonus lived in the eastern lands for a long time and participated in battles and only recently returned to his homeland, as I heard, to recruit soldiers to participate in the campaigns of the Hittite emperor. While Emathion and Memnon are still children, with an experienced and authoritative regent, each of them can become a king.

"But Laomedon also has a cousin, the ruler of Dardania, Capys, the son of the great warrior Assaracos. He is a proven military leader who has led the Dardanian warriors on campaigns more than once. Capys is respected both in Troy and beyond. He has close ties with the Thracian kings. He is a real candidate for the post of regent. If not the king himself, many Trojans would follow him.

"Capys and his son Anchises were in the city yesterday and, apparently, were supposed to participate in the night campaign. I don't know what happened to them. If Capys did not perish in the battle, then he will play an important role in choosing a candidate for the throne of Ilion, and I don't think he'll support Podarces.

"Divine Hercules, if you make Podarces the king of Ilion, he will not be able to protect his throne and, possibly, his life. He has no supporters, no experience, and most importantly, no desire to bear the burden of royal power. To be a king, he must become a different person. The best of all, Hercules, is if you yourself will agree to become the king of Troy. You have already saved her once, and you will be able to protect her from future dangers. Many Trojans respect you. People say that you are the son of a deity, and if so, you deserve to be king."

Hercules silently listened to the speech of the Trojan princess. Telamon and the returned Iolaus looked at him, waiting for a decision.

"Hesione, you are not only beautiful but also wise, as befits a princess," said Hercules. "You Trojans especially revere Apollo, the bearer of the silver bow. Maybe you know about the oracle of Apollo at Delphi, where every mortal can receive a prophecy. I have been there many times, seeking guidance from the gods and healing from ailments. The deity gave me wise guidance to get rid of my illnesses. The deity also foretold me the will of Zeus the Thunderer. It is not possible to become a king against the will of the almighty ruler of Olympus.

"Know, Hesione, if I enthrone Podarces, he will reign in Troy. But now Podarces is among the captives who are to be sold into slavery. To release him just like that, without a ransom, would mean depriving the Achaean warriors of their lawful prey. This may also cause the disapproval of the Trojans, who will think that Podarces succeeded due to the death of his father and brothers. To avoid such conversations, Podarces must be redeemed from captivity.

"Tell, beautiful Hesione, can you offer something as a ransom? Do you know of some kind of hiding place where Laomedon could keep some of his treasures? Maybe your mother knows about such a hiding place and wants to tell about it in order to save her son."

"Divine Hercules," answered Hesione, "Father was very cautious and did not divulge his secrets to anyone, especially women. Only Hicetaon could be aware of the king's hiding places. He became close to the king when the eldest son, Tithonus, left for foreign lands, but the king did not reveal everything even to him.

"I don't know the location of the hiding place, and I'm sure neither my mother nor my sisters and Podarces does. The only item of value I can offer is this peplos of mine. This cape, woven from a magical, miraculous thread with gold spinning, was brought from distant eastern lands. As the merchant said, the wife of the pharaoh of Egypt has such capes, and she is the wife of a living god. Look, all of it can fit in my fist. Isn't that magic? The merchant asked for forty bulls for this peplos but agreed to take twenty and a detachment of guards to the borders of the Hittite empire."

"Well, Hesione," Hercules said after a moment of silence, "let it be your way. Now we will go to the square, where, in the presence of the soldiers and the citizens of Ilion, Iolaus will put up Podarces for sale, and you, as the wife of Telamon, can buy him for the agreed price and set him free. After he becomes free, I will appeal to the inhabitants of Ilion. Then I will proclaim your brother the ruler of the Trojan kingdom and make him able to bear the burden of royal power. Noble Telamon, inform all the leaders that after the new Trojan king takes the throne, we will leave Ilion and head for the ships."

CHAPTER 5

EXIT FROM ILION

Hercules decided to be the last to leave Ilion. Standing on the tower of the Scaean Gate, he watched as a long convoy with booty and captives stretched out from the city on the road along the banks of the Scamander and farther by the edge of the gentle hills to the Hellespont. The entire path from the city to the strait was opened from the height of the tower, and only the very shore of the Hellespont was hidden by coastal hills. Hercules was pleased with the number of trophies; they were quite enough to reward the Achaean warriors and leaders. His share as a commander in chief promised to be sufficient to begin the implementation of his plans.

Hercules recalled how Podarces, a slender young man, rejoiced at the ransom from captivity, how a feeling of gratitude to his sister for the newfound freedom and grief from the impending separation mixed up on his face. He noticed how fear appeared in the eyes of Podarces in response to the command to come and listen to the will of the gods and how Podarces turned to stone when he heard that from now on he would become the king of Troy.

Recalling how many years ago the Delphic Pythia gave him a new name, implying that changing a name would help change the fate, Hercules named the new Trojan king Priam and proclaimed that Priam, according to the will of the gods, would be a wise and just ruler. In conclusion, he released several lightly wounded Trojan captives from his quota, announcing that he was doing this at the request of King Priam, the son of King Laomedon and the grandson of King Il.

"Yes, King Laomedon did not expect that the retribution for the broken oath would fall on him after so many years. But even more, he did not expect that his youngest son would become his heir," said Hercules, looking at the Trojan plain, which reached the foothills of Ida.

He remembered another king, Augeas, who ruled at Elis in western Peloponnese. Augeas, like Laomedon, hired Hercules to do hard work and, when work was completed, refused to pay off the contract. It was a long, long time ago, when Hercules was still in the service of King Eurystheus, but broken contract had no expiration date.

"Let Augeas prepare for retribution. He is next after Laomedon," Hercules said a moment before he saw Iolaus, who went out to the observation deck.

To resemble his champion, Iolaus did not take off his armor during campaigns while warriors usually put on heavy armor only immediately before the battle. But if Hercules did not feel the weight of the multilayered armor made from the skin of a lion, bronze leggings, and shoulder pads, then for Iolaus, the full uniform turned out to be burdensome. Therefore, he gradually reduced the load to a copper breastplate lined with boar skin and a small round copper shield that he wore on his back. And now his appearance was preceded by the sounds of the shield tapping against the wall.

Hearing the words uttered by Hercules, Iolaus could not help asking, "Invincible Hercules, have my ears deceived me, or you are contemplating a trip to Elis, the kingdom of Augeas, rich in herds?"

"You heard right, son of the noble Iphicles. I intend to punish Augeas, because he, like Laomedon, violated the contract and did not pay for my work. The time has come to collect from him the debt, as we have collected from Laomedon. However, first, we have a rough journey home. Tell me if everything is ready for departure. What have you heard from the watchers on the towers and how things are in the city?"

"Divine Hercules, the Achaean detachments and the convoy, together with the captives, have already left the city to the ships. Our fighters guard all the gates and are ready to withdraw. The new king of Ilion, Priam, apparently took your advice and spread the news throughout the city that, by agreement with you, all Achaeans would leave the city before sunset. Thus, he strengthened his authority and saved us from unnecessary anxiety, because the residents are waiting for our departure in their homes.

"Everything is calm in the city. However, the soldiers guarding the tower of the Dardanian gate saw chariots on the Dardanian road several times. The drivers did not approach the walls, but the warriors believe that they are watching the city."

"They know that there are Achaeans in the city and are waiting to gather enough forces to attack or take the city under siege," Hercules replied. "I believe that it will happen soon, so it is time for us to go to the ships. Announce total withdrawal. We move as soon as all the fighters gather. Let the warriors at the Dardanian gate quietly abandon the observation deck, leaving a few helmets on the parapet. Also, don't forget to post a rear guard. Let them follow us at four spear throws."

With these words, Hercules, letting Iolaus forward, began to descend the narrow stairs. Leaving the tower, he noticed Priam standing with some elderly Trojan near the high wall of the temple, separated from the tower by a passage.

Hercules slowed down for a moment and turned to Priam.

"King of the Trojans, Priam, as I promised, the Achaeans are leaving Ilion and will go to their homeland. Soon, Trojan warriors scattered in the battle will begin to flock to the city from the surrounding area. Reinforcements may also come. My advice is to keep all the gates closed and demand an oath of allegiance from everyone who comes. As soon as enough warriors are gathered, organize a replaceable guard at the gate and put watchers on the walls.

"Do not forget yourself, and do not let the Trojans forget, you are the inherited ruler of Ilion, King Priam, the liberator of the city. The fate of the people of Troy is in your hands. It is always hard to start, but the longer you reign, the more you will enjoy the royal scepter."

After waiting for all the warriors to gather at the Scaean Gate, the Achaeans left the city and moved to the ships. Descending from the hill on which the city was located and crossing the Simois, the detachment headed down the road leading along the Scamander to the coast.

Soon, Iolaus caught up with Hercules and began to report.

"Invincible Hercules, I was the last to leave the city and saw how the new king, Priam, and the group of old people gathered by him began to close the Scaean Gate. All other gates are closed. Chariots have not been seen on the Dardanian road lately. Experienced warriors have been sent to the rear. They will not lose sight of us and will immediately notify us if the enemy appears."

"Well done, son of wise Iphicles," replied Hercules. "If the gods will be pleased, we can leave Trojan coast tomorrow morning. When we arrive at the camp, post guards on the hilltop and order them to watch Ilion all night. If they notice movement between the town and our camp, they should report at once. We need a good meal and rest, because the previous night was sleepless for everyone."

Soon, the road began to turn behind a hill, and the walls of Ilion disappeared. Around the twist of the road, a broken chariot was hidden on the side of the road.

"Laomedon was apparently in a hurry on his way to the seashore," Hercules said. "But even more had he hastened back when he realized that he had left Ilion unprotected, and the enemy had deceived him. Look, Iolaus, this chariot, finished with copper and wood carvings, was not thrown down into the river but dragged up the slope.

"Apparently, they expected to return for it. This suggests that the chariot was lost on the way to the shore, when the king was counting on a quick and decisive victory. After a clash on the shore, the king assessed the strength of the attackers. He probably realized that they were well-armed and led by an experienced leader. On the way back, Laomedon was concerned with keeping his throne, not some chariot."

"You are right, invincible Hercules," answered Iolaus. "The gods, undoubtedly, clouded the mind of the arrogant Laomedon. Trying to correct one mistake with another, he brought himself to an inevitable end."

The road, rounding a couple more hills, turned away from the river and climbed in a wide arc up the coastal hill. A view of the Hellespont, rolling its waters into the boundless Aegean Sea, opened from a hill. In the distance, to the west, was the mountainous Imbros. Leaving the mouth of the Scamander behind and turning along the shore of the strait, the travelers almost immediately saw the Achaean ships and soon entered the camp.

CHAPTER 6

DEPARTURE FROM TROY

Hercules was immensely saddened by the news of the death of the courageous Oikles, who fell in a night battle on the shore with Trojan detachment. Lighting a funeral pyre, he urged the Achaeans to remember the hero who saved the ships for the return and vowed to visit the children of Oikles in Arcadia to tell what a great warrior their father had been. A share of the booty of Oikles was given to the Arcadians to give to his family.

The burial ceremony was short, as the soldiers had to prepare for departure. When Hercules returned to his tent, he saw Telamon, who was waiting for him at the entrance.

"Divine Hercules, conqueror of Troy, I came to say goodbye, as we intend to sail at dawn if the wind will not change. I heard that everything is calm in Ilion, and there is no need to fear an attack this night."

"Glorious Telamon, your exploits during the assault on Ilion will be chanted by storytellers for many years," Hercules spoke in response. "I also believe that the pursuers will not threaten us. Do you think that King Priam will be able to secure himself on the throne, or will Capys, returning from Dardania with strong reinforcement, challenge his dominion over Troy?"

"It seems to me that King Priam is quite capable of staying on the throne," answered Telamon, "especially if enough Trojan warriors will gather in the town or more fighters will come from nearby villages before Capys arrives. In addition, Capys's wife and Laomedon's sister, Themiste, is in Ilion and does not want a confrontation between her husband and nephew. It is possible that Capys was wounded in the battle at the Scaean Gate. Then he will send his son Anchises with a detachment.

"In this case, the risk of Priam losing the throne will be even less. After all, Anchises will not take decisive action without consulting his father, which will take time. And the longer the king stays on the throne, the stronger the royal power. I have experienced that at Salamis. Troy is a rich and fertile country, and Priam will be able to quickly restore the power of Ilion."

"In your words, I hear the wisdom of your father, Aeacus, with whom even the gods consulted," answered Hercules. "I agree that the new king has a good chance to keep the throne, so help him, the patron of the Trojans, the bearer of the silver bow, Apollo. And the time has come for the Achaeans to leave the Trojan coast. Tell, Telamon, which route you are going to take."

"Invincible Hercules, we intend to return the same way we came here. First, our ships will go to Imbros. If the winds are favorable, from there, we will head straight west to Lemnos and continue to Cape Athos. If not, we shall take a long way—first north to Samothrace, then to Thasos and farther along the coast of Thrace to Chalcidice. Most of the ships are already loaded, and we expect to sail at sunrise. Your ships are also ready to sail. Tell me if you are going to leave tomorrow or have other plans."

"I wish you, brave Telamon, a fair wind and a successful return to Salamis. We, too, will set sail in the morning, but we will take a course to the south. We will bypass Lesbos, where Laomedon's allies may wait, and head for Chios. There I intend to sell the prisoners, and if there are difficulties, we will go down farther south. There is always demand in Samos and Miletus.

"From Samos, one can head for the sunset and pass by Ikaria, Mykonos, and Tinos. If you sail between Mykonos and Tinos and keep straight at sunset, you will pass several islands and come to Argolis. This is a good route, as traders from Asia and Phoenician merchants tell us. Think, Telamon. Maybe you'll go with us. After all, for the captives, you can get much more in the cities of Asia. There you can also buy overseas goods and sell profitably in Peloponnese."

"Divine Hercules, you are right, it is more gainful to sell captives on Chios or Samos. But I do not intend to sell. I want to deliver my captives to Salamis. The population on the island is not large, and they will be very useful for fieldworks, household chores, and for caring for the herds on the mainland. I even traded a few captives with other chieftains for trophies and weapons from my share of the booty."

Telamon was silent for a while and continued.

"However, I would be glad to go with you if it were not for my brother Peleus. You know that after being expelled from Aegina, Peleus wandered the world for a long time, but then he found a new home with the king of Phthia, Actor, who gave him his daughter in marriage. Everything went well, but some god whom Peleus had the misfortune to anger took revenge on him. This is what happened last year when you were still in Asia with Queen Omphale.

"The king of Calydon, Oeneus, summoned heroes from all over Hellas to hunt the monstrous boar that was devastating his lands. I was there too. There are many stories about the hunt itself and what happened after, but what happened there with Peleus is a very sad story.

"He came hunting from Phthia with the son of King Actor, Eurytion. When the boar was surrounded, Peleus threw his spear at the beast, but it pierced Eurytion, who jumped on the boar with a sword from the bushes and was just in the path of the spear.

"All the hunters who were there testified that this death was the result of an accident. However, Peleus again turned out to be an exile accused of unintentional murder. Since then, he wandered around Hellas, finding no shelter, driven by evil fate.

"There is hope that Acastus, who became the king of Iolcus after his father suffered the inevitable fate, will agree to receive him and cleanse him of the murder. Peleus went to Troy hoping to get good gifts for Acastus, and now he has them.

"Peleus asked me to accompany him since I know both Acastus and Actor. If he is lucky enough to find a home in Iolcus, I can bring his wife from Phthia. It is for this reason that we want to go back along the coasts of Thrace and Macedonia. After all, the path from Chalcidice to Iolcus is very close. And on the other route, the travel can take a long time."

"Son of wise Aeacus, generous Telamon, you are a true support for your worthy brother. If the matter with Acastus does not settle down, advise Peleus to go to Mount Pelion, which is situated north of Iolcus. Centaurs live there. Let him turn to their leader, Chiron, and refer to me, because Chiron and I have been longtime friends.

"I hope everything goes well for the noble Peleus. Maybe in the future, he should visit Delphi, ask the Pythia for advice, and make sacrifices to the thrower of fast arrows, Apollo. This god is very insidious and loves to show his displeasure by arranging incidents like what happened to Peleus."

"Thank you, invincible Hercules. I will convey your words to Peleus. Perhaps you have not heard that Peleus considers his patroness the sister of Apollo, the far-reaching Artemis. He makes sacrifices to her before every hunt. I hope Artemis will put in a good word for Peleus to her brother.

"I wish you a peaceful voyage and great success in all your endeavors, godlike Hercules. Let the news of your exploits go ahead of you all over Peloponnese. You will always be an honored guest on Salamis."

Hercules sent a torchbearer to escort Telamon to his tents in the coming darkness. When he left, Iolaus spoke about the preparations for departure and mentioned that there was no activity from Ilion.

After receiving a nod of satisfaction from Hercules, Iolaus asked, "Unbeatable Hercules, you are seriously considering a campaign against king of Elis, Augeas. If so, then why didn't you invite Telamon to take part in this endeavor? After all, Elis is a rich kingdom. There are many brave warriors. King Augeas, I have heard, has plenty of relatives and allies. And Telamon and his brother are powerful fighters and could be very useful."

"Indeed, Iolaus, there are many brave warriors and experienced leaders in Elis. King Augeas can put up a large defense force. A powerful army is needed to crush such a force. I have long thought of punishing the lying king for breaking his sacred oath and refusing to pay for my labors.

"Many years ago, when I was still serving with King Eurystheus, he sent me to Elis to provide military support. That time, your father was my companion. During our stay with Augeas, he suggested that I work for him and clean the royal stables. The king swore to give a herd of bulls when the work is finished and took his sons as witnesses.

"Of course, you have heard about the Augean stables, but maybe you don't know that your farsighted father, Iphicles, warned me that if Eurystheus calls me back to Mycenae before the job is over, I will not get a single oxtail. Iphicles even suggested that in his cunning, Augeas could send a messenger to Eurystheus with a related request. I myself did not trust Augeas, but I was able to complete this work very quickly, much to his surprise.

"As you know, the worthless Augeas refused to pay, justifying himself by the fact that I am not a civilian but serve the king Eurystheus, and all arrangements should be carried out through him. He also said that it was not I who cleaned the stables but the waters of the river, which belongs to Elis, and bombarded me with other false arguments.

"When I called his sons as witnesses, but only one of them, the noble Phileas, confirmed that the king had promised to give me the herd. For this, he was expelled from Elis by his own father. It was then that your father told Augeas that if he does not give me the promised herd now, then in time, by the will of the gods, all his herds will become mine. Angry, Augeas ordered us to leave his kingdom and never return.

"Arguing with kings is not easy, but now that I've defeated Laomedon, I'm confident that I can handle Augeas as well. However, the war with him will require a lot of expenses, and the treasures of Ilion will come in handy."

"Invincible Hercules, I am sure that the trophies and glory you have earned at the walls of Ilion will help to gather an army of worthy fighters," answered Iolaus. "Father often talked about campaigns with you, because there were always enough people who wanted to listen. Recalling the events in Elis, he often added that Augeas had broken his oath. And according to the law of the gods, sooner or later, all his herds would go to Hercules.

"Once, I asked what kind of law that is, and he explained. Suppose, he said, that there is a pond in some town into which several kinds of fish have been released. One day, the king issued a decree that the Crucians living in the pond are dedicated to the gods, and the king forbade catching these Crucians. If you catch a Crucian, you must release it back. So the townspeople did, and over time, only Crucians remained in the pond.

"The same story is with the bulls in the herds of Augeas. If we mark the bulls of Hercules and their offspring, then only unmarked animals can be taken for the needs of Augeas. After all, Augeas has no right to use bulls that do not belong to him. As in the example with the Crucians, over time, only the bulls of Hercules will remain in the herds. And whether the bulls are marked or not, it does not matter, because the laws of the gods are inevitable, as Father explained."

"Your wise father is right, Iolaus," said Hercules. "I'll tell you that by the will of gods, the perjurer Augeas will lose not only all his herds but also the kingdom itself. I want to recruit experienced fighters in Miletus. This is one of the reasons why our return trip follows the coast of Asia. I also count on warriors from Arcadia, because Augeas has long been at enmity with the inhabitants of this region. I hope that Iphicles will be able to join this campaign.

"As for Telamon, then, of course, his participation would be useful, and I wanted to invite him to go against Augeas. However, upon consideration, I decided not to. I told you that Telamon was not eager to go to Ilion. Only long persuasion and reminders of his oath could convince him. But Troy is far away, and Elis is a prominent kingdom in Peloponnese.

"King Augeas makes friends with the lord of Mycenae, Eurystheus, with the king of Sparta, Hippocoon, and with the Messenian ruler Aphareus. Telamon, who rules on a small island, has no need to come into conflict with the powerful kings of Peloponnese. After all, in the event of defeat, he risks losing everything."

"Invincible Hercules," asked Iolaus, "the king of Mycenae has been envious of you since the glory of your exploits overshadowed his deeds. Do you think that he will try to obstruct your campaign against Augeas?"

"If Eurystheus can hurt me, he will," Hercules replied. "Having learned of my intentions, he will undoubtedly notify Augeas. Therefore, he must remain in the darkness as long as possible. If we manage to recruit enough warriors in Miletus, I want to march on to Elis without delay. Success in Troy should help the conquest of the kingdom of Augeas. I hope Elis, rich in herds, will fall as swiftly as the strong-walled Ilion."

Will I be able to pull together sufficient force to deal with the king of Elis? Hercules thought. *Augeas became one of the most powerful rulers of Peloponnese from the time when the king of neighboring Pisa, Pelops, suffered an inevitable fate. There are several rich towns under his rule. Maybe it's worth testing my strength on the ruler of Pylos first. He is much weaker.*

The insidious Neleus, years ago, refused to purify Hercules from the murder and behaved arrogantly. Previously, Neleus had enjoyed the patronage of the Messenian ruler Aphareus. But Hercules had heard that in recent years, their relationship had deteriorated.

The king of Elis does not like Neleus either. Maybe I should start with Neleus and, after conquering Pylos, go to Elis. Perhaps it is worthwhile to ask the oracle of Apollo. If you seek the advice of the bearer of the silver bow, he at least will not become your adversary.

DEIANEIRA

CHAPTER 1

MEETING AT THE GATE

Agamemnon and Menelaus were returning to Mycenae from a trip to Argos. Leaving the city in the afternoon, they crossed the full-flowing Inach and found themselves on the well-worn Corinthian road. Menelaus skillfully drove the chariot, and after making a stop in the sanctuary of Perseus, by sunset, they were in sight of the walls of the Mycenaean citadel.

The young men, tired of the road, had been looking forward to a hearty dinner by a hot fireplace when the horses suddenly came to a stop not far from the fortress gates. Seeing that the wanderer who came out of the twilight had no weapons, Agamemnon removed his hand from the spear mounted in the chariot holder. The man removed his cloak, and Agamemnon recognized Calchas, a well-known priest and fortune teller in Mycenae, who in recent years had been the mentor of the sons of King Atreus.

"Calchas, son of the wise Thestor, your disciples greet you," Agamemnon said as he got off the chariot. "Surprised to see us at the city gate at such a late hour. Are you here in such a cold evening by your own will or by the will of the gods? Your path leads to the city, or you are leaving Mycenae?"

"Valiant son of Atreus," replied Calchas, "to the first question, both. To the second, neither. I expected that you could return at this time and went out of the gates hoping to intercept you. Menelaus, turn the chariot around and take it away from the gate so it will not attract attention. We need to talk urgently. Find out that while you were absent, your father, King Atreus, suffered an inevitable fate."

"What happened?" Menelaus interrupted Calchas. "Tell me how it happened. And why can't we go into the citadel now and discuss everything there?"

"Valiant sons of Atreus, you can certainly enter the gate. But no one can guarantee that you will be able to get out alive. The gods have announced to me, and I tell you that by entering the citadel, you will put your life at great risk. I was waiting here to warn you."

The priest's voice sounded hollow and tense. Agamemnon realized that the matter was serious and began to help Menelaus turn the chariot on the narrow road going up to the Lion Gate, the main gate of the Mycenaean citadel. Calchas went ahead, pointing the way away from the walls of the city to where the road widened before merging with the main road to Corinth.

Having stopped the chariot not far from the Corinth road, the young men eagerly turned to the mentor. Calchas leaned on his staff and began his story.

"Sons of the great king Atreus, listen to me and then ask questions. Last night, I learned that King Atreus, in his eighth decade, suffered an inevitable fate. As I was told by trusted servants, your father died in his bedchamber. His death was sudden. The king did not appoint an heir, as he had good health and counted on years of rule. After all, despite his advanced age, he was full of energy, conducted state affairs, administered the court, and was able to drive a chariot.

"The Council of Elders gathered this morning and has entrusted the reins of government to your uncle Thyestes as the eldest in the family. He has supporters in the city who helped sway the council's opinion in his favor. They said that you, Agamemnon, are still too young to reign in Mycenae and take control of the vassal regions and towns.

"Besides, you weren't there, and Thyestes convinced the council that your time would come and promised to take care of your decent upbringing. He told about his plans to use treasury funds to strengthen the walls and reconstruct the well in the citadel, as well as to resume the construction of ships for trade expeditions. These plans have resonated with many influential citizens."

"Wait, Calchas," Menelaus exclaimed, interrupting the priest. "If Thyestes has already been proclaimed the king of Mycenae, what danger threatens us? The enmity between him and our father is a matter of old days. Yes, I have heard stories about their fight for power. Now that Father is gone, the fight is over. Thyestes has achieved his goal.

"Agamemnon and I were not at enmity with him. On the contrary, we have delivered him an invitation from our father to return to Mycenae in peace. While he lived in Mycenae, I did not notice any hostility and hatred from him. Do you really think he's going to pursue us?"

"Noble Menelaus," replied Calchas, "you and your brother do not know everything. But telling about the past will take a lot of time. We will postpone it for later. I want to tell you that for the whole day today, the day when Thyestes ascended to the throne, he gave many orders and spoke with many citizens of Mycenae and other Argives. He summoned Aegisthus and ordered him to stay in the room next to the throne room.

"I was in the throne room all the time, but I never heard him say your name, Agamemnon, or yours, Menelaus. No, he never mentioned you, although he knew that you were out of town, and it would be wise to send a messenger to you with a notification of your father's death. For me, this served as a hint that Thyestes has an insidious plan for you.

"You may not know, but he has accused Atreus of sacrificing his children, and maybe with good reason. But this is part of a long history connected with the Phrygian traditions of the Tantalus family, which I will tell you when we have time. Now I suggest we head to my friend's house located not far from here, along the road to Argos, close to the sanctuary of Perseus. There we can spend the night and discuss what to do next."

Menelaus looked at Agamemnon. He was silent. Menelaus followed his gaze and saw the last rays of the sun glide over the top of the mountain rising behind the Mycenaean citadel.

A light wind from the sea blew Menelaus's hair. He smoothed his hair with his hand and said, "Worthy Calchas, I understand that you are concerned, but you don't think that Thyestes will want to deal with us right in the citadel, where we have allies and not a few? He's our uncle, and we don't stand in his way. You said yourself that he has already become a king. After all, Atreus gave shelter in Mycenae to his son Aegisthus and never offended him, even while Thyestes was in exile. We joked with him sometimes but always in a kind way. I think nothing will happen if we return to Mycenae, honor the memory of our father, and discuss everything with a fresh head tomorrow."

Calchas looked from Menelaus to Agamemnon, who remained silent. He looked at the gates of the citadel and saw torches being lit above them. The night watch had come. The priest thought that if his assumptions were correct, then turning the chariot away from the gates would mean the difference between life and death. If he was mistaken, the worst that could happen was the brothers not honoring the burial of Atreus and spending a few days outside Mycenae.

"Sons of Atreus," he said slowly, "when I stood at your father's deathbed, I had a vision. As before a thunderstorm, for a moment, all the sounds died down, and I heard a whisper. These are the words I heard: 'The gods love Agamemnon, the son of Atreus. Many heroes have to travel to distant lands and fight mighty enemies to find a worthy death. But Agamemnon, son of Atreus, the favorite of the gods, will find death right in his home.' That's what I have heard. Now decide whether you are going home to Mycenae or coming with me."

Menelaus, speechless, looked at Calchas. Then he turned to the closed gate and wondered if the ambush was already lurking behind. They could abandon the chariot, go around the citadel, and enter through the Corinthian gate or a secret gate. There in the citadel, they would be able to gather a squad of loyal warriors.

His thoughts were interrupted by Agamemnon's voice.

"Calchas, show us the way to your friend's house."

Calchas, as it turned out, had informed his friend about a possible visit in advance, so dinner and a prepared overnight stay were waiting for them at the estate, which the travelers had reached in complete darkness. The priest added almost nothing to the story of the events in the citadel, saying only that Thyestes was not with the king on his final day, but the servants saw Aegisthus coming out of the royal chambers. Deciding to talk about future plans in the morning, everyone went to bed.

CHAPTER 2

CHAT WITH THE PRIEST

The gloomy morning sky foreshadowed the imminent rain. Having refreshed themselves with goat cheese and cakes, Agamemnon and his brother sat down on the stones near the path leading to the sanctuary of Perseus to wait for Calchas. He, as the servant said, went to the sanctuary, located not far from the Argos road, to make sacrifices to the hero, the founder of the city.

"How the world changed overnight," said Agamemnon. "When yesterday we visited the temple of Perseus, everything around was smiling in the light of the sun. And today, the bleak haze does not promise well."

"Listen," Menelaus uttered, turning to his brother, "you don't think that Thyestes will try to deal with us without waiting for the burial of Father? Even if he harbors malicious intent, he will not act until the funeral ceremonies are completed. We will wait for Calchas and go to Mycenae without expressing our suspicions in any way. In the citadel, we will honor the memory of our father and take part in the burial. At the same time, we will talk with the leaders of the warriors, the townspeople."

Seeing Calchas walking along the path, Menelaus made a short pause and, when he approached, voiced a greeting, settled down, and continued.

"Hello, wise Calchas. Agree that no matter how villainous Thyestes is, he certainly will not dare to attack us until the funerals are over. And if we do not participate in the ceremonies, then we will deserve universal condemnation. Let the Argives see that we are worthy heirs of King Atreus. Say what you think, Agamemnon."

"It is important that in Mycenae they know that we honor the memory of our father and are not afraid of Thyestes," Agamemnon said slowly. "There are many people in the city and throughout Argolis who are ready to take our side. On the other hand, I don't see much benefit in Thyestes getting rid of us now. After all, such an act would provoke the indignation of the Argives. We can stay in Mycenae for a few days, arrange a decent burial for our father, and go to Midea or even to Argos if we feel danger. How do you like this plan, Calchas?"

"Your plan is not bad, Agamemnon, but on one condition," Calchas replied after a short pause. "You will manage to live it to the end, which I strongly doubt. After all, I visited the temple not only to make sacrifices to the son of the almighty Zeus, Perseus. There, I was waiting for a man from the citadel with whom I had arranged a meeting in advance. He told me that they were already looking for you on the orders of King Thyestes. The guards at the gate are instructed to escort you to him immediately upon arrival.

"Understand one simple thing. What you think of your uncle doesn't matter. What matters is what the lord of Mycenae, Thyestes, thinks of you. He has already been promoted to royal authority and with a wave of his hand can turn his thoughts into actions. The king can exile or impose other punishments for disturbing public order or crimes against citizens. However, in the eyes of Thyestes, you are a threat to royal power, and there is only one punishment for threatening king authority."

The young men were silent, sensing the seriousness of the situation in Calchas's tone.

"Now listen to why I think Thyestes intends to get rid of you. To understand this, you need to recall the past, about which you know far from everything. But it is not for nothing. The legends tell that whoever does not know the past is not capable of understanding the present and will not be able to get ready for the future. However, many believe that not all events of the past deserve remembrance.

Indeed, the participants themselves frequently prefer to forget about their deeds.

"Atreus and Thyestes were born and raised at the court of their father, King Pelops, in glorious Pisa. When Pelops quarreled with his wife, Hippodamia, the brothers sided with their mother and were expelled from Pisa. As far as I know, Thyestes was his brother's best friend when they were young. They experienced many hardships until the then king of Mycenae, Sthenelus, the father of King Eurystheus, invited them to rule in Midea, a small city, subordinate to Mycenae.

"But over time, a quarrel broke out between the brothers, caused by a power struggle. They say that Eurystheus deliberately inflated their enmity, giving preference to one or the other. I also heard that the brothers began to openly feud after their mother, Hippodamia, suffered the inevitable fate. When Atreus marries the daughter of the Cretan king Aerope, his influence at the Mycenaean court increased significantly. One way or another, Thyestes fought for a long time with Atreus for a place at the court of Eurystheus but lost and fled.

"Over time, from the ruler of the small town, Atreus becomes a recognized military leader and closest associate of the king of Mycenae, Eurystheus. Years later, Thyestes returned to Argolis and plotted against Atreus in Sicyon and Corinth. When Atreus became king of Mycenae, he first expelled Thyestes but later changed his mind, returned him to Mycenae, and even made him his counselor. You know about this and that Thyestes has since lived in Mycenae, acting as an adviser to the king and an envoy to Delphi.

"What you probably don't know, however, is that Atreus, once many years ago, wanted to kill Thyestes when rumors reached him that he was after Aerope in his absence. It was then that Thyestes fled from Mycenae. Shortly thereafter, Aerope suffered an inevitable fate. You were very young children then and do not remember those events, and contemporaries do not want to recall them, fearing to provoke the anger of the king.

"Atreus, burning with revenge, ordered the sacrifice of the sons of Thyestes. According to the testimony of Thyestes, which he did not repeat after returning to Mycenae, Atreus ordered his children to be boiled in a cauldron and served to him as a dinner. Perhaps having cooled down, Atreus was ashamed of what he had done, so he allowed Thyestes to leave the city without hindrance. But Thyestes believed that Atreus wanted to doom him to long-suffering, and his death would only be a relief.

"One way or another, they say Thyestes cursed the Atreus family and swore revenge. He tried to find opportunities for revenge among the kings of Peloponnese, traveled to Pisa, where after the death of Pelops, the brother of Pelops, Broteas, reigned. However, the power of Mycenae and the military might of Atreus were reliable protection.

"In recent years, the anger of Atreus subsided. And becoming king of Mycenae, he offered reconciliation to his brother. As you know, Thyestes agreed and settled in Mycenae. However, I believe that he never forgave Atreus and only waited for an opportunity to take revenge. Now such a case has come. However, this is not all. In addition to revenge, Thyestes most certainly wants to arrange the fate of his son, Aegisthus. Now, Agamemnon, you are the eldest in the family after Thyestes. He can make Aegisthus the legitimate heir to the throne only by getting rid of you.

"Judge for yourself if blood feud and concern for an heir are not sufficient reasons for Thyestes to seek your death. The legends say that the winner can pardon, but the vanquished will never forgive, and Thyestes was defeated more than once by Atreus.

"And know that Thyestes will not wait until the end of the funeral or even until tomorrow, because he has been waiting for many years, and his patience has run out. Moreover, having gone through a series of failures, he fears that you can slip away and destroy his plans. Therefore, I believe that the reprisal will be immediate and merciless."

Having finished his speech, Calchas took a sip of water from a wineskin and sat down on a roadside stone. He looked at the slopes of the two mountains, Euboea and Acrea, framing the surroundings of Mycenae. Between them was Heraion, the sanctuary of the great goddess Hera.

Maybe we should have gone there, where the boys would have been safer, Calchas thought.

Indeed, of all the Achaean gods, Thyestes most of all revered Hera. He identified with the great mother goddess, the main deity of the Phrygians. He could not dare attack those who had taken refuge in the temple of Hera, and in former years, he committed no such sacrileges.

Calchas told far from everything that he knew about the history of the enmity between Atreus and Thyestes. He did not mention the role of the mother of Agamemnon and Menelaus and the involvement of Atreus's wives, Aerope and Pelopia, in the cruel and bloody vicissitudes of their struggle. He did not mention why the grandfather of the young man, the king of Pisa, Pelops called his brother the cripple Broteas from Phrygia and shortly before his death gave him the throne of Pisa. Nor did he mention the prophecy that the curse of Myrtilos, the charioteer of King Oenomaus, would haunt Pelops and his heirs until the third generation.

Like many prophecies, this is, if you look at it, quite ambiguous, Calchas thought. *But what is the reason for such ambiguity? That I cannot interpret it correctly or that the deity leaves us freedom of choice, and the outcome will depend on the actions of the people?*

King Pelops himself believed in the curse of Myrtilos, whom, according to rumors, he first persuaded to betray and then killed. He erected a sanctuary to Myrtilos, made sacrifices to him, and as they said, begged for forgiveness for his crime. Perhaps it was the fear of retribution passing on to children and grandchildren that prompted him to summon brother Broteas from Phrygia.

Calchas's thoughts were interrupted by Menelaus.

"Wise Calchas, I see now that you are right. We shouldn't go to Mycenae and put ourselves at the mercy of Thyestes. Of course, there are many different stories. I also heard that in the old days, Thyestes accused Atreus for the death of his sons. It may be true or not. We do not know.

"We can try to gather our supporters and confront Thyestes. If we manage to enter the city, we will have a chance of success. If not, we'll challenge him to battle on the plains or besiege him in the citadel. I do not argue that Thyestes has supporters, but he is already old and will not participate in the battle himself. Aegisthus always kept aloof from military exercises, and the Mycenaean warriors would not follow him. What do you think, Agamemnon?"

"Menelaus, do you really suggest to go up against the king of great Mycenae?" replied Agamemnon. "I have no doubt that Thyestes has surrounded himself and Aegisthus with trusted fighters. We will never get to them. Think for yourself. If the guards are warned and we still manage to get into the city, then every moment will play against us. Sooner or later, the guards will get to us, and the Atride family will come to an end.

"Now about the battle on the plain. Thyestes will never leave the walls of the citadel on his own but will send out more and more warriors until the goddess of fortune turns her back on us. And finally, don't you seriously think about storming the walls that have stood impregnable for hundreds of years. The citadel of Mycenae is designed to resist a huge army, and for the sake of us and a handful of supporters, they will not even close the gates. No, Menelaus, military confrontation will not bring us the success."

"Yes, fearless Menelaus, I agree with Agamemnon," Calchas seconded, entering the conversation. "Now you have the support of many Achaeans in Mycenae and Midea, as well as in Argos and Tiryns—in a word, throughout Argolis. This is your main asset, because people respected your father and consider you his worthy and rightful successors. But having unleashed a war, you will become the enemies of Mycenae as soon as you shed the blood of the first Achaean warrior, and this is what Thyestes needs. He will only be glad for his losses.

"Do you know the history of the struggle between the lords of Argos, Acrisius, and Proteus? How many Argives died in a fratricidal war until the brothers agreed and divided the war-ravaged Argolis among themselves? This is how the Mycenaean and Argos kingdoms appeared. And remember the struggle for Thebe between the sons of Oedipus. It was recently when Argives, under the leadership of the lord of Argos, Adrastus, set off on a campaign against Thebe to help the son of Oedipus, Polyneices, overthrow his brother, the usurper.

"Of course, you have heard the stories of wandering singers about this campaign. All who came out of Argos perished under the walls of the city, except for Adrastus himself. He was the only one of the leaders who returned home. Boeotia is ruined. What is left of the herds of Oedipus, famous throughout Hellas? No, starting a military campaign would be a very rash step."

"So what do we do?" said Menelaus. "Flee from Thyestes in fear with tail between our legs?"

Calchas saw that both young men were looking at him, waiting for an answer. He thought that youth very easily inclined to decisive actions, not caring about fatal consequences, and thanked the gods that they had agreed to stay out of the city.

"Sons of the invincible Atreus," he began, "planning your steps according to common sense and the command of the gods does not mean being afraid. On the contrary, it means having the courage to look fate in the eye and proceed from the real state of affairs. This is the only way to earn the patronage of the almighty Zeus the Thunderer.

"I guess until you openly oppose Thyestes, he won't publicly harass you. At the same time, secretly, he will do everything possible to eliminate you. Therefore, you should not stay in Argolis, where he has now become all-powerful. Perhaps the whole Peloponnese will become unsafe for you. Embark on a journey to distant lands, such as Aetolia, and wait for the will of the gods to return to Mycenae.

"In your travels, avoid the lands inhabited by the Heraclids and their allies. After all, they believe that King Atreus closed for them the road to Peloponnese, and they can unleash their anger on his sons. Always be on your guard. Thyestes won't be able to sleep peacefully until he gets rid of you. It is best to leave the limits of the Mycenaean possessions today. I will return to the citadel and make sacrifices so that the invincible Athena and the almighty Zeus, who were merciful to your father, do not leave you with their patronage.

"When you find shelter, send word with a reliable person. I will let you know when the circumstances change in your favor. Wherever you decide to go, avoid Corinth. Thyestes has connections with the lords of Corinth and could send soldiers to the Isthmus to intercept you. There is only one road there."

The brothers were silent for a long time, trying to comprehend the new reality. From careless offspring of the royal house, they had turned overnight into persecuted exiles. Agamemnon, for a moment, thought that rather than lead such a life, maybe they could put everything at stake and, having penetrated the citadel, enter into an open confrontation with Thyestes. But he immediately discarded this thought, understanding that there were practically no chances to win, and he felt that there were no chances to stay alive.

"Wise Calchas," he said, "it seems to me that you are right. The new king will stop at nothing to secure the Mycenaean throne for his heir. We should leave Argolis and Peloponnese as quickly as possible. However, the Isthmus is the only route by land. If we do not stop at Corinth but send the chariot straight across the Isthmus, then by evening, we will be in Attica. Theseus rules there, and the warriors of Thyestes will be left behind. What do you think?"

"Yes, the road through the Isthmus is the fastest way from Peloponnese," answered Calchas. "But it is also the most dangerous. How many great warriors and heroes laid down their lives on the Isthmus? There is nowhere to hide from the pursuers. You were teenagers, but you must remember how King Eurystheus died on the Isthmus in battle with the Heraclids. When the Mycenaean army was demolished in Attica, Eurystheus realized that the goddess of victory had turned away from him and drove the chariot back to Mycenae. After all, it was on the Isthmus that son of Hercules, Gill, overtook him in a narrow place behind the Molurida rock and defeated him."

"I have heard that Eurystheus was defeated by Iolaus, the nephew of Hercules," Menelaus said, entering the conversation. "So the son of Hercules, Tlepolemus, told. Of all sons of Hercules, only Tlepolemus so far had a chance to settle in Peloponnese. He talked a lot about Iolaus, about how he was the squire of Hercules and accompanied him in his travels."

"Indeed, Iolaus is an experienced warrior and leader," Calchas replied. "He participated in many campaigns of great Hercules. Iolaus was chosen as the commander of the army, which then set out to repel the attack of King Eurystheus on Attica. Therefore, they say that Iolaus defeated Eurystheus as one commander defeats another in a battle of armies. However, Eurystheus himself was overtaken and slain by Gill. I heard it from Gill himself on the battlefield in the presence of many witnesses.

"It was on that great day when your father, King Atreus, led Mycenaean warriors and their allies from Argolis and Arcadia to repel the Heraclids' invasion to Peloponnese. The troops met on the border of Megara and Corinth, not far from the place where King Eurystheus fell. Gill, the son of Hercules, that day was the leader of the Heraclids and the Dorians who marched with them. He stepped forward before the ranks of the warriors and told about the claims of the Heraclids to the possessions in Peloponnese, conquered by their father.

"Gill announced that he had slain Eurystheus in a fair fight and now wanted to avoid unnecessary casualties. He called the best warrior to battle on the condition that the army of the loser must admit defeat and leave the battlefield. As everyone knows, this challenge was accepted by the king of Arcadia, the valiant Echemus, the son of Aerop from Tegea. He defeated Gill in a single combat.

"It was a duel of great warriors. Both were in their prime. Echemus won eternal glory in Arcadia and throughout Peloponnese, and Gill was buried on the Isthmus, not far from the grave of Eurystheus. The Heraclids remained true to the word of Gill and left Peloponnese."

Calchas wanted to continue the story about the events of those days, but he thought that now was not the time for long stories. He saw that both Agamemnon and Menelaus felt the reality of the threat, and by staying, he would only delay them. Calchas decided it was time to give the brothers free rein. After saying goodbye, the priest went out onto the road and slowly headed toward the Mycenaean citadel.

CHAPTER 3

JOURNEY TO PISA

Left alone, Agamemnon and Menelaus sat for a while in thought.

Menelaus watched the priest until he disappeared around a bend of the road, turned to his brother, and said, "Listen, Agamemnon, I think Calchas is right. We should not appear on the Isthmus. If Thyestes really organized the hunt, his messengers are waiting for us in Corinth and, most likely, have set a trap on the road from Corinth to Megara. No wonder this road is notorious. The robbers have long used it to ambush travelers. And we don't even have armor with us, just spears and swords. Let us go back to Argos and discuss with friends what to do next.

"We shall talk, first of all, with Sthenelus, the son of King Capaneus. He is a young but influential Argive leader. Then with Diomedes, the son of Tydeus. He is my good friend. Let's meet with Tlepolemus if he's still in Argos and not back in Tiryns. If it doesn't work out in Argos, we'll go to Tegea, to King Ehemus. He always supported our father.

"I know Agapenor, the son of Ancaeus, if he is in Tegea, we can count on his help. From Arcadia, we can go to Lacedaemon and then to Pylos to King Nestor. I have long dreamed of visiting Pylos and listening to the stories of the wise Nestor about the heroes and battles of the past. After all, he personally met Hercules. I am sure he has lots of stories to tell. What do you say, Agamemnon?"

"Yes, it's a good plan for a leisure trip," Agamemnon replied after a short pause. "But remember what the priest said. It's dangerous for us to stay in Peloponnese. What if we turn for help to King Broteas, to whom his brother and our grandfather Pelops left the throne in Pisa? I hope King Broteas will help his relatives. He can send a messenger to Thyestes, who owes him a favor or two.

"I remember, it was Broteas who gave Thyestes shelter when he fled Mycenae. If Broteas talks to Thyestes, he may agree to leave us alone, and we can live in peace. Perhaps Broteas will be able to convince Thyestes that we have no claims on the Mycenaean throne and will be satisfied with a small realm in the far reaches of Argolis or even in Aegialeus."

"I agree, brother," Menelaus exclaimed in response. "This is a good idea. Let's go to Uncle Broteas. We can avoid Argos if you think it's unsafe to go there. Argos is a stone's throw from Mantinea, and we could get there by chariot before sunset. The next day, we will head to Orchomenus. And from there, there is a direct road to Pisa. I suggest we move in the chariot as long as possible and then trade in horses and a chariot.

"So it is time to hit the road, brother. The sun is already high, and the road is long."

"Wait a little longer, Menelaus," Agamemnon replied. "The way to Elide through Arcadia is probably the shortest but not the safest. If Thyestes knows about yesterday's trip to Argos, he may send his men to Argos or set up an ambush on the road. Arcadia is also not a salvation for us. Many of the rulers there are closely associated with Mycenae. I think Corinth and Argos are the places we should avoid.

"There is another way to Pisa—through the Aegialeus along the coast of the Gulf of Corinth. It is longer, but in my opinion, it is much safer, because Thyestes will not think that we will move along the coast. Our father said that although many cities of Aegialeus pay tribute to Mycenae, they have long gravitated to Athens. Aegialean Ionians live there. We will take the Corinthian road, turn onto the mountain path, circle Corinth from the west, and head straight to Sicyon.

"I met the ruler of Sicyon, King Zeuxippus, when he was in Mycenae. Zeuxippus enjoys the patronage of Adrastus of Argos and will not fear the wrath of Thyestes. We can expect to get support or at least good advice from him. From there, along the coast through Pellene, Helice, Aegion, and Olenus, we will reach Elide and, bypassing Elis, will go straight to Pisa. And if we feel like being followed, we will find a ship and cross the gulf."

After a short discussion, the brothers decided to go along the shore of the bay and, having equipped themselves, set off on their way. Quickly passing the turn to Mycenae, they found themselves on the Corinthian road. A well-worn old road passed between mountains and hills, sometimes curving to the north, then deviating toward sunrise. The sun had long since passed noon when they approached the outskirts of Corinth, and finding the right fork, they turned west and soon found themselves on the road to Sicyon.

The meeting with the king of Sicyon, Zeuxippus, was short. Agamemnon greeted the king and told him about the death of Atreus and the accession of Thyestes. He decided not to talk about the proposed visit to King Broteas and limited himself to the message that the brothers were going on a trip to Aetolia, Boeotia, and Thessaly. Zeuxippus honored the memory of King Atreus and offered to help with supplies for the journey. He did not mention the intrafamilial feud of the Pelopides but advised them not to linger in Sicyon.

"There are Thyestes supporters in the city who can send a messenger to the king. Mycenae has long expressed a desire to take Sicyon under vassalage," Zeuxippus added. "And I do not want to provoke the Mycenaean lord."

After spending the night in the allotted rooms and loading the donkey presented by the king with provisions, the brothers set off along the seashore. The journey along the coast of the Gulf of Corinth between Sicyon and Elide was not burdensome. The road was mostly deserted, and residents of coastal towns were friendly and not curious.

In the vicinity of Helice, Agamemnon and Menelaus visited the temple of Poseidon Heliconius and offered sacrifices to the great earthshaker, asking for good luck on the way. A few days later, having reached Olenus, the travelers questioned the townspeople and chose a road leading south to Olympia and Pisa.

CHAPTER 4

KING BROTEAS

The walls of Pisa suddenly appeared after the sharp turn of the road. The town, surrounded on all sides by vineyards, was small. The ancient city wall was significantly inferior to the walls of the Mycenaean citadel and was even lower than the walls of Argos. After approaching the city gate and asking to see King Broteas, the travelers were directed to the royal residence. When they arrived, they informed the guard that nephews of King Broteas had arrived on a family visit.

After a short wait, the young men were led into the throne room. King Broteas looked at the newcomers inquisitively, sitting on a high dark wooden throne trimmed with copper and silver. Around him were several warriors and an elderly priest. Stepping forward, Agamemnon identified himself and his brother and uttered words of greeting to the king of Pisa. Then he announced the death of King Atreus and the accession of Thyestes.

King Broteas kept silence for a long time, considering the news.

"I am glad to welcome the grandchildren of King Pelops to the land of Pisa. It is sad to learn about the death of Atreus. He was a brave warrior and a wise ruler. We are the descendants of the great Tantalus, the companion of the gods, the ruler of vast lands in Phrygia. Pelops, your grandfather, was the eldest son of Tantalus, and I was the youngest.

"Tantalus had a daughter, our sister Niobe, whose beauty was famous throughout Phrygia. Pelops married her to Boeotia. She became

72

the wife of the lord of the Boeotian Thebe, King Amphion. You probably heard about it from King Atreus. Despite the many years spent in Thebe, she did not want to worship the local gods. Apparently, because of that, Niobe and her children suffered a tragic end."

Broteas was quiet for a moment, remembering the events of the past, and returned to his story.

"In the wars with powerful kings of Dardania and Troy, Tantalus lost many assets but retained Mount Sipylus and the lands near the river Hermus. When Tantalus suffered the inevitable fate, your grandfather, Pelops, inherited his throne. King Il, the ruler of Ilium and Troas, went against him, having secured an alliance with the powerful Hittite empire lying in the east of Asia. The war lasted for several years. Pelops was a great warrior, but the enemy's forces far outnumbered his army, and he preferred to negotiate with Il.

"Having secured the rights to small region on the mount Sipil, Pelops left it to me, and he himself, with the remnants of the army, went on ships to look for his kingdom. He performed great feats and established himself on the throne of Pisa. And after many years, Pelops called on me and handed over his kingdom. I am happy to repay the kindness and help of Pelops to his grandchildren.

"Now wash, refresh yourself, have a snack, and relax after a long journey. And tomorrow, I invite you to a dinner, where we will continue talking about the past and discuss the events of recent days. I hope that my son Tantalus Jr. will return from Olympia and join us. He is a famous horse tamer, and his chariots always participate in competitions at the Olympic hippodrome."

King Broteas gave instructions to the servants and dismissed the young men with a wave of his hand.

*****

The next day, in the late afternoon, Agamemnon and Menelaus were invited by the steward to dinner. They entered the dining hall and saw Broteas sitting at the head of the table, surrounded by courtiers and servants. To his right was a tall, slender young man, Prince Tantalus Jr.

Agamemnon greeted King Broteas, the son of Tantalus, beloved by the gods; Prince Tantalus Jr., an unsurpassed horse tamer; and the worthy residents and warriors of Pisa and wished everyone good luck and prosperity. The king returned the greeting, introduced the young men as relatives from Argolis, and invited them to his table. The servants began to deliver cakes and meat; the cupbearer mixed wine with water and offered it to those sitting at the tables.

After the guests had satisfied their hunger, King Broteas told about the latest news. He spoke about the victory of the chariots of Tantalus Jr. at the races in Olympia, about the recent skirmishes on the border with Elide, and about the death of King Atreus and the reign of Thyestes in Mycenae. The king announced that he would soon send a messenger to Thyestes with gifts and congratulations.

After the words of Broteas, Tantalus Jr., who had remained silent during the meal, volunteered to go to Argolis and try to enlist the support of the king of Mycenae in an ongoing dispute with Elide over the borderlands. King Broteas supported his son's intention and said that they would continue discussing the details the next day. Now it was time to listen to the songs of the storytellers.

The cupbearer began to deliver the wine, and the storyteller sang a ballad about the campaigns of Hercules in the lands of Elide. He sang about how the mighty Hercules destroyed the invincible generals of King Augeas, the Molion brothers; crushed the army of Augeas; and captured the city of Elis and how Hercules kept the peace and prosperity of Pisa. At the direction of the Oracle of Delphi, he erected the altar of Pelops and gave peace to the city out of respect for the favorite of the gods, Pelops, and the great king Broteas.

The brothers listened to the ballads with great interest. Seizing the moment, Agamemnon approached the king and said that he would like to talk with the lord of Pisa face-to-face. Broteas nodded and suggested the young men to be ready in the morning, promising to send a servant for them.

*****

The next day, early in the morning, Agamemnon and Menelaus were conducted to the private room of the ruler of Pisa. Broteas was waiting for them, sitting in a comfortable chair. He greeted the young men briefly and asked what they wanted to talk about.

Agamemnon, who thought over the conversation more than once the day before, took a step forward.

"Great king Broteas, son of the companion of the gods, Tantalus, Menelaus and I are grateful to you for your hospitality. Pisa is a blessed city, enjoying the patronage of Zeus the thunderer, and the wines of Pisa are among the best in the entire Peloponnese. We really like Pisa, but we have something to worry about.

"At the moment when our father, King Atreus, died, we were not in Mycenae. We learned about the reign of Thyestes returning from Argos and decided to go to you, as the oldest in the family of Tantalides, for help and advice. After all, you've probably heard about the long-standing quarrel between our father and Thyestes. As they say, in those distant years, their enmity was fierce. Under the threat of death, Thyestes fled from Argolis several times and even blamed Atreus for the death of his sons.

"Although Atreus and Thyestes have recently reconciled, we are afraid that, having reigned in Mycenae, Thyestes has planned to take revenge on us for the insults received from our father. That's why we want to ask your advice, wise Broteas, the oldest of the Tantalids. Advise us what to do to avoid the revenge of Thyestes. Is it a time for us to leave Peloponnese and find shelter in Aetolia or Thessaly? Or we can say goodbye to Hellas and go to the ancestral lands in Phrygia. Thyestes won't be chasing us there.

"We also want to ask if you could speak on our behalf and inform Thyestes that we do not dispute his sovereignty and will willingly agree to rule in some small city of Argolis, such as Midea, where Atreus and Thyestes began. We will always be grateful to you, great king Broteas, and we will gratefully accept any answer you offer."

King Broteas was silent for a long time.

"I told you about how your grandfather Pelops left Asia for Hellas, losing in the war to King Il, the ruler of Troas and Dardania. After the victory, Il chose as its capital an ancient trading city lying on the Trojan plain between the mighty Hellespont and the wooded Mount Ida. Residents began to call the city, in his honor, Ilium.

"Il gave his daughter to his nephew Kapis and sent him to rule Dardania and left Ilion and extensive possessions in Troas and adjacent lands to his son Laomedon. After becoming king, Laomedon fortified Ilium, built new walls, and continued to collect tribute from ships passing through the Hellespont. He increased his wealth, began to expand his possessions, and decided to finally expel the Tantalids from Asia. I had to leave the ancestral lands near Mount Sipil and go to Pelops in Pisa.

"The remnants of the kingdom of Tantalus were given to the ally of Laomedon, the ruler of Mysia, Teuthras. However, the plans of Laomedon were put to an end by the great Hercules, capturing Ilium. Laomedon himself and his eldest sons perished during this assault, and the throne of Ilium passed to Laomedon's youngest son, Priam. At first, Priam was weak. But over the past decades, he has consolidated his power and has many tributaries and allies.

"I don't think you'll be safe crossing to Asia. Many Phrygian rulers have a long-standing enmity towards the Tantalid family. They may see you as applicants for ancestral lands. If I were you, I would go to Aetolia or Thessaly."

Broteas plunged into thought and, looking intently at the brothers, continued.

"I'll tell you what I know about the long-standing troubles between Atreus and Thyestes. Both brothers inherited their father's arrogant character. In later years, he regretted that he expelled them from Pisa, but what he had done could not be undone. I can only guess at Thyestes's plans for you, although I agree that your concerns are reasonable. Thyestes visited me several times, and his feelings towards Atreus leave no doubt. You should not put your head into the lion's mouth even if he is full.

"I'll think about it and decide how to help you. Tomorrow, I will talk about this with my son, whom I am going to send with gifts to the king Thyestes. In the meantime, be honored guests in Pisa. Relax. Visit Olympia. Honor the grave of your grandfather, Pelops, with a sacrifice. It is located near the city walls of Pisa on the way to

Olympia, and the altar of Pelops was erected in Olympia by the great Hercules himself.

"One day, I will show you the royal scepter. This is a sign of the royal power of the Tantalites, made by the son of Zeus, Hephaestus, himself. I inherited it from Pelops, who claimed that this scepter was given to him by the messenger of Zeus, Hermes. However, if memory serves well, I still remember this scepter in my father's hands. The brother believed that the scepter was the source of royal power and did not part with it until his death.

"The scepter has become too heavy for me, and I keep it in the treasury. I will summon you as soon as I make a decision, but in the meantime, you are always welcome at the royal table. Go ahead now."

With these words, the king dismissed the young men.

CHAPTER 5

ESCAPE FROM PISA

Agamemnon woke up from the touch of a hand.

"Get up, Agamemnon," he heard Menelaus say, "and come out into the courtyard armed."

A few moments later, Agamemnon, with a sword on his back and a spear in his hand, was in the courtyard of the palace assigned to them for the night. Menelaus was waiting for him at the threshold. A loaded donkey was standing next to him.

"We must leave Pisa immediately, brother. Tantalus Jr. has returned from Mycenae, and what he brought does not look well for us. Let's hurry out of town, and on the way, I'll tell you everything I've learned."

Agamemnon, realizing from his tone that the situation was serious, silently nodded and followed his brother. After leaving the palace, they walked quickly through the city and soon found themselves at the city gates, which were open at night on the occasion of peacetime. Once outside the city wall, Menelaus slowed down, breathed a sigh of relief, and began to explain.

"Brother, if I did wrong, we only lost the shelter in Pisa. But if I'm right, we saved our lives. After all, even this morning, I could not imagine that we would have to run for our lives again. However, I will tell you everything in order.

"The night before, I went to the royal stables to observe the horses. Remember, King Broteas suggested that we pick up a pair to

78

participate in the races at the Olympic racetrack. It was in the stable that the old priest found me as if he knew that I would be there. You probably saw him. The old man often stood behind the throne of King Broteas.

"He said that he knew our father when he was still a young man and was famous in Pisa as a skilled charioteer. It was as he said about five decades ago, when Pelops was the king, and his fame thundered throughout Peloponnese. The priest said that Tantalus Jr. returned today from a trip to Mycenae and appeared before King Broteas with a message from King Thyestes. Although the ruler of Pisa was ill, he nevertheless received his son in his bedchamber. The old priest said he was looking for me to warn me about the threat that was hanging over us. Here is what he told about the meeting of King Broteas with his son, which he attended.

"Tantalus Jr. reported that King Thyestes promised to send a detachment of soldiers with a leader to fight the lords of Elis, and he himself asks that the sons of Atreus, whom he accused of evil intent against his power, be detained and escorted to Mycenae for the royal court. This is the message that Tantalus Jr. brought from Mycenae. He urged Broteas to support the alliance with the lord of Mycenae and grant his request.

"The king, after listening to his son, said that we were guests in Pisa, and we were guarded by Zeus the thunderer, the patron saint of wanderers and travelers. Tantalus Jr. replied that without the help of Thyestes, it would be difficult to contain the onslaught of the lords of Elis. Many years have passed since Hercules overthrew King Augeas and devastated Elide. A new generation of warriors has already grown up there and is anxious for revenge.

"He also said that Mycenae might be a powerful ally that Pisa needed in the upcoming war. Thereafter, he offered to send us, the sons of Atreus, out of the city under a plausible pretext, and there the faithful warriors would do their job. King Broteas listened to Tantalus Jr. and said that he would announce his decision the next morning. Then he ordered to summon the priests in the morning and prepare everything for divination to find out the will of the gods and told his son to wait for the results of divination. When Tantalus

Jr. left, the king called the priest and told him to do as the precepts of the gods command."

"I suspected that Tantalus Jr. harbored malicious intentions against us," Agamemnon confessed, interrupting his brother. "He always behaved very arrogantly. May Athena, the daughter of Zeus, the lord of heaven, send us a chance to repay his treachery. King Broteas does not want to spoil relations with his son or initiate an open feud with the mighty Mycenae. Neither does he want to violate the laws of hospitality. So he sent a priest to warn us."

After a short silence, Menelaus resumed his narrative.

"Brother, this is not the end of the story. This priest is not just a messenger of the king. He knew our father and said that already in his youth he had the makings of a great leader, which he became. He also said that he sees in us many traits of Father, and we are destined for great military glory. But now according to the priest, we need to leave Pisa immediately and beware of Tantalus Jr.

"The old man revealed to me a great secret, which, according to him, few people know about, but it will help us to correctly assess the motives and actions of Tantalus Jr. You won't believe it, brother, but the priest said that Tantalus Jr. is not the son of Broteas at all. According to the priest, the father of Tantalus Jr. is most likely none other than Thyestes himself.

"Yes, the priest told me that Thyestes, on one of his long-standing visits to Uncle Broteas, seduced his young wife, and she gave birth to Tantalus Jr. The child was born after Thyestes left Pisa, so he was not aware of the son until recently. But during a visit to Mycenae, Tantalus Jr. probably revealed to him the secret of his birth, which he himself learned from his mother. So Tantalus Jr. will do his best to serve his real parent and grab us.

"He probably won't do anything until morning, as he is not afraid of our flight and intends to maintain good relations with King Broteas as long as possible. However, having discovered our absence in the morning, he will most likely try to catch up with us. Therefore, we need to hurry and leave the borders of Pisa.

"The priest said that it would take two or three days to get to Elide at a brisk pace. If we need a ship, the harbor of Elis, Killena, lies one day's journey from the city. At parting, the priest advised us to find Amphimachus, the son of Cteatus, or Thalpius, the son of Eurytus, in Elis if we had difficulties with the ship. Their fathers, the Molion brothers, were killed by Hercules when he was at war with the king of Elide, Augeas. Although many years have passed since then, they do not like the Heraclids and will surely not refuse to help the sons of King Atreus, who stopped the invasion of the Heraclids in Peloponnese.

"The priest also suggested to leave Pisa through the northern gate, leading to the mountain road by which you and I arrived from Olenus. They are always open. After walking a little, we should turn left along the city wall and get out on the road to Elis, which goes across the plain through Letrini. That's what the old priest told me in the stable."

Menelaus had finished his story.

After a short pause, Agamemnon said, "Let's do it. It's better to get to Elide as soon as possible. If we walk all night at a fast pace, then tomorrow, we will leave the borders of Pisa. This scoundrel Tantalus Jr. will not get ahold of us there."

In silence, the young men approached the fork of the road and turned left. After walking along a well-worn trail, they soon came to the wide Elis road. The road, visible in the moonlight, stretched out between the vineyards. Having rested during the days in King Broteas's palace, the brothers did not feel tired, and the coolness of the night and the premonition of the chase quickened their pace.

The sun was already high when the weary travelers reached Letrini, a small town lying near the sea about halfway to Elis. According to local residents, the Letrini was a longtime ally of Elis and did not obey the will of the king of Pisa. The brothers agreed that they no more needed to be afraid of the chase and decided to take a break and have a snack at a picturesque lake located near the city.

Agamemnon and Menelaus reached Elis safely the next evening. They saw from afar a new city wall, rebuilt instead of the old one, destroyed in the war with Hercules. From their inquiries with the townspeople, the young men learned that Amphimachus and

Thalpius were respected in the city, corulers of King Agasthenes, the son of Augeas.

Of these, Thalpius was more engaged in trade and owned merchant ships. He had a second home in Cyllene, the harbor of Elis on the shore of the Ionian Sea, where he conducted his trading business and stored goods. Agamemnon and Menelaus decided to visit Thalpius, ask for a night's lodging, and find out if there was a passing ship to Aetolia.

Although Thalpius himself was not at home—he had just gone to Cyllene on trade business—permission for overnight stay was granted, and the manager told them that the ship to Aetolia was preparing to sail. If they hurried, they could catch it.

*****

The next morning found the brothers, provided with instructions on how to find Thalpius, on the way. The journey to Cyllene took most of the day. As the brothers learned from fellow travelers, ships from the ports of Peloponnese, Ithaca, Cephallenia, and Zacynthus, as well as from Thesprotia and the Corinthian Gulf, were frequent guests of the harbor. The sun was already falling into the sea when they found Thalpius.

A tall, broad-shouldered man was watching the loading of a merchant ship.

"Beloved by Olympian gods, Thalpius, son of the great Eurytus, travelers from distant Mycenae, Agamemnon and his brother Menelaus, sons of Atreus, greet you."

Thalpius looked at the young men with awareness.

"Greetings to the sons of mighty Atreus. We have heard of your father's exploits. What brought you to the lands of Elis?"

"Worthy Thalpius," Agamemnon replied, "thank you for your words about Atreus. The rumor about the deeds of your father, the incomparable Eurytus, and his brother Cteatus, the sons of the godlike Actor, goes all over Peloponnese. Recently, our father, King Atreus, suffered an inevitable fate. His younger brother, Thyestes, ascended to the throne of Mycenae, and we decided to go on a trip to Hellas. We ask you to provide us with seats on the ship, which, as we have heard, you are equipping for Aetolia."

After a short pause, Thalpius said, "King Atreus was a great warrior and leader. It is remembered in Elis that Atreus stopped the invasion of the Heraclids in Peloponnese. We are thankful to your father for preventing another devastating war. Now about the ship. Indeed, I am sending a ship to Corinth with a call at Naupactus and Cyrrha, the harbor of Delphi. It is almost ready to leave and, if the wind is fair, will set off the day after tomorrow. I don't see what will prevent you from sailing on it. There always will be a place for good rowers.

"I suggest you stay at my house for a while before sailing and invite you to dinner. After all, dinnertime has come, and you are probably hungry after a long journey. Wait a bit. I'll give orders, and we'll go together."

On the way to his house, Thalpius asked the young men how they got to Elis. Agamemnon replied that the brothers visited King Broteas, and after staying in Pisa, they decided to go to Aetolia and, possibly, farther to Thessaly.

Soon, they arrived at the seaside dwelling of Thalpius, an extensive building with stables and warehouses located at some distance from the waterfront. The travelers washed themselves and, leaving their belongings in the designated room, soon joined Thalpius and his guests at the dining table.

The conversation was about the deeds of King Augeas, the father of the current king of Elis, Agasthenes. The brothers learned that Thalpius and his cousin Amphimachus had become corulers of Agasthenes under a treaty, concluded between King Augeas and their grandfather Actor before the war with Hercules. Augeas had great wealth and powerful enemies, so he needed reliable allies. For a long time since the reign of King Oenomaus and his successor, King Pelops, Pisa had been skirmishing with Elis for border territories.

After the death of Pelops, his younger brother, Broteas, became the lord of Pisa. He was peaceful and did not seek war with Elis. But by that time, Augeas was much more afraid of an assault from Hercules. After all, in the old years, the king of Elis had a quarrel with the great son of Amphitryon because of a broken contract.

Many citizens believed that King Augeas was wrong. Even the son of Augeas, the noble Philaeus, begged his father to settle the contract but, in response, was expelled from Elide.

Hercules, who at the time of this quarrel was in the service of King Eurystheus, left Elis without a fight but vowed to return for a settlement. When Hercules's term of service with the king of Mycenae came to an end, King Augeas became worried and started looking for allies who could help protect his possessions. And so it happened that he agreed to share the power with his brother, the influential leader Actor, the father of two famous warriors, Eurytus and Cteatus, nicknamed the Molions.

Fortunately for Augeas, Hercules went to Asia for a long time and then decided to attack the Trojan king Laomedon. One merchant from the guests of Thalpius knew an Arcadian warrior, a participant in the campaign to Troy. According to this warrior, Hercules conquered Ilium in one day, punished Laomedon, and seized huge riches. But on the way back from Phrygia to Peloponnese, Hercules's ships were caught in a storm, and many sank. With only one ship and part of the spoils, Hercules managed to return to Tiryns, adding to the reputation of an invincible fighter the glory of the conqueror of the walls of Ilium.

"Yes," Thalpius said, entering the conversation, "having found out about the return of Hercules, Augeas and Actor began to prepare for war, recruited soldiers, strengthened the walls of the city, looked for supporters. Then they accepted into their union Amarynkeus, the famous Thessalian leader of the warriors. My cousin and I were still children, because these events happened more than twenty years ago. Actor's sons, my father and his brother, who were popularly called Molions by their mother' name, led the army.

"Many cities of Elide sided with Augeas, but Pisa refused to oppose Hercules. Hercules did not go on to Elis immediately after returning from Troy. This gave Augeas time to prepare the defense. When Hercules and his army came to Elide, a strong and well-organized army came out to meet him. Hercules did not expect such an opponent and was completely defeated in the first battle. A significant part of his soldiers died, his brother Iphicles was mortally wounded, and Hercules himself was wounded and went to Arcadia with a group of followers. Yes, this victory forever glorified in Elide the names of Eurytus and Cteatus, the sons of Actor, the only ones who managed to defeat the army of Hercules in open battle."

Agamemnon, who was listening to Thalpius with great interest, said, "Noble Thalpius, son of the divine Eurytus, the glory of the exploits of your father and uncle goes far beyond the borders of Elide. The whole Peloponnese is talking about them. I was born a few years after the Elide war, but my father, Atreus, told me that the defeat suffered by Hercules in the battle with the troops of Eurytus and Cteatus greatly undermined his authority. According to Father, it was after this battle that King Eurystheus decided to banish Hercules. Never again until his death did Hercules enter the borders of Argolis."

Menelaus joined the conversation.

"If you wish, noble Thalpius, we would love to hear more about that war."

"The war left devastating mark on the life of Elis for a long time. The losses were huge," Thalpius replied. "Although the army of Elis won, hundreds of fighters perished in the battle. While Elis was still counting the losses, Hercules healed his wounds and gathered a new army. Having insidiously ambushed and killed my father and uncle, he invaded Elide for the second time. He knew that Augeas had nowhere to find such leaders as Molions and nowhere to recruit another army.

"Hercules captured the city of Elis on the second attempt. After the victory, he took away all the herds of Augeas but did not show cruelty. He did not turn the remaining inhabitants into slaves, allowed the city to exist, and enthroned Phyleus, the son of Augeas.

"However, the hour is already late. And tomorrow, I have to finish the loading. If it pleases the gods, the ship will leave the next morning, and there is a place for you on board. So you also need to have a good rest."

Thalpius hesitated a little.

"Your interest about the war, Menelaus, is understandable to me. But at that time, I was a child, and I know about the events only from the storytellers and songs of the bards. It is better for you to ask the contemporary about the affairs of those days. I advise you, when you are in Aetolia, to visit the lord of Calydon, Oeneus. King Oeneus, the son of Porthaon, is famous for his hospitality, fine wines, and hunting grounds. By age, he belongs to the generation of Augeas, Sisyphus, Eurystheus, and Neleus. All his peers from that generation, apart from Oeneus, have already suffered the inevitable fate. The king of Sparta, Tyndareos, remains among the living, although, in my opinion, he is much younger. Oeneus was well-acquainted with many participants in those events, both with Hercules himself and with King Augeas. Over a cup of wine, he will tell you a lot of interesting things. In the meantime, I wish you pleasant dreams. A place to stay for the night has already been shown to you."

*****

The next day was spent in preparations for departure. The young men learned from the helmsman that the way by sea from Cyllene to Corinth was not considered dangerous; most of it passed through the inland waters of the Gulf of Corinth, and the captain hoped to overcome the section running through the open sea in a day, especially if the gods sent a fair wind.

Agamemnon and Menelaus helped with the loading, and in the late afternoon, having washed in the sea, they sat down to rest on the coastal rocks.

"Listen, Agamemnon," Menelaus began the conversation, "it seemed to me that Thalpius was displeased with my question at the dinner yesterday. But I just wanted to hear about the battles that Hercules fought. Storytellers often tell about the conquer of Pylos, about the terrible battle at the gates of Pylos, when all the sons of King Neleus died except one, Nestor. I would like to visit King Nestor in Pylos someday and listen to his stories, but we chose a different road. But until now, I knew almost nothing about the war of Hercules with Augeas."

"I haven't heard much about this war either," Agamemnon replied. "When King Eurystheus died in the battle with the Heraclids, my father spoke several times about the relationship between Hercules and Eurystheus. According to him, Hercules was not so much the gods' gift as the gods' punishment for the king. After all, following the directives of the Oracle of Delphi, Hercules served Eurystheus faithfully but never hid that he was doing it, fulfilling the will of the gods and not out of devotion to the king.

"Eurystheus also believed that if a strong army is useful for the king, then a strong commander may be rather destructive. According to Father, Eurystheus wanted to get rid of Hercules but never tried to do it. He believed that a mortal could not defeat Hercules, because such a prophecy was given to Hercules at Delphi. And when the term of service of Hercules came to an end many years before my birth, Eurystheus was seized with fear for his life. He became so afraid of Hercules that he exiled him from Mycenae to Tiryns.

"Yes, Father repeatedly told me that this decision of the king is an example that the true causes of events are often opposed to the apparent ones. After all, then Atreus himself hoped to get the post of ruler of the rich Tiryns. When he learned that Eurystheus was appointing Hercules there, he was upset. At first, he thought that the king rewarded Hercules for his service, and his own merits remained unmarked. However, Father soon noticed that Eurystheus never summoned Hercules to Mycenae but always sent a herald to him with an announcement. Over time, he realized that Eurystheus was afraid of Hercules and found a convenient way to remove him from Mycenae without infuriating him.

"I am telling you this story so you would understand how delighted King Eurystheus was when he learned about the defeat of Hercules in Elis. Father said that he did not hide his joy and announced that he was expelling Hercules from Argolis. He sent a herald to Tiryns and ordered his mother, Alcmene, and other relatives to leave Argolis. When Hercules recovered and managed to defeat Augeas, Eurystheus was very worried. He was afraid of revenge.

"Having learned that Hercules and his army stopped to rest near Pisa after the victory, Eurystheus feared that from there the army would move to Mycenae. Father did not go into details but mentioned that Eurystheus sent a herald to King Broteas and tried to find out about Hercules's plans through him. Broteas reported that he had persuaded Hercules not to go to Argolis. Whether this is so or whether Hercules himself did not have such an intention, I do not know."

"Yes, brother, how sorry I am that we asked Father so little about the events of those days," Menelaus exclaimed. "Tell me, what else did Father tell you about this war?"

"I can't add much from Father's stories. He was usually brief, and I was a child and was more eager to play with my peers. And then after becoming the king of Mycenae, my father did not return to this topic, because he believed that it was inappropriate for a king to criticize his predecessor. I remember that when Eurystheus and his sons perished in the battle with the Heraclids, Father said that the king had brought this fate upon himself.

"After all, when Hercules left this world, his children, the Heraclids, were scattered throughout the country and thought little of any conquests. However, King Eurystheus transferred his hatred of Hercules to his descendants and began to pursue them throughout Hellas. These persecutions for several years rallied them and gathered around them many loyal companions and old fighters of Hercules. My father often said that nothing unites people like a common enemy.

"Then the Heraclids were led by the famous Iolaus, who returned from an overseas trip. Iolaus managed to negotiate with the king of Athens, Theseus, a mighty warrior and admirer of Hercules, and he took the Heraclids under his protection. Father advised Eurystheus to leave them alone and wait for them to quarrel among themselves or with Theseus and the Athenians. He said, 'Let time win this battle for us.' After all, there were many hot young warriors among the Heraclids, and everyone wanted to be a leader.

"But King Eurystheus did not listen to our father. In addition, the lord of Mycenae has long had no special sympathy for King Theseus. Eurystheus sent several heralds to Theseus with a demand to expel the Heraclids from Attica, and when he refused, he gathered a Mycenaean army and went to Athens to make war. You know what happened next."

"Yes, I have heard that the spirit of Hercules helped his sons in this battle, because almost no one returned from the army that went out with Eurystheus," Menelaus answered. "The king himself and all his sons perished. True or not, their father's fame certainly has helped the Heraclids. I would like to know everything I can about the war of Hercules against King Augeas and other campaigns of the great hero. As far as I know, Thalpius is right, the battle with the Molion army is the only battle that Hercules lost."

"I agree with you," said Agamemnon. "But listen, Thalpius gave us excellent advice. Let's go to Aetolia to King Oeneus. As far as I know, Oeneus was on good terms with our father. He will not refuse us shelter, and he can tell a lot about the events of old times."

"That's what we'll do," Menelaus replied. "I have heard about King Oeneus and his fine wines from his grandson, Diomedes, in Argos. Diomedes, the son of the great warrior Tydeus, and his mother is the daughter of Adrastus himself. You know that Tydeus, the son of King Oeneus, participated in the Argosian campaign against Thebe under the leadership of Adrastus and fell at the walls of the city having performed many glorious feats."

"Of course I've heard about it," Agamemnon remarked. "And Diomedes himself has already become a good fighter. He has mentioned that the sons of the leaders who fell under the walls of Thebe want to avenge the death of their fathers. I saw the mighty Tydeus when he was in Mycenae, and Diomedes looks like his father. I was a child then, but I remember how skillfully he drove the chariot. Atreus treated him with great respect.

"But I do not know whether it is worth mentioning Tydeus when we are in Calydon with his father, the king Oeneus. After all, I heard that Tydeus went into exile from Calydon after committing a murder. That's how he ended up in Argos. However, we can discuss this on the way. I suggest getting off the ship in Naupactus. This is the first port on the way. From there, we will get to Calydon on foot through the Aetolian land in a day or two."

"I agree, brother," Menelaus replied. "And now let's eat and sleep. The ship departs at dawn."

The sun had not yet risen when the merchant ship, which had been loaded the day before, was ready to leave the shore. Agamemnon and Menelaus came up to thank Thalpius, who was seeing the ship off.

"Worthy Thalpius, son of the invincible Eurytus, my brother and I thank you for the shelter and a place on the ship. We decided to take your advice and visit King Oeneus to listen to his stories about the battles of bygone times. Would it be right for us to get off the ship at Naupactus and get to Calydon by land?"

"Sons of Atreus, I wish you a safe journey," Thalpius replied. "The road to Calydon via Naupactus is considered not dangerous. Aetolian robbers and pirates have subsided in recent years. If you like my advice, I'll give you another one. Whatever you talk about with King Oeneus, do not ask about his sons unless he himself talks about them. All his sons were mighty warriors, and they all have perished. Rumor has it that he himself killed the first in a quarrel. The second was ruined by his own mother, Oeneus's wife, with slander. The third, the invincible Tydeus, having gone into exile from Calydon, not so long ago fell under the walls of Thebe. Whether Oeneus was given such a prophecy or he insulted some god, I have heard different stories. But keep in mind that the king does not like to talk about it."

"Thank you for your wise words, noble Thalpius," Menelaus replied. "We have heard about the great warrior Tydeus, and we met his son, worthy Diomedes, in Argos. It is a pity that King Oeneus has no sons left alive. Have you heard about the daughters of Oeneus?"

"Are you aware that the king's oldest daughter, Deianeira, was the last wife of Hercules and did not survive him for long? There are various legends about the death of Hercules. Maybe the king will tell you about it. I don't know about the fate of the other daughters."

After farewell, the brothers hurried to take seats on the benches for rowers; and soon, the ship, driven by powerful strokes of the oars, turned northeast to the Gulf of Corinth.

CHAPTER 6

DWELLING IN CALYDON

Menelaus and Agamemnon disembarked from the ship at Naupactus and, after a long journey along mountain road, reached Calydon. King Oeneus received the travelers cordially and, having listened to their greetings, offered them to stay as long as they wished, mentioning that such great heroes as Theseus, Jason, Telamon, Peleus, Bellerophontes, and many others were guests of Calydon, abundant in wines.

Upon learning of the death of the king of Mycenae, Oeneus said that Atreus, the son of the favorite of the gods, Pelops, was a great commander and a wise king. Having invited the young men to dinner, the king asked if they had a chance to meet with his grandson, Diomedes, son of Tydeus, in Argos.

"Lord of Calydon, we know Diomedes well," answered Agamemnon. "He is an outstanding young warrior who is respected in Argolis and promises to be a worthy heir to his father. Quite recently, before leaving Mycenae, we met with him in Argos. He is in great shape."

The king was pleased with this answer and ordered that the brothers be given quarters and let them go to bathe and rest before dinner.

*****

Having settled in the palace, Agamemnon and Menelaus found themselves in the circle of the offspring of royal and aristocratic families who were forced to leave their hometown for various reasons and found refuge at the court of King Oeneus. Time passed in hunting trips, military exercises, and royal dinners with fine Aetolian wines accompanied by the tales of skillful bards.

As Menelaus once remarked, King Oeneus was, at one time, a mighty warrior and a skilled charioteer. Now at a venerable age, he could no longer participate in hand-to-hand combat. He did not have sons capable of protecting him from conspiracies of contenders for the throne. The wise king welcomed wandering warriors in Calydon, counting on their presence as a barrier against the intrigues of enemies.

In the second year of the stay of the sons of Atreus in Calydon, several refugees from Boeotian Thebe arrived in the city. They said that the children of the Argive leaders who fell during the first attack on Thebe grew up and organized a new campaign led by Alcmaeon, the son of the famous Argive soothsayer Amphiaraus. King Oeneus, in the circle of his courtiers, listened with interest to the stories of eyewitnesses about the campaign of the Epigones, as they were called, against Thebe.

In a fierce battle under the walls of the city, the lord of Thebe, the grandson of Oedipus, Laodamas, fell. After that, the defenders closed in the city. Soon, there was a shortage of provision. Supporters of the former ruler and many residents fled. Thebe fell. The city was plundered and given over to another grandson of Oedipus, the son of Polyneices, Thersander. Young warriors well-known to Agamemnon and Menelaus took part in the campaign against Thebe.

In the stories of the refugees, the names of Alcmaeon, the son of Amphiaraus; Sthenelus, the son of Capaneus; Euryalus, the son of Mesistius; and Diomedes, the son of Tydeus sounded frequently. Agamemnon noticed that the king listened with obvious pleasure to stories about the valor of his grandson Diomedes. After dinner, he shared this observation with Menelaus.

"Yes, brother. After all, not much time has passed since I played dice with Sthenelus at the walls of the Argive citadel," exclaimed

Menelaus. "And look, Sthenelus, Euryalus, and Diomedes have already distinguished themselves in battles, avenged the death of their fathers, and became recognized warrior leaders. King Oeneus has every right to be proud of his grandson. Diomedes, son of the invincible Tydeus, and other Argive warriors performed great deeds under the walls of Thebe. They can only be envied."

"Do not be jealous, valiant Menelaus. Your share of great battles is yet to come," Agamemnon replied. "But Alcmaeon's participation in this campaign surprises me. If refugees are not mistaken, he was the one who led the attack on Thebe. But when we talked with him in Argos about two years ago, he was in a completely different mood.

"Alcmaeon told me that his father, the illustrious leader and soothsayer Amphiaraus, did not want to participate in the first assault on Thebe. That campaign Adrastus himself has started to reinstate his son-in-law Polyneices on the Theban throne. According to Alcmaeon, the prophecies received then by Amphiaraus did not sound well for the campaign. Amphiaraus agreed to join only in response to the persuasion of his wife, Eriphyla, to whom he once swore an oath to fulfill her any request.

"Alcmaeon could not forget how Amphiaraus told him that taking this oath, he expected that Eriphyla would ask for a precious jewelry, but she demanded his life. He did not violate the oath given by the name of Zeus the Thunderer. And after all, his prophecies came true. He perished in that campaign. He and all Argive leaders perished under the walls of Thebe, all except Adrastus himself.

"Alcmaeon told me then that he saw no point in bloodshed in order to replace one grandson of Oedipus on the throne of Thebe with another. After all, Laodamas, the son of Eteocles, the grandson of Oedipus, is not responsible for the blood of the Argive leaders shed in the first campaign against Thebe. Neither is Thersander, the son of Polyneices, the grandson of Oedipus. So Alcmaeon spoke about a new campaign against Thebe when we talked last time in Argos."

"Probably Thersander, Sthenelus, and Diomedes were able to persuade him," Menelaus answered, "because they all thought about a new campaign against Thebe, and Adrastus himself supported them. Thersander was a particularly zealous supporter of the war. He angrily talked about how Eteocles deprived his father of the Theban throne. To be honest, at that time, I thought about joining them. Maybe Alcmaeon had already forgotten that he did not want to go, because the campaign turned out to be successful."

"Perhaps," said Agamemnon, "someday we will find out why he has changed his mind."

*****

A year had passed after the fall of Thebe, and a messenger arrived in Calydon from Phthia from King Peleus. He brought King Oeneus an invitation to the wedding of Peleus with Princess Thetis, the daughter of an overseas ruler. Peleus decided to arrange grandiose celebrations and sent out invitations to Achaean kings and the rulers of Crete and many other islands. Agamemnon was present at the meeting of King Oeneus with the messenger and was very interested in the news.

At the royal dinner, the messenger told about the exploits performed by Peleus and the upcoming feast on the occasion of marriage with the appearance of bards, competitions of warriors, and chariot races. King Oeneus was thankful for the invitation and said that perfectly remembered the son of the wise Aeacus, noble Peleus. Many years ago, he visited Calydon and participated in the legendary hunt for a giant boar. The king complained about advanced age and illness, which made long journeys very burdensome, and said that he would send an envoy to Phthia with expensive gifts for Lord Peleus and his beautiful wife.

The messenger of Peleus departed the next day, having received a farewell gift. At dinner, Agamemnon found himself in a narrow circle of close associates of the king. One of the dignitaries, raising a cup of wine, wished that the gods would send worthy heirs to King Peleus.

King Oeneus apparently thought of Peleus himself and, having drunk his wine, said, "I believe that the gods will not deprive the valiant Peleus of their favor, because from the first meeting, I noticed the seal of their attention on him. There were rumors in old times that Peleus and his brother Telamon were involved in the death of their brother, Phocus. For this, they were expelled by their father, King Aeacus, from their native Aegina.

"Peleus went to Phthia, where he was cleansed of spilled blood by King Actor, and then received the royal daughter as his wife and a third of the kingdom as a dowry. Shortly thereafter, a giant boar appeared in the vicinity of Calydon, devastating the lands and killing the inhabitants. To get rid of him, my son Meleager invited heroes from all over Hellas to hunt. Among the arrivals was the young Peleus, and then I met him."

King Oeneus paused and, turning to Agamemnon, continued.

"These events, son of Atreus, happened before your birth, long before, but I remember them as now. After all, this hunt began a series of misfortunes that led to the death of my valiant Meleager. I lost my son, and Calydon lost a great warrior and heir to the throne. However, now we are talking about the glorious Peleus, who came to hunt with the son of the king of Phthia.

"In the midst of a raid, Peleus threw a spear at a boar but accidentally hit the Phthian prince. My son Meleager and other hunters saw this with their own eyes and confirmed that this death was an accident. After all, Peleus, a skilled spearman, threw from afar, and the prince jumped out from the side of the bushes right on the boar and was hit. Then I thought that the hunting goddess Artemis favors Peleus and prepares the Phthian throne for him. That is how it eventually turned out.

"As you know, years later, after the death of King Actor, Peleus became the sole ruler of the fertile Phthia. However, at that time, Peleus, accused of an accidental murder, was forced to leave Phthia for another exile. I heard that then he went with the great Hercules on a campaign against the Trojan king and got rich trophies. Shortly thereafter, he took refuge in Iolcus, which lies under Mount Pelion. The king of Iolcus, Acastus, cleansed him of spilled blood and received him as a guest at his court. But the evil fate did not leave Peleus alone.

"King Acastus suspected Peleus of courting his wife, or maybe the wife herself slandered Peleus. One way or another, the king, unable to find out what really happened and not wanting to execute the innocent, took Peleus to the slope of Mount Pelion and left him unarmed, and some say he was even bound to the tree, entrusting his fate to the gods. And the gods did not leave their favorite. Neither wild animals nor robbers touched him, but he was soon found and saved by the leader of the centaurs, the wise Chiron.

"After many years of life as a mercenary warrior, Peleus gained both fame and fortune. And after the death of the king of Phthia, who left no heirs, Peleus ascended the Phthian throne as the husband of the king's daughter. I will tell you that once upon a time, I thought of marrying my daughter Deianeira, the one who could drive a chariot like a warrior, to Peleus. But the gods have prepared a different fate for her."

Oeneus finished his story, and the dining room was plunged into a long silence.

After the long pause, the son-in-law of Oeneus, Andraimon, replied, "When you consider how many great heroes died or were injured on that hunt, it becomes obvious that the boar was sent by some god, maybe the very daughter of Zeus the Thunderer, Artemis. Having struck the monster, Meleager performed a great deed. He saved Calydon but incurred the wrath of the goddess. In order to take revenge, Artemis inflated a dispute over tusks and a boar skin between Meleager and his uncles from the Curetes tribe. It came to fight and murder, which caused the war between Curetes and Calydon."

"I know some say that Artemis, the patroness of hunters, was offended by the lack of sacrifices and sent a monstrous boar to Calydon," Oeneus replied. "I believe that the goddess, from the very beginning, wanted to unleash a war between Calydon and Curetes. After all, the gods find pleasure in the spectacle of bloody battles. How many mighty warriors died under the walls of Calydon on both sides? How many lands were devastated? How many years did it take to restore what was lost? But the dead cannot be returned. I still think about what the fate of Meleager would have been if I had not persuaded him to leave the city and give battle to Curetes."

Agamemnon wanted to hear the continuation of Oeneus's story about Meleager, wanted to ask about Deianeira, but the king, apparently tired of the sad memories, wished his companions pleasant dreams and left. After sitting a little longer, the courtiers began to disperse, and Agamemnon went to his chamber.

A few days later, when Menelaus returned from hunting, Agamemnon told him about the wedding of Peleus and the stories of the king.

"May the gods send a worthy wife to the glorious Peleus," Menelaus answered. "I'm sorry that the king refused to go to Phthia. We could accompany him and take part in the festive competitions. Brother," he continued, "you remember what Thalpius told us in Elis? Then I thought that these were legends, but after listening to the locals, I begin to believe them.

"In the presence of the king and his attendants, you will not hear about this, but many in Calydon believe that the wife of Oeneus, the mother of Meleager, Althaea, was guilty in the death of her son. Althaea was the daughter of the lord of Curetes. And you know the old saying that Cretans are skilled in theft and Curetes in witchcraft.

"The Calydonians say that Althaea cursed Meleager when she learned that he killed her brothers in a fight after the quarrel. She burned sacrifices and prayed to the gods of the underworld for retribution for her son. They say that when Meleager found out about the curse of his mother, he was terribly upset, shut himself up in his house, and did not want to see anyone.

"Even the invasion of the Curetes left him unresponsive. And keep in mind that he was not only the heir to the throne but also chief military leader and most powerful warrior in Calydon. But the curse of his mother crushed him, or maybe he really thought that the gods heard her because she comes from Curetes.

"One way or another, the townspeople say that no one could convince him—neither friends nor his wife or the king himself. Even his mother, having come to her senses, came to him, but he remained deaf to her words. Only when the Curetes, after the long siege, began to climb the walls and throw spears and stones into the city did Meleager seem to realize that he could not escape fate. Residents believe that he saved the city from destruction when he went out of the gate and utterly defeated the Curetes. At the same time, he himself received a mortal wound, which as they claim was exactly the same that he inflicted on the boar.

"There is a legend among the townspeople that Meleager killed as many Curetes leaders as Achaean heroes fell from the fangs of the boar. They say that both the invasion of the boar and the war with the Curetes are all the works of Artemis. The goddess wanted to take revenge on King Oeneus for some kind of misconduct. Either he did not bring her the promised sacrifices, or he killed her beloved doe while hunting. And she retaliated by killing those he loved. Indeed, the day after the death of Meleager, his mother was found hanged. Many believe that she killed herself in desperation, but not everyone agrees."

Agamemnon considered for a while what he had heard.

"Yes, Thalpius did not warn us in vain. Tell, Menelaus, have you heard what they say in Calydon about the eldest son of King Oeneus?"

"Few people remember him, because he suffered an inevitable fate many years ago, long before the war of Calydon against Curetes, which everyone here remembers," said Menelaus. "I have heard that from a young age, he liked to start quarrels, violated the decrees of the king, and publicly challenged his will. In the end, as one old warrior told me, Oeneus's patience snapped, and his son got what he deserved. So maybe there is a truth to Thalpius's words.

"And about the daughter of the king, Deianeira, I heard that the king gave her for the great Hercules, as Thalpius said. Having married Deianeira, Hercules, at the request of Oeneus, went with the Calydonian army on a campaign against the Thesprotians. The victory of the Aetolians in that war is mainly the accomplishment of Hercules. It is a joke in Calydon that the Thesprotians still tremble at the sound of his name. It is said that when Hercules lived in Calydon, he was friends with the young Tydeus and taught him the military arts."

"It may be helpful to ask Andraimon at a convenient time about the war with the Thesprotians and about the fate of Deianeira," Agamemnon answered. "After all, he is married to her younger sister and should know about these events firsthand."

CHAPTER 7

THE TALE OF MELEAGER

A long time passed before Agamemnon managed to talk with the son-in-law of Oeneus. First, the king sent Andraimon as an envoy to the wedding of Peleus; and on his return, he was provided with the set of gifts to be delivered to Delphi. An opportunity presented itself one day many months later while hunting in the mountains. Agamemnon, sitting next to Andraimon in the evening by the fire, asked him if it was true that his wife's sister, Deianeira, was a skilled hunter.

"Yes, it is so," answered Andraimon. "She was still a teenager when the best hunters from all Hellas gathered in Calydon to rid the country of the sinister boar. Among the arrivals was Atalanta, the famous huntress from Arcadia, who, according to storytellers, hunted with Artemis, the daughter of the almighty Zeus. Deianeira was bewitched by the beauty and dexterity of Atalanta and followed her as if on a leash. And not only Deianeira.

"It is not customary to talk about this at the court, but Meleager himself did not remain indifferent to the virtues of Atalanta. After all, when he received the main trophy, the skin and fangs of a boar, which he deserved by inflicting a mortal blow on the monster, he immediately handed them to Atalanta. Meleager proclaimed that the huntress from Arcadia deserved the trophy because she shed first blood by hitting the beast with an arrow, and no one rejoiced at his act more than Deianeira.

"Years later, she told my wife how this moment inspired her. But to tell you the truth, not everyone shared the opinion of Meleager and Deianeira. The famous Nestor, who later became the king of Pylos, said that the arrow of Atalanta only angered the beast and prompted him to rush at the hunters in a rage. The monster devoured several people. The brother of Hercules, the glorious Iphicles, who was also on this hunt, noticed that the bow is good when hunting a deer but not a seasoned boar. After all, few people, except for the great Hercules, could shoot an arrow with such force that it pierced the skin of such a beast as the Calydonian boar.

"Other hunters also said that Atalanta's shot was well-aimed but reckless. However, of all those present at the party, only two of Meleager's uncles challenged his decision aloud. They acted against the will of the first prince of Calydon and, in my opinion, were themselves responsible for the quarrel unleashed. After all, since Meleager received the trophy, he had the right to dispose of it at his discretion. Meleager could not endure such an insult in the presence of heroes from all over Hellas and, most importantly, Atalanta. Swords quickly replaced words, and both uncles were hacked to death.

"Having learned about the murder of members of the royal family, Curetes decided to take revenge. So because of the skin of a boar and, others say, because of the beautiful eyes of Atalanta, a war broke out with Curetes, which led to huge losses for Calydon and the death of Meleager himself. The inevitable fate befell both Meleager's mother, Queen Althaea, and his wife, the beautiful Cleopatra. King Oeneus was left without an heir and without a wife. He was inconsolable.

"Curetes failed to take Calydon, but many warriors perished, the city was almost destroyed, and the country was ruined. The people said that the long-reaching Artemis wanted to punish Calydon and sent not only the boar but also Atalanta to help him. The beautiful huntress finished what the boar could not accomplish."

"I understand," said Agamemnon. "Atalanta, willingly or unwittingly, fulfilled the desire of the goddess and plunged the city into the abyss of disaster. She caused the death of Meleager, his wife, mother, and mother's brothers. And she herself went back to Arcadia with trophies."

"Yes, with trophies," repeated Andraimon. "There was even a rumor in Calydon that Atalanta did not remain deaf to the courtship of Meleager and, upon returning home, gave birth to a son by him. But I believe this is all fiction. After all, as the storytellers say, the farsighted Artemis is very vindictive and does not share her favorites with anyone."

Andraimon was silent for a while, took a sip of water from a flask, and continued.

"Deianeira, after the war, was all absorbed in hunting and exercises. Trying to imitate her idol, she mastered the art of hunting, archery, and learned to perfectly control the chariot. King Oeneus said more than once that with such skills, only a great warrior can become Deianeira's husband. And his wish came true, but not in the way the king saw it."

"Thank you, noble Andraimon, for your story," said Agamemnon. "But why do you say that King Oeneus was left without an heir by the death of Meleager? Was not the mighty Tydeus worthy of the royal throne?"

"Agamemnon, son of the great Atreus," answered Andraimon, "find out that Tydeus was not the son of King Oeneus from his lawful wife. He was born of a concubine and by birth could not claim the throne. I remember that Tydeus was born before the war with Curetes and was a teenager during the campaigns of Hercules against the Thesprotians. He was very unhappy that due to his age he could not go out with the army.

"Hercules was friendly with the young Tydeus, taught him martial arts, and predicted that he would become a great warrior. He gave Tydeus a shield with a boar's head, which he did never part with. Tydeus was saddened when Hercules decided to leave Calydon due to an accident. When Hercules suffered the inevitable fate, Tydeus was very upset. He was even more struck by the death of Deianeira, with whom he had been friends since childhood.

"After these events, Tydeus often said that Hercules was the greatest hero and deserved more honors than those given to him. When rumors spread that Deianeira, tormented by jealousy, could be involved in the death of Hercules, Tydeus threatened with reprisal for such slander. In general, like Hercules in his youth, he easily lost his temper, started quarrels at the slightest provocation.

"One of these conflicts turned into a fight. Tydeus killed his opponent and was forced to leave Calydon for exile. They say that he found refuge at the court of Argos, participated in the campaign of the great Adrastus against Thebe, and laid down his head under the walls of the city."

"You are right, worthy Andraimon," said Agamemnon. "I saw Tydeus many years ago in Mycenae on the eve of the Argives' campaign against Thebe. He was one of the leaders who went with Adrastus to Thebe in order to return Polyneices to the throne. The Argos warriors who were on that campaign said that Tydeus killed many enemy leaders. He inspired fear in Theban fighters. Hercules taught him not in vain. In hand-to-hand combat, he had no equal. Eyewitnesses said that no one could defeat Tydeus in a duel.

"I heard that he was struck down by a spear thrown from the side during a fight with one of the Theban commanders. It hit him in the stomach, but Tydeus pulled out a spear and, despite a mortal wound, managed to defeat the enemy. When he died, Polyneices stopped the battle and offered to decide the fate of the Theban throne in a duel with his brother. In the fight, the sons of Oedipus inflicted mortal wounds on each other.

"With the death of Polyneices, the Argives had nothing to fight for, and they left Thebe. Tydeus fell in that war, but he left a son, born from the daughter of Adrastus. Menelaus and I know well the son of Tydeus, the young Diomedes of Argos. He has all the makings of a great warrior, and as I have heard, he performed many feats during the recent campaign of the Epigones against Thebe. Someday, he might visit Calydon and meet his grandfather."

"Yes, King Oeneus said more than once that he would like to see his grandson," Andraimon answered. "He was glad to hear about the exploits of Diomedes under the walls of Thebe. But it's time to rest, noble Agamemnon. Tomorrow, we have to face a worthy opponent. The beaters say that this boar is only slightly inferior to the monster that Meleager slew and has already managed to string two hunters on his fangs. Get a good night's sleep before hunting. Wish you sweet dreams."

Wishing good dreams to Andraimon, Agamemnon went to his hut, where Menelaus was already sleeping. He thought that the young Tydeus, who had warm feelings for Hercules and for Deianeira, could not bear to hear that one of them could plot against the other.

It was a pity that Andraimon went to bed so quickly. One could have asked him to tell more about the life of Hercules in Calydon, his marriage to Deianeira, and the war against Thesprotia. However, if there is some truth in the rumors about the involvement of Deianeira in the death of Hercules, it should be unpleasant for Andraimon and King Oeneus to talk about it.

We, as guests, should not ask about such matters. It may be helpful to consult with Menelaus, thought Agamemnon, falling asleep.

*****

A messenger arrived at the hunters' camp the next day. King Oeneus urgently demanded Andraimon to the palace. Saying good-bye and ordering to continue hunting without him, Andraimon went to Calydon.

A few days later, on the way to the city after the hunt, Agamemnon returned to his thoughts about Hercules. He knew quite well about Hercules's life in Argolis from eyewitnesses. His campaigns and fights were on everyone's lips and glorified the military power of Mycenae. But a few years before the birth of Agamemnon, King Eurystheus expelled Hercules from Mycenae; and after that, only echoes of the events associated with the great hero reached the townspeople.

Even in Mycenae, Agamemnon heard that the leader of the Heraclids, Gill, who laid down his head on the Isthmus, was the son of Hercules from the daughter of King Oeneus, Deianeira. Hercules left a deep mark on the life of Calydon, but as in Mycenae, they preferred not to mention him at the court.

Agamemnon overtook Menelaus, who was walking a little ahead.

"Listen, Menelaus," he said, turning to his brother, "I recently talked with the worthy Andraimon and learned new details about the famous Calydonian hunt. According to Andraimon, the famous Arcadian huntress Atalanta was the cause of the quarrel between

Meleager and his uncles. When Meleager decided to give her the skin of a boar, which he received as a trophy, these uncles objected and challenged his will. The dispute turned into a fight, and Meleager hacked them to death.

"Having learned about the murder of their fellow tribesmen, Curetes invaded Calydon. It turns out that the troubles that Calydon had suffered were caused not so much by the monstrous boar as by the beautiful Atalanta, the favorite of Artemis."

"I don't know, brother," Menelaus replied. "With equal success, they can be blamed on the mother of Meleager, Queen Althaea. With her curses, she deprived her son of the will to fight. After all, if he had joined the battle immediately, Curetes would most likely have been defeated. However, crushed by his mother's curse, he remained dormant until Calydon was on the brink of destruction. The more I hear about that hunt and subsequent events, the more I recall the words of King Oeneus. He once said that the boar was sent to Calydon to start a war for the amusement of the gods."

"Yes, I remember well, and now I understand what the king meant," Agamemnon answered. "The gods wanted bloody battles. In obedience to their will, Atalanta came to hunt, turned Meleager's head, and caused a quarrel that led to murder and war. Meleager, like a mighty beast, followed his feelings, fell into a trap, and could not find a way out. He is the true Calydonian boar.

"Calchas once said, if the gods want to punish a person, they deprive him of his mind. But it is not clear whether the long-reaching Artemis wanted to destroy Meleager from the very beginning. Or she went jealous of him for her favorite, Atalanta, and took her revenge."

"Perhaps it could be the second," Menelaus remarked. "Artemis is known for her vindictiveness. Do you remember how Father told us about her merciless revenge on Pelops's sister Niobe? Or maybe Meleager was just trying to win the heart of beautiful Atalanta. His uncles, the brothers of Queen Althaea, sought to take possession of trophies in order to show off their hunting exploits among Curetes in their homeland. Many agree that the curses of Queen Althaea removed Meleager from the battlefield and dragged out the war for a long time, which led to huge losses for Calydon.

"No one can say for sure whether those events were due to the actions of people or the plotting of the gods. Only the appearance of a boar is beyond doubt. Someday, I will ask old Architelos about these events. He participated both in the hunt itself and in the war with Curetes. But enlighten me on what else the wise son-in-law of King Oeneus told you."

"I wanted to know about the accomplishments of Hercules," replied Agamemnon. "However, Andraimon told a little, only that Hercules was friends with Tydeus and taught him martial arts. But Hercules lived in Calydon for a long time. He married Deianeira, had children, and led an army on a campaign against the Thesprotians.

"You know, the son of Hercules Gill, who slew King Eurystheus and led the Heraclids on a campaign against Peloponnese, was born here in Calydon. This was a few years after the war with Curetes and the death of Meleager.

"Andraimon said that after Hercules and Deianeira suffered the inevitable fate, Tydeus was heartbroken. He started a quarrel with some city dweller and killed him. That is why Tydeus was forced to go into exile and ended up in Argos."

"Listen," Menelaus interrupted, "I noticed long ago that at the court they do not like to talk about Hercules. Maybe this is due to the rumors about the role of Deianeira in his death. And after all, Gill is the son of Deianeira, and Deianeira and Tydeus are brother and sister. It turns out that Diomedes, the son of Tydeus, is the cousin of Gill, son of Hercules. Diomedes has never mentioned that his father was so intimately acquainted with Hercules himself."

"Gill was much older than Diomedes, and they have never met," replied Agamemnon.

After a long silence, Menelaus said, "Look, the walls of the city are already visible. Our journey is coming to an end. I wonder why King Oeneus needed to urgently call in his son-in-law. Andraimon was very disappointed, because he is a big fan of hunting. I hope all is well in the city."

"I think nothing threatens Calydon," answered Agamemnon. "Otherwise, the king would have called not only Andraimon but all warriors who were on the hunt."

CHAPTER 8

THESEUS VISITS CALYDON

Arriving in the city, the brothers washed and went to the throne room. There was a conversation at the dinner table about a recent hunt. The king listened favorably to the stories of the participants. After waiting until all guests had gathered, Oeneus brought the proper sacrifices to the gods and ordered the dishes to be served and the wines to be poured. Menelaus noticed that the conversations gradually subsided. The audience seemed to be waiting with interest for the royal word.

Oeneus finished his meal and, after drinking a good sip of Aetolian wine, began to speak.

"Noble citizens, Calydon has long been famous for its hospitality. Many great heroes honored our city with their presence. Hercules, the greatest hero, whom some consider the son of Zeus the thunderer, lived in Calydon. Bellerophontes, whose exploits are legendary, was a guest here.

"I want to tell you that a few days ago, we welcomed the conqueror of the Amazons: the king of Athens, the godlike Theseus; and the winner over centaurs and the leader of the Lapiths, the incomparable Periphoy. It wasn't the first time these illustrious warriors had been guests of Calydon. But their visit was short-lived.

"Theseus and Periphoy are heading to Thesprotia on their own business and stopped in Calydon for a short rest. I wanted to organize competitions of Calydonian warriors and presentation of story-

106

tellers in honor of the great heroes. But King Theseus said that their affairs were urgent. He has promised to stop at Calydon on the way back, and then we can have a party."

The king took a sip of wine and continued.

"When the detachment of Theseus and Periphoy was about to leave the city, several young warriors, delighted with the exploits and glory of Theseus, wished to accompany him. I stopped them and forbade the citizens of Calydon carrying weapons to follow Theseus and Periphoy. They didn't tell us about the purpose of their trip. But if their actions lead to an armed clash with the Thesprotians, Calydon and all of Aetolia may again be on the verge of war.

"You remember the last war with the Thesprotians. These are the events of twenty years ago. The Calydonian army then won with the support of the great Hercules. But how many glorious men did not return from the campaign. Many still remember the war with Curetes. About thirty years have passed since then. The city was almost taken, the walls were destroyed, and the land was looted. And how many soldiers died? The best warriors of the Calydonian army and Meleager himself gave their lives for the victory.

"Only recently, Calydon began to recover from two devastating wars, and the prosperity of the old times began to return to our homes. A new generation of valiant warriors is growing. We don't need a war. And rash actions can provoke the Thesprotians, many of whom are thinking about revenge. That's why none of the Calydonians should go with Theseus's squad."

"God-wise king Oeneus," one of the king's confidants, Architelos, entered the conversation, "no one will dispute the validity of your words, but what grounds do we have to suspect Theseus and Periphoy of evil intentions? They can go to Thesprotia to purchase horses or visit the oracle in Dodona. I have heard that the daughter of the ruler of Molossia, the worthy Aidoneus, attracts many suitors from all over Hellas. So far, no one has been awarded her hand. Maybe this is the purpose of their trip."

"You speak sensibly, worthy Architelos," Oeneus replied. "I respect the illustrious kings Theseus and Periphoy, but first of all, I think about the welfare of Calydon. I didn't want to mention it until I get confirmation, but it's probably better to say it now. Merchants who had recently arrived from Corinth brought news from Peloponnese.

"They reported that the youngest daughter of the king of Sparta, Tyndareos, the golden-haired Helen, whose beauty, despite her youth, is already being praised by storytellers, was abducted. King Tyndareos laid the responsibility for this on Theseus. If the merchants are telling the truth, then I fear that Theseus and Periphoy may continue their series of exploits.

"According to Architelos, the daughter of King Aidoneus, Cora is beautiful as a goddess, and her father demands huge gifts for her hand. After all, since Theseus and Periphoy kidnapped Helen, they may have the same intentions with regard to Cora. If King Aidoneus finds out that they were helped by Calydonian fighters, a war with the Thesprotians will be inevitable."

"The great king and the worthy citizens," Andraimon said, rising, "we know that Thesprotia is abundant with brave fighters and can raise a large army. And the detachment of Theseus and Periphoy is not so great and does not pose a threat to the kings of the Thesprotians. If they were aiming for war, they would have brought hundreds of fighters. If they expected to recruit soldiers in Calydon, this did not happen. I have reinforced the guards at all the city gates, and I guarantee that the decree of the king is carried out. Not a single warrior of Calydon left the city with Theseus's detachment."

"Thank you, Andraimon," Oeneus replied. "Young warriors do not understand this, but in mature years, after going through many trials, you begin to feel the approach of danger like an ache in the bones. At the time when Hercules lived in Calydon, I sometimes felt in his presence the approach of inevitable blows of fate, and these premonitions always came true.

"You remember, Architelos, that unfortunate day when your son suffered the inevitable fate due to the carelessness of Hercules. That day, in the morning, I felt the approach of fatal events, but I could not foresee what would happen. But it happened, and Hercules went into exile, never to return.

"In the old days, the priest of the great Hera told me that some people are able to feel the presence of the deity, even without comprehending the nature of their perception. The feeling of the gods' presence is perceived by such people as a premonition of fatal events. It was how I perceived the presence of the god who was willing to attend such fateful moments but did not want to reveal himself. After all, the gods are not interested in the daily life of mortals, but they like to watch tragic events, catastrophes, and bloody battles."

Oeneus paused, sipped his wine, and continued.

"This is exactly the feeling that I had with the arrival of Theseus and Periphoy. I was afraid that they would start a quarrel or start a conflict with one of our neighbors, and the war would come to the Aetolian land again. It was then that I summoned Andraimon and ordered him to strengthen the guard at the gates and make sure that not a single Calydonian warrior went with their squad."

"Glorious king Oeneus, son of the great Porthaon," said Architelos, "you reminded me of the saddest day in my life, the day when I lost my beloved son. Although it has been about two decades, but the pain of loss is alive. I forgave Hercules, because he did not want evil, and feeling guilty, he acted according to the law and went into exile.

"Over the years, I have often thought about that day. I want to say that I agree with you, That day, a certain god arrived in Calydon. The gods loved to watch Hercules, because his whole life was full of fights and battles. Only in Calydon he lived peacefully for several years in a marriage with Deianeira. But perhaps the gods missed the sights and decided to send Hercules back on the warpath. To this end, a certain god pushed the hand of the great hero so that the blow inflicted by him turned out to be fatal.

"Many say that Hercules was the favorite of the daughter of the almighty Zeus, the invincible Athena. Whether it was her or another deity, I do not know, but the plan of the gods succeeded. Hercules left Calydon and gave up his peaceful life. His last years spent in the north, rumor has it, were a continuous series of deadly duels, battles, and sieges of cities."

After a pause, Architelos spoke again, slowly pronouncing his words.

"King Oeneus, I believe that you felt the presence of the deity when Theseus and Periphoy were in the city, and the presence of the gods truly foretells fatal events. Therefore, I agree with your order. However, this order was violated. Calydonian warriors marched with Theseus's detachment. Yes, I know from eyewitnesses that Agrius's two sons joined his squad outside the city walls."

"This is bad news, but you did right by telling me about it, Architelos," Oeneus said quietly. "Agrius has long loved to sow quarrels and start troubles, but so far, we have managed to avoid his intrigues. I hope everything will work out this time. Tomorrow, I will make sacrifices and ask the gods to turn away adversity from Calydon.

"I know that glorious warriors who intended to join Theseus's squad are saddened by my ban. They may be interested in the upcoming funeral games in Olympia. A messenger from Pisa arrived in Calydon shortly before Theseus. He told that the king of Pisa, the wise Broteas, suffered an inevitable fate. His son, Tantalus Jr., ascended to the throne of Pisa. King Tantalus Jr. invites warriors from all over Hellas to Olympia, to the games dedicated to the memory of Broteas. Let the herald notify the young Calydonian fighters. Here is a worthy place where a brave warrior can show his prowess and seek glory. However, the time is already late. I wish you all good dreams."

With these words, the king left the throne room.

"It's a pity we couldn't see these great warriors," Menelaus said to his brother after the dinner. "I hope King Theseus will stop by Calydon on his way back. I would like to hear his stories about the campaigns to Crete and the duel with Minotaur, about the wars with the Amazons, about meetings with Hercules. Theseus is the most powerful warrior and the most famous in Hellas after the death of Hercules. Do you believe that Theseus kidnapped the daughter of King Tyndareos, the golden-haired Helen?"

"I don't know, brother," Agamemnon answered. "Our father said that when Eurystheus marched with an army to Athens against the Heraclids, Theseus was over forty. More than ten years have passed since then, so the king of Athens must be over fifty by now. The following year, Father repelled the attack of the Heraclids, and envoys from all over Peloponnese frequented Mycenae. The ambassador from Sparta also arrived. Then he told about the younger daughters of King Tyndareos. He said that Clytemnestra would soon be ten, and Helen was not even three. So Helen can't be more than twelve or thirteen years old. Think about why King Theseus would kidnap a child.

"And it may be for the best that we didn't meet him. It's hard to guess how a man like Theseus would react to the sons of King Atreus. After all, Theseus, together with the Heraclids, opposed King Eurystheus. My father believed that without the help of Theseus and the Athenian army, Eurystheus would not have been defeated. He feared that Theseus might join the Heraclid invasion of Peloponnese."

"However, he did not," Menelaus replied. "So Theseus and Atreus didn't clash on the battlefield, and Theseus has no reason to dislike us. Listen, brother, if we manage to establish a good relationship with King Theseus, it may help in the struggle for the Mycenaean throne. After all, six years have passed since we left Mycenae. It's time to think about the return."

"I think about it all the time," Agamemnon replied. "But you must admit, the day has not come yet. Tell me, have you heard that Tantalus Jr. became the ruler of Pisa after the death of King Broteas? This scoundrel is a longtime ally of Thyestes. Do you remember how we had to flee Pisa when Tantalus Jr. returned from Mycenae? Even then, he was plotting against us together with Thyestes. When the Mycenaean throne becomes vacant, he will almost certainly support Aegisthus. Having become king, Tantalus Jr. is already looking for ways to attract allies. With that in mind, he arranges the games in Olympia.

"We also need to seek support in the struggle for the Mycenaean throne. Argos probably will not want to interfere in the affairs of the Mycenaean kingdom. This is the tradition of the ancestors. I have heard that Adrastus and his son, who knew us well, have perished during the second war of the Argives against Thebe. Diomedes could support us, but he most likely has little influence at the Argos court. According to rumors, Sthenelus, the son of Capaneus, Cyanippus, the son of Aegialeus, and Alcmaeon, the son of Amphiaraus now reign in Argos. We know Alcmaeon, but we are not well-acquainted with the others.

"I think you're right, brother, an alliance with the king of Athens may be helpful for us. When Theseus visits Calydon on his way back from Thesprotia, I will try to talk to him. If Theseus really kidnapped Helen and did not pay the ransom, he faces a serious conflict with King Tyndareos. I think he may support our claim to the Mycenaean throne in exchange for help in the struggle against Sparta."

THE TALE OF HERCULES

King Theseus did not appear in Calydon a month later and neither with the onset of cold weather or by the next spring. However, his name was often mentioned in the stories and rumors that came to Calydon with caravans and ships from Attica and Peloponnese. The kidnapping of Helen, the youngest daughter of the king of Sparta, Tyndareos, broke the peace between Athens and the Spartan kingdom.

The sons of the king of Sparta, Castor and Polydeuces, experienced leaders known in Peloponnese as the Dioscouroi, gathered a large army and invaded Attica. Encountering no resistance in the absence of Theseus, they plundered the land and laid siege to Athens. The Dioscouroi demanded that Helen be handed over and threatened to storm the city. The Athenian citizens found themselves in a critical situation.

Learning about these events, the inhabitants of Calydon said that after the conquest of Boeotia by the Argives, it was the turn of Attica. They wondered where Theseus had gone. At one of the royal dinners, Agamemnon heard the opinion that the Spartans, having learned about the rich trophies collected by the Argos army in Boeotian Thebe, also decided to go for prey. They took advantage of the absence of King Theseus and put forward the abduction of Helen as a pretext for war. The courtiers feared that having plundered Boeotia and Attica, the Peloponnesian conquerors might reach Aetolia.

How could these events turn out for Menelaus and me? thought Agamemnon. *Thebe is already devastated. Athens is waiting for a similar fate. If Thyestes wants to follow the example of Argos and Sparta and embark on the path of conquest, where will he go? To the north lies the kingdoms of the mighty Peleus and his vassals and the regions of the Dorian tribes ruled by the Heraclids. Aetolia remains.*

We have been living in Calydon for seven years, and Thyestes is undoubtedly aware of our whereabouts. If the Mycenaean ruler demands our extradition, what will King Oeneus do? Wouldn't he give up the laws of hospitality to keep Calydon out of the war? No, thought Agamemnon, *Thyestes would not attack Calydon. He is too old. And old kings don't like wars. During his entire reign in Mycenae, Thyestes never started hostilities.*

Now if in his place there was such a ruler as Theseus, then it would be a different story. Where could Theseus disappear while his kingdom is on the verge of destruction? King Oeneus said that Theseus has promised to visit Calydon on his way back. He must be also surprised by the long absence of the great warrior.

However, King Oeneus only listened to the table conversations and remained silent.

*****

Two months passed, and new news came from Attica with another ship. The merchants told that the noble Menestheus, the son of Peteos, came to the aid of Athens. He initiated the talks with the Dioscouroi and dissuaded them from storming Athens.

Menestheus opened the gates of Athens to the Spartans, and they were assured that Helen was not in the city. The Dioscouroi believed his words that the Athenian citizens were not involved in the abduction of Helen, that this was the work of Theseus alone. They did not touch anything in the city and concluded a peace treaty with Menestheus, who was proclaimed the ruler of Athens.

According to the stories of merchants, it soon became known to the Dioscouroi that Helen was hidden in Aphidna, a small town located half a day's journey from Athens, where several loyal supporters of Theseus guarded her. The Spartan army took Aphidna by storm, and many famous warriors were killed in a fierce battle. The Dioscouroi plundered the city, freed Helen, and captured many prisoners, after which Spartan troops went back to Sparta.

The merchants praised the Dioscouroi for not causing damage to Athens although they entered the city. No one in Athens, according to the merchants, knew what happened to Theseus, but many blamed him for the troubles that befell them. It was said that among the prisoners captured in Aphidna and taken away to Sparta, there was even the mother of Theseus, Aethra.

The sons of Atreus often discussed the news from Attica, wondering what could happen to Theseus and Pirithous. Agamemnon was inclined to think that they suffered an inevitable fate at the hands of robbers, or they were attacked by centaurs, who had long been at enmity with the leader of the Lapiths, Pirithous. Menelaus believed that such mighty warriors would not become easy prey for robbers and had more than once emerged victorious from battles with centaurs.

During one of these disputes, Menelaus offered to question old Agrius.

"Do you remember, it was said at a king's dinner that two sons of old Agrius joined Theseus's detachment," he said. "Maybe I will try to find out from Agrius himself or someone from the household about what happened to them."

"Listen, Menelaus," replied Agamemnon, "after all, we are the guests of King Oeneus, and the king has been in dispute with his brother Agrius for a long time. Old Agrius, I have heard, has had claims on the throne of Calydon. Perhaps he sent his sons with Theseus, trying to persuade him to take his side, in the struggle with Oeneus for power. I believe it is not proper for us to turn to the king's ill-wishers. I'd rather try to talk to Andraimon. He is the son-in-law and trusted adviser of Oeneus and probably knows something."

A convenient opportunity to speak with Andraimon presented itself a few days later, when the king's son-in-law invited several young warriors to inspect a herd of horses recently brought in from Thessaly. On the way back from the royal meadows, where horses were grazing, Agamemnon caught up with Andraimon and, praising the dignity of animals, started a conversation on a topic of his interest.

"Noble Andraimon, do you remember about six months ago, the king of Athens, Theseus, visited Calydon on his way to Thesprotia? Menelaus and I were then hunting and could not meet this great warrior and his companion, King Pirithous. I have hoped that illustrious Theseus would stop by King Oeneus on his way back. However, this did not happen, and visiting merchants say that Theseus did not return to Attica either. According to them, the worthy Menestheus now rules in Athens, and everyone forgot about Theseus. Tell, Andraimon, do you know what happened to these glorious warriors, whether they are alive or they have suffered an inevitable fate?"

Andraimon listened to the question but was in no hurry to reply. It was only when the road rounded the overhanging cliff and they came to a long, gentle slope that he answered, speaking slowly, as he was used to.

"Son of the great Atreus, what I say is intended for you and your brother, because there are people in Calydon who are ready to use my words to the detriment of the king. You know how King Oeneus honors the glorious Theseus, whose deeds are well-known throughout Hellas. When Theseus and Pirithous visited the king on their way to Thesprotia, they asked for guides who would know this northern region. However, the king, fearing that Theseus had dangerous intentions, decided not to send Calydonian soldiers with him, and here's why.

"Thesprotia is a large country inhabited by mighty fighters. The leaders of the Thesprotians have tried to attack our lands more than once in the past. The last war was about twenty years ago. The divine Hercules, who was then married to Deianeira, took the side of Calydon. He defeated the Thesprotians, conquered their capital city, and captured the king and his household. They say that from Hercules, the daughter of the Thesprotian king gave birth to the glorious Tlepolemus.

"In exchange for their lives, the Thesprotians then swore to Hercules never to start a war with Calydon. However, if Calydon attacks first, the oath given to Hercules will cease to be valid. Therefore, King Oeneus forbade the Calydonian warriors to go with Theseus. You understand that the presence of Calydonian warriors in Theseus's detachment could lead to war. Indeed, in the event of a conflict with Theseus, the Thesprotians might say that the Calydonians were the first to violate the agreement. And after all, the king saw it through this time.

"A couple of months ago, Oeneus learned that a battle had taken place between the soldiers of King Aidoneus, who now rules in Molossia, and the detachment of Theseus. Theseus was defeated. King Oeneus sent a messenger to Thesprotia to find out about his fate and also about the plans of Aidoneus. The messenger returned and reported that Pirithous had perished in a fight with the soldiers of King Aidoneus, and Theseus had been taken prisoner. According to the herald, Aidoneus is not going to start a war with Calydon. He also said that the ruler of the Thesprotians was holding Theseus in chains, hoping to receive a big ransom from Athens."

Agamemnon considered what he had heard for a while.

"Tell me, worthy Andraimon, whether it is known what caused the collision of Theseus's detachment with the army of the Thesprotian ruler. Surely, King Aidoneus has many hundreds of warriors. It is hard to imagine that, with few companions, Theseus expected to defeat the Thesprotian army, which is a threat even to Calydon."

"You are right, son of wise Atreus," Andraimon replied. "Theseus is a great warrior and leader. He accomplished many feats, managed to win a victory in Crete with a small detachment, and repelled the invasion of the Amazons on Athens. Pirithous is also a mighty warrior, but like all Lapiths, he is distinguished by recklessness. King Oeneus learned that in Thesprotia, Theseus's detachment was attacked by surprise by far superior force. We do not know whether Pirithous died in the fight or was executed. Theseus, most likely, did not have time to arm himself and was captured. He was alive when the messenger of Oeneus left Molossia.

"King Aidoneus announced that Theseus and Pirithous suffered a worthy punishment, because they came to the country with evil intentions. According to him, they wanted to kidnap the daughter of the king, the beautiful princess Cora. Wise Oeneus suggests that this was the case. After all, you heard that Theseus and Pirithous were accused of kidnapping the beautiful Helen, the daughter of the Spartan king Tyndareos.

"As the rumor says, Theseus kept her for himself. Probably, Cora was intended to be the wife of Pirithous, who was widowed in the recent past. And since Pirithous was not rich and could not pay gifts for the bride, he persuaded Theseus to help kidnap Cora, as he himself helped kidnap Helen. In the end, Pirithous is dead, and Theseus languishes in captivity, awaiting a ransom."

"If everything is like this," Agamemnon noted, "then Theseus will never get out of captivity. After all, as you know, Menestheus came to power in Athens. I do not think that he will be in a hurry to ransom Theseus. I heard that when the Dioscouroi freed Helen, they killed many of Theseus's supporters and took away many more, including his mother, Aethra, as prisoners. Who will pay the ransom to Aidoneus? I hope that the king of the Thesprotians has not yet found out about the events in Athens. Otherwise, Theseus's life would not be worth anything."

"You are right," Andraimon answered, not hesitating. "King Oeneus also spoke about this the other day. He believes that the Dioscouroi would not have gone to Attica if Theseus had been in Athens. They would most likely keep negotiations going. And Theseus himself, according to the king, was captured because he tried to repeat what he has accomplished in Sparta. But he did not take into account that rumors about his exploits had already reached Thesprotia, and King Aidoneus was ready to protect his daughter. Oeneus said that he wanted Theseus to gain freedom. However, only the great Hercules could help him now. The Thesprotians would not refuse him. But Hercules is no longer among the living."

Agamemnon realized that the king of Calydon did not want to interfere in the affairs of the Thesprotian ruler and Theseus. He decided to change the topic of conversation and ask Andraimon a question that had long interested him.

"Worthy Andraimon, thank you for your story. You can rest assured that I will keep everything I have learned a secret. You know, my brother and I have always been fans of Hercules, admired his campaigns and exploits. In Argolis, little is known about the last years of the great hero in this world. I hope you do not mind if I ask you about the life of Hercules in Calydon, his marriage to Deianeira, the trip to Thesprotia, and how the inevitable fate befell the great hero. I will be grateful for anything you can tell."

Andraimon was silent for a long time, considering the question.

"Agamemnon, son of Atreus, why are you interested in the affairs of those ancient days?" he finally asked. "Perhaps you have heard the rumors spread by old Agrius and his sons. So know that there is not a drop of truth in them. Here's what I know about those days. Deianeira had many suitors, but after learning that the god-equal Hercules was the pretender, all of them, except for one, abandoned their intentions.

"This last one, Achelous, was a mighty Thesprotian warrior who did not know defeat in the battle. He was named after the river stretching deep in the lands of Thesprotia with the sources reclining high on Mount Pindus. He considered this river to be his ancestor. I saw this giant in a horned helmet. It seemed that nothing could resist his pressure.

"But Hercules defeated him in a duel arranged by King Oeneus to choose a husband for his daughter. Three times the fighters converged, and three times he threw Achelous to the ground. And the last time, he did not rise. In order not to overshadow the wedding celebrations, Hercules did not take the life of Achelous but let him go for a large ransom.

"Soon after the wedding of Hercules and Deianeira, a war began with the Thesprotians. These events took place about twenty years ago. I was very young then and did not participate in battles, but my father went to war. The younger sister of Deianeira had not yet become my wife. It happened much later, after the death of Hercules and Deianeira.

"The beginning of the war is told in different ways. Some say that Achelous began to devastate the border Calydonian lands and steal cattle out of revenge for losing the battle with Hercules. Others say that the Calydonian pilgrims, on their way to the oracle at

Dodona, were robbed in Thesprotia, and when they asked for justice from King Phylas, then ruler of the city of Ephyra, he ordered them to get out.

"King Oeneus had long harbored enmity toward the lord of Ephyra, and here, counting on the help of Hercules, he decided to teach the Thesprotians a lesson. Oeneus was right. Hercules, at the head of the Calydonian army, reinforced by his hardened fighters, defeated the Thesprotians in several battles and captured Ephyra, along with the king and his family. He took a huge ransom and forced the Thesprotians to swear in the temple of Dodona in the name of the almighty Zeus never to be the first to start a war with Calydon.

"This is how King Oeneus speaks about it. The king told me that in Dodona, Hercules was given the prophecy. It said that he was not destined to die neither by the hand of a mortal nor by the will of an immortal. Hercules then told the king that he had received a similar prophecy from Apollo.

"After spending about a year in Thesprotia and collecting tribute from the cities there, Hercules returned to Aetolia with an army. I have already told you about the years of his life in Calydon. I sat at the same table with him many times. Each time, I experienced a feeling of colossal power emanating from this incomparable warrior. Hercules was modest in his movements, but his every gesture spoke of superhuman strength. He was stingy with words, but from each of his phrases, a feeling of irresistible fate emanated. It seemed that nothing in the world could stop him, hold back his onslaught, and yet he was not a young warrior then. He must have been over fifty years old.

"I have heard stories of fits of rage and indomitable anger that visited Hercules in his younger years, but in Calydon, he was calm and benevolent. He and Deianeira had children. He loved to practice martial arts with young Tydeus. However, a peaceful life was not destined for him. King Oeneus believes that the gods forced Hercules to take the roads of war again. One way or another, Hercules inadvertently caused the death of the young son of worthy Architelos.

"King Oeneus and Architelos himself, who were present at this unfortunate event, forgave him. All the witnesses confirmed that the death of the boy was not intentional but accidental. But

Hercules decided to pay for his guilt and voluntarily go into exile for a year, leaving Deianeira and the children in the care of the king. So Hercules again got involved in the bloody deeds of the war, because there always were people who wanted to use his strength and experience. The year turned into two and three.

"The day came when Deianeira found out about the love affairs of Hercules and caught fire with jealousy and a desire to return him to Calydon. She found a medicine man from the tribe of centaurs who promised her a love potion to turn Hercules away from other women. But instead of a love potion, the malicious healer gave her poison, which she sent to Hercules, hoping to regain his affection. Deianeira is not guilty of wickedness. She loved Hercules and wanted to keep him for herself. When she found out what happened, she could no longer live and laid hands on herself. And so the Dodona prophecy came true.

"You see, it is known for certain that the healer from the tribe of centaurs died on the same day that he supplied Deianeira with a deceitful potion. It was said that he was either the father of a centaur killed by Hercules, or he himself received a severe wound from Hercules. So the prophecy came true. Death came to Hercules not from the hand of a mortal but from a dead man.

"More than fifteen years have passed since then. Many in Calydon believe that Hercules was the son of Zeus the Thunderer himself. Every year, on the day of his death, they make sacrifices to him and his wife, Deianeira."

"I was still a child when Hercules suffered the inevitable fate," Agamemnon said after a long pause. "In Mycenae, they say that he was a hero chosen by the gods for great endeavors. I also have heard about the prophecy that Hercules was not destined to die at the hands of a mortal. Maybe there is truth in the words of King Oeneus, that gods did not allow Hercules to indulge in a peaceful life. They wanted him for other things."

Travelers continued the rest of the way in silence and reached the city in the evening. Arriving in his chambers, Agamemnon had time to bathe and was waiting for Menelaus when a herald from King Oeneus appeared and announced that a messenger had come from Mycenae and wanted to see the sons of Atreus as soon as possible.

CLYTEMNESTRA

RETURN OF THE ATRIDES TO MYCENAE

A twenty-oared ship driven by mighty rowers was on its way to Corinth. The sons of Atreus watched the coast of Aegialeus pass by on the starboard side, remembering how they traveled along these shores many years ago. The helmsman decided to land for the night in the harbor of Pellene. He intended to reach the harbor of Corinth, Lecheum, by the middle of the next day.

"It is a pity that we did not manage to visit the oracle in Delphi," said Agamemnon. "However, King Thyestes demanded us to come as soon as possible. I hope he will be able to lift the veil of the future as good as Apollo himself."

"Hopefully, the bearer of the silver bow, Apollo, will not hear you," Menelaus replied. "The son of Zeus may see in your words a lack of respect for his divinations. Think again, Agamemnon, how sure you are of our safety. Talthybios told us only that Thyestes was unwell and expected our arrival every day. Perhaps sensing the approach of the inevitable end, the king decided to get rid of us and finally clear the way for Aegisthus to the Mycenaean throne."

"We have discussed this many times in Calydon."

There were notes of impatience in Agamemnon's voice.

"The messenger of the king said that Thyestes swore for our safety in the name of the almighty Zeus. I knew Talthybios as a young teenager in Mycenae. He would not lie to me. I believe the king wants to discuss succession to the throne. It is better to try to negotiate peacefully than to unleash civil war. Everyone knows that after Thyestes, I am the rightful heir to the throne by seniority in the family.

"In addition, news from Calchas came with Talthybios. He conveys that he hopes to see us soon and will be waiting at the city gates. In my opinion, the priest wants to inform us that there is no threat to our lives from the king. If Talthybios can be deceived in his youth, the wise Calchas would have warned us if he suspected the king of bad intentions. You yourself spoke many times in Calydon about returning to Mycenae. King Oeneus did not see the danger in our journey, and the fortune-telling of the court priest promised a favorable outcome.

"Look. The ship is already entering the harbor of Pellene. There is a short passage from here to Corinth, and according to Talthybios, the king's chariots are waiting in Lecheum. It's too late to retreat, brother. Tomorrow evening, we will be in Mycenae."

The harbor of Pellene, although situated far from the city, was large and convenient for anchorage. Having unloaded their belongings and supplies for the meal, the rowers anchored the ship not far from the shore. A simple meal cooked on a fire consisted of goat meat and barley cakes. Travelers made sacrifices to the lord of the seas, Poseidon, with a request for the successful completion of the voyage. Having finished the meal, the helmsman wished the sons of Atreus pleasant dreams and promised to be at Corinth before evening tomorrow.

*****

The sky was just beginning to turn pink when the helmsman took the ship out to sea and sent it to the sunrise. The rested rowers leaned on the oars, and soon after noon, the ship, having passed Sicyon, arrived in Lecheum. As Talthybios had promised, three chariots with charioteers were waiting in the harbor.

The journey to Mycenae along the Argos road took the rest of the day. It was already dark when the tired horses turned off the road to the left and began to climb to the entrance to the Mycenaean citadel. The gates of the citadel were lit, and torches burned on the walls.

The chariots stopped at the gate. Agamemnon, who was in the first chariot, looked at the figures standing at the gate—two warriors with spears and two men in cloaks. One of them stepped forward, throwing back the cover from his head. Agamemnon recognized Calchas and felt relieved. For some time, he had considered what to do if the priest was not at the gate.

The second cloaked man holding a torch turned and disappeared through the gate. Descending from the chariot, Agamemnon took a step toward Calchas, but the priest himself rushed ahead.

"Noble Agamemnon, I welcome you in famous Mycenae," the priest said in a loud voice. "You became a mature warrior and came home after many years of wandering. Your father would be delighted to see you in your prime. Glorious Menelaus, welcome to your native city," he continued when he saw Menelaus and Talthybios approaching the gates. "Talthybios, you have fulfilled the orders of the king and are worthy of a reward. Now go to rest. The guards will take care of the chariots."

"We are glad to see you in good health, wise Calchas," answered Agamemnon. "The years have not changed you much. You are almost the same as the last time we met at this gate."

"Worthy Calchas, I greet you in the great Mycenae," Menelaus said, entering the conversation. "We often remembered you in the past years. Tell me how long you have been waiting for us, and who was your companion who retired to the city at our approach?"

"Sons of the great Atreus, I have been waiting for your return for a long time, and I came out to the gate recently, when I learned from the messenger of the king that you were approaching the city. As usual, when someone important is expected, King Thyestes sends a warrior to the mountainside in advance with the order to set alight two torches at your approach. He recognized three chariots on the Argos road, because the charioteers were ordered to return altogether only if the sons of Atreus arrived.

"Seeing the signal, the observer on the tower alerted the king. The king sent me and his assistant to the gate to meet you. This was my companion. As soon as I made sure that it was really you, he went to report to the king. King Thyestes asks you to dine and rest in the allotted chambers and expects you tomorrow morning for a conversation. Follow me. I will lead you, arrange a meal, and call for maids to wash after a long journey."

The travelers passed the gate and began to climb along the slope of the hill along the wide ramp leading to the palace. Passing the outbuildings on the right side, the priest turned left toward the palace. But before reaching it, he turned again and began to bypass the royal palace on the left, heading toward the northern gates. Having passed them, the travelers went to the watchtower. There, in the halls located at the foot of the tower, the brothers were to spend the night.

While Agamemnon and Menelaus were bathing, the servants prepared a meal, and Calchas invited the brothers to the table.

"Wise Calchas," said Agamemnon, having tasted the offered treats, "during the years of wandering and life at the court of the glorious king Oeneus, the ruler of Calydon, we received limited news from Peloponnese. Tell us what is new in Argolis and the neighboring lands."

"But first of all, venerable Calchas," Menelaus interjected, continuing the words of his brother, "tell, if you know, why King Thyestes called us. For me, his first message in so many years was a complete surprise."

"First of all, I want to say that the king did not discuss with me the purpose of your visit," Calchas began. "He called me recently, said that he wanted to see the sons of Atreus, and asked me to inform the messenger that nothing threatens you in Mycenae. After all, I have rarely seen the king in recent months. For a year or so now, he does not go out in a chariot, royal dinners have become rare, and receptions in the throne room have almost ceased.

"The king's health is said to have deteriorated. I can also add that the son of the king, Aegisthus, is in Mycenae and not so long ago was sick for a long time. The king called to him healers from Crete. Now he feels better. He is often seen in the city and surrounding

areas. However, he is not involved in state affairs and does not participate in military exercises.

"You left Mycenae as young men who had barely begun to bear
arms. Now you are both mature men, leaders, ready to lead warriors.
You have the blood of the Pelopides. I believe the king wants to discuss the succession to the throne with you, but I don't know what he
wants to propose. I hope King Thyestes understands that Aegisthus is
unable to organize the defense of the Mycenaean possessions. Many
citizens believe that Mycenae needs a strong ruler capable of leading
troops, and Agamemnon, the son of Atreus, is worthy to take the
throne."

Calchas was silent for a while and took a sip of wine, and making sure that the brothers were listening attentively, he continued.

"Sons of the great Atreus, you have been absent for almost ten
years. Much has changed in Peloponnese. Of course, you have heard
about the second campaign of the Argives against Boeotian Thebe.
This war was led by the sons of the leaders who went on the first
campaign. The leader was the glorious Alcmaeon, the son of the wise
Amphiaraus, who perished in the first campaign. Many mighty warriors from Argolis and Arcadia went with him.

"The Argos army besieged the city after heavy battles with the
Thebans. Worthy Aegialeus, the son of Adrastus, fell under the walls at
the hands of the ruler of Thebe, Laodamas, the grandson of Oedipus.
The great Adrastus suffered an inevitable fate when he learned of
the death of his son. The city was surrendered after the death of the
ruler Laodamas. Another grandson of Oedipus, Thersander, the son
of Polyneices, reigns now in Thebe. You must have met him in Argos
before.

"New kings also rule in the mighty Argos. As has been customary since ancient times, there are three kings in Argos. These
are Sthenelus, the son of the great Capaneus, Amphilochus, the son
of the wise Amphiaraus, and Cyanippus, the son of the glorious
Aegialeus. They rule over the dominions of Argos, including Troezen,
Hermione, Epidaurus, Aegina, and other cities."

"Tell me, wise Calchas," Agamemnon said, interrupting the
speech of the priest, "was it not Alcmaeon, by seniority, who should

have inherited the throne of his father, Amphiaraus? We have heard, and you confirmed that Alcmaeon has taken Thebe and returned to Argos with the victory. How did it happen that the youngest son of Amphiaraus, Amphilochus, became the king?"

"Valiant Alcmaeon, the oldest son of Amphiaraus, is no longer in Argos," Calchas replied. "He indeed was the king but went into exile, ceding the throne to his younger brother Amphilochus shortly after the victory over Thebe. They say that Alcmaeon discovered that his mother, Eriphyla, accepted a valuable gift in order to persuade her husband, Amphiaraus, to march on Thebe. Amphiaraus was the seer and knew that he was not destined to return from Thebe, but he was bound by a sacred oath. Observing it, Amphiaraus went on a campaign and perished.

"Alcmaeon believed that his mother received a gift in exchange for the life of her husband, and before the second campaign, she also received a gift for the promise to persuade her son to go to Thebe. Avenging the death of his father, Alcmaeon slew his mother and, tormented by the goddesses of vengeance, went into exile. What happened to him afterward is unknown to me."

"May the gods be merciful to the noble Alcmaeon, and he will find relief in his wanderings," said Agamemnon.

Calchas was silent for a while and continued his narrative.

"Probably, you have heard in Calydon about the recent conflict between Sparta and Athens. This war was started by Castor and Polydeuces, nicknamed the Dioscouroi, who are the sons of the Spartan king Tyndareos and seasoned military leaders. They have chosen the time when Athenian king Theseus was out of town and invaded Attica with a Spartan army, accusing Theseus of kidnapping their sister Helen.

"The Dioscouroi occupied Attica, besieged Athens, and ransacked the town of Aphidna, where Theseus kept his treasury. The sons of Theseus were forced to flee to Euboea to avoid persecution. Furthermore, Menestheus, the son of Peteos, was promoted to the leadership in Athens, as some say, with the Dioscouroi support.

"None of that would have happened if Theseus had been in place. But in his absence, the Dioscouroi seized rich booty and helped their ally Menestheus to become the ruler of Athens. They say that Theseus has no reason to return now. He has lost his kingdom, his family, and his treasure all thanks to Castor and Polydeuces. In recent years, the sons of Tyndareos have become a force to be reckoned with in Peloponnese. They seek to expand the possessions of Sparta and often wage wars with the neighbors."

"Wise Calchas," Menelaus began, entering the conversation, "we have heard about the invasion of the Dioscouroi to Attica but not exactly as in your story. In Calydon, it was said that Theseus and the leader of the Lapiths, Pirithous, kidnapped the daughter of King Tyndareos, Princess Helen. Theseus settled her in Aphidna under the supervision of his mother and under the protection of his companions while he himself went to Thesprotia with Pirithous. There, they intended to capture another princess, the beautiful daughter of King Aidoneus, Cora, who was destined for Pirithous.

"On the way to Thesprotia, Theseus visited King Oeneus in Calydon, so we learned about his campaign. Although we were not in Calydon at this time, we heard about it from King Oeneus himself. Theseus told Oeneus that he was going to Thesprotia, but he did not say why. Unlike Sparta, where everything turned out as they wanted, things in Thesprotia did not work out for Theseus and Pirithous. A small detachment of Theseus's entered into battle with the soldiers of the Thesprotian king and was utterly defeated. Pirithous perished, and Theseus was captured. The king of the Thesprotians demands a huge ransom for his head. This is what we have heard about Theseus."

Menelaus took a sip of wine and continued.

"The Corinthian merchants also told a lot about the attack of the Dioscouroi on Attica. According to them, the Dioscouroi demanded that the Athenians hand over their sister Princess Helen. And when they did not, they invaded Attica at the head of the Spartan army and besieged Athens.

"Worthy Menestheus saved the city from being ruined. He convinced the Dioscouroi that the abduction of Helen was the work of Theseus alone and that the Athenians had nothing to do with it. He swore that Helen was not in the city, that the Athenians did not know about her whereabouts, and opened the gates of Athens for

Spartans to see for themselves. The Dioscouroi entered the city but did not sack it after making sure that Menestheus told the truth.

"Soon, they found out that Theseus had hidden Helen in the town of Aphidna, which lies not far from Athens. The Spartan army took Aphidna by storm. The Dioscouroi freed Helen and seized the treasury of Theseus and returned to Sparta, and Menestheus took the Athenian throne with the support of the citizens. So they say in Calydon."

Calchas listened to Menelaus with great interest.

"What you told about King Theseus is deplorable. Himself in captivity, sons in exile, treasury seized by enemies—it looks like the gods have abandoned their favorite. However, I want to mention that there are two sides to the story of the Spartan invasion. Your version is a view of events from the side of the Dioscouroi and their ally Menestheus.

"I do not argue that Menestheus has the right to the Athenian throne, because, like Theseus, he is the great-grandson of King Erechtheus. However, while Theseus ruled, Menestheus could only dream of power. His influence in the city was not even enough to make a noticeable opposition to Theseus. And so in the absence of Theseus, the Dioscouroi came and, by force of arms, erected Menestheus to the throne of Athens. As a reward, they received the treasury of Theseus, captive slaves, a faithful ally on the throne in Athens, and the glory of a victorious war."

"You forget, wise Calchas, that the Dioscouroi came to Attica to free their sister, captured by Theseus," Agamemnon interrupted. "And their trophies are the legitimate booty of war. Menestheus saved Athens from ruin and received the throne as a reward, and Theseus brought danger to Athens and threw the city at the mercy of the enemy.

"And keep in mind that it is not for the first time that the deeds of Theseus have been a source of trouble for the glorious Athenians. In old times, Athens was invaded by the Amazons. Father said that they also came to take revenge on Theseus for the kidnapping of their princess. Then Theseus was in the city, organized the defense, and defeated the army of the Amazons, killing their leaders. And this time, he acted imprudently and left the city to the mercy of fate. The Dioscouroi just took advantage of it."

"I'm not trying to protect Theseus, but I want to understand what really happened and what the possible consequences are," the priest replied. "After all, everything you say is the version of one of the parties. Nobody has heard the story of Theseus himself. I can add that no one also knows what really happened to Princess Helen. I can't even rule out that Theseus didn't kidnap Helen. Maybe he had an agreement with King Tyndareos, because there is such a custom in Arcadia.

"Who, after the abduction, saw Helen in Aphidna or at least spoke with a witness who saw her with his own eyes? Nobody. After all, all the defenders of Aphidna were either killed or enslaved and taken to Sparta. The Dioscouroi could argue that Helen was kidnapped by Theseus to have an excuse for invading Attica.

"Now let's look at Theseus. Would you believe that such an experienced ruler, having committed an act that could provoke a war, will leave his family and his throne without protection? It seems to me that the situation is not exactly the same as Menestheus, and the Dioscouroi are trying to present it. To learn what really happened is important for understanding the situation in Peloponnese. Therefore, I wanted to discuss this with you before tomorrow's conversation with King Thyestes."

"Wise Calchas, I agree with you," Agamemnon said after a pause. "We are not aware of all events of this war. Tell me, what else do you know?"

"The sons of King Tyndareos have been trying for many years to expand Spartan boundaries by capturing adjacent lands," the priest continued. "They wanted to seize lands in Arcadia but without success and then turned their eyes to Messenia. This rich country surpasses Sparta both in land and in population. There, the Dioscouroi found worthy opponents and experienced warriors Idas and Linceus, the sons of the local ruler Aphareus.

"The confrontation went on with varying success, but in recent years, Idas and Linceus gained the support of the king of Pylos, the favorite of the gods, famous Nestor, who took the throne from the hands of Hercules. The Dioscouroi had to look for allies for themselves, and they have found them both in the west and in the east. More recently, the Dioscouroi arranged the marriage of their sister Clytemnestra to the young king of Pisa, Tantalus Jr. Pisa is a rich city, now probably the richest in Elide, because it was not plundered during the wars of Hercules with King Augeas.

"As you remember, Hercules came to Elide twice. The first time, his army was defeated before reaching Elis. But the second time, he crushed and sucked whole Elide but did not touch only Pisa. The ruler of Pisa has sufficient funds to provide assistance to Spartans to continue the confrontation with Messenia. And the Dioscouroi, in turn, can support Pisa's expansion in Elide and, possibly, in the north of Aegialeus. And as you know, Aegialeus is subject to Mycenae.

"King Tantalus Jr. came to Mycenae to King Thyestes several times over the years. The last time was quite recently, after his marriage to Clytemnestra. After his visits, King Thyestes was always unwell. I don't know for sure, but I guess they were talking about the cities of Aegialeus. Now you see that as a result of the Dioscouroi invasion of Attica, the union of Sparta and Pisa was strengthened by Athens. Perhaps they may decide to move from words to deeds in their territorial claims.

"King Thyestes must be quite concerned about those claims. During all the years of his reign, he relied more on the strength of the city walls than on the prowess of the Mycenaean warriors, and now the Mycenae may have to defend their possessions on the battlefield. The king is old and weak. He is not able to lead the troops. His son Aegisthus is not involved in military affairs. Mycenae needs a strong, dependable commander. I think the king will talk about this tomorrow."

Calchas hesitated, assessing whether he had said everything he wanted, and finished with the words, "Consider your terms, Agamemnon, if you decide to make an agreement with the king. And now I propose to rest. May the gods send you pleasant dreams."

CHAPTER 2

ACCESSION OF AGAMEMNON

Early in the morning, the sons of Atreus went to meet their uncle, King Thyestes of Mycenae. The priest Calchas visited their quarters at the watchtower closer to noon and, making sure that the brothers had not yet returned, decided to wait for them, sitting under a canopy not far from the tower. When he noticed the brothers slowly walking along the road from the royal palace, the sun had already passed past noon.

"Greetings, worthy sons of Atreus," said the priest, rising from the steps.

"Hello, wisest Calchas," Agamemnon answered, stopping. "It's good that you met us. Your assumptions were largely justified, but you were mistaken in one important circumstance. The king of Pisa, Tantalus Jr., does not seek to seize a couple of cities in Aegialeus from the Mycenae. This scoundrel wants to get all the Mycenaean possessions and the throne of Mycenae in addition. Let's go into the chambers, away from prying ears, and I will tell you about our conversation with King Thyestes."

Refreshed and settled down for a conversation, Agamemnon continued his tale.

"Perhaps I'll start with the story told to us by King Thyestes. Did the rumor reach you, Calchas, that Tantalus Jr. is the bastard son of Thyestes himself? We have heard about this when, many years ago during our travels, we visited the old king Broteas in Pisa. There, in the city, we learned from an old priest that Tantalus Jr. considers himself the son of Thyestes. As such, he is a pretender to the Mycenaean throne, and my guess is that Tantalus Jr., already then, saw me as a competitor and tried to eliminate us."

"Yes, such gossip reached Mycenae, even in the reign of King Eurystheus," answered Calchas. "Thyestes was then in exile. But they didn't inspire confidence, and I would never have imagined that Tantalus Jr. would use them to claim the Mycenaean throne. What else does King Thyestes say?"

"To this I turn," Agamemnon replied, continuing his story. "In short, King Thyestes offered me to ascend the throne of Mycenae tomorrow after sunrise on one condition. I must offer sacrifices on the altar and swear by the name of Zeus the Thunderer that I myself will not harm his son Aegisthus and will not let others harm him. Menelaus is my witness. These were the first words of the king after our meeting. He also said that he was ready to immediately proclaim me coruler and hand over the reins of government while he himself would step back from power, the burden of which he was tired of bearing.

"After that, he said that if I agreed, then I should know that the war of Mycenae with the king of Pisa, Tantalus Jr., and his allies was inevitable. I asked the king what gave him such confidence, whether he learned the oracle's predictions or received messages from trusted persons. No, the king replied, Tantalus Jr. himself informed him. It was then that he told me about the claims of Tantalus Jr. to the throne of Mycenae.

"Tantalus Jr. announced to King Thyestes that he considers himself his eldest son and demands to recognize himself as the legitimate heir to the Mycenaean throne. Tantalus Jr. also reported that his first child was born to Clytemnestra, daughter of the ruler of Sparta, Tyndareos. The Spartan king supports the claims of Tantalus Jr. This is what Thyestes told us. The king said he would give me time to think before sunset."

After listening to the story of Agamemnon, Calchas looked at Menelaus, waiting for him to add something. However, Menelaus remained silent. The priest understood that the eldest son of Atreus had seen himself at the head of the Mycenaean state for many years but did not know whether he was ready to go to war with superior forces for the sake of the Mycenaean throne.

It is difficult to offer worthy advice in this matter, Calchas thought and said, "Noble Agamemnon, son of the great Atreus, there is still a lot of time before sunset. You probably want to be left alone to think about the situation and make a worthy decision. Let me leave."

"There is no need for this, wisest Calchas," Agamemnon replied. "I made a decision in the throne room and informed the king of Thyestes. In the presence of the king and his attendants, I swore on the altar of Zeus that Aegisthus was inviolable. Now the courtiers are gathering a council of elders, and tomorrow morning, I will officially be elevated to the rank of ruler of Mycenae. Calchas, in how many days you think this news will reach Pisa?"

CHAPTER 3

CONVERSATION WITH DIOMEDES

Agamemnon watched the Argos road from the observation deck located on the top of the Mycenaean citadel. Shortly after noon, he saw the chariot approaching from Argos. It turned off the main road onto the road leading to the main gate of the fortress.

"Menelaus," said Agamemnon, "is this the one we are waiting for?"

"Yes, it is," replied Menelaus. "In the chariot is Diomedes. I will meet the guest at the gate, offer to freshen up after the journey, and escort him to the throne room."

Agamemnon waited until the chariot approached the gates of the citadel and went to the throne room. Many days had passed since he became the rightful ruler of Mycenae, and the greetings of those he met had ceased to cause pleasant excitement.

Diomedes, entering the hall, paid his respects to the king and conveyed greetings from the lords of Argos. Expressing his gratitude, Agamemnon offered to share a meal and ordered to serve dishes. The conversation around the table began with hunting and wines of Argos and soon turned to recent military campaigns. Agamemnon turned to Diomedes with a request to tell about the campaign against Thebe.

"Diomedes, son of the god-equal Tydeus, I heard a lot about the glorious deeds of the Argives during the second campaign against the seven-gated Thebe but never from its participant. Tell us about the events of this campaign, about the battles and the assault on the walls of the city."

"Lord of Mycenae, Agamemnon," answered Diomedes, "let the Argives, who shared with me the hardships of this war, be my witnesses. The sons of the leaders who fell in the first campaign against Thebe united to avenge their fathers. We called this campaign the war of the Epigones against Thebe and, at the behest of the oracle, chose the fearless Alcmaeon, the son of Amphiaraus, as our leader. With him went his brother, now king of Argos, Amphilochus.

"Also went the king of Argos, Sthenelus, the son of the fearless Capaneus, Aegialeus, the son of the great Adrastus, Promachus, the son of Parthenopaeus and the brave Euryalus, the son of Mecisteus, and others. But the most impatient was Thersander, the son of the valiant Polyneices. After all, some of the Argives did not seek war, but Thersander managed to persuade most of them. It was especially difficult for him to convince Alcmaeon. We did not know then, but Thersander made a deal with Alcmaeon's mother, Eriphyla, who had accepted expensive gifts from him. She convinced her son to lead Argives to Thebe."

Diomedes drank wine and, after a pause, continued.

"When we arrived in Boeotia, Alcmaeon did not approach the walls of Thebe. Neither did he challenge the enemy to battle. Instead, he sent detachments of soldiers to ravage small settlements and surrounding towns subject to Thebe. Alcmaeon said that the Theban army would not come to their aid, and so it happened. We took a lot of booty without suffering losses.

"When at last the Theban leaders realized that these raids weakened their defenses and increased our strength, they withdrew their army from the city and decided to fight a big battle at Glisant. Thebans fought bravely in this battle. Their leader, Laodamas, son of Eteocles, slew the brave Aegialeus, son of Adrastus. In the end, however, Argives began to gain the upper hand.

"Finally, the Thebans could not stand it and retreated behind the walls of the city. Alcmaeon did not want a long siege and entered into negotiations with them. The Thebans offered a ransom. Alcmaeon demanded to surrender the city, promising to leave all the inhabitants alive and give the throne to Thersander. Otherwise, he threatened to storm.

"The Thebans played for time. When on the second day we saw that there were no soldiers on the walls, Alcmaeon ordered the gates of Thebe to be broken. We met no resistance, as the remnants of the Theban army and leaders had left the city the day before. Having collected the booty and enthroned Thersander, we returned to Argos, learning along the way that the glorious Adrastus suffered an inevitable fate when he heard about the death of his son. After all, Adrastus was the only one of the Argive leaders who returned alive from the first campaign against Thebe.

"The noble Alcmaeon avenged the death of his fathers and achieved victory in this campaign. Returning to Argos, he judged Eriphyla, who had betrayed her husband and son for gifts. Although Alcmaeon did what the oracle of Apollo commanded him, the goddesses of revenge pursued him as a mother killer, forcing him to suffer daily. Seeing no end to his torment, he handed over the royal scepter to his younger brother and left Argos, going into self-imposed exile. That is how Argives lost their best commander," Diomedes finished.

"You are right, worthy son of Tydeus," Agamemnon said after a pause, "Alcmaeon is a great commander. His departure is a painful loss for Argos. Do you know what happened to him?"

"They say that the noble Alcmaeon wandered for a long time through the mountains of Arcadia," answered Diomedes. "Finding no consolation anywhere, he arrived at the Arcadian ruler Phegeus. Phegeus performed a ritual of purification over Alcmaeon. Not so long ago, I heard that he married the daughter of Phegeus, Arsinoe. I hope Alcmaeon has found a worthy sanctuary."

"Is there any news of the glorious Tlepolemus?" inquired Menelaus. "I have heard that he left Argos several years ago."

"Tlepolemus, the son of the invincible Hercules, went into voluntary exile after the accidental slaughter of an elderly relative,"

Diomedes replied. "He sailed from Nafplion, accompanied by followers on several ships. Obeying the oracle, Tlepolemus went to Rhodes. The local inhabitants received him cordially, and having learned that the son of Hercules himself had arrived, they allocated a place for him to settle. Rumor has it that things are going well with Tlepolemus. The city he has founded is growing."

"Glad to hear good news of the worthy Tlepolemus. What do they say about the other Heraclids?" asked Agamemnon. "Do they intend to return to Peloponnese?"

"After your father, the great king Atreus, defeated them on the Isthmus more than fifteen years ago, they restrained their claims," Diomedes replied. "I talked about this with Tlepolemus shortly before he went into exile. According to him, Hercules planned that his older children, those who were born from the daughters of Thespius, would go to the blessed island of Sardinia and settle there. He ordered Iolaus to lead this campaign. And so it happened.

"And the rest of the Heraclids who remained in Hellas were given a prophecy that they would return the possessions conquered by their father only in the third generation. By this, they explained the failure of Gill's campaign and decided to wait for the time set by the oracle. In addition, after the departure of the descendants of Thespius and the losses in the war with the Mycenae, the ranks of the Heraclids thinned out. Therefore, the lords of Argos believe that there are no reasons to fear the return of the Heraclids."

"And what do you think about the recent campaign of Sparta?" Agamemnon asked. "What do they say in Argos about the attack of the Dioscouroi on Athens?"

"The Dioscouroi have informed kings of Argos in advance of their crusade against Attica. I watched as the Spartans came along the Tegean road, passed the walls of Argos, and headed for the Isthmus along the Corinthian road. It was a strong, well-trained army. Not many days passed, and we saw that Spartan warriors were returning with booty.

"As you probably know, they did not ravage Athens but captured the small town of Aphidna, where King Theseus kept his treasures. They did not find the king himself in Attica. Otherwise, the victory would not have been given to them so easily. Theseus is a famous fighter and leader. He has accomplished many deeds and went on campaigns with Hercules himself. In Argos, many wondered where he had gone."

"Valiant Diomedes," said Agamemnon, "your grandfather, King Oeneus, often talked of you when Menelaus and I were staying in Calydon. He listened with pleasure to the stories of your exploits under the walls of Thebe. The great Theseus visited King Oeneus about a year ago and went farther to Thesprotia. We have heard gloomy news about Theseus's adventures."

"Someday, I will go to Calydon to visit my grandfather and taste the Aetolian wines," Diomedes replied. "But tell me what you know about Theseus, because the most incredible rumors are circulating about him. His enemies and, above all, Menestheus, who is now in power in Athens, say that he is already in the underworld, from where there is no return. The Dioscouroi accused him of kidnapping their sister Princess Helen. But only one thing is known for certain—that he has not been in Athens for more than a year."

"When we were visiting your grandfather," Agamemnon said in response, "Theseus, along with the ruler of the Lapiths, fearless Pirithous, visited Calydon for a couple of days. It was over a year ago. They went to Thesprotia with a small detachment. Theseus did not tell the king about the purpose of the trip but promised to stop at Calydon on the way back. For a long time, there was no news of Theseus and his companions. Then rumors reached Calydon that Theseus was languishing in captivity in Thesprotia.

"Not wanting to remain in the dark, King Oeneus sent an envoy to Thesprotia with an order to find out about the fate of Theseus. Returning, the messenger told that the king of Thesprotia, Aidoneus, accuses Theseus and Pirithous of plotting to kidnap his daughter, Princess Cora. When King Oeneus heard about this, he said that probably, Princess Helen was intended for Theseus, and Cora, for Pirithous.

"But if in Sparta everything worked out as they planned, in Thesprotia, they failed. Either the Thesprotians found out about their plan, or the princess was well-guarded, but the abduction did not succeed. The messenger reported that Pirithous perished in the fight, and Theseus was captured. King Aidoneus demands a huge ransom and has sworn to keep Theseus in chains until he gets it. This is what we heard at the court of King Oeneus shortly before returning to Mycenae."

"This is a fascinating story," exclaimed Diomedes. "Now I can believe that Theseus abducted the Spartan princess Helen, as they say, also with the help of Pirithous. And since they could not share the princess, they decided to kidnap another one so that everyone got a princess. I am sorry that such an illustrious hero as Theseus is doomed to end his life in chains.

"I do not know if you have heard, but a long time ago, Theseus rendered a great service to Argos. After the first campaign of Argives against Thebe failed, the ruler of Thebe, Creon, forbade the burial of the bodies of the Argive warriors who had fallen under the walls of the city. My father, Tydeus, was one of them. Upon learning of this, Theseus went to Thebe and persuaded Creon to hand over the bodies of the dead to their relatives. My father was buried in accordance with the tradition thanks to King Theseus.

"In gratitude for this, I would like to help Theseus, but I do not know how. Who will pay the ransom to the Thesprotians? Theseus's treasury is captured by the Dioscouroi, his sons are in exile, and in Athens, there is another king."

Agamemnon ordered to pour the wine and spoke after a pause.

"Son of the invincible Tydeus, I share your feelings and also want to help the glorious Theseus. I am ready to pay a ransom from the treasury of Mycenae. But a reliable messenger will be needed to deliver it to King Aidoneus. He will take a trip to Calydon and from there, with the support of King Oeneus, will go farther to the Thesprotian ruler. I'm sure there is no better candidate than you for this mission. The journey will be dangerous, especially the trip to Thesprotia. The decision is yours, Diomedes.

"However, whether you agree or not, I ask you not to disclose this part of our conversation. You know that in Athens and in other cities there are influential leaders who do not want Theseus to return. They can interfere with the delivery of the ransom. Therefore, everything must be done in secret. Except me and Menelaus, no one will know about the real purpose of the trip. In Argos and Mycenae, we will announce that you are going to Calydon to visit your grandfather, King Oeneus. What do you say, valiant Diomedes?"

Diomedes was silent for a long time. Agamemnon thought that if he refused, all that remained was to send Menelaus. Moreover, Menelaus himself wanted to go with the ransom. But he had less chances of reaching the goal than Diomedes. After all, King Oeneus would definitely give his grandson reliable protection and would help in any way possible. Or maybe it was better to abandon the plan to bring back Theseus and deal with internal problems instead.

Not all vassals confirmed their loyalty to the new ruler of Mycenae. Only a few days ago, messengers arrived from Pellene and Helice, but Sicyon and Corinth kept silent. Agamemnon remembered King Thyestes, who had not left Mycenae in recent years. Old Thyestes recognized well the risk of undertaking even a small campaign, leaving the city without dependable supervision. No, it was better for Menelaus to stay in the citadel.

"A fast ship is ready to take the envoy to Aetolia," Menelaus said, interrupting the pause. "Reliable helmsmen and rowers are waiting in the Lecheum harbor."

"Son of the great Atreus, lord of Mycenae, Agamemnon," Diomedes finally replied, "I will deliver a ransom for Theseus to the lord of Thesprotia Aidoneus. I will go through Calydon and visit my grandfather, King Oeneus, for the first time. But the journey through the boundless lands of Thesprotia will be a dangerous one. From the storytellers, I have heard that there are many wild tribes and ferocious robbers. Only godlike Hercules dared to wander there alone.

"Even the invincible Theseus went there with a trustworthy companion. Therefore, I want to invite the brave Euryalus, the son of Mecisteus, the descendant of the famous king Talaos, to share with me the dangers of this trip. Euryalus is a mighty warrior. He went with me to Thebe and performed many feats under the walls of the city. And I can guarantee that he will keep the secret, and no one will know the real purpose of our journey."

Agamemnon breathed a sigh of relief. He had been afraid that Diomedes would request Menelaus to be his companion.

"I remember the glorious Euryalus and have heard about his exploits. He will be a worthy companion. There is no need to delay your departure. If you wish to leave for Argos tomorrow morning and return with Euryalus the next day, we will get everything ready. We will prepare a ransom in well-worn duffel bags so as not to attract unnecessary attention."

"I will leave tomorrow at dawn," replied Diomedes. "And if I find Euryalus in the city, I will try to return to Mycenae the next day."

"Invincible Diomedes," Menelaus said, entering the conversation, "ask glorious Euryalus to swear on the name of Zeus the Thunderer to keep private the purpose of your trip. If supporters of the current ruler of Athens or their Spartan allies find out about this, your journey will become even more risky. You might even get lost along the way."

"I also ask you, Diomedes, to keep this secret in the future," added Agamemnon. "It is better that Theseus does not know who made a ransom for him. He can, in the heat of a quarrel, tell Menestheus. And for Menestheus and the Dioscouroi, anyone who helps Theseus will be a sworn enemy."

"I understand you, King," Diomedes replied. "But Theseus himself and the king of Thesprotia will ask who gave the ransom. In fact, my grandfather, King Oeneus, will also want to know."

Agamemnon considered the risks. If Theseus returned to the Athenian throne, Athens would most likely cease to be an ally of Sparta and Pisa. But if this did not happen and instead Menestheus and the Dioscouroi found out who tried to rescue Theseus from captivity, then in the event of a military conflict, they would undoubtedly support Tantalus Jr. by the force of arms.

"We will think about it, Diomedes, and we will have a convincing answer by the time of your return from Argos," he said at last. "And now it's time to rest. Sweet dreams."

C H A P T E R   4

MISSION TO THESPROTIA

The next day, after seeing off Diomedes, Agamemnon sent Menelaus with a court official to the treasury to prepare a ransom and invited Calchas to the throne room.

"Wise Calchas," he began when the priest had settled down and all the courtiers, obeying the order, had left the hall, "I called on you to discuss how to rescue King Theseus from Thesprotian captivity. The brave Diomedes agreed to deliver the ransom to Thesprotia. To those who inquire about the purpose of his trip, he will say that he is going to Calydon to visit his grandfather. However, Diomedes expressed serious concerns.

"He will have to answer the questions of both Theseus himself and the king of Thesprotia, as well as his grandfather, King Oeneus, about who is making the ransom. I do not want to reveal the role of Mycenae in this matter for fear of setting against me the current ruler of Athens, Menestheus, and moreover, the Dioscouroi. What would you recommend? Is it necessary to reveal to Theseus and others where the ransom came from or to leave them in the dark? How to answer their questions?"

The priest was silent for a long time, considering what he had heard. He understood that the deliverance of Theseus from captivity did not mean that he would be able to return the Athenian throne. At the same time, if the Dioscouroi learned about the role of the king of Mycenae in the release of Theseus, they would have a strong reason to support Tantalus Jr. in his claims to the Mycenaean throne. Menestheus would feel the same way. Then the plan of Agamemnon would achieve the opposite result. Instead of weakening the coalition of enemies of Mycenae, rescuing Theseus would strengthen it. If the Dioscouroi openly opposed Mycenae and supported Tantalus Jr. with all their might...

No, Theseus could not learn about the role of Agamemnon. It was necessary to offer him another version, one that would not infringe on his pride, and the king of Thesprotia must respect the one who would be the liberator of Theseus. Otherwise, he might not comply with the terms of the contract.

The priest looked at Agamemnon.

"Tell me, king of Mycenae, when Diomedes is going to leave for Thesprotia."

"Diomedes promised to return from Argos tomorrow, and the next day, he could sail from the Lecheum harbor to Aetolia," Agamemnon replied. "He is going to invite Euryalus, son of Mecisteus, as a companion."

"Then I will go without delay to the sacred Heraion and bring worthy offerings to the all-glorious Hera on the altar of the temple. Then I will perform fortune-telling, and tomorrow morning, I will report to you what the gods have advised."

*****

Diomedes and Euryalus arrived at Mycenae the next evening. Having washed and freshened up from the road, the travelers were led to a room located behind the throne room, where four were waiting for them—the king, Menelaus, the priest Calchas, and a young Mycenaean warrior.

In response to the greetings of the guests, Agamemnon said, "Welcome, valiant leaders of the Argives. You are embarking on a long and dangerous journey. The wise Calchas made suitable sacrifices in Heraion and completed fortune-telling about the intentions of the gods. Hear what was revealed to him and rejoice."

Calchas spoke after a long pause.

"King of Mycenae, the favorite of the gods, Agamemnon, the worthy Menelaus, and you, the famous conquerors of Thebe, Diomedes and Euryalus, the beautiful Hera, the wife of Zeus the Thunderer, in her temple, which lies under Mount Euboea, revealed the will of the gods. The invincible Hercules performed great feats in honor of the wife of Zeus, and for this, after his departure from this world, he was exalted by the gods to Olympus. He wishes to liberate the glorious Theseus from captivity and give the king of Thesprotia, Aidoneus, the due ransom.

"You, the executors of this sacred mission, are under the sponsorship of the great Hercules. Notify the king of Thesprotia that the godlike Hercules does not blame him for the death of Pirithous and does not seek revenge. He wants Theseus to be freed and given all due honors. Your journey will be successful, as it is done according to the will of the deity and for its fulfillment."

"Young Periphetes, son of Kopreus, will go with you," said Agamemnon. "Kopreus served as a messenger for the Mycenaean rulers and at one time often went with messages from Eurystheus to Hercules. The great hero treated Kopreus well, although he was often angry with King Eurystheus. Kopreus told his son a lot about the life and incomparable exploits of Hercules. If King Aidoneus asks about Hercules, Periphetes will have something to tell him.

"Remember that the ransom for Theseus is given by the godlike Hercules. By his will, you will go to Thesprotia. Let both King Aidoneus and the glorious Theseus know about this. And now I invite you to share a dinner in the throne room."

CHAPTER 5

VASSALS OF MYCENAE

The speech of the court official about the cities subjected to Mycenae was short. Since Agamemnon ascended the throne, Corinth, Cleonae, Araethyrea, Pellene, Gonoessa, Aegion, and Helice had confirmed their loyalty to the treaties with Mycenae and sent messengers with greetings and gifts. Only three cities did not express obedience to the new ruler. These were Sicyon, Hyperesia, and Orneiae.

The official said that messengers were sent there with a reminder of the annual tribute. The messenger from Orneiae and Hyperesia returned with a request for a delay. The messenger sent to Sicyon was not admitted to King Hippolytus and returned with nothing. King Hippolytus, who recently replaced King Zeuxippus on the throne of Sicyon, was the grandson of Festus, one of the eldest sons of Hercules. He had never paid tribute to the Mycenae. Having finished the review of the vassal estates, the official told about the completion of the repair of the city wall and the progress of other works.

After listening to the report and releasing the courtier, Agamemnon asked, "Tell me, brother, do we already have enough military power to start a campaign? If Hippolytus's challenge is not answered now, the lords of Hyperesia and Orneiae may follow his example. Previously, Sicyon was under the patronage of Adrastus and did not pay tribute to Mycenae. Hippolytus wants to continue this tradition. He is a descendant of Hercules and well-versed in military arts.

"I have heard that the father of Hippolytus went with the Heraclids to the Isthmus against Mycenae when his grandfather, Festus, the son of Hercules, was still ruling in Sicyon. Then Zeuxippus reigned in Sicyon. He was determined to make peace with Mycenae. Hippolytus succeeded Zeuxippus on the throne recently but is said to have the support of the townspeople. Although Sicyon is located on a plain, its walls are high. If Hippolytus manages to find allies, the city can offer serious resistance."

*****

Menelaus had returned the day before from Tiryns, where he recruited soldiers for a mercenary squad. In addition to the squad in Mycenae, Agamemnon decided to create detachments of mercenaries in Corinth and Tiryns and instructed his brother to recruit and train warriors.

After listening to the king, Menelaus said, "Mycenae must immediately respond to the challenge of Sicyon. We will march with the whole army, withdraw troops from Tiryns and Corinth, and call on the militia from Pellene. With such forces, we can take Sicyon in a complete siege. The townspeople will not starve to please King Hippolytus. I believe he did not prepare for a long siege and will soon solicit for peace."

Agamemnon replied, "I agree, brother. I used to think of waiting for Theseus to return from Thesprotia because I was afraid that Hippolytus might get support from the current Athenian ruler, Menestheus. However, time passes by, and we do not know when Theseus will return. Go to Tiryns for a detachment of mercenaries. Also, call on volunteers from the young warriors. I will prepare the Mycenaean troops. We'll start as soon as you get back.

"A detachment from Corinth will join us on the way. We shall not notify them beforehand. Otherwise, rumors may reach Hippolytus, especially if there are Sicyonians in the city. We will also send a messenger from the road to Pellene and Phlius with the demand to send a militia near Sicyon. Let's see what Hippolytus will say when he sees the Mycenaean army from the city wall."

CHAPTER 6

MARCH ON SICYON

Leaving Menelaus to guard the citadel, King Agamemnon set out early in the morning along the Corinth road. This was the first campaign of the king at the head of the Mycenaean armed forces. Having reached Corinth in the afternoon, the army rounded it and moved along the road to Sicyon. The city, founded by the legendary Aegialeus, had a well-fortified acropolis and strong walls.

Agamemnon considered on the way from Corinth that Sicyon had successfully repelled several attacks in the old days. He remembered his father's stories about the long-lasting war of Thebe against Sicyon, a war started because the beautiful princess Antiope was kidnapped by the king of Sicyon, Epopeus, from her father, the ruler of Thebe, Nycteus. The Sicyonians then won, and the Theban army, which was superior in strength, left with nothing.

Then there was the war of Sicyon against Archander and Architeles, the sons of the great Achaeus. This war was won by the commander Sicyon, repelling all the attacks of the Achaeans. From him, the city got its present name. Adrastus was the king of Sicyon at the time of his exile from Argos. Atreus told his son that the support of the Sicyonians helped Adrastus regain the power in Argos.

In recent years, Sicyonians had not experienced attacks. How many days of siege would Hippolytus endure? Agamemnon once again recalled the orders given to the troops before leaving Corinth, trying to figure out if he had forgotten something. In a discussion

151

with Menelaus, they decided not to send messengers to Hippolytus. The demands and threats from Mycenae could only help him prepare Sicyon for a siege. The troops were ordered not to destroy the farms and not to oppress the population. The reward from the king was promised at the end of the siege.

The advanced detachments of the Mycenaean army must block the roads leading from the city to Phlius and Pellene, as well as occupy the Sicyon harbor and block the road leading from it to the harbor of Pellene. As the troops approached, the entire city should be surrounded, and the supply of provisions stopped.

The king of Mycenae established his headquarters where the view of Sicyon opened from the Corinthian road and sent messengers to the harbor to await the arrival of ships with supplies from Corinth. Soon, messengers began to arrive with reports of the deployment of detachments, and then the leaders began to gather for dinner in the king's tent. All the gates in the city were closed, and soldiers were seen on the walls. Apparently, they were preparing for a siege.

After dinner, Agamemnon ordered the night watch to be strengthened and the detained messengers, if any, to be brought to the king's tent. The next day, the troops should tightly surround the city and impede the passage and transport of provisions but not attack.

*****

On the morning of the next day, a herald, Talthybios, appeared in the king's tent with a report—that two messengers had been caught during the night. They were trying to get to Corinth. Both admitted that they were sent to the king of Athens, Menestheus, with a request for help.

While Agamemnon was thinking about what to do with them, the herald entered the tent and reported that an ambassador had arrived from King Hippolytus of Sicyon and had asked for a meeting.

"Let him enter," ordered Agamemnon.

After expressing proper greetings, the ambassador moved on to the purpose of his visit.

"The great king of Mycenae, Agamemnon, son of the divine Atreus, the king of ancient Sicyon wants to know why you brought an army to our walls. The city built by the great Aegialeus has never been taken, and it has enough supplies for a long siege. All problems can be solved through negotiations. Withdraw your troops from the city and send an envoy to King Hippolytus. He is ready to discuss your requirements."

After a long pause, Agamemnon replied, "Go to Sicyon and take with you two messengers captured by my soldiers this night. Tell King Hippolytus that if he wants to remain king, he must come to my tent and take an oath of obedience to Mycenae. He will pay the tribute due to Mycenae in triple size. He will also have to give a reward to the soldiers who came with me. I give him time until tomorrow morning. Otherwise, he will lose his kingdom. And if he dares to start hostilities, he will lose his life.

"If Sicyon is taken by storm, all the men in the city will be enslaved, the king and his family will be executed, and the walls will be torn down. Those who leave the city and take an oath of obedience to Mycenae will be saved from repressions and left in their homes. My herald Talthybios will announce these terms at the main gates of the city this afternoon. Go and pass my words as you have heard."

After the departure of the ambassador, King Agamemnon ordered messengers to be sent to Pellene and Phlius to hasten the local militia, and he himself, accompanied by several soldiers, went around Sicyon to check on the troops. The city stood on a small hill adjacent to a wide plain gently descending to the sea and was surrounded by an ancient stone wall. Nearby, about four to five stadiums toward sunrise, the river Asop carried its waters to the sea.

Heading toward the Sacred gates, Mycenaean warriors passed several temples located along the road and approached a structure resembling a large rectangular gazebo located on a small hill and based on two rows of stone columns. The warrior approached and explained that there is a spring in the cave under the gazebo. Locals use the waters for everyday needs. Now the Mycenaean put a tight barrier in front of the source. In the acropolis, they say there is another source, but its water is only enough to quench thirst.

In response to a question about the temples, the warrior explained that one of them was dedicated to Athena and, according to the local priest, was built by Epopeus himself in honor of his victory over the Theban army. The temple houses statues of Athena and Hercules, whom the locals revere as a god. The next ancient temple is dedicated to Apollo, and next to it is the temple of Hera, Heraion, built by the Argive leader Adrastus during his reign in Sicyon.

"Many years ago, on the way to Pisa, my brother and I visited the king of Sicyon, Zeuxippus," said Agamemnon. "He said that his predecessor on the throne, Festus, the grandfather of the current king, ordered the townspeople to sacrifice to Hercules as a god. He revealed to them that by the will of Zeus the Thunderer, Hercules was ascended to Olympus and became a god. Festus probably erected this statue of Hercules in the temple.

"We should offer sacrifices to Hercules and Athena in this temple so that they send down good luck for our undertakings. Let them arrange this and select worthy sacrificial animals. The priests will perform a ceremony around noon today so that the people of Sicyon will see that we honor the gods in their temple. And now let's go to the road to Phlius."

Having completed the detour of the Mycenaean detachments stationed around the city, Agamemnon and his companions descended along the plain to the harbor, which lay at about thirty stadia. The ships that arrived the day before from Corinth were unloading. Some of the soldiers who arrived by sea were preparing to go to the city and take their places in siege positions. It was nearing noon when Agamemnon returned to his tent. He sent messengers to organize sacrifices in the temple of Athena and summoned Talthybios to discuss the announcement at the Sacred gates.

Sicyon held out for four days. When shortage of water in the city became unavoidable and citizens began to talk that all roads were blocked and reinforcements to Mycenaean were arriving every day, Hippolytus sent a herald with consent to the demands of the king of Mycenae. The Mycenaean army entered the city, and in front of the acropolis, the lord of Sicyon took an oath of allegiance to the king of Mycenae. After distributing rewards to the warriors and loading wagons with tribute, Agamemnon set off on his return journey.

CHAPTER   7

FREEING OF THESEUS

The new moon managed to replace the old twice after campaign against Sicyon, when Diomedes, Euryalus, and Periphetes returned to Mycenae. Having washed and freshened up from the road, the envoys joined the royal dinner.

Agamemnon did not want to publicize the news from Thesprotia and waited until the end of the meal. The king sent the courtiers away and remained in the throne room with Menelaus, Diomedes, Euryalus, Periphetes, and the priest Calchas.

"Fearless warriors, you have returned from a long and dangerous trip. Welcome back. Tell us about your journey to Thesprotia," said Agamemnon and ordered the wine to be poured into goblets.

"King Agamemnon," replied Diomedes, "it appears that godlike Hercules has given us his blessing, so we did not have any serious problems. Lord of Calydon, Oeneus, provided us with two dozen experienced fighters and guides who knew well Thesprotian lands. Therefore, we were not disturbed by wild tribes or robbers.

"After many days of travel through Thesprotia, we reached the city of Molossia, where we found King Aidoneus. Appearing before the king, we introduced ourselves, presented the ransom, and asked to release Theseus in exchange for a payment. The king replied that he was true to his promise, but Theseus was not in Molossia. As soon as he recovered from his wounds, he was sent to Kihira, which is located on the river Acheron. Aidoneus promised to send messengers

155

to Kihira with the orders to release Theseus and his companions, return their weapons, and let them be on their way.

"Having received a ransom, the king asked to whom Theseus owed the return of the freedom, Athens or Argos. We answered that neither Athens nor Argos had anything to do with it. Godlike Hercules himself has conveyed his will through a prophecy and provided the means through his earthly possessions to liberate Theseus. We have been chosen to execute his will. Aidoneus contemplated our words for a long time and finally replied that the will of Hercules should be fulfilled. He would immediately dispatch messengers and arrange to give Theseus guides to the borders of Thesprotia.

"In our presence, the king summoned military commanders and gave his orders. We stayed in Molossia, expecting to see Theseus, until the messengers returned. They said that Theseus, after his release, asked who made a ransom for him. Learning that he owed his freedom to Hercules himself, he said that he will prize the god-like Hercules upon his return to Athens and departed, accompanied by his companions and the guide. We decided that our mission was accomplished, said goodbye to King Aidoneus, and set off back to Calydon.

"It seems to me that Theseus could go either at sunrise to Phthia or Iolcos and from there to sail down to Athens or at sunset to the sea and from there go down to the Gulf of Corinth. He did not come to Molossia or Calydon."

"You have fulfilled your task with dignity," Agamemnon said after a short pause. "And the reward for your labors will not be long in coming. Tell Diomedes how the king Oeneus, beloved by the gods, is doing. Menelaus and I lived under his roof for many years and will always be grateful to him for his hospitality."

"For his age, my grandfather feels well. But in the performance of royal duties, he is increasingly relying on his son-in-law, Andraimon," Diomedes answered. "As Andraimon told me, the brother of the king, the rich landowner Agrius, lives in Calydon. This Agrius has been intriguing against Oeneus for a long time, and recently, he has been spreading rumors that Oeneus is too old to satisfactorily perform royal duties. Agrius and his sons whisper that, by the will of Artemis, Oeneus has no sons left. So the townspeople must choose a new king from the descendants of the great Parpheus, and those are Agrius and his many sons. Thus, he lays claim to the throne of Calydon."

"Old Agrius did not change his attitude since we left Calydon," Menelaus said. "I am sure that King Oeneus and the worthy Andraimon will find a way to curb him. But tell me, did I understand correctly that you did not see Theseus and cannot testify that he is free?"

"Yes, it is so," replied Diomedes. "King Aidoneus kept him in Kihira and, having received a ransom, ordered to be released right there. Theseus decided not to go to Molossia and went his own way. However, we were present at the return of the messengers, and they confirmed that Theseus, with a supply of provisions and a guide, left Kihira as a free man."

"At first, I thought that Theseus would arrive in Molossia and from there go with us to Calydon," Euryalus said, entering the conversation. "But apparently, this was not his intention, and he chose a different path."

"I am sure that King Aidoneus has released Theseus as promised," Agamemnon said. "And Theseus did not want to meet his captor again. He was in a hurry to return to Athens."

*****

The next day, seeing off Diomedes and Euryalus to Argos with valuable gifts, Agamemnon said to Menelaus, "Glory to Zeus the Olympian, everything turned out for the better. Theseus does not know who delivered the ransom and will glorify Hercules for his salvation. We will hear about it. Even if he took the long way through Thessaly, he would soon arrive in Attica. When he takes the power in Athens back, our chances of defeating Tantalus Jr. will increase significantly.

"In the meantime, we will continue to recruit warriors. The campaign in Sicyon showed that we have a strong detachment in Tiryns, and the Corinthian mercenaries are poorly trained and few in number. Maybe you should visit Corinth. There are no experienced military leaders in the city. The city council does not want to spend money on the maintenance of the soldiers. Go and see what can be done there."

"Very well, brother," replied Menelaus. "I will go tomorrow. There are few warriors in Corinth but many merchants. They will probably be the first to know about the return of Theseus. Athens, under him, will cease to be an ally of Sparta and Pisa. But Tantalus Jr. will still have a Spartan army behind him, and now it is the strongest in Peloponnese. If he decides to invade the Mycenaean possessions, Castor and Polydeuces will come with him. In such a situation, it is very important which side Athens will take."

"I think, brother," Agamemnon said after a pause, "that Tantalus Jr. would already be on his way to Aegialeus if he suspected that Theseus might return and the reign of his ally in Athens would soon come to an end. He can even march on Mycenae, not to miss the last chance to have Athens on his side when rumors of Theseus's return reach him.

"We need to know what's going on in Athens. Take Eurymedon, son of Ptolemy, with you tomorrow. He is a skillful warrior, experienced charioteer, and will help with the training of warriors. In the meantime, have him go to Athens. Listen to what they say and see if there's any news about Theseus."

Eurymedon visited Athens, but no one knew anything about Theseus even there.

CHAPTER 8

THESEUS COMES
BACK TO ATHENS

Theseus appeared in Athens many days after the return of Diomedes. As Agamemnon later became aware, he went to Aphidna first and found the city destroyed and abandoned. He learned that the Dioscouroi came from Sparta and took Aphidna by storm. In the battle, his most loyal supporters were killed, and his mother and many others were taken into slavery.

Learning that Theseus was in Athens, Agamemnon sent Eurymedon there to find out what the people were saying and who ruled the city. Returning a few days later, he told the following: Arriving in Athens, Theseus found out that his sons had escaped to Euboea under the protection of Elephenor. He had sent for them.

Theseus was one of the biggest landowners in Attica and had many renters, who always were his supporters. Returning from Thesprotia, he transferred part of his lands in favor of Hercules and ordered that the proceeds from these plots be used for sacrifices and the construction of the temple of the great hero. Upon learning of this, the renters stopped responding to his calls.

There were still many followers of Theseus in Athens, but he did not have the same popularity as before. His orders related to the administration of the city were often not carried out. He met with expressions of discontent several times when citizens openly blamed him for the disasters that fell on the city during the Dioscouroi invasion. Theseus tried to see Menestheus and sent messengers to him, but he avoided a meeting.

After listening to Eurymedon, Agamemnon turned to Menelaus.

"If things are as Eurymedon describes, Theseus is far from power in Athens. His most devoted supporters were destroyed by the Dioscouroi or fell during the campaign in Thesprotia. It doesn't look like the arrival of his sons will change the situation. I thought that Athenian citizens saw in Theseus the king and would support him.

"Apparently, Menestheus had managed to lure the people to his side. After all, he is also one of the richest landowners of Attica and, like Theseus, a descendant of King Erechtheus. If Theseus is completely removed from power, Menestheus will have no internal opposition. He will be able to offer full military support to Tantalus Jr. In that case, our position will be unenviable. What do you think, brother?"

"We were mistaken in believing that Theseus will return to Attica the same person who left it—the king of Athens," Menelaus replied. "Eurymedon's story is similar to what Athenians are saying. I talked in Corinth with Iyas and Elements. Many Athenian citizens blame Theseus for the misfortunes that the city experienced from the Dioscouroi. But most of all, Athenians fear that Theseus will drag the city into a new war with Sparta. After all, Theseus will not stay calmly in Athens knowing that his mother is languishing in slavery in Lacedaemon. He will not forget the death of his friends and associates from the swords of the Dioscouroi.

"There is no need to mention the treasury of Theseus, the main trophy of the Dioscouroi. Elements noticed in our conversation that the treasures of Theseus, hidden in Aphidna, were great—so great that the Dioscouroi were satisfied and left Athens without sacking it.

"Many in Attica believe that if Theseus comes back to power, war with Sparta is inevitable. After all, we also expected that Theseus would want to take revenge. This is what our plan was based on. If we manage to return Theseus to the throne in Athens, he would be the best ally in the war with the Dioscouroi and their sister's husband, Tantalus Jr.

"You see, brother, the citizens of Athens agree with us, but they do not want this war. Therefore, they are against the return of Theseus to power. Apparently, he will not be able to return to the throne by relying on the will of the people, and time is working against him. After all, as soon as Menestheus is convinced that the people will not support Theseus, he will most likely drive him out of the city.

"However, not all is lost. There are still enough supporters of Theseus in Athens. We can negotiate with Theseus and move our soldiers to the city. Let us do what the Dioscouroi did but in reverse. We will elevate Theseus to the throne by force of arms, and when he consolidates his power, we will move together with him against Tantalus Jr. and the Dioscouroi. But we must act swiftly. Otherwise, it may be too late. I am ready to go to Athens and discuss this matter with Theseus. What do you say?"

Agamemnon was silent for a long time, contemplating what he heard.

"Of course, the city walls in Athens are much weaker than the Mycenaean ones," he finally said. "But still, Menestheus would hold out for several days, and the Spartan army will have enough time to reach Attica and join the battle. And if Menestheus manages to deal with Theseus, then we will find ourselves exactly in the situation which we are trying to avoid. We will be left alone against three opponents. Mycenae will have to fight with Sparta, Athens, and Pisa."

"Yes, Menestheus, son of Peteos, is far from stupid," Menelaus replied. "If Theseus is in the city when Mycenaean troops approach, he will be immediately destroyed. But I will persuade him to leave Athens. He may gather his supporters in one of the suburbs or in the harbor."

"If Theseus leaves the city before the attack and, even more so, if he joins the attackers, he will become the enemy of Athens," said Agamemnon. "He will no longer have any influence. And Athens, Sparta, and Pisa will unite against us. No, I believe that going against Athens is not the right thing to do. However, while Theseus is in Athens, Menestheus's hands are tied. He cannot leave Theseus in the city and come to the aid of the Dioscouroi and Tantalus Jr."

"It turns out that the ransom for Theseus was not given in vain," Menelaus remarked. "His presence holds part of the enemy's forces. With the troops we have, we can defeat Tantalus Jr. We might even have a chance in the fight against the Dioscouroi. But we can't stand the battlefield if they join forces, and here in Mycenae, we are safe."

"You are right," replied Agamemnon, "it is dangerous to go against Pisa now. But here, we are not afraid of Tantalus Jr. and the Dioscouroi. We can wait. I will ask Calchas to offer sacrifices to the gods and ask for a sign. Let's rely on the help of the ruler of the sky, Zeus, and prepare the soldiers for the campaign. After all, Theseus still might be able to regain the power in Athens."

THE PLAN FOR ATTACK ON TANTALUS JR.

Autumn came, and the vast barns of Mycenae began to fill with abundant tribute. On one of the rainy autumn evenings, when preparations for dinner were going on in the throne room, the herald announced the arrival of an envoy from King Agapenor of Arcadia. The messenger reported that the herds belonging to the king Agapenor and other owners were stolen. According to eyewitnesses, the sons of the king of Sparta, Castor and Polydeuces, as well as the sons of the Messenian ruler Aphareus, Idas and Linceus, participated in the attack.

The king of Arcadia sent messengers to King Tyndareos and to the lord of Messenia, Aphareus, but received no answer. Agapenor recalled the friendship of the Arcadian rulers with King Atreus and asked for help in returning the stolen herds. After listening to the message, Agamemnon promised to give an answer the next morning and invited the envoy to join the royal meal.

When the guests and courtiers dispersed and the servants began to clear the tables, Agamemnon and Menelaus went up to the observation deck of the palace.

"What do you think about the request of King Agapenor?" Agamemnon asked, turning to his brother. "Until now, I have not heard of the abduction of the herds of the Arcadian ruler by the Dioscouroi."

"I know little about King Agapenor. He took the throne recently, shortly before our return to Mycenae. I remember his predecessor, King Echemus. He was a mighty warrior and answered the call of our father when he led an army to battle with the Heraclids. King Echemus was married to Timandra, the eldest daughter of King Tyndareos and the sister of Castor and Polydeuces. Therefore, while he was in power, the Dioscouroi did not touch his herds and did not raid Arcadia. I heard that Agapenor's father, Ancaeus, was also a glorious warrior. He went with Jason to Colchis. Shortly after returning, Ancaeus went to Calydon at the call of Meleager to hunt for a boar.

"Maybe you remember the stories of King Oeneus about this hunt. Ancaeus of Arcadia was one of those killed by the fangs of the Calydonian boar. Agapenor, the son of Ancaeus, is a young ruler. He does not have strong support yet. That's why the Dioscouroi, together with the sons of Aphareus, decided to profit at his expense. I would like to help Agapenor, but I don't think we need a feud with Sparta right now."

"There is a truth in your words," answered Agamemnon. "But Arcadian kings have always supported Mycenae, and now they have the right to count on our help. King Echemus not only led his warriors to the battle with the Heraclids, but he also accepted the challenge of their leader Gill and defeated him in a duel. And Agapenor himself is not without military might. I believe he can field more than a thousand warriors."

"We can send heralds demanding the return of the cattle," Menelaus suggested. "The king of Sparta and the ruler of Messenia will most likely disregard our message or answer that they do not know anything about the stolen herds. A thief will never admit to stealing until he is caught red-handed. Then we have to react. Otherwise, the reputation of Mycenae will suffer. But to act against Sparta and Messenia is a big risk when Tantalus Jr. is waiting for our misstep. Wouldn't it be better to promise Agapenor support if the attack is repeated? Cattle rustle is common and will soon be forgotten."

"We can offer King Agapenor to forget about the herds stolen by Idas and Linceus but demand a return only from the Dioscouroi," said Agamemnon. "Let him once again send an envoy to their father, King Tyndareos, demanding the return of the herds. If the Spartans refuse, Agapenor will gather soldiers and march to the border with Sparta. We will support him and come with an army to Arcadia. It wouldn't be the first time that a kingdom in Peloponnese has been destroyed for refusing to return the herds to their owner. You remember Father's stories about the war for the Augean herds. This was before I was born, probably more than thirty years ago.

"After returning from the campaign against Troy, Hercules sent messengers to the king of Elis, Augeas, demanding to repay the debt. Augeas did not even think of repaying the debt. Instead, he assembled an army and recruited many famous fighters, including his nephews, well-known warriors. The king of Elis thought that with such powers, he could fear nothing, but Augeas misjudged. Hercules destroyed his army. King Tyndareos was in exile at that time, but he must remember these events well. I don't think he wants to risk his kingdom in a war over stolen cattle."

"But Tantalus Jr. will want to," Menelaus replied quickly. "If we lead an army against Sparta, the ruler of Pisa will immediately side with the Dioscouroi. He can pass through Aegialus and appear at the gates of Mycenae. Or he will begin to occupy one by one the cities of Aegialus. To support Agapenor means to start a war not only with Sparta. Remember, we discussed Athenian affairs.

"I have heard that Menestheus, son of Peteos, is no longer so afraid of Theseus. Theseus failed to gain enough supporters to try to regain power. They say Theseus is now thinking about leaving Athens. Although he himself is still in the city, his sons are said to have left Attica and returned to their families on Euboea. If Menestheus comes out on the side of his allies in Sparta, we will have to fight not against two but against three opponents."

"I agree," answered Agamemnon. "If we march on Sparta, Tantalus Jr. will not stand aside. The king of Pisa will not miss such an opportunity to stab us in the back and try to capture cities subject to Mycenae or even the Mycenaean throne. King Thyestes, until his last day, repeated that while Tantalus Jr. reigns in Pisa, we cannot sleep peacefully.

"There is no doubt that we can help Agapenor only if we eliminate Tantalus Jr., so let the king of Arcadia help us in this. He has many brave warriors. I hope Agapenor will be able to hold the Dioscouroi in Arcadia and give us time to deal with the king of Pisa. And the Athenian lord will not come forward, fearing to leave Theseus in the city.

"You see, brother, the gods are giving us a last chance. As long as Theseus keeps Menestheus and his army in Athens and Agapenor detains the Dioscouroi by threatening to invade Sparta, we will have time to defeat Tantalus Jr. and take Pisa. And then we will return to Agapenor his herds."

"You have really decided to march on Pisa, brother," exclaimed Menelaus. "This is a real war, the first in many years after the victory of Mycenae over the Heraclids. We have more warriors than our father had when he set out for the Isthmus. I think we will be able to take Pisa, but only if Spartans do not come to the aid of Tantalus Jr. I remember the walls of the city. They are not so tall. The main thing is not to let Castor and Polydeuces come to the defense of Pisa. The Dioscouroi are famous throughout Peloponnese as mighty warriors and experienced leaders. Their march to Attica is still on the lips of storytellers.

"Will the king of Arcadia agree to enter into open war with Sparta? I hope that Agapenor's desire to return the stolen cattle will overcome his fear of the Dioscouroi. We need to act as quickly as possible while Theseus is still in Athens and the thirst for revenge boils in the blood of Agapenor. We must convince him to send his soldiers only against Sparta and in no case against Messenia. If he will not unleash active actions but only will defend himself, he might be able to hold out."

"I do not believe that such favorable disposition of forces will continue for a long time," said Agamemnon. "As soon as Theseus leaves Athens, the hands of Menestheus will be untied. He will be able to lead an army to Sparta or to Pisa to help his allies. Agapenor is young, ardent, and ready to fight for his herds. But time will pass, anger will cool down, and maybe Tyndareos will even return some of his livestock. We must act immediately.

"Send messengers at dawn to Tiryns and Corinth with an order for the military leaders to arrive at Mycenae with troops and be ready for a long march. You, Menelaus, will take over the protection of Mycenae. I can entrust only to you the defense of the citadel. Set up outposts on the Argos road towards Argos and Corinth. The enemy can come from any direction. If an enemy appears, do not take warriors out of the gates. It is impossible to foresee how long this war will drag on. In any case, after the capture of Pisa, I will have to go to Tegea and to help Agapenor."

"Well, brother," Menelaus answered after a long pause, "do not worry about Mycenae. After all, for hundreds of years, no one has been able to take the citadel by storm. And with new fortifications and the current supply of provisions, we can easily hold out for a year. The work to deepen the fortress well, which began even during Thyestes's time, is coming to an end. But tell me where you want to meet King Agapenor. Which road are you using to get to Pisa?"

"The best way for the troops lies through Arcadia," replied Agamemnon. "Tomorrow, I will announce a campaign. And the next day, I will set out with an army along the Argos road and farther along the road to Mantinea. I will send Agapenor's envoy back tomorrow morning with a promise of help and an offer to come immediately to Mantinea for negotiations. I believe that Agapenor will agree to march against the Dioscouroi and keep them at the borders of Arcadia until my return from Pisa. After all, he asked for help, and we came to his aid.

"From Mantinea, I will move to Orchomenus. From Orchomenus, the road leads to Phegia and farther to Thelpusa. Everywhere, there are abundant sources of drinking water. Then one day to Gerea, and from there is a direct path to Pisa along the river Alpheus. Eurymedon told me that the road from Orchomenus to Olympia and Pisa is passable for pack animals and chariots. According to legends, Oenomaus himself used this road to travel in chariot from Pisa to Orchomenus in less than a day. I expect the army will reach Argolis to Pisa in five to six days in dry weather. I want to take Tantalus Jr. by surprise and personally notify him of my arrival."

"This is a good plan," said Menelaus. "Since Agapenor turned to you for help, he must accept your conditions or forget about his herds. May your path to Pisa be easy and the return difficult because of heavy weight of prey."

Menelaus paused and added, "You have not forgotten our recent conversation about Alcmaeon, the son of Amphiaraus? Do you remember how Diomedes said that after long wanderings around Arcadia, he settled in Phegia and married the daughter of a local ruler? This was about the time we returned from Calydon. When you will be passing through Phegia, find out how noble Alcmaeon is doing."

CHAPTER 10

CAPTURE OF PISA

Menelaus watched the Argos road from the observation deck of the Mycenaean citadel. Traffic along the road intensified as sunset approached. Travelers hurried to reach their destination before dark. The messenger who arrived the day before reported that King Agapenor met with Agamemnon in Mantinea and promised to bring the Arcadian soldiers to the border of Sparta. Agamemnon reported that the Mycenaean troops were moving quickly and had already passed Gerea, crossed the river Erymanthus, and entered Elide. The signs of the gods were favorable, and the king ordered to move straight to Pisa.

The messenger reported that being near Phegia, King Agamemnon inquired about Alcmaeon. According to local residents, Alcmaeon, the son of Amphiaraus, arrived in the city several years ago. He married the daughter of a local ruler and lived in the city. But it had been almost two years since Alcmaeon left Phegia, and no one knew where he was.

The messenger went back to the king with the report that everything was calm in Mycenae. Menelaus thought that the army of Agamemnon should already be near Pisa. Tantalus Jr. would either bring his fighters to battle, or he would defend himself in the city. If he counted on the help of Sparta, he would be waiting it without leaving the walls of Pisa. Agamemnon could not prolong the siege.

If the Mycenaeans managed to capture Pisa quickly, the campaign would turn into a great victory. If the troops of Agamemnon got stuck under the walls of the city, the Dioscouroi would receive news from the king of Pisa. They might come to his aid despite the threat from King Agapenor.

At the other end of Peloponnese, near the walls of Pisa, in his camp tent, King Agamemnon thought the same thing. Mycenaean warriors approached Pisa, surrounded the city, and set up camp near the road leading from Pisa to Olympia. The king did not count on a long siege. The outcome of the war was to be decided in a few days. He posted an advanced patrol at a small distance from the walls of the city, hoping that Tantalus Jr. would decide to leave the city and give battle. But that did not happen. On the offer to surrender with the promise of life to all the townspeople, the defenders refused.

The roads leading from Pisa to Arcadia were blocked. Agamemnon ordered to send a long-range patrol along the road leading from Olympia to Triphylia and farther to Messenia. It was this path that the Dioscouroi would have chosen to come to the aid of Pisa. The road on the plain leading from Pisa to Latrine and the mountain road to Eleian Pylos were also secured. The warriors who were watching the roads did not notice attempts to enter the city.

Talthybios entered the tent.

"Lord of Mycenae, valiant Agamemnon," he said, "a messenger arrived from a detachment sent along the Messenia road. He reports that the soldiers reached almost Skilliount and not far from the city found a broken chariot by the road. Apparently, the breakdown happened a day or two ago. It is possible that this was a messenger from Tantalus Jr., sent to ask for reinforcements, although it is impossible to say for sure."

Agamemnon got up and said, "Worthy Talthybios, send a messenger back with a word that the soldiers not approach Skilliount. They should watch the path and not get involved in the collisions unless attacked. The inhabitants there may be frightened and set in favor of Tantalus Jr. Then call the military commanders for counsel. Let them come after sunset. I'm going to talk to Calchas, and I'll be right back."

Armed and leaving the tent, Agamemnon walked along the road leading to Olympia. The road was wide and well-worn. Going around the city, it passed into the Arcadian tract. There were vineyards on both sides of the road. Agamemnon approached the fork. Here, the direct path to the gate departed. The main city gate with tower was located at a distance of three to four spear throws. Warriors were visible on the walls and tower of the city gates; many stood with bows in their hands.

Agamemnon passed the fork and headed along the Arcadian road. Near the road, not far away from the city walls, was the tomb of Pelops, built in the form of a small quadrangular temple with a pedestal inside. Next to the tomb was the temple of Artemis. Entering there, Agamemnon saw Calchas near the altar. The priest had just finished the sacrifice.

"Venerable Calchas, I greet you," said Agamemnon. "You make sacrifices to the fast-cutting Artemis, but she is engaged in hunting and not in the battles between people. Are you going to ask about the victory the lord of heaven himself, Zeus the Thunderer, in his temple in Olympia?"

"Son of Atreus, King Agamemnon, I made sacrifices to Zeus the Thunderer and patroness of Pelopides, Athena," the priest replied. "But now I pray to the daughter of the almighty Zeus, Artemis. She, as legends say, foretold the victory of your grandfather Pelops when he came to Pisa many years ago to win the hand of Hippodamia, the daughter of the king of Pisa, Oenomaus. That was more than a hundred years ago.

"Here, in this temple of Artemis, Pelops and his companions made sacrifices and performed divination about the victory in the chariot race. If you leave the temple, you will see a large mound about a stadium farther along the road. Those pretenders to the hand of Hippodamia who competed with King Oenomaus before Pelops are buried there. In total, as they say, Oenomaus won the races and sacrificed about fifteen people. Among them were the descendants of kings, skilled charioteers, and valiant warriors. They all wanted to marry the daughter of Oenomaus, but instead, they laid down their lives.

"Pelops knew this and hesitated for a long time before venturing into a chariot race with King Oenomaus. After all, defeat meant death. Artemis gave him hope. Pelops, your grandfather, prevailed and destroyed King Oenomaus. He became the husband of Hippodamia and king of Pisa. According to your father, Pelops honored those buried in the mound as heroes. Every year, he made memorial sacrifices on the mound and thanksgiving sacrifices to Artemis in this temple."

"The memory of the exploits of Pelops will never fade, wise Calchas," Agamemnon said after a pause. "But we need to take care about the events of today. The Mycenaean warriors may tomorrow storm Pisa. Everything is ready. Rams and protective covers are located at the two gates of the city. Old warriors say that the gates will not last long, and there are more of our fighters than the defenders of the city. Tell me what your divination promises. Will the fast-destroying Artemis grant us victory, or is it better to wait for a more favorable day? Be honest. There is no one here, and I have not yet announced my intentions to the leaders of the warriors. They will gather in my tent after sunset to discuss plans for tomorrow."

The priest spoke after a long pause.

"Lord of Mycenae, you want to know what Artemis predicts. The goddess announced that you are destined for good luck in the upcoming battle. However, divination says that victory will not avert danger from you. Do not rush to rejoice after the capture of Pisa. When you decide the fate of Tantalus Jr., don't forget that he is the son-in-law of the king of Sparta. The sons of King Tyndareos will take revenge. Everyone knows how the Dioscouroi paid back King Theseus for kidnapping their sister. Theseus lost the royal throne in Athens and all his treasury.

"After defeating Tantalus Jr., you shall decide the fate of Clytemnestra. You can keep her as a hostage or send her with honors to her father. In any case, the capturer of Pisa would incur the wrath of the Dioscouroi. Get ready for war with Sparta. The military commander has to worry about winning the battle, but the king bears a heavier burden. Your destiny is to take care of maintaining and increasing the power of Mycenae. Know that the fall of Pisa may not be the end of the war but its beginning."

Agamemnon was silent, considering what he had heard. He regretted that Menelaus was not here. He could offer sincere advice. But who else could be entrusted with the protection of Mycenae? It was getting dark outside; the sun was coming down. Agamemnon thought that time had come to go to the council of military commanders.

"Wise Calchas," he addressed the priest, "we do not need to clash with the Spartan kingdom. Ask the gods how to avoid war with the Dioscouroi. We will do what is in our power and in our interests."

*****

The assault on Pisa dragged on. The city was taken only a few days later. The defenders protected the palace for another whole day. Resistance ceased only after the death of Tantalus Jr. Mycenaeans assumed full control of the city.

In the throne room, Agamemnon found the scepter of Pelops. The king knew about this relic from the stories of his father, who described in detail a spear-shaped scepter, tall with human height, with a skillfully forged handle and tip. According to Atreus, the scepter was a symbol of the royal power of the Pelopides, bestowed by the gods. It was forged by Hephaestus himself for the father of Pelops, Tantalus, who was at that time a mighty king and a friend of gods in Phrygia. Holding the scepter in his hands, Agamemnon thought that if his father could see him now, he would be pleased.

Ordering to put up a reliable guard at the women's quarters of the palace, the king gave the city to the mercy of the winners and went to the camp. A messenger from Mycenae and Eurymedon was waiting for him at the tent. The king decided to first listen to the messenger. Menelaus reported that everything was calm in the citadel. Recently, the Athenian citizen Arcesilaus, one of the supporters of Menestheus, visited Mycenae. According to him, Theseus left Athens and went on ships to Skyros, where he had extensive possessions. Arcesilaus was interested in the whereabouts of the lord of Mycenae.

Having dismissed the messenger with an order to wait for an answer, the king called Eurymedon. The charioteer reported that the enemy's resistance was crushed throughout the city and its vicinity. Most of the city's defenders fell. However, the losses of the Mycenaean army are also great. Many soldiers died during the storming of the walls of Pisa. Considering the wounded, the army decreased by almost a third. Eurymedon offered not to linger in the city but retreat to Arcadia after collecting booty and laying to rest fallen soldiers.

"Yes, you are right, worthy Eurymedon," the king replied. "It is unknown who would have been the winner today if the Dioscouroi had appeared under the walls of Pisa on time. However, the gods were on our side. We will leave the city as soon as memorial services are completed."

Following a long deliberation with the priest Calchas, the king sent a messenger for Talthybios with an order to wait near the tent.

After listening to the greeting, the king said, "Worthy Talthybios, you have a difficult mission ahead. I am sending you to Sparta to King Tyndareos. Whether there will be peace or war between Sparta and Mycenae depends on your success. You will head south from Olympia along the Messenian road through Triphylia to Messenia. There you will cross the mountain range and descend to Sparta. When you come to King Tyndareos and convey greetings and gifts from the lord of Mycenae, ask him to listen to you without witnesses. You will say as follows.

"You will say that the king of Pisa, Tantalus Jr., has suffered an inevitable fate. The daughter of King Tyndareos, Clytemnestra, is now a widow. The lord of Mycenae, Agamemnon, asks the king of Sparta for the hand of his daughter Clytemnestra. The daughter of Tyndareos, beloved by the gods, will not remain a widow but will become the wife of King Agamemnon and queen of Mycenae.

"Further, inform the king that Clytemnestra enjoys the honors due to the wife and daughter of the king and is waiting for the blessing of Tyndareos. King Agamemnon hopes for the approval of the lord of Sparta. In gratitude, he will provide wedding gifts and is ready to settle the conflict over the missing herds between the sons of the king of Sparta and the king of Arcadia, Agapenor. The lord of Mycenae promises that the glorious Dioscouroi will keep all the herds that they have, and King Agapenor will not make claims against them.

"If the king asks where his daughter is, answer that she is waiting for your return in Mycenae. If you get the consent of King Tyndareos, ask him to send his envoy with the message to the Dioscouroi. I believe the sons of the king are lingering somewhere in Laconia, near the borders with Tegea.

"With the envoy of the king, set off from Sparta by direct road to Tegea and farther to Argolis and arrive at Mycenae as soon as you can. If the king does not give his consent, return the same way that you have arrived—through Messenia to Olympia. From there, you will go to Arcadia.

"Take the gifts for King Tyndareos with you. Here in the chest are golden goblets and other precious things."

CHAPTER 11

RETURN TO MYCENAE

The king's chariot drove under the vaults of the gate and, turning to the right, slowly rolled up the ramp. Having reached the foot of the palace stairs, the charioteer stopped the horses, and Agamemnon, holding the scepter of Tantalus in his hand, descended onto the steps. Menelaus, informed of his brother's return, waited at the bottom steps of the stairs. The sons of Atreus greeted each other. Then the noble citizens greeted the king.

Agamemnon climbed several steps of the stairs and, turning to the audience, said, "Worthy citizens, the enemy of Mycenae is defeated. Our army is returning with huge trophies. I invite everyone tomorrow to celebrate the great victory of the Achaean warriors."

When Agamemnon refreshed himself and went out into the throne room, Menelaus was waiting for him at the table, which had been set for a meal.

"Brother, you have destroyed strong enemy, captured rich trophies, and returned from the war as a famous commander. And I had to sit in Mycenae, guarding the impregnable walls, instead of going to Pisa and sharing with you the exploits and dangers of war."

"Menelaus, you have contributed as much for victory as any other," said the king. "I could not have left with an army to the other end of Peloponnese if I was not sure that Mycenae was under reliable protection. Who else but you could I leave here to guard the citadel? Don't worry, you will have enough endeavors in the future. And now we need to think about a peaceful life. Soon, Clytemnestra will arrive at the citadel. Are chambers and servants ready for her?"

"Everything is done, as your messenger requested," Menelaus replied. "The servants had to work hard. You know that Mycenae has not had a queen for about twenty years. The wife of King Eurystheus suffered an inevitable fate during his reign. Our father came to the throne as a widower, just the same as Thyestes. The chambers of the king's wife, where no one lived all this time, were repaired, cleaned, and put in order. The maids are ready to meet their mistress when she arrives."

Menelaus poured wine into goblets and continued.

"You have won a great victory, brother. Pisa was a rich city with a strong army. The Achaeans all over Peloponnese recognize now that a mighty king and a great commander reigns in Mycenae. However, you are right. The war is over. We must think about a peaceful life. Tell me, what have you heard from Sparta? Does the king Tyndareos agree to approve you as the husband of Clytemnestra? How did you make a deal with Agapenor? Who will return the livestock to him?"

"I expect Talthybios with answers to these questions from day to day," answered Agamemnon. "But for now, look here, Menelaus. You see the legendary scepter of Tantalus. Yes, this is the same scepter made by Hephaestus himself, about which our father told us. It was received by Pelops from Tantalus or directly from Hermes as a gift from Zeus the Thunderer.

"According to Father, Tantalus received a scepter with parting words that while you have this scepter, you will be king by the will of the gods. Do you remember, when we visited Pisa many years ago, King Broteas mentioned that he owns a scepter and even promised to show it. When Tantalus Jr. inherited the throne of Pisa from Broteas, he inherited also the scepter. I believe that possession of the scepter gave him that confidence which Thyestes told me about. That is why he was so bold in his claim to kingship in Mycenae."

"Listen," Menelaus said, interrupting his brother, "if this scepter is truly a gift from almighty Zeus, why didn't it help Tantalus Jr. in the battle for Pisa? Maybe it's not the right scepter. Although I have not seen a more sophisticated work. It was clearly not made by human hand. It is said that in the Hittite empire, there are blacksmiths who trace their lineage back to Hephaestus himself. They might be able to perform such a skillful work. But let me ask you, brother. If you knew that Tantalus Jr. had the scepter in his possession, how could you dare to go into battle against the owner of the gift of gods?"

"I guessed that Tantalus Jr. had the scepter," Agamemnon replied. "According to Father's stories, it always stood by the royal throne in Pelop's palace in Pisa. King Broteas inherited the scepter, along with the kingdom, from Pelops. Remember, Broteas told us that he keeps it in the royal treasury. Father was not sure whether the scepter was given to our great-grandfather Tantalus or to our grand-father Pelops. King Pelops alleged that the scepter was given to him by gods, but it looks like Tantalus already had it.

"Tantalus was a mighty ruler of vast lands in Phrygia and had a well-fortified capital on Mount Sipylus. His kingdom, as Father said, surpassed the entire Peloponnese. Shortly before his demise, Tantalus quarreled with the gods. Father once said that after this quarrel, the scepter most probably lost its magical power and ceased to help the owner. Tantalus soon lost most of his possessions and then his life itself. Pelops hoped that someday the scepter would return to Phrygia, and there it would restore its former power. And its owner, the heir of Tantalus, will return the lands of ancestors."

"Are you thinking about going to Phrygia?" exclaimed Menelaus, looking at his brother with admiration. "If so, then I will not stay in Mycenae."

"We don't have enough power for such a campaign now," Agamemnon replied. "Phrygian kings have enough brave warriors and many powerful allies. Pelops was a famous warrior and an expe-rienced commander, but the Dardanian king Il, the son of Tros, defeated him. He was forced to give up his lands to the winner and leave Phrygia. Pelops went on ships to Peloponnese, where he overthrew King Oenomaus and got himself the throne of Pisa and Hippodamia as a wife. That's how powerful Pelops was, and yet he yielded to King Il.

"I think that even if the troops of all the cities of Peloponnese were united, their forces would not be enough for a successful invasion of Phrygia. But we must not forget about our ancestors and their victories and defeats. Let the scepter be in the throne room and remind us of the greatness of the Tantalides family. You know, brother, it's not worth saying that the scepter was in the possession of this scoundrel, Tantalus Jr. This would undermine and discredit the gift of gods. Let people believe that the scepter was given by Pelops to Atreus, passed from him to Thyestes, and from him to me. Surely that was the true will of the gods. But as you know, Atreus and Thyestes had to suddenly and forever leave the court of Pelops in Pisa."

CHAPTER 12

TREATY WITH SPARTA

A few days passed, and Talthybios arrived in Mycenae. He brought a message from the king of Sparta. Tyndareos decided to give Clytemnestra as wife to the king of Mycenae, Agamemnon, and accepted his terms. In addition to the herds already in the possession of the Dioscouroi, King Tyndareos demanded a herd of horses previously owned by Tantalus Jr., along with the shepherds. The king claimed that the horses were promised by the former ruler of Pisa to his sons, the Dioscouroi, and it was not their fault that he left this world without having time to fulfill the promise.

Also, on the account of the ransom for the bride, the king would have to receive the amount of gold, silver, and copper indicated by him. King Tyndareos pointed out that Tantalus Jr. had agreed to these terms on the condition that he would not pay immediately but over time. Since the lord of Pisa suffered an inevitable fate, what he did not have time to provide was now due from King Agamemnon. In addition, the king of Sparta asked to provide patronage to Spartan merchants in the ports of Corinth subject to Mycenae. Tyndareos invited the king of Mycenae and his wife to visit him at a convenient time.

After listening to the envoy, Agamemnon thanked him for the implementation of the important mission and asked him what caused the delay in his return and if he had any difficulties and surprises along the way. Talthybios replied that there were no difficul-

180

ties, but the king of Sparta asked him to wait in the city until he communicated with his sons, who were away. The king sent messengers in several places. When he received word from the Dioscouroi, he summoned them to Sparta. After a discussion with his sons, King Tyndareos called for Talthybios.

When the Mycenaean envoy appeared in the throne room, there were the Dioscouroi, whom Talthybios described as mighty warriors in magnificent armor who looked sternly at him. In the presence of the Dioscouroi, King Tyndareos enumerated the terms of the contract and, having given Talthybios the escort, allowed him to leave for Mycenae. The king of Sparta sent his own herald with Talthybios to deliver the answer to Agamemnon.

In Sparta, Talthybios also met the youngest daughter of King Tyndareos, Helen. He had not seen a young girl more beautiful in appearance. When the time came for her to marry, there would be no shortage of suitors.

After listening to the envoy, the king of Mycenae expressed gratitude and asked him to take care of the Spartan herald, whose answer would be given the next day.

When Talthybios retired, Menelaus turned to his brother.

"Will the lord of Mycenae agree to the demands of King Tyndareos? After all, Clytemnestra is captured by you as a trophy of war, and the Spartan ruler demands a ransom for her exceeding everything that could be expected for the bride. Assuming that Tantalus Jr. has been destroyed and the king Agapenor is firmly on our side, his appetite could be more moderate."

"I think that the demands of the king were dictated by the Dioscouroi," answered Agamemnon. "They have lost an ally and want compensation. Although their requirements are huge, we can afford thanks to the trophies obtained in Pisa. May the Dioscouroi get what they want and recognize Clytemnestra as my wife. It is better to have them as relatives than as enemies. The herds captured in Pisa will be enough to cover the losses of King Agapenor. He won't have to regret supporting us in this campaign."

CHAPTER 13

NEWS FROM CALYDON

A year passed after the victory of Agamemnon in the war against the king of Pisa, and queen Clytemnestra gave birth to a daughter. The girl was named Iphigenia.

A few days after the birth of the child, the king of Mycenae and his brother, Menelaus, dined in a narrow circle of courtiers. The companions were discussing the prospects for the harvest when the servant reported that Diomedes from Argos had arrived at the citadel and asked the king to receive him. Agamemnon ordered that Diomedes be offered to bathe from the road and invited him to dinner.

"I greet the lord of Mycenae, Agamemnon, beloved by the gods," said Diomedes, entering the throne room. "I salute the worthy Menelaus and you, noble warriors."

"Welcome, son of the famous Tydeus," answered Agamemnon. "We are glad to see you in Mycenae. Join our meal."

When Diomedes satisfied his hunger, the king ordered the wine to be poured and asked, "Valiant Diomedes, tell us what's new in great Argos."

"Lord Agamemnon, everything is well in Argos. We recently received news of King Amphilochus's brother, the fearless Alcmaeon. Merchants who arrived from Aetolia said that not so long ago, he was a guest in Calydon and then went to the country of Curetes. Their possessions are spread near the mouth of Achelous, on the south of

Thesprotia and at sunset from Aetolia. According to the merchants, Alcmaeon settled among them and married the daughter of a local ruler."

"I hope the son of Amphiaraus, valiant Alcmaeon, will find peace and calmness in the country of wise Curetes," Menelaus said. "We know that he lived in Arcadia for some time, in the domain of the venerable Phegeus. But the disease pursued him, and he went on wandering again. May the thrower of silver arrows, Apollo, command that the spirits of vengeance leave him."

After taking a sip of wine, Diomedes continued.

"I have heard from King Amphilochus that when Alcmaeon went into exile, he had two objects of divine origin, a peplos and a necklace, with him. Legends say, these are the gifts from the gods to Harmonia in honor of her marriage to Cadmus. They were inherited by Oedipus.

"His son Polyneices took them with him when he left Boeotian Thebe. He gave the necklace to Amphiaraus's wife, Eriphyla, in exchange for her assistance in the first Theban campaign. And then she also received the peplos from the son of Polyneices, Thersander, for supporting the campaign of Epigones.

"After Alcmaeon went into exile, King Amphilochus asked the oracle at Delphi about the fate of his brother. It was revealed that Alcmaeon will be followed by the spirits of vengeance while he keeps these fatal gifts of gods. If he brought the peplos and the necklace to the country of the Curetes, calamity will haunt him there too."

"There are great fortune tellers among the Curetes. The almighty Zeus especially loves this tribe," said Menelaus. "We heard stories about them when we lived at the court of your grandfather in Calydon. Since King Oeneus was at enmity with Curetes, we did not have a chance to visit their land. But in Calydon, people often talked about the art of Curetean fortune tellers. I hope they will warn Alcmaeon of the fatal necklace and peplos.

"The wife of King Oeneus, Althea, was the daughter of the lord of Curetes, and as they say, she had a prophetic gift. The adviser of King Oeneus, wise Architeles, told me this story. Many years ago, a huge boar appeared in Calydon. The queen announced that this was the punishment of the gods, the punishment for King Oeneus, who did not make the prescribed sacrifices to the well-aimed Artemis. Only sacrifices to Artemis could tame the monstrous boar and save the king and the city from hardship and suffering.

"But Meleager did not listen to his mother. He gathered hunters and killed the boar. He was very proud of his victory and said that the mother's prophecy had not come true, and the boar had been defeated without the help of Artemis. But the queen's brother, a Curetean priest, objected to him and said that the goddess would take revenge even after the boar's death. He wanted to take the skin and fangs of the beast to lay them at the altar of Artemis and beg her for forgiveness. In this way, he hoped to tame the wrath of the goddess. However, Meleager decided to give the skin and fangs to the beautiful Atalanta.

"This was, according to the Architeles, the cause of the conflict. A quarrel began between them, which grew into a fight, and Meleager killed both him and the second brother of the queen. Architeles said that having learned about the death of the brothers at the hands of her son, Queen Althea was in great anger. She predicted that her son would incur the punishment of Artemis.

"Shortly after, Curetes went to war against Calydon, avenging for the death of their citizens. The fighting was fierce. But learning about the prophecy of his mother, Meleager stopped participating in battles. After that, the army of Calydon suffered one defeat after another. Finally, when the city was almost taken, Meleager went out of the gate and crushed Curetes, but the victory was given to him at the cost of his own life. Shortly after, inevitable fate befell the queen.

"The king suffered deeply from the loss of his wife and son. So according to Architeles, the prophecies of the queen came true."

"I talked to the old Architeles when I was in Calydon," Diomedes replied. "He is really very devout and convinced that all the hardships of mortals are coming from divine punishment. Almost every day, he makes sacrifices to the gods. But not everyone believes that the events that occurred after that hunt were caused by Artemis. I remember my father, Tydeus, talking about it. He was then still a child. He did not participate in the hunt itself, and about the fight with the boar, he could only tell what he had heard from others. Father did not say anything about the predictions of Queen Althea and her brothers, the Curetean priests. Tydeus told about subsequent events as follows.

"According to him, Meleager had a weakness for the beautiful Atalanta from the very first day of the hunt, but she was not very responsive. A quarrel happened at a feast, and everyone who was there drank a lot of wine. Meleager received the skin and fangs of a boar as a reward for killing the boar. Under the influence of wine and passion, he decided to present it to Atalanta, who was the first to hit the boar with an arrow. She was very pleased.

"But his uncles, who also participated in the hunt, got into an argument. They said that the skin should remain in the family, and if Meleager does not need it, then they want to take it. They made their request right in front of Atalanta, and she just could not tolerate it. A quarrel began. Meleager got angry, joined the fray, and in the heat of anger, hacked them to death. After that, everything is as in your story."

"Both stories largely coincide," said Agamemnon. "Those events are often chatted about in Calydon. For example, I heard from Andraimon that the beautiful huntress Atalanta, like the boar, was a servant of Artemis. Just like the boar, she was the accomplice of the goddess's plans. After all, it was under the influence of her spell that Meleager got involved in a fatal quarrel that led to murder and war. And she was the only one, as Andraimon noted, who left Calydon with the trophies.

"In Aetolia, many believe that Artemis severely punished King Oeneus for some misconduct. By her will, Calydon was devastated and almost destroyed. The queen suffered an inevitable fate. The heir to the throne, Meleager, perished. But Curetes also suffered greatly. The old Calydonian warriors said that their losses during the assault on the walls of the city were enormous. Maybe they also provoked the wrath of the goddess, or she simply used them for her own purposes. But enough about that. Tell me, valiant Diomedes, by what fate did you end up in Mycenae?"

"Lord of Mycenae, I came to ask for your help," Diomedes replied. "The same merchants who brought news of Alcmaeon delivered a message from my grandfather, King Oeneus. He reports that his brother Agrius with sons are making claims to power in Calydon. For a long time, they have been spreading slander that King Oeneus has become old and unable to perform royal duties. Since all the sons of Oeneus have passed away, the next in the royal family is Agrius, who has several sons.

"Now Agrius demands from the council of elders to recognize Oeneus as incapable of ruling and elevate him to the throne. King Oeneus himself wants to transfer the throne to his grandson Thoas. Thoas's father, the noble Andraimon, is Oeneus's chief assistant and will remain commander in chief when the king leaves the throne. The king invites me to come to Calydon and expects that, as the son of Tydeus, I will be able to influence the outcome of the dispute.

"I ask King Agamemnon to give me a ship to sail to Aetolia. Leaving the Lecheum harbor, I can reach Calydon in a few days while sailing from Nafplion will take much longer. I want to arrive in Calydon before Agrius moves from words to deeds."

"Your request will be fulfilled, noble Diomedes," said Agamemnon. "I will be glad to help King Oeneus to show appreciation for his hospitality. Tomorrow morning, a messenger will set out for the Lecheum harbor with orders to equip the ship urgently. If you like, you can sail the next day. My brother and I enjoyed the generosity of King Oeneus for years, and we owe him a lot. I propose to send a squad of Mycenaean warriors with you in case the dispute with Agrius cannot be resolved peacefully."

"Thank you, King Agamemnon," Diomedes answered. "I intend to depart as soon as the ship is ready. I appreciate your offer of military assistance. However, I want to try to settle the dispute peacefully, without the use of weapons. Agrius and his sons have not yet come out with weapons against King Oeneus, so there is a hope that they will not move on to direct clashes. And if I arrive in Aetolia with a squad of Mycenaean warriors, the citizens of Calydon may think that I am trying to force my will on them, and this will induce them to take the side of Agrius.

"When I visited King Oeneus last time, it seemed to me that most of the townspeople did not consider me their fellow tribesman.

In order not to set the citizens against me, I do not want to appear in Aetolia at the head of Mycenaean warriors. However, in case Agrius supporters decide to go into armed confrontation, let the ship wait at the harbor for word from me. If King Oeneus and Andraimon need armed support, I will send a messenger from Calydon to the harbor. Then the ship will quickly rush to Corinth and return to Aetolia with a group of Mycenaean warriors."

"Well, Diomedes," said Agamemnon, "let it be your way."

The next day, Diomedes departed for Lecheum. Menelaus went to see him off. After the departure of Diomedes, Menelaus met Athenians in Corinth, from whom he learned the news about Theseus. The ship on which the great warrior sailed to Skyros had returned to Athens. The helmsman said that on the island, Theseus had suffered an inevitable fate. When he arrived, he was received with honor. Theseus had estates on Skyros left to him by King Aegeus.

The great warrior was invited by the lord of Skyros, Lycomedes, to stay in his palace. Once he went for a walk, accompanied by Lycomedes, they walked around his possessions; and as Lycomedes reported, he fell off the coastal cliff and crashed to death. After the burial of Theseus, his companions decided to sail back to Attica. Upon learning of the death of Theseus, his sons decided to stay on Euboea, where they had property inherited from him.

CHAPTER 14

VISIT OF KING OENEUS

Two months had passed since the departure of Diomedes. One evening, a guard came to the royal chambers with news from Corinth. A messenger arrived and reported that Diomedes's ship had anchored in Lecheum harbor. King Oeneus came ashore with Diomedes. They spent the night in Corinth and arrived in Mycenae the next day.

"Worthy king Oeneus, we welcome you and the esteemed Diomedes to Mycenae," said Agamemnon, meeting the travelers in the throne room. "We are happy to repay your hospitality. I hope the charioteer drove skillfully, and the road was not tiring. I invite you to bathe from the road, quench your hunger and thirst, and then spend time with wine and pleasant conversation."

"Thank you, son of the famous Atreus," answered Oeneus. "The road to Mycenae is well-rolled, and I do not feel tired. We shall be glad to join your meal."

When dinner came to an end, Agamemnon turned to King Oeneus.

"King of Calydon, Oeneus, tell us how things are in Aetolia and how the feud with Agrius ended."

"King of Mycenae, Agamemnon, find out that I am no longer the lord of Calydon," answered Oeneus. "The glorious Thoas, my grandson and son of Andraimon and my daughter Gorge, reigns in the city now.

"As you know, my brother Agrius claimed the throne of Calydon for many years. And recently, he began to promote his eldest son to the kingdom. Agrius won over several respected citizens to his side, intimidating them with an attack by the enemy during the change of ruler. Agrius argued that only he could prevent a war with Curetes. He knows the leaders of Curetes, and if his son becomes the king, peace will be preserved. It was then that I decided to send a message to my grandson, the valiant warrior Diomedes.

"Diomedes arrived in Aetolia and helped win the feud with Agrius. He went to the lands of Curetes and met there with Alcmaeon, the son of Amphiaraus, with whom he fought together under the walls of Thebe. Alcmaeon visited Calydon more than a year ago, but his illness still tormented him. He continued his wanderings until he arrived at the lands of Curetes, where, as they say, he found refuge and peace.

"With the help of Alcmaeon, Diomedes entered into negotiations with the leaders of Curetes. They said that they still blame me for the last war, although more than thirty years have passed. They will not make peace while I reign in Aetolia. But if there is another king in Calydon, they are ready to forget about the old enmity. With these news, Diomedes returned to Calydon. It was then that we decided that my grandson Thoas would become king of Calydon, and I would go to live with Diomedes in Argos."

"We hope, the great king Oeneus, that everything is resolved to your satisfaction," said Agamemnon. "You are our honorable guest, and we are always glad to receive you in Mycenae. Be our guest for as long as you wish. Noble son of Tydeus"—the king turned to Diomedes—"tell us about your journey to the country of Curetes and meeting with Alcmaeon. Was he able to get rid of his long illness?"

"Lord of Mycenae, the great Agamemnon," replied Diomedes, "I thank you for the fast ship and experienced helmsman. We reached the Aetolian coast in three days. The next day, I was in Calydon. The struggle for the throne flared up in the city. Old Agrius, with his acolytes, decided to take the throne of Calydon for his eldest son. He promised the townspeople peace with the Curetes, who had been at enmity with my grandfather for many years. King Oeneus did not want civil strife, which could only weaken the city and invite the enemy.

"After consulting with the king and his son-in-law Andraimon, we decided to try to reduce the threat of war with Curetes and deprive Agrius of his main argument. The king confirmed the story of the merchants that Alcmaeon settled down in the country of Curetes and, according to rumors, married the daughter of their ruler. I decided to go to the lands of Curetes and ask Alcmaeon to help reconcile them with Calydon.

"I traveled on land through Pleuron and soon reached the ostium of Achelous, where the lands of Curetes lay. I tracked down Alcmaeon without difficulty. It was a joyous meeting after so many years. Alcmaeon told me about his wanderings. Leaving Argos, he wandered for a long time in Peloponnese until he arrived in Arcadia. There he felt relieved and decided to settle down. Having settled in the possessions of the ruler Phegeus, he hoped that the spirits of vengeance would leave him, but that did not happen. A year passed after another. Still, disease continued to torment him. Then he turned to the oracle at Delphi.

"In her answer, the Pythia said that he must part with everything that witnessed the death of Eriphyla. Therefore, the spirits of vengeance would not locate him. He can find peace only on the earth that was not in the world when the blood of Eriphyla was shed. Having received this prophecy, Alcmaeon left the magic necklace and peplos to his wife, the daughter of the ruler Phegeus. He also left his sword and spear and, armed with a freshly cut staff, went in search of the newborn land.

"Alcmaeon visited many lands. He was in Calydon. From there, he was going to the lands of Thesprotia to visit the oracle in Dodona. A stranger whom he met in Thesprotia advised him not to go north in the winter but to head south to the land of Curetes. Heeding the advice, Alcmaeon arrived at the ostium of Achelous in the country of Curetes. From them, he learned that the lands at the mouth of the river have been growing for centuries. Year after year, the mighty Achelous washes up new areas at its confluence with the sea.

"Alcmaeon realized that this is the land that the oracle spoke of. He appeared to the ruler of Curetes, told about himself and about the prophecy given in Delphi. The ruler received him cordially, said that he knew the father of Alcmaeon, the wise seer Amphiaraus, and his uncle, the illustrious leader Adrastus. The ruler of Curetes gave Alcmaeon a plot of land at the mouth of Achelous, washed over in recent years, and gave him his daughter Callirrhoe as a wife. Curetes helped Alcmaeon build a house, and he already had his firstborn, Acarnan. He told me that the spirits of vengeance could not find their way to him. Such is the story of Alcmaeon."

After a pause and having a drink of wine, Diomedes continued.

"I told him why I arrived in the country of the Curetes. Alcmaeon introduced me to the leader of Curetes, who agreed to listen to my appeal. When he learned that Calydon wanted peace with the Curetes, the chief replied thus. He said that Curetes did not harbor enmity towards the people of Calydon but would not negotiate peace with King Oeneus. They believe that the blood of Curetean leaders and warriors remains on Oeneus, son of Portheus. As long as he reigns, there will be no peace with Calydon, said the ruler of Curetes.

"With such news, I returned to Calydon. After considering the situation, the king decided to transfer power to his grandson Thoas and go with me to Argos. Thoas became the lord of Calydon and promised the townspeople peace with Curetes. He was supported by the followers of Oeneus, and old Agrius had nothing to say. On the day of our departure, Thoas sent an envoy to Curetes to inform them that Oeneus is no longer in Calydon and to negotiate peace."

"I am glad to hear that worthy Alcmaeon has found deliverance from the disease in the country of Curetes," said Menelaus. "I remember well Thoas, son of Andraimon, grandson of King Oeneus. He was a most skilled young warrior in Calydon. I'm sure he'll make a worthy ruler.

"News of King Theseus came to us in your absence, Diomedes. I do not know if you heard that Theseus suspended the struggle for power in Athens and sailed to Skyros, where he had possessions inherited from his father. Not so long ago, his ship returned to Athens, and the helmsman told that the illustrious warrior suffered an inevitable fate. During a walk in the company of the king of Skyros, Lycomedes, Theseus fell off a cliff and crashed. He was buried in Skyros."

"The death of Theseus reminds me of the death of the great Hercules," said Diomedes after a long pause, "far from the homeland, far from family. One fell victim to deceit. The other, an accident. Indeed, in battle, both Hercules and Theseus were invincible. Theseus did not even lose his last battle with the Thesprotians. As I learned in the country of the Curetes, he and his companions were captured in their sleep. Only Pirithous managed to wake up, joined the fight, and was killed."

"If King Lycomedes was the only witness to the death of Theseus," said Oeneus, "then I'm not sure that the accident was the cause. I have heard of the deeds of the lord of Skyros. Lycomedes reimburses for the small number of his warriors with cunning and deceit. Previously, he had dealings with Theseus. Probably because of that, the great hero decided to go to Skyros.

"But in recent years, he began to make friends with the king of Phthia, noble Peleus, the son of Aeacus. Peleus has a powerful Myrmidon army and a significant fleet. His son, Achilles, is still a teenager but shows unmatched ability in the martial arts. Lycomedes enlisted the support of Peleus, and now Theseus, who became the enemy of Sparta and was expelled from Athens, is more of a hindrance to him than a support.

"Theseus had large landholdings on Skyros and perhaps was going to settle there, and Lycomedes made enemies on the island during the years of his reign. He was concerned that local population could support Theseus. All this made Theseus more of a rival to Lycomedes than the valuable ally he had previously been. I wouldn't be surprised if Lycomedes decided to get rid of Theseus and appropriate his lands. He probably knew that the ruler of Athens, Menestheus, would not seek justice."

"Honorable king Oeneus," answered Agamemnon, "I also thought about it. Theseus was probably about sixty years old. He was in good shape. Otherwise, he would not have been able to make the long journey from Thesprotia to Attica. A small child or a frail old man can stumble and fall off a cliff, but not such a mighty warrior. Someday, we will know whether the death of Theseus was a decree of fate or the result of human deceit."

The king of Mycenae invited Diomedes and Oeneus to stay, but Diomedes decided not to linger and went home to Argos. He was going to settle Oeneus on his suburban estate, located on the road to Mantinea at the foot of Mount Artemision.

CHAPTER 15

BIRTH OF ORESTES

Shortly after the departure of Diomedes and Oeneus, Clytemnestra was relieved of her burden with a boy. Few things could bring more joy to King Agamemnon than the birth of an heir. The child was named Orestes. A messenger was sent to Sparta with good news. Returning, he brought gifts for Clytemnestra and a message from King Tyndareos.

The king decided that it was a good time for his youngest daughter, Helen, to get married and called on everyone who wanted to become a husband of the Spartan princess. The courier said that the king sent messengers to all parts of Hellas and to the island of Crete.

Learning about the plans of Tyndareos, Menelaus decided to go to Sparta and compete for the hand of Helen, stories of whose beauty he had heard more than once. Agamemnon supported his brother and advised him to talk to Clytemnestra before leaving.

After inquiring about the health of the newborn, Orestes, Menelaus told the queen about his intentions. Clytemnestra was silent for a long time.

"Worthy Menelaus," she said at last, "Helen is really beautiful. Her beauty surpasses all descriptions. Many compare her to Aphrodite herself. From childhood, she used this gift, and all her desires were immediately fulfilled. Whatever Helen asked for, she was not used to accepting refusal. My brother Castor once said that seeing Helen is a delight, but hearing her is a torment."

After a pause, the queen continued.

"You must know the story of our sister Timandra, the eldest daughter of King Tyndareos. She is much older than Helen and me. As my mother said, when Timandra was born, my father did not make the required sacrifices and angered the patroness of marital bonds, the beautiful Aphrodite. The goddess, through the mouth of a priest, predicted that the children of Tyndareos would be unhappy in marriage.

"You, of course, heard about what happened long ago between Timandra and her husband, the king of Arcadia, invincible Echemus. You also know what happened to me. Every full moon, I make sacrifices to Aphrodite and pray for indulgence. Do not forget to make sacrifices to the golden-haired daughter of the almighty Zeus if you decide to fight for Helen's hand, and if you get her, remember this prophecy."

HELEN

CHAPTER 1

HELEN'S WEDDING

The finest grooms of Hellas had gathered in Lacedaemon. They had all heard the rumors of the bride's virtues and wished to become related to the powerful ruler of Sparta. King Tyndareos welcomed the suitors but was in no hurry to make his choice, nor did he accept their wedding gifts. Every day, the king gave abundant feasts and entertained his guests with sport competitions, bards, and dancers.

The favorites among the suitors were Philoctetes, son of Poeas, ruler of Meliboea of Thessaly, and Menelaus, son of Atreus, brother of the king of Mycenae. In his youth, Philoctetes had participated in endeavors led by the great Hercules and was considered an exceptional archer. The bride's brothers, Castor and Polydeuces, were on his side.

Menelaus was supported by Agamemnon, ruler of the great Mycenae, married to Helen's older sister, Clytemnestra. Agamemnon sent a herald with a message and gifts to King Tyndareos and the bride's brothers. Among other suitors were Ajax, son of King Telamon of Salamis; Protesilaus, son of Iphicles, king of Phylacia of Thessaly; Menestheus, ruler of Athens; Elephenor, the leader of the Abantes of Euboea; and Idomeneus, son of Deucalion from Crete.

Many illustrious leaders offered gifts and awaited the decision of the ruler of Sparta. King Tyndareos soon realized that Helen's success exceeded his expectations. He hesitated to choose out of fear of the revenge of the rejected suitors and spent every day thinking of a way to resolve the situation without causing conflict. One such day, he was visited by Odysseus, son of King Laertes, from Ithaca. He conveyed wishes for prosperity and gifts from his father, who was Tyndareos's longtime close acquaintance.

"Noble Odysseus, son of Laertes," the king greeted, "I am glad to see you in our realm. Certainly, you have heard that we are marrying off our dearest daughter. There is no shortage of suitors, the best in glory, valor, and wealth, who have come to seek the hand of the beautiful Helen. Accept our invitation to dinner, where you will see all the suitors. In the meantime, tell us how your father is doing and what business brings you to Lacedaemon."

"The great lord of Sparta, Tyndareos," replied Odysseus, "my father is thinking of retiring and making me the ruler of his kingdom. He wishes me to bring a worthy wife to Ithaca. I want to marry Penelope, your brother Icarius's daughter. I visited him yesterday and spoke of marriage, but he was evasive. I fear Icarius will not marry his daughter to Ithaca and will refuse me or ask an exorbitant ransom. Lord Tyndareos, my father says you can help me and persuade Icarius to concur to this marriage. Please, great king, talk to Icarius and persuade him to agree. My father and I will be forever in your debt."

King Tyndareos contemplated Odysseus's words for a while.

"Valiant son of Laertes," he finally said, "I will fulfill your request and speak to Icarius. But in return, I also ask you to do me a favor. I told you how many mighty fighters and glorious leaders are gathered in Sparta. You see how hard it is to make a choice. It's even harder to guess how the other suitors will feel about the verdict and what they might do. When there are two or three suitors, it's easy to decide. But how to avoid problems when the number of suitors is comparable to a small army? And I do not want to delay the choice, as the grooms eat herds of fattened bulls and rams.

"In the old days, a duel between the grooms was used to choose the best suitor. You must have heard how the king of Calydon, Oeneus, gave his daughter Deianeira in marriage. Two best fighters of the time, the invincible Hercules and the finest warrior of Thesprotia, valiant Achelous, came to seek her hand. Their superiority was so obvious that all other suitors refused to compete."

Tyndareos paused and continued.

"Many illustrious warriors have arrived in Sparta, all ready to fight for Helen's hand. But it is our wish that the choice of the groom should be made peacefully and cause no strife. We want no bloodshed. You, Odysseus, are the son of the wise Laertes and the grandson of the cunning Autolycus, whom they call the offspring of Hermes himself. I remember so many legends about his endeavors. You must have heard from Laertes some of them.

"Your father told me that you are like Autolycus in the sharpness of mind and that you had been dealing since nine years old. I wish you to figure out how to make sure that all the suitors agree with Helen's choice of husband, and no one expresses displeasure or becomes violent. If you can do that, I promise to convince Icarius. He won't be able to refuse me, because I have saved him from the wrath of Hercules himself."

Odysseus pondered the king's proposal for a long time.

Finally, he said, "Great lord of Sparta, I can offer a solution that will calm the discontent and eliminate the strife. Your choice will be accepted by all suitors, and when they leave, they will not harbor anger. Here is what you must do. Gather all your guests in a sacred place and make sacrifices to the gods. After that, demand that suitors swear on the blood to protect Helen's chosen husband from all offenses. Let all the suitors swear one by one. Call upon the gods to witness this oath. After that, the chosen one may be declared."

"Odysseus, beloved of the gods, I will follow your advice," replied the king after a short pause. "But you will have to go out and take the oath first. For as the shepherds say, until the first sheep moves, the whole flock will stand still."

A few days passed, and the lord of Sparta carried out Odysseus's plan. He assembled all the suitors at the small town of Pellanus, which lay on the road from Lacedaemon to Arcadia. There on the altar, King Tyndareos offered a horse as a gift to the gods. When he had cut it up, he made all the suitors, in turn, stand on the parts of the horse's body and dip their hands into the blood to swear an oath.

Each man swore in the name of the lord of Olympus that he would protect Helen's husband from all harm. Each swore to pursue and punish the one who would forcibly take possession of Helen. Then the horse was buried in the ground in front of the altar, and Tyndareos announced that the decision would be made in the evening at the feast.

When all the suitors had assembled in the throne room, the king came out with Helen and announced that his daughter had chosen Menelaus, son of Atreus, as her husband. The brother of the lord of Mycenae became the husband of Helen, daughter of King Tyndareos, and remained to live in Sparta.

Castor and Polydeuces were not present when the suitors took their vows. They knew that Menelaus would be chosen, and they left Lacedaemon so as not to hear reproach from their favorite, Philoctetes. Many of the suitors were not very upset, because they did not expect to win and had come to Sparta for the feasts and entertainment. They got what they wanted.

When Talthybios returned from Sparta, he told Agamemnon about the wedding.

"Lord of Mycenae, your brother, the noble Menelaus, was chosen from many worthy leaders. He became the husband of Helen. But the other suitors cannot complain either. King Tyndareos was not stingy. He gave a rich wedding feast and distributed farewell gifts to all suitors. I have not seen so many illustrious chiefs and warriors gathered in one place in a long time, and they were pleased with the reception and the refreshments.

"Among the suitors was Patroclus, son of Menoetius. He lives in Phthia, in the court of the illustrious Peleus, son of Aeacus. You remember, Lord Agamemnon, how Mycenae was visited by the king of Calydon, Oeneus, with his grandson Diomedes. He told of the son of King Peleus, young Achilles. Patroclus, like Oeneus, praised the young Achilles and said that he was far superior to his peers in martial arts and that in endurance and skill he had been compared to the young Hercules.

"King Peleus sent Achilles to the centaur Chiron, who lives on Mount Pelion. The centaur teaches Achilles not only combat skills but also wound healing and the art of divination. According to Patroclus, in two or three years, Achilles will be an excellent young warrior and a worthy heir to his father."

"King Oeneus and his grandson, valiant Diomedes, visited us about a year ago," answered Agamemnon. "I have heard that Oeneus had settled in Diomedes's estate not far from Argos. And the young Achilles, judging by the reviews, promises to grow into an outstanding leader. King Peleus was wise to send him to be raised by centaurs. This would help Achilles avoid the weakness and pampering often inherent in the sons of kings brought up at court. When Orestes grows up, I also think of sending him to live with the shepherds for a year or two. Thank the gods that Achilles is still so young. If he were three or four years older, he could have competed for Helen's hand."

"Your words are true, king of Mycenae," Calchas intervened. "Achilles would be a worthy rival for Menelaus. Phthia is a rich land, and King Peleus himself has participated in several successful overseas campaigns. To mention only that he went with Hercules himself to the land of the Amazons and to Troy. In both campaigns, they captured great riches. Indeed, with these funds, Hercules raised an army and conquered half of Peloponnese. And he could have taken the whole Peloponnese, as King Eurystheus feared, but the gods stopped him. Of course, the portion of the spoils that went to Peleus and his brother Telamon was much smaller."

"Lord Agamemnon is, of course, right," said Talthybios. "Patroclus expressed the same opinion at the feast in the palace of Tyndareos. I have heard Protesilaus, son of Iphicles, speaking to Patroclus. He was praising his father and proclaimed him to be the fastest runner, who in his youth beat even the wind and was second only to Apollo himself. Patroclus replied that young Achilles was already faster than any adult in running, and if he had been a peer of Iphicles in his prime, he would have overtaken him in the contest. Then he added that if Achilles were five years older, he would have been the strongest contender for Helen's hand."

"The valiant Achilles is the grandson of the illustrious Aeacus of Aegina," said Calchas. "Aeacus did many worthy deeds and for his wisdom was even called the son of Zeus the Thunderer. I have heard that in his youth, he visited Troy and took part in building the walls of Ilion. But the Trojan king Laomedon did not pay him what he had been promised.

"Aeacus left the Hellespont by ship, but in his heart, he fore-told that he would return. And if not himself, his descendants would return to Ilion until the debt was paid. And the gods heard these words of Aeacus, which became a prophecy. His sons, Telamon and Peleus, went to Ilion with Hercules. If this prophecy applies to all his descendants, then Achilles is also destined to go to Troy."

"Every Achaean knows of the deeds of Aeacus, the favorite of the gods," replied Agamemnon. "King Oeneus said that Zeus the Thunderer was willing to respond to Aeacus's requests. No wonder the lord of heaven fulfilled that prediction. I see that it came true for his sons. And you say that his grandson Achilles, son of Peleus, is also destined to go to Ilion. If you are right, such a fate awaits the other grandsons of Aeacus, Ajax, and Teucer, the sons of King Telamon of Salamis, and the descendants of Aeacus's oldest son Phocus. Tell me, wise Calchas, how many generations of Aeacus's descendants are doomed to come to Ilion?"

Agamemnon was quiet for a while and continued.

"I think to invite King Oeneus to Mycenae and ask what he thinks about it. Wise Oeneus knows a lot about the deeds of the gods and heroes of the past. He told me that he himself had been in the presence of the gods, and more than once. Talthybios, send to Argos young Periphetes. Tell him to go to Diomedes, who knows Periphetes well, and ask when it is convenient for him and Oeneus to come to Mycenae for a visit."

"Lord of Mycenae," answered Talthybios, "tomorrow morn-ing, Periphetes will depart for Argos. I will give him two chariots with drivers so that he can return with King Oeneus if he wishes to visit Mycenae. I am very curious how many generations of Aeacus's descendants are destined to fulfill his prediction. I think that Aeacus himself did not want his words to turn into a spell. Why would he condemn his descendants to such a fate? I wonder what the wisest Calchas thinks about this."

Everyone looked at the priest.

Calchas was silent for a long time, and finally, he said quietly, "The will of the gods is unbreakable. Everyone knows how Zeus the Thunderer condemned Prometheus to be chained to the rock forever.

Even when he forgave Prometheus many years later, this command remained in force. Prometheus must forever wear the rock chained to his finger in the form of a ring. This ring always reminds him that Zeus's will is unbreakable. If Zeus, ruler of the heavens, has turned Aeacus's words into a prophecy, it will last as long as Aeacus's descendants live." The priest paused and added, "Or as long as the walls of Ilion stand."

Periphetes, who had been sent to Argos, returned with the news that King Oeneus was troubled by an old ailment. His visit to Mycenae had to be postponed. Soon, a sad message came from Diomedes. King Oeneus had met his inevitable fate.

CHAPTER 2

BIRTH OF HERMIONE

A year had passed since the marriage of Menelaus, son of Atreus, and Helen, daughter of Tyndareos. A daughter was born in their family and named Hermione.

King Agamemnon, in the throne room of the Mycenaean citadel, listened to Talthybios, who had returned from his journey to Lacedaemon. In the room were the priest Calchas, the king's charioteer Eurymedon, and several advisers.

"King of Mycenae," Talthybios reported, "I have completed my errands. Menelaus has received your congratulations, message, and the gifts for his wife. I also have delivered to King Tyndareos your gifts. He sends valuable gifts in return."

"Thank you, Talthybios," replied Agamemnon. "Have you brought from Sparta any other news?"

"I have learned about sad rumors from the worthy Menelaus. The merchants from Arcadia told that noble Alcmaeon, son of Amphiaraus, met his inevitable fate. It happened in the realm of Phegeus. According to the merchants, Alcmaeon was killed by the sons of the ruler and buried near the road not far away from the city. Menelaus has already sent an envoy to Arcadia with instructions to find out what had happened."

"I regret to hear of the unhappy fate of the worthy Alcmaeon," replied Agamemnon after a pause. "But I am not sure whether we can believe these rumors. As I know, the sons of the lord Phegeus are not noted for military exploits, and Alcmaeon is an experienced and skilled fighter.

"I knew him many years ago, during my father's reign. Even then, he was first among his peers. All the Achaeans know that he conquered Thebe, where he performed many great exploits. I think of those warriors living today, only the glorious Ajax, son of Telamon, could have gone into battle with him and withstood.

"But most importantly, Alcmaeon has left Arcadia for some years now and lives in the country of Curetes, near Aetolia. Why would he return to Phegeus's realm in Arcadia, violating the oracle's foretelling?"

"King Agamemnon, you are right about Ajax," said Talthybios. "I saw him a year ago in Sparta. He is indeed an outstanding warrior, worthy of his father's glory. Perhaps he could stand his ground against Alcmaeon. His brother Teucer is not as mighty, but he is a skilled archer. He is said to be second in marksmanship only to Philoctetes, who trained under Hercules himself."

"Did you know that Teucer is only half brother of Ajax by his father?" Eurymedon interjected. "He is the son of Telamon by the Trojan princess Hesione. Yes, Teucer's mother was a Phrygian. I heard that on a campaign to Ilion, the great Hercules captured the daughter of King Laomedon, Hesione, and gave her to Telamon as his wife. She arrived with Telamon at Salamis and bore him a son, Teucer.

"A few years later, Hesione expressed a wish to visit her family in Troy. Telamon did not object but did not want to accompany her. Hesione hired a Phoenician merchant ship and sailed for Phrygia. That was many years ago, back under King Eurystheus. She never came back, and Teucer grew up to be a worthy warrior."

"You said correctly, worthy Eurymedon," replied Agamemnon, "that Teucer's mother, Hesione, is the daughter of a Trojan king. But do not call her a Phrygian. Long ago, the son of Zeus the Thunderer, Dardanus, brought warriors from across the sea and conquered the land along the Hellespont and around Mount Ida from the Phrygians. He founded a city on the banks of the Hellespont and named it in his honor as Dardanus. The lands he conquered was called Dardania, and later, when Dardanus's grandson Tros reigned, it became known as the kingdom of Troy.

"Hesione is a descendant of Dardanus, and you can call her a Dardanian or a Trojan but not a Phrygian. My grandfather Pelops, son of Tantalus, was the Phrygian. Tantalus once reigned in the Phrygian lands from his capital by Mount Sipylus. Tantalus and the Dardanian king Tros fought for many years.

"After Tantalus died, his son Pelops came to power. He continued the war against Tros's son Il and his allies. Pelops was a great warrior, but he could not hold back such a powerful enemy. But he did not surrender. He left Phrygia and sailed to Peloponnese, where he won himself a new kingdom. And Il, after his victory, chose as his capital a city near Mount Ida, on the bank of the Scamander River. That city has been called after him Ilion ever since. Il's son, Laomedon, inherited his father's throne. Now Priam, son of Laomedon, reigns in Ilion. Correct me, honorable Calchas, if I am mistaken."

"Your words are true, lord of Mycenae," answered Calchas. "Not much has come down to us of the wars of Tantalus with Dardanians, for more than a hundred years have passed since then. The legends say that Tantalus and Tros began to fight for the fertile lands by the river Kaikos. For a long time, they fought as equals, luck changing hands. Before the decisive battle, two rulers asked the famous oracle of Cybele in Phrygia, situated by the white hills. The same answer was given to both. He who offered the gods the most valuable sacrifice would win.

"King Tros, as the legends say, gave his eldest son to the gods. Tantalus also prepared a sacrifice, but he could not take his son's life. He kept Pelops but lost the favor of the gods. Tantalus was defeated and perished in that battle. Soon, Tros passed away as well. Tros's son Il completed the conquest of Tantalus's kingdom. But Dardania did not retain power over Tantalus's realm.

"Most of his lands are now part of Mysia, where the lord Teuthras ruled. And Il reigned in the Trojan kingdom and left it to his son Laomedon. When Hercules conquered Ilion more than forty years ago, he put Laomedon's son Priam on the throne. Now Priam is the ruler of the Trojan kingdom."

"Yes, it is so, wise Calchas," replied Agamemnon. "Most of the former kingdom of Tantalus has been under the rule of Teuthras for many years. He rules in Mysia over the lands lying from the southern bank of river Kaikos to the river Hermus and Mount Sipylus. The east part of Tantalus's kingdom became the possession of King Mygdon, who left it to his son Coroebus. But the lands to the north of Kaikos were acquired by Dardania and now belong to the Trojan kingdom."

The king paused for a moment and then went on.

"We could talk about the Phrygian lands for days. Tell, Calchas, what do you think of the news we have received from Arcadia?"

"As for the fate of Alcmaeon," replied the priest, "it is too early to believe the rumors of his death. For Alcmaeon left Arcadia long ago. He wandered for a long time, then finally, fulfilling the will of the oracle, came to the country of the Curetes and stayed there. Why should he go against the prophecy and incur the wrath of the demons of vengeance that had tormented him so long?"

"It's not like Alcmaeon," Agamemnon said. "He has always shown proper respect for the gods. The lord of Calydon, Thoas, may know more of his fate. After all, Alcmaeon helped him negotiate peace with the Curetes. Perhaps it is time to send an envoy to Aetolia.

"Talthybios, take a few days to rest after your visit to Sparta and head out to Calydon to King Thoas. Present him with gifts and ask him how the worthy Alcmaeon is doing. Inquire if the king has heard of his journey to Arcadia. If he starts asking any questions, tell him about the rumors about the sons of Phegeus. Tomorrow, send a messenger to the Lecheum harbor with the order to prepare a ship."

CHAPTER 3

WARS OF ARGOS
AGAINST THEBE

A month after Talthybios's departure, King Agamemnon received news from Sparta. Menelaus reported that the merchants' stories were confirmed. Alcmaeon had found his demise at the hands of the sons of the lord Phegeus.

Envoy sent to Arcadia learned that Alcmaeon had arrived in Arcadia and asked the daughter of Phegeus for the return of the necklace and peplos he had given her years before. He told her that he wanted to bring them as a gift to the oracle of Apollo in order to heal himself entirely of his illness. The woman complied with his request.

But the lord Phegeus and his sons learned from one of Alcmaeon's companions that he was not going to leave the gifts at Delphi but would take the necklace and the peplos to the land of the Curetes, to his new wife, Callirrhoe. The lord's sons became infuriated at this treachery and, after catching up with Alcmaeon at night, slaughtered him. He was buried by the roadside, not far from the city. And they, it is rumored, intended to go to Delphi and bring a necklace and a peplos as a gift to the oracle.

"Let Calchas take care of the memorial sacrifices," said Agamemnon, dismissing the messenger. "A courier should also be sent to Argos to King Amphilochus. Though it will be better to wait

210

for Talthybios. His journey to Calydon must have been in vain, and he will not bring good tidings."

Another month passed, and Talthybios returned from Aetolia.

"Lord of Mycenae," he began, "King Thoas was surprised to hear that Alcmaeon had left his residence. The last news that reached him from the country of the Curetes was about the birth of Alcmaeon's second son. I told the king about the rumors from Arcadia, and he was very concerned. The lord of Calydon said that Alcmaeon had promoted reconciliation with the Curetes. If inevitable fate befell him, the Curetes might reverse from peace to enmity.

"To find what really happened, King Thoas's father, Andraimon, decided to visit Pleuron. I volunteered to accompany him. Many merchants dwell in Pleuron and trade with Curetes. We have found among them some who were well-acquainted with Alcmaeon. From them we learned that few months ago, Alcmaeon left by ship for Elide. The merchants knew men of Alcmaeon's estate and suggested we contact them. Upon consultation, we sent a courier to the country of Curetes with the order to inquire about Alcmaeon's associates. His words I now pass on to you."

Talthybios was silent for a moment and then continued.

"The messenger went to the mouth of Achelous, where the Curetes live, and found the estate of Alcmaeon. He met and spoke with an Argive warrior who had wandered with Alcmaeon for many years and had come with him to the country of the Curetes. This warrior had not gone with Alcmaeon to Arcadia because he was afflicted with a serious illness. He confirmed that Alcmaeon had indeed left by ship for Elide some months ago, and here is why.

"When Alcmaeon told his wife Callirrhoe of his wanderings, he mentioned the necklace and the peplos and called them gifts from the gods. And among the Curetes, all items of divine origin are considered the objects of worship from the ancient times. They believe that the owner of such an object is under the patronage of a deity. From then on, Callirrhoe wanted to become the owner of these objects or at least one of them. She constantly persuaded Alcmaeon to go to Arcadia to get the necklace and the peplos, but he refused, because he remembered the precept of the oracle and his torment from the demons of vengeance.

"Finally, after the birth of her second son, Callirrhoe managed to persuade her husband. She promised to send with him a Curetes priest who would turn away the demons. The priest came to the house of Alcmaeon and said that he would help him, but the gifts of the gods must be delivered to the sanctuary of the oracle of Dodona. Callirrhoe, however, wished to have them for herself. The priest then advised them to first take the items to the oracle and receive his blessing. Thereupon, they agreed and set sail by ship, intending to sail as far as Elide, then through Olympia to reach Arcadia and the possessions of Phegeus.

"The ship returned not so long ago, but without Alcmaeon. The helmsman said that he had met his inevitable fate in Arcadia. That was all Alcmaeon's companion knew."

"Thank you, Talthybios," said Agamemnon after a long pause. "What you have told me corresponds to the news I received from Menelaus. He learned that Alcmaeon was killed in Arcadia by the sons of the lord Phegeus. Send a messenger to Argos tomorrow to tell King Amphilochus of his brother's fate."

"King of Mycenae," Calchas said, entering the conversation, "the fate of Alcmaeon is indeed sad. Just like his father, Amphiaraus, who went against Thebe at his wife's request, he went to Arcadia at his wife's will, both to never return. Remember what Menelaus's messenger said about the necklace and the peplos. According to him, they were the cause of Alcmaeon's death. The sons of the lord of Phegeus decided to kill him when they found out that Alcmaeon was going to give these objects to his wife. Only someone in Alcmaeon's entourage could have revealed this.

"Talthybios said that a Curetes priest was among Alcmaeon's companions. He must have been the one who gave the secret away. After all, the priest had a claim to the necklace and the peplos. It is not known what became of them. Were they brought as a gift to the Delphi oracle, or did the sons of Phegeus keep them, or did they fall into the hands of the Curetes priest? I dare to say that if these objects remain among people, Alcmaeon would not be the last victim in their fatal journey. Maybe we should ask the oracle about the fate of the necklace and the peplos. I am ready to go to Delphi, if it is your will."

"We in Mycenae do not need to worry about this magic necklace," Eurymedon interjected. "If it didn't go to Delphi, it might stay in the possession of Phegeus, where it has been for years without doing any harm. And if the Curetes priest got ahold of it, he intended to bring it as a gift to the oracle in Dodona. Even if we believe in its fatal properties, the only one who suffered from it is Alcmaeon. But he disregarded the oracle's command, counting on the protection of the treacherous priest."

"Worthy Eurymedon, you probably do not know the whole history of the necklace," replied Calchas, "if you think that Alcmaeon was its only victim. Let me enlighten you. It is said that the magical power of the necklace is such that it makes the recipient fulfill the wishes of the giver. According to Theban legends, many years ago, the necklace and peplos were given by the gods to Harmonia, the beautiful wife of the founder of Thebe, King Cadmus. They were kept in the treasury of the kings of Thebe until Eteocles learned of their magical power.

"However, I have also heard another version. Some say that Oedipus received a necklace and a peplos after defeating the sphinx by cunning or by military force. The sphinx wished in return immunity for himself and his cohorts and advised him to visit Thebe and give the necklace to the queen. Oedipus showed up at Thebe and presented the necklace and the peplos to Jocasta, the widow of King Laius. After receiving the necklace, the queen granted Oedipus's wish. She married him and made him the king of Thebe.

"Many years passed. Jocasta and Oedipus met their inevitable fate. There are various accounts of their deaths. Some say the necklace played its fatal role here too. The sons of Oedipus agreed to take turns in reigning. When they were discussing how to divide power, Eteocles handed Polyneices a necklace with the words, 'Take this necklace, brother, leave Thebe, and concede the first year of the reign to me.' So according to his wish, Eteocles remained to rule in Thebe while Polyneices left Boeotia. He arrived in Argos, where he became the son-in-law of the great Adrastus and awaited his turn to take the throne in Thebe.

"When Polyneices realized that Eteocles was unwilling to honor the treaty and transfer power, he plotted to take it away by force of arms with the help of Adrastus. It was hard to persuade Argives to attack Thebe. Although Adrastus supported his son-in-law, Amphiaraus and some other leaders were against the war.

"After exhausting all other means, Polyneices used the magical necklace to get his way. He gave it to Eriphyla, who was the sister of Adrastus and the wife of Amphiaraus, the two most influential leaders in Argos at the time. Eriphyla, receiving the necklace, granted Polyneices's wish and convinced her husband to march on Thebe. Thus began the first war of the Argives against Boeotia.

"Everyone knows how it ended. All the leaders except Adrastus and many valiant warriors perished under the walls of Thebe. Polyneices and his brother Eteocles also departed this life. And now judge for yourself, worthy Eurymedon, whether the necklace may be regarded as the cause of their destruction. Would Eriphyla have persuaded her husband to risk his life and march on Thebe if the necklace did not have magic power?"

"Listening to you, wise Calchas, the necklace does have certain powers," answered Eurymedon. "So the farther away it is from Mycenae, the better."

"King Sthenelus, son of Capaneus, told me that his father was also against the march on Thebe," Talthybios interjected. "But he agreed when Amphiaraus decided to go. The illustrious Capaneus never returned from that campaign. But Sthenelus went on a second march to avenge his father. I myself heard his account of these events in Argos.

"According to Sthenelus, Adrastus supported his son-in-law Polyneices's intention to go to war against Thebe and was prepared to give him Argos soldiers. But Amphiaraus, Capaneus, and some other Argive leaders were against the war. They thought that the chances of Polyneices taking Thebe were very slim.

"Capaneus said that Boeotia was a rich and vast region with many brave warriors. Cadmea, the citadel of Thebe, was built by overseas masters and was impregnable. If Eteocles and his uncle Creon gather the Boeotian militia, they will defeat Polyneices. And Amphiaraus feared that having repelled the attack of the Argives, Thebans might take the Heraclids as allies and come to Argolis with a return visit.

"Amphiaraus made divinations, and the result was unfavorable for the campaign against Thebe. That is when Polyneices employed his necklace. He acted wisely in choosing Eriphyla as his ally. Everyone in Argos knew that in the past, she managed to resolve in peace the deadly quarrel between Adrastus and Amphiaraus. As a reward for this, she had taken an oath from them to fulfill one wish of hers.

"And now after receiving the necklace, she reminded her husband of that oath. She asked that he help Polyneices regain the throne of Thebe. Amphiaraus could not break his oath, but before the march, he told his son that Eriphyla had exchanged his life for the necklace. The rest is as you told. Of the whole army, only Adrastus and a handful of warriors survived."

"I do not see a big difference in the stories of Calchas and Talthybios," said Agamemnon. "But there is a difference, and it comes to manifestation of magic powers. Those who believe in the magical power of the necklace believe that it made Oedipus king of Thebe. Others say that Oedipus defeated the sphinx by his wits or weapons and received the Theban throne as a reward, and he found the necklace in the king's treasury. Some say that the magical power of the necklace helped start the first Theban war, and others, like Alcmaeon, blame it all on Eriphyla's greed. They believe that she sacrificed her husband and son for the sake of the necklace and the peplos.

"It seems to me that without the necklace, magical or not, Argives would not have gone to Thebe. Therefore, the necklace could influence events, so we should try to find out where the necklace is now and who owns it. Calchas, you will go and bring the gifts to the Oracle of Delphi. You will also take my message to Strophius, son of Crisus, the ruler of Phocis. He recently asked for the hand of our sister Anaxibia. We have decided to accept his offer."

The king was silent for a while and then turned to the priest.

"Wise Calchas, I know that Amphiaraus was a great leader and an acclaimed fortune teller. Many of the Argives believed his prophecies. The noble Diomedes considers him a prophet. What do you think of the mention of the Heraclids in the story of Sthenelus? Do you believe that Amphiaraus foresaw the attack of the Heraclids on Peloponnese, or is it simply his attempt to discourage the Argives from the war?"

"Lord of Mycenae," replied the priest, "Amphiaraus was not the only one who feared the invasion of Heraclids in those years. The march of Adrastus on Thebe took place about twenty-five years ago. At that time, King Eurystheus, too, thought that the Heraclids were preparing an attack on Peloponnese. That is why, it seems to me, he refused the request of Tydeus and Polyneices to give warriors for the war against Thebe.

"During the lifetime of Hercules, Eurystheus kept saying that the great warrior wished to unite the whole Peloponnese under his rule. And after Hercules was no longer among the living, Eurystheus transferred his fears to his descendants. When he learned that the Heraclids had gathered in Athens, he was sure that an invasion was just around the corner. To defend against them, he gathered an army and marched on Athens himself. You know how that ended.

"And your father, the godly Atreus, also feared the Heraclids. As soon as he came to power after the death of Eurystheus, he began to prepare for their attack. He recruited warriors and negotiated with allies. As a result, when the Heraclids did move into Peloponnese, Atreus was able to meet them at the Isthmus at the head of an powerful army. As Atreus himself recounted, the Heraclids did not expect this. They did not want to die in the battle and offered to decide the outcome of the battle in a duel.

"Now you see, King Agamemnon, that Amphiaraus was not the only one who anticipated the attack of Heraclids, but Eurystheus and Atreus also foresaw and prepared for it."

"You are right, wise Calchas," said Agamemnon. "I think that Amphiaraus wanted to avoid a confrontation with the Heraclids, and his fears were justified. But I have heard from my father that King Eurystheus was not so much trying to avoid the attack of Heraclids but provoking it himself by his own actions. When Hercules left the world of the living, his descendants were scattered all over Hellas. Eurystheus transferred his hatred for their father to them and began to pursue them.

"The Heraclids tried to seek refuge in many cities of Boeotia and Thessaly, and Eurystheus forced the local rulers to refuse them by threats and bribery. This persecution gradually forced the Heraclids to unite and establish friendship with the Dorians, who had come to Hellas from the north—as they say, from beyond the Pindus mountains.

"Finally, after years of wandering, the Heraclids found refuge in Athens with Theseus. My father said that Eurystheus had long persuaded Theseus to expel the Heraclids, and when persuasion failed, he threatened to march on Athens. But Theseus was an admirer and friend of Hercules and decided to protect his descendants. I do not know what pushed Eurystheus to the fatal step. My father never talked about it. Maybe it was Theseus's determined refusal to expel Heraclids, or maybe, as Calchas says, he wanted to prevent them from attacking. But he led an army to Athens.

"Either way, I agree with what my father said. If Eurystheus had not gone to Athens and suffered a crushing defeat, the Heraclids would not have begun the campaign in Peloponnese. King Atreus was no less perceptive than Amphiaraus. He supposed that the Heraclids would want to take advantage of their victory over Eurystheus and invade Peloponnese, and so they did, especially since they knew that the Argive army had also recently been defeated at Thebe and believed that Peloponnese was defenseless. However, my father had time to prepare for their attack and managed to repel it."

Agamemnon paused and continued.

"Calchas, when you will be in Delphi, listen to what they say about the Heraclids. Nothing has been heard from them for a long time. After the defeat at the Isthmus and the death of Hyllus, the Heraclids left Attica and went north. More than twenty years have passed since then. Hyllus's sons have matured. A new generation of warriors has grown up.

"I know that the king of the Dorians, Aegimius, adopted Hyllus when Hercules left this world. His descendants became Dorian leaders. Try to learn if the Heraclids are plotting a new campaign against Peloponnese. To find out about this is as important as finding about the fate of the magical necklace."

"I will do my best, lord of Mycenae," replied the priest.

C H A P T E R   4

THE ROYAL SCEPTER AND OTHER GIFTS OF GODS

More than a month passed before Calchas returned from Delphi. Although the voyage from Corinth to the harbor of Delphi took only a day or two, one of the rare storms occurred in the Gulf of Corinth and delayed the sailing for a long time.

On his arrival in the Lecheum harbor, Calchas found a chariot with a charioteer, who delivered him to the Lions Gate just before sunset. Walking up the wide, newly rebuilt ramp, the priest climbed the palace steps and entered the reception chambers. The gatekeeper at the door of the throne room greeted him and informed him that King Agamemnon was receiving an envoy from Crete. The priest waited on one of the benches until the envoy left and then entered the hall.

"Greetings, son of the godly Atreus, King Agamemnon," he said as he approached the throne. "At your command, I made a trip to Delphi and brought gifts to the oracle. Also, I delivered your message to the lord of Phocis, Strophius."

"Welcome back, Calchas," replied the king. "Your journey took a long time. But make no excuses. We know that a winter storm has been raging in the bay for nearly a month, and not a single ship has left the harbor. Today, we received noble Merion, an envoy from Crete. He brought an invitation from King Idomeneus to visit

Knossos at the end of the summer and participate in a feast in honor of our grandfather, King Catreus, son of the great Minos. All the relatives of the illustrious ruler would gather there.

"Merion has come from Crete to the port of Sparta, Gythium, and has already visited Menelaus. He has brought an invitation to me, Menelaus, Palamedes, and the sons of Theseus, Acamas, and Demophon. As you know, wise Calchas, our mother and mother of Palamedes were daughters of King Catreus. And the mother of Acamas and Demophon, Phaedra, is the sister of Catreus. So in the line of Minos, Menelaus and I are nephews of Acamas and Demophon.

"I offered Merion a chariot to go to Nafplion to see Palamedes and then through the Isthmus and Boeotia to Euboea to convey an invitation to the sons of Theseus."

The king stood up and, heading for the side door, said, "Come to the observation deck tomorrow morning, wisest Calchas, and we'll talk about your journey. Now it is time to prepare for dinner."

*****

The next morning, after climbing a long stairway, Calchas stepped onto an observation deck located at the top of a Mycenaean citadel. From the deck, one could enjoy a view of neighboring lands as far as the city of Argos. Agamemnon often invited his advisers and guests there for conversation.

The king met the priest with the words, "Greetings, wise Calchas. I hope you rested well. Tell me now what you have seen and heard in Delphi."

"Lord of Mycenae, may the favor of Zeus the Thunderer, patron of the Atreus family, be with you. I visited Delphi and spoke to the priests and servants of the temple and to the guardian of the treasury," reported Calchas. "The priests remember how years ago Alcmaeon came to Delphi and received a prophecy. But none of them had heard of the visit of the sons of the lord Phegeus. Nor had there been any offerings to the oracle such as the necklace and the peplos.

"It is not known what happened to these objects. Perhaps the sons of the lord Phegeus had not yet reached Delphi. Or maybe the Curetes priest managed to get ahold of them. If so, I hope he went straight to Thesprotia and brought them as a gift to the oracle of Dodona."

"You are right, Calchas," replied Agamemnon. "Let us hope that these gifts of the gods have gone to Dodona forever. I remember well the fatal story of the necklace and the peplos as you have conveyed it. It began in Thebe with the death of Oedipus and his wife or maybe even earlier. It was followed by the death of their sons, the destruction of the Argive army, and then the ransacking of Thebe. Alcmaeon was their last known victim. Hopefully, there are not many objects possessing such overwhelming power in the world."

"Lord of Mycenae, you yourself hold one such object," said Calchas. "In fact, the royal scepter, which is kept in the storage space of the throne room, is the creation of Hephaestus himself. Your great-grandfather Tantalus befriended the gods, and either he or your grandfather Pelops received the scepter of power as a gift from Zeus, the lord of heaven. Like the necklace, this scepter can wield great powers."

"I don't think the scepter has magical powers," Agamemnon replied. "As you know, it did not help its owners protect their kingdoms. Tantalus was defeated by the Dardanian ruler Tros and perished in the battle. True, I am not sure if Tantalus owned the scepter. My father told me that he did not know whether Pelops inherited the scepter from his father, Tantalus, or, as Pelops himself liked to tell, personally received it from Hermes, the herald of the gods.

"According to my father, Pelops had ambivalent feelings about his parent Tantalus and was often contradictory in his judgments of him. Perhaps Thyestes could tell more about it, but I never asked him. I shall have to ask Aegisthus if Thyestes told him anything about the history of the scepter."

Agamemnon looked at Calchas, but the priest kept silent.

"My grandfather Pelops possessed the scepter, but he lost both his kingdom and his ancestral lands on Mount Sipylus. He was forced to leave Phrygia and sail to Peloponnese. There he became king of Pisa, lived a long life, and passed away in his palace. The next holder of the scepter, King Broteas, also ended his days peacefully in Pisa. After him, that scoundrel Tantalus Jr. became the ruler of Pisa. But the scepter did not help him escape retribution. Only a few years after he ascended the throne of Pisa, inevitable fate befell him.

"If this scepter was received from the gods, it may have magical power. But there are no evidences of it. However, if you look closely at the scepter in the sunlight, you can notice that it was not made by human hands, and my father called it a gift from the gods. Still, I do not know any proofs of its powers."

"Lord of Mycenae, let me tell you what I think," answered Calchas. "I, too, have heard your father say that the royal scepter is a gift from the gods. Indeed, Atreus said on several occasions that descendants of Tantalus would have the royalty as long as they hold the scepter. Tantalus fought a long war and died in battle. I know Pelops did not fight in that battle. He was far away. And Pelops ended up with the scepter. So either Tantalus did not take the scepter in his last battle, or it was given not to Tantalus but to Pelops himself.

"I am trying to show that Tantalus didn't have the scepter when he lost the battle and died. You say that the scepter has no magical power because Pelops had it and still lost the war and was forced to leave Phrygia. Yes, that's true, but consider the power of his opponents.

"As your father was reciting Pelops's stories, Dardanian army was joined by Lycians, Paphlagonians, and detachments from Thrace. Despite the superior forces of the enemy, Pelops was able to avoid total defeat, escape to Peloponnese, and take enough warriors with him. He did not remain a wandering commander but soon won the royal throne.

"I can suppose that the scepter helped him become king of Pisa. The scepter also protected the next descendant of Tantalus, King Broteas. During the reign of Broteas, Hercules conquered and ravaged almost all of Elide, but he did not touch Pisa and Olympia, where Broteas reigned.

"Now about Tantalus Jr. Yes, he had the scepter when he lost his kingdom and his life. How to explain this? If we believe the words of Atreus, that the scepter guards the royal power of the Tantalides, I will say this. Tantalus Jr. was not a descendant of Tantalus. Maybe he didn't know it himself, but gods know everything.

"After all, King Broteas was already old when he ascended the throne. Broteas's wife needed to give birth to an heir to the king. If she could not accomplish it with Broteas, she found another father for the child and told the king that the son was his. She was not the first to do so. Tantalus Jr. himself claimed to be Thyestes's son, but Thyestes always denied it, and he denied it very confidently, as if he knew it was impossible.

"Tantalus Jr. must have been told of Thyestes's paternity by his mother in order to tie him to herself. I don't know who Tantalus Jr.'s real father is, but it's not Broteas or Thyestes. Tantalus Jr. was not Tantalid, and so the scepter did not serve him. But it will serve you, lord of Mycenae."

"You are right about Tantalus Jr.," Agamemnon replied after a pause. "I do not believe that this rascal belonged to the Tantalid family. However, there is nothing to support what you say about the magical powers of the scepter. It may be a creation of Hephaestus, but it has no magical power. Just because certain events took place in the presence of the scepter does not mean that it has influenced them. After all, the necklace and the peplos were explicitly used to influence people's actions.

"It can be argued that without them, there would have been no Theban wars, hundreds of warriors would not have perished, and Amphiaraus and Alcmaeon would not have died. I would not be surprised if they were originally handed over to Harmony by some deity to destroy the great city founded by Cadmus. After all, the gods do their business with mortals according to their habits. Some send a monstrous boar to punish the unworthy. Others use a necklace for that same purpose.

"And speaking of the scepter, it has shown nothing of itself in many decades. No, Calchas, if there are objects endowed with magical powers, the scepter of Tantalids is not one of them. Tell me, are you aware of any other gifts of the gods? And if so, how have they manifested their powers?"

"Lord Mycenae, of course, I've heard the legends about the gifts of the gods to King Minos," answered Calchas. "Storytellers say that Perseus, Bellerophontes, and some other heroes received from gods objects with magical powers. In the old days, the gods often appeared among people, and there were many such gifts. These days, items of divine origin are very rare. However, they still exist.

"For example, during my stay at Delphi, I met Phoenix, the son of Amyntor. He dwells in Phthia, at the court of King Peleus, son of Aeacus. Phoenix said that Peleus received armor made by Hephaestus himself as a gift for his wedding with the daughter of an overseas king.

"In this armor, as Phoenix said, Peleus alone, without an army or even a few companions, captured Iolcus. However, Iolcus is not some kind of village. It is one of the most fortified cities in Thessaly. The soldiers guarding the walls were not afraid of a lone traveler and did not close the gates when Peleus approached them. He entered the city, and no one could stop him. This armor, according to Phoenix, makes the warrior invulnerable. Neither the sword nor the spear or the arrow takes them."

"I heard a lot about the noble Peleus, the son of Aeacus," said Agamemnon. "He is one of those warriors who went with the great Hercules to Troy. The fact that he single-handedly was able to capture Iolcus gives credibility to the rumors about the magical properties of his armor. I wouldn't be surprised if this is a gift from the farsighted Artemis, the daughter of Zeus.

"I remember, in Calydon, King Oeneus said that Artemis has a fondness for Peleus and helps him deliver a mortal blow in every battle. Oeneus said that sometimes this blow falls on an ally of Peleus, but this does not bother Artemis much. According to him, when Artemis sent a boar to Calydon, she not only took revenge on Oeneus but also reserved the Phthian throne for her favorite, Peleus.

"And the son of Peleus, Achilles, from a young age enjoys the favor of gods as well. He is marked by success in military arts. According to rumors, he excels in weapons exercises and chariot races. Perhaps Phoenix told you about the successes of young Achilles."

"You are right, lord of Mycenae," Calchas answered. "Phoenix talked about Achilles frequently. He himself participated in the upbringing of the young prince—taught him how to drive a chariot, build troops for battle, and other military skills. Achilles spent his last years on Mount Pelion. There he matured and learned a lot from the leader of the centaurs, Chiron. Wise Chiron knew many great heroes, including Hercules himself. He has something to remember.

"But last year, the father called the young Achilles from Pelion and sent him to the island of Skyros in the possession of King Lycomedes. Phoenix told me that war was brewing between Dorians and centaurs in Thessaly at that time.

"More and more Dorians are coming from northern lands surrounding Mount Pindus. From there, they move at sunrise toward the areas settled by centaurs. Clashes between centaurs and Dorians over hunting grounds and pastures threatened to escalate into war. King Peleus was afraid that Achilles, who had already become a young warrior, would enter the fight on the side of the centaurs.

"According to Phoenix, at one time, the oracle predicted to the mother of Achilles that her son would become famous on the battlefield but would not return from it. The king sent his son to Skyros in the care of King Lycomedes in order to protect him from participating in the war. About a year has passed since then. Skirmishes between Dorians and centaurs continue as before, but neither seeks a major war. Phoenix arrived in Delphi to receive the oracle's prediction for Achilles."

"King Peleus acted wisely by sending his son to Skyros," answered Agamemnon. "And what side the king was going to take in the case of war, centaurs or Dorians?"

"Phoenix told me that the king does not want war," said the priest. "When he sent Achilles to Skyros, he gave him his armor. Peleus is no longer at the age to lead warriors into battle. He is waiting for approval from the oracle for his son to return in order to transfer to him the throne of the Phthian ruler."

"One may say that Dorians are becoming more active in Thessaly," Agamemnon said after a long pause. "Few people have heard about them in previous years. And now Dorians became a problem for King Peleus himself. Tell me now, Calchas, how are their allies, the Heraclids, doing?"

"Lord of Mycenae," replied Calchas, "the Heraclids and Dorians are frequent guests in Delphi. Dorians are settling in the lands from Mount Pindus down to Mount Eta, and Mount Eta is located not far from the oracle. The priests know them well and are willing to share many interesting stories.

"They conveyed that the king of the Dorians, Aegimius, who reigned at the time of Hercules, had no children of his own. In those years, Dorian leaders wanted to take power away from him, referring to the old age and the lack of an heir.

"With the support of Hercules, King Aegimius defended the throne and was reinstated as supreme ruler of Dorians. In gratitude, he adopted Hyllus, the son of Hercules, when the great hero left this world. As you know, Hercules's funeral pyre was on Mount Eta. And since then, the Heraclids and Dorians have been offering him sacrifices over there.

"When King Aegimius himself suffered an inevitable fate, the descendants of Hyllus became his heirs and the leaders of the Dorian tribes. Do not forget that by that time, the leaders of the Heraclids, Hyllus and Iolaus, were no longer alive. But this was not their only loss, not by far. Even before, many powerful Heraclids perished in the battle with King Eurystheus. We in Mycenae thought only about our own defeat and losses at that time. But as I have heard in Delphi, although they have won the battle, the losses of the Heraclids were extremely significant.

"What you have said in our previous discussion, lord of Mycenae, looks very plausible. Having defeated the Mycenaean army and knowing the disastrous results of Argos's war against Thebe, the Heraclids decided to invade. They decided that there was no force in Peloponnese that could stop them.

"But your father, the godlike Atreus, managed to assemble a strong army at the Isthmus. The sight of his warriors astonished the Heraclids. They probably realized that one more such battle as with Eurystheus and there would be almost no sons of Hercules left. I think that is why they did not engage in battle with King Atreus.

"Realizing that even if they are victorious there would be no one left to conquer Peloponnese, Hyllus proposed to decide the outcome of the battle by a duel. He wanted to save his warriors for the invasion of Peloponnese. Hyllus took a risk and lost. After that, the Heraclids had no choice but to retreat. They did not have enough strength to continue the war. So they moved north and settled in the lands of Dorians.

"In Delphi, they say that the Heraclids asked the oracle when they were destined to return to the lands conquered by their father in Peloponnese. The oracle replied, 'Come back after the third fruition.' Having learned the prophecy, they decided that the oracle promised them to return after the third harvest—that is, in the third year.

"But after the events on the Isthmus, substantial losses of warriors, and the death of Hyllus and Iolaus, they came to the oracle again. Following his response, they changed their interpretation. Now they believe that the oracle predicted their return in the third human generation. So in the next thirty or forty years, we shall not expect the invasion of the Heraclids."

CHAPTER 5

TRIP TO CRETE

King Agamemnon was waiting for his brother in the port of Cythera, an island located near Cape Maleas in the very south of Peloponnese. Agamemnon's ships came from Nafplion after a long journey down the east coast of Laconia. Menelaus was supposed to arrive from the seaport of Sparta, Gythium, on his ship. From Cythera, the brothers intended to sail together to Knossos, the residence of the Cretan kings.

The ruler of the island welcomed Agamemnon on the shore. He said that Cretan merchants set up their trading settlement on Cythera. The island had convenient harbor and had long been considered the best port for sailing from Peloponnese to Crete. In the middle of the passage lay a small deserted island, Antikythera, which served as a good guide. To reach Crete, one must sail south with a shift toward sunrise; and if you saw Antikythera, you must deviate even more toward sunrise. A merchant ship usually traveled from Cythera to Crete in two or three days, and it took another day to sail along the northern coast of Crete to the sunrise to reach Knossos.

Menelaus arrived the next day. At sunset, his twenty-oared ship entered the harbor of Cythera. The brothers decided to spend two more days on the island, expecting the arrival of Palamedes. The ship of Palamedes stayed behind in Nafplion, waiting for the sons of Theseus, Acamas, and Demophon coming from Euboea. Palamedes invited them on his ship for a voyage to Crete and offered to meet at Nafplion.

When Palamedes did not show up on the third day, Agamemnon and Menelaus made the prescribed sacrifices and put out to sea. Driven by a fair north wind, their ships headed for Crete.

*****

Palamedes arrived at Knossos when the celebrations in honor of King Catreus, the son of the great Minos, were already in full swing. Competitions of warriors and athletes were replaced with performances of Cretan dancers and acrobats on bulls. They were substituted by presentations of bards and storytellers. Every evening, dinner tables were waiting for guests, bursting with magnificent Cretan dishes.

At one of these dinners, Palamedes approached Agamemnon with a greeting, accompanied by two young warriors. He introduced them as Acamas and Demophon, the sons of Theseus and the Cretan princess Phaedra, the sister of King Catreus. Palamedes said that his ship arrived at Knossos only today.

Responding to the greeting, the lord of Mycenae invited Palamedes and his companions to share a meal. When the arrivals were satisfied, Agamemnon turned to Acamas.

"Tell me, son of famous Theseus, how was your journey from Euboea? Menelaus and I waited in vain for you at Cythera, and before we sailed, we ordered the local ruler to notify Palamedes."

"King Agamemnon," answered Acamas, "Poseidon kept us from misfortunes at the sea. At Carystus, the southern port of Euboea, we found a ship bound for Aegina. Having reached the island in three days, we made sacrifices at the grave of the god-equal Aeacus and began to look for a ship sailing to Argolis. We had no luck, but wandering in the harbor, we heard that the ships from Phrygia had lately called into Aegina.

"According to local residents, Paris, the son of King Priam, arrived from the Trojan kingdom and was heading for Salamis. Two days later, we found a boat and crossed over to Troezen. From there, we came by land to Nafplion, where Palamedes was waiting. He said that your ships departed five days ago, and most likely, we would be able to catch up with you only at Knossos. And so it happened."

"Worthy Acamas," said Agamemnon, "we are glad to see you at the celebration in honor of our common relative, the great king Catreus. I was interested in your words about the visit of the son of the king of Troy. Tell me what the locals told about Paris and his companions. Do they know why he arrived in Attica? And what are his future plans?"

"There was a lot of talk on Aegina about the visit of Paris," said Acamas. "According to local residents, Paris came from Troy in search of Hesione, the sister of King Priam. Hesione married Telamon, son of Aeacus, and followed him to Salamis. That was, as they say, forty to fifty years ago. Since then, no one has heard of her in Ilion.

"The Trojans wanted to know how to get to Salamis, where Paris hoped to find Hesione. The people of Aegina explained to them how to sail to the island. They also told the guests that many years ago, Hesione left Salamis and went by ship to Ilion. Since then, nothing is known about her. The Trojans were surprised and upset. According to them, Hesione has never returned to Ilion. Therefore, the king of Troy, Priam, sent his son in search of her.

"Paris decided to ask the king of Salamis, Telamon, who might know more about Hesione's fate. He sailed a few days ago on a course for Salamis. We ourselves did not see the ships of Paris, but before leaving Aegina, we heard from locals that ships coming from the direction of Salamis were seen east of Aegina. They looked like Trojan ships. Passing by Aegina, the ships went to open sea."

"I also have heard from inhabitants of Aegina that the ships of the Trojans left Attica and were seen headed for the sea," Demophon said, entering the conversation. "They passed by shortly before our arrival. As for the reason for the visit of the Trojans to Hellas, it is not easy for me to accept as true that they were led by the search for Hesione. After all, Hesione became the wife of Telamon more than forty years ago, during the reign of Eurystheus. So told our father, King Theseus.

"Telamon received Hesione as a reward during the campaign of Hercules in Ilion. My father said that when Telamon returned from Ilion with a lot of booty, Hesione was with him. It is hard to believe that forty years later, King Priam recalled his sister and sent ships to Attica to uncover her fate."

"Demophon speaks sensibly," said Menelaus. "We also have heard stories about the campaign of great Hercules in Troy. With a small detachment, he defeated the army of King Laomedon, took the city, and placed Priam on the throne. It is said that Hercules seized countless treasures in Ilion but lost much of it on the way back when his ships were caught in a storm.

"Now almost fifty years later, Priam is the ruler of a rich king-dom in his seventies. Is it possible that he feels the approach of the inevitable end and sends the ships to search for his sister? After all, legends say that Hesione saved the life of Priam. But I do not rule out that Paris may have other motives."

"I heard many stories from the helmsmen about the Trojan kingdom," Palamedes joined. "After all, ships from Nafplion often travel to Lesbos and Chios. The king of Troy, Priam, has many sons, but only two claim the throne, Hector and Paris. Hector has always been considered the heir as the eldest son. He is a powerful warrior and an experienced commander.

"However, not so long ago, King Priam announced that he also had a son, Paris, who grew up far from the palace, among the shep-herds on Mount Ida. They say that Paris can be older than Hector in age and by seniority can claim the throne. But he has not partic-ipated in campaigns, and he has neither personal military glory nor the experience of a leader of warriors. I would assume that the king decided to give Paris a chance to prove himself in a sea voyage and sent him in search of Hesione."

"Worthy Palamedes," replied Agamemnon, "I think there is truth in your words. The participants in the campaign against Troy said that Hercules killed all the sons of King Laomedon except for Priam and was going to kill him too, but Hesione begged Hercules to let Priam live. There is no doubt that those events made an unfor-gettable impression on Priam, and having become king, he decided to protect himself from the risk of losing all his sons as a result of a surprise attack.

"Priam hid his firstborn on Mount Ida with the shepherds without revealing to anyone his true parents, so he guaranteed that his family would not be interrupted even if Ilion was taken and all the sons of the king were destroyed. But decades passed. Paris grew up, matured, and the king no longer could hide his origin. Now Paris has the right to the throne as the eldest heir, but Hector has earned this right in battles and has authority among the people. It is difficult for the king to choose. He loves both his sons.

"And he decided to send Paris on a risky sea voyage. If Paris disappears at the will of the gods in the abyss of the sea, Hector will become the only contender for the throne. If Paris returns, having acquired military glory, then he can claim the throne as the oldest son, and Hector will have to yield. This is how I see the purpose of this trip."

"What will Paris do when he finds out that Hesione is not on Salamis?" said Menelaus. "True, her son Teucer, the cousin of Paris, lives on Salamis. But I do not think that Teucer agreed to sail to Troy instead of Hesione. Moreover, delivering Teucer would not be a great feat in the eyes of the king and the people of Ilion. If the purpose of this trip was to find Hesione, Paris would have to go home with nothing and give up hope of the throne."

"You are right, valiant Menelaus," Palamedes replied. "I believe Teucer, son of Teamon, will not board the ship of Paris no matter what he promises. However, Paris would not like to return empty. This would mean giving up the throne to Hector. If he were an experienced leader, I would say that he may try to capture the booty and increase his military glory by attacking a rich coastal city or island. But Paris has no combat experience. I'm not sure what he decides to do."

"Let Paris think about his fate," Agamemnon said, reentering the conversation. "His ships left Attica and sailed to the sea. If this is his first sea trip, he will be wise to avoid direct confrontation."

Idomeneus came up to the table.

"King of the great Mycenae, Agamemnon, noble warriors, am I correct to recognize the sons of invincible Theseus?"

"Yes, you are, son of the glorious Deucalion," answered Agamemnon. "Acamas and Demophon were delayed on their way and arrived only today on Palamedes ship."

"We are glad to see you, worthy Idomeneus, grandson of the god-equal Minos," said Palamedes.

"We greet you, lord of Crete, Idomeneus," said Acamas.

"Welcome, worthy Palamedes, grandson of Catreus," said Idomeneus. "Grandchildren of the great Minos, Acamas and Demophon, welcome to Crete, cradle of the lord of mortals and immortals. Your father, the invincible king Theseus, was here many times. The first time, he came to Crete as a young, unknown warrior. It was in old times, in the reign of Minos, the son of Zeus the Thunderer. Theseus fought the unbeatable Minotaur, defeated him, and won Princess Ariadne as his wife.

"For the last time, he arrived at Knossos many years later, in the reign of Catreus, already a celebrated hero, the conqueror of the Amazons. King Catreus gave him his sister, Princess Phaedra, your mother, in marriage. We are glad to see all relatives of the great Catreus. Enjoy the food and the performance."

After dinner, Agamemnon and Menelaus went to their chambers.

"Tell me, Agamemnon," Menelaus said, turning to his brother, "do you think that the Trojan prince Paris has another objective besides searching for the sister of King Priam? Hesione left Ilion over forty years ago. Why did Priam remember her only now?

"Let me remind you about the Phoenician merchant who visited Mycenae several years ago. He told us how the Hittites started a war with the pharaoh of Egypt in Syria and could not defeat him. The pharaoh did not allow them to grab hold of lands to the south and east. To the north of them lay the sea. So the Hittites could expand their empire only to the west, toward Thrace, Thessaly, and Peloponnese.

"More than once, we have heard about the close associations of the Hittite empire with Trojan rulers. Is it possible that the Hittites are preparing an invasion? At their request, Priam sent Paris to explore the coast and find suitable places for landing troops, and the search for Hesione is just a convenient excuse."

"You are right, brother. If the Hittites decide to attack us, Trojans will be on their side," answered Agamemnon. "They did not forget how Hercules ravaged Ilion and almost destroyed the ruling dynasty. King Priam knows that we also remember how his grandfather, Il, expelled Pelops from the ancestral lands in Phrygia. Therefore, he is ready to support our enemies.

"But I do not think that the Hittites themselves are ready to start a war in the west. As the Phoenician said, in the war with the Egyptian pharaoh, the Hittites threw all their forces into battle but could not defeat him. The losses on both sides were enormous. Pharaoh went back to Egypt to gather a new army. The Hittites will not go west until the great pharaoh Ramses threatens them from the east."

"So you think that Paris went in search of the king's sister?" Menelaus asked.

"It is hard to believe that after so many years, the lord of Troy suddenly remembered his sister and sent ships to look for her," Agamemnon replied. "Probably, wise Palamedes is right. King Priam is thinking about the transfer of the throne. He is probably already over seventy. Priam does not want to offend his sons and tries to put the choice of the heir in the hands of fate.

"The fact that the king sent Paris confirms once again that he is not planning an attack. After all, a battle-tested commander should choose places for landing troops, and Paris has no military experience and is not trained to lead warriors. If King Priam were preparing for war, he would send Hector or another seasoned leader."

"I hope you are right," said Menelaus. "What will Paris do? After all, there may be a hundred or two warriors on his ships. This is enough to sack a small coastal city. Shouldn't we send a ship to Argolis with a warning?"

"Once again, I agree with Palamedes," replied Agamemnon. "Paris is not experienced in battles and did not go on military campaigns. I don't think he would dare a pirate raid. Moreover, when Acamas and Demophon arrived at Nafplion to meet with Palamedes, they must have spread the news of the visiting ships from Troy. But even if Paris is willing to take the risk, our herald will be too late.

"When we return home, I will send Talthybios to Salamis to King Telamon. He may know more about the fate of Hesione and may tell Paris's whereabouts."

"Perhaps this is the best thing to do," Menelaus said after a long pause. "There is one more issue that I wanted to discuss. During lunch, Acamas approached me with a request for help. We are talking about his grandmother Aithra. You remember the Dioscouroi invasion of Attica? When they captured the town of Aphidna?"

"Of course. It was not long ago," answered Agamemnon. "If memory serves, about fifteen years ago, shortly before our return to Mycenae."

"Yes, you are right," continued Menelaus. "The Dioscouroi took into slavery all the surviving inhabitants of Aphidna. Among the prisoners was Theseus's mother, Aithra. Since then, she has been a servant to Helen. Acamas and Demophon, on the way to Nafplion, visited Troezen and learned that Aithra continues to serve Helen.

"They turned to me with an appeal to release their grandmother and deliver her to them on Euboea. Acamas does not want to go to Sparta because of the Dioscouroi, who harbor hatred for Theseus. The sons of Tyndareos are known for their irascible temper. What would you advise, brother?"

"Aithra, the mother of Theseus, the daughter of Pittheus, is among the servants of Helen," Agamemnon repeated after his brother. "And her captivity has been going on for fifteen years. Tell me, brother, have you ever talked to your wife about Aithra?"

"Yes, brother. We talked about it more than a year ago. I asked if Helen thought it would be better for Aithra to be released. Helen replied that Aithra was happy in her service and was not looking for a better life. Her duties are not burdensome, and the household treats her well. And where will she go at that age? Her son has suffered the inevitable fate, and her grandchildren live in exile."

"It is hard to argue with beautiful Helen," Agamemnon said after a long pause. "But try to talk to her again. Try to convince her to let Aithra go. Tell her that Aithra's father, Pittheus, is our father's older brother, and Aithra is our cousin. Don't remind Helen of Theseus. Say that Aithra is our relative, and therefore, I ask for her.

"I am ready to present a worthy ransom if there is a need for it. Tell her that if Helen cannot decide for herself, I will have to turn to King Tyndareos. This should have an effect on her. Tell Acamas that you will help Aithra find her freedom when you arrive in Sparta. She will go wherever she wishes—to her grandchildren on Euboea or to her native Troezen."

After a pause, the king added, "Not so long ago, in Mycenae, a storyteller from Corinth performed a ballad about the exploits of Bellerophontes, the son of Glaucus. I remembered the stories of King Oeneus about Bellerophontes. I don't know if you've heard how young Bellerophontes left Corinth and went to Argos.

"On the way, he visited King Pittheus in Troezen and wooed Aithra. At that time, Pittheus, son of Pelops, predicted that Bellerophontes had many exploits and battles ahead, and the time had not yet come to marry. And so it happened. Soon, Bellerophontes sailed on a ship to Lycia, where he performed great feats. Subsequently, when King Aegeus arrived in Troezen, Pittheus made another prediction, which also came true.

"When you return to Sparta, ask Aithra if she remembers the visit of Bellerophontes to Troezen."

CHAPTER 6

KIDNAPPING OF HELEN

Returning to Knossos after a successful hunt, Agamemnon, Menelaus, Idomeneus, and their companions settled down at dinner in one of the chambers of the royal palace. To entertain the guests during the meal, a court storyteller hummed hunting stories to the sounds of a cithara.

He told about a dog named Laelaps, from which no game could escape. The magical dog was given by the gods to the king of Crete, the great Minos. At the same time, in Boeotia, near Thebe, an insidious and elusive fox emerged, which many considered the gods' punishment. She destroyed crops and attacked animals and even people. Many hunters tried to overtake her, but the fox was able to get away from any chase. Amphitryon himself, the father of the great Hercules, pursued this fox day and night but could not catch it.

One day, the Athenian Cephalus appeared in Thebe with the magical dog Laelaps, which was now in his possession. He offered the dog to Amphitryon on one condition.

Listening to the bard, Menelaus suddenly felt that someone touched his shoulder. Raising his head, he saw one of Idomeneus's heralds.

"King Menelaus," he said, "a ship arrived with news from Sparta. The messenger is waiting for you."

After dinner, Agamemnon went to his chambers, located in one of the wings of the huge palace of Knossos. At the threshold, the servant of Menelaus was waiting for him.

"Lord of the great Mycenae," he said, turning to the king, "your brother asks you to come if you are not very tired. He wants to speak to you immediately."

"I'm sorry, brother, that you have left the feast early," said Agamemnon, entering the chambers of Menelaus. "The narrator told a lot of interesting tales. You would have learned that Cephalus, an Athenian, owned more than just a magical dog that he received from King Minos. He was also the owner of a magical hunting spear that never missed a beat. With this spear, Cephalus participated in the legendary war of Amphitryon against Teleboans.

"In that campaign, he, for the first time, used this spear in battle and performed many feats. As a reward, Cephalus received from Amphitryon an island named later Cephallenia in his honor. Now this beautiful island is part of the realm of Odysseus, son of Laertes. But no one knows what happened to Cephalus's spear."

"Brother, you will forget the legends of the past when you find out what is happening right now," Menelaus replied. "A herald from Sparta arrived today with a message from King Tyndareos. He reported that my wife, Helen, was missing. Tyndareos suspects that she has been kidnapped, and by none other than the same Trojan prince Paris. Yes, brother, son of King Priam, as it turned out, visited Sparta quite recently. He only missed me by a dozen days.

"Castor and Polydeuces were not in the city on the day of the abduction. As soon as Tyndareos found out of the disappearance of Helen, he sent out soldiers in pursuit, but they were too late. By the time they made it to the harbor, the ships of Paris had managed to put out to sea.

"Learning that Paris had slipped away, King Tyndareos decided to notify me. Four days after Helen's disappearance, the ship with the messenger went to sea. He was on the road for five days. Even if I sail tomorrow morning, the ships of Paris are ahead of me by many days. We can assume that he is already in Troy. What should I do, brother? What do you advise?"

Agamemnon considered the news for a long time.

"Brother," he said at last, "first of all, you should find out what really happened and then decide what to do. I believe Paris could have gone for the kidnapping of Helen. After all, he failed to find Hesione, and to return with nothing means to give in to Hector in the struggle for the throne.

"Arriving in Attica, Paris learned that Achaeans consider Helen to be the most beautiful woman, or maybe he heard about it back in Troy. Having kidnapped her, he wants to declare himself as a worthy contender for the Trojan throne. Although he could not return Princess Hesione, he got the beautiful princess Helen.

"That is how I see it. If everything is confirmed, we will send an embassy to Ilion and demand the return of Helen. But what if Paris refuses to let her go?"

"Then I will gather Achaean warriors and go to Troy," Menelaus replied.

"Don't get excited, Menelaus," continued Agamemnon. "We need to think it over well. When the eldest daughter of King Tyndareos, Timandra, left her husband, King Echemus, he did not pursue her. Echemus was a great warrior, but he did not start a war for the sake of an unfaithful woman. When the Phoenician merchants kidnapped in Argos Princess Io, Argives did not go to war. And when the Cretans went to the Phoenician Tyre and kidnapped the daughter of the local ruler, Europe, the Phoenicians did not attack Crete.

"We must begin negotiations with King Priam. The lord of Troy can return Helen or offer a worthy ransom. Ilion is a rich city. You can get huge treasures from the king."

"You speak correctly, brother," Menelaus said after a long pause. "But you forget one detail. King Echemus reigned in Arcadia by hereditary entitlement. When Timandra left him, he did not start a war because he had not lost anything but got rid of a bad wife. And this scoundrel Paris did not just kidnap Helen. He stole my kingdom.

"When Helen gave birth to our only daughter, King Tyndareos announced that he would divide the Spartan kingdom into two parts— one he will leave to his sons, Castor and Polydeuces, and the other to the husband of his beloved daughter. The Dioscouroi were not very pleased but resigned themselves to the will of their father. And now I'm no longer Helen's husband. If I don't get her back, I'm nobody in Sparta. I will have to return to Mycenae and become the king's adviser again."

Menelaus was silent for a while and continued.

"It seems that some god heard the prayers of the Dioscouroi and decided to help them. Do you remember the campaign of the Dioscouroi to Attica to save Helen? They joked in Sparta that Zeus the Thunderer takes good care of the Dioscouroi as their own father. He forced Theseus to kidnap Helen to give the Dioscouroi an excuse to invade and then sent Theseus away so that he would not deter the Dioscouroi from sacking Attica.

"And now the deity decided to give Sparta to the Dioscouroi and sent Helen to distant lands with the hands of this scoundrel Paris. If only Helen gave birth to a son, he would have become the rightful heir. But she gave birth to a daughter. Now there is no Helen, and there is no heir. Even the Dioscouroi themselves could not have wished for better. Although I do not exclude that they not only wished but also had a hand in the kidnapping of Helen."

"Do you think that the Dioscouroi conspired with the Trojan Paris," exclaimed Agamemnon, "and gave Helen away? This is truly a win-win deal. Paris proved that he was a worthy contender for the Trojan throne, and the Dioscouroi got all of the Spartan kingdom. None of them gave up anything, but both gained everything they wanted."

"I don't know, brother," Menelaus answered. "But if it is so, I won't be surprised. And how could Paris, without help, organize the abduction of Helen from Sparta, which is located two days away from the sea? He knew he was risking his life. But guessing about it is useless. Even if I come to King Tyndareos with evidence of the involvement of the Dioscouroi in the kidnapping, he will not listen to me. These are his sons and now his only heirs."

"Of course, King Tyndareos will not listen to accusations against his sons," repeated Agamemnon. "But he wants to return his beloved daughter, the beautiful Helen. I'm sure Tyndareos will give you troops to rescue Helen. We need a large army. King Priam has many warriors and numerous vassals and allies. Only with superior forces will we have a chance of success.

"The first step is to convince as many Achaean leaders as possible to participate in the campaign, and it won't be easy. After all, the

Trojan kingdom is across the seas, and the Achaeans are not used to long-distance military campaigns. Do you remember, brother, how Polyneices convinced Argives to go against Thebe with the help of a magical necklace? It would help us now. At one time, I have tried to track down the necklace's trail, but without success."

"We have something better," Menelaus replied. "This is the oath that Helen's suitors gave to Tyndareos. After all, they all swore on the blood of a horse to protect Helen's husband from rivals. Tyndareos told me that cunning Odysseus, son of Laertes, advised taking such an oath from the suitors. Now we can call on all those who swore then to march on Ilion and punish this scoundrel Paris."

"I have heard about this oath," answered Agamemnon. "Do you think the suitors still remember it? Maybe it's worth telling them about the treasures of Troy, especially those who have forgotten the oath. The promise of bountiful spoils may also attract those who have not been the suitors. The legends are still being told about the booty Hercules took in Ilion. Today, the Trojans are much richer than they were under King Laomedon. Shores of the Hellespont and nearby islands are covered with flourishing cities, tributaries of King Priam. Those who did not take an oath will go with us for the sake of the riches of the Trojan kingdom."

"Even such a mighty ruler as Priam cannot stand against the combined forces of Achaeans," said Menelaus. "Brother, you have said in the past that the Achaeans should unite in order to resist the invasion from outside. United army under the control of one leader is needed for a war against a powerful common enemy. You are the ruler of the most influential Achaean state, and you must lead it. You will lead the united Achaean army against Troy."

Agamemnon was silent for a long time, thinking over the words of his brother.

"I think we should not start with the call to war, because some may prefer to stay at home. We will call Achaean leaders to discuss Helen's kidnapping by the Trojans. At the council, we'll propose to send a herald to Priam, demanding the return of Helen, and if he refuses to march on Troy with all Achaean forces.

"We should not delay. In the morning, we will talk to Idomeneus and the guests, tell them what has happened, and invite them to the council. We sail out tomorrow. You go straight to Sparta and find out all the details of this case. Promise King Tyndareos that you will return Helen no matter what the cost. Find out how many warriors Tyndareos will provide and what the intentions of the Dioscouroi are.

"I will send a herald to Salamis to ask Telamon about the visit of the Trojan prince. Arrive at Mycenae as soon as you sort out the situation. From there, we will send messengers and convene a council of the Achaean leaders."

CHAPTER 7

DEBATE OF RESPONSE

Menelaus and Odysseus arrived at Mycenae shortly before sunset. Each drove his own chariot to reduce the burden on the horses. Thanks to this, in two exhausting days, they were able to overcome the path from Sparta to Mycenae.

Having washed and refreshed after a long journey, the travelers came to the throne room, where they greeted the lord of Mycenae and, following his invitation, joined the royal meal. When those present were satisfied and the cupbearer had filled the goblets again, Agamemnon ordered the singers and dancers to leave.

"Valiant Menelaus, noble Odysseus, son of the wise Laertes, if you are not tired of a long journey, it is time to talk. Tell me, Odysseus, if you know about the recent visit of the Trojan prince Paris and subsequent events."

"Worthy Menelaus told me about this, lord of Mycenae," answered Odysseus.

"Odysseus knows as much as I do," Menelaus remarked, "and has a suggestion on the course of action. That is why we were hurrying the horses all the way to Mycenae."

"The wise Odysseus will get the floor, but first, let's listen to Talthybios," said Agamemnon. "He returned the day before yesterday from Salamis. Worthy Talthybios, repeat for the guests what you learned from the lord Telamon."

"Glorious Achaean leaders," Talthybios began, "having arrived at Salamis, I appeared before King Telamon and his sons Ajax and Teucer. I informed them about the abduction of Helen by the Trojan prince Paris. I said that this insidious crime happened when Menelaus went to Crete to honor the memory of his grandfather, King Catreus. Taking advantage of the absence of Menelaus, Paris abducted Helen in Sparta and managed to sail from Gythium before the chase overtook him. The ruler of Mycenae, Agamemnon, respectfully inquires what Telamon knows about the visit of Paris and his intentions."

Talthybios paused and continued.

"King Telamon told me that Paris, the son of Priam, was on Salamis for a short time. He came on three ships and told Telamon that he was sent by the king of Troy, Priam, in search of the king's sister Hesione. She became the wife of Telamon in Ilion many years ago, long before the birth of Paris. King Priam wants to know if Hesione is alive. If inevitable fate befell her, he wants to receive her remains for burial in her homeland and is ready to give gold and copper as a reward.

"King Telamon listened to Paris and answered that there is neither Hesione nor her remains on Salamis. She left the island of her own free will about eighteen years ago. Then Hesione expressed a desire to visit Ilion and see her relatives. The helmsman of the Phoenician ship from Sidon, which disembarked at the time in Athenian port of Phalerum, promised to deliver her to Troy. Telamon did not object and paid the helmsman. The ship sailed, and Hesione was never heard from again.

"Paris asked about the name of the helmsman, his trading goods, and Telamon told him everything he could remember. After listening to the king, Paris said that he will visit Phalerum to find out if anyone had heard of this helmsman in recent years, and there he would decide whether to go to Sidon. At this, Paris said goodbye and sailed towards Athens. Telamon never saw him again."

"Now tell us, Menelaus, what happened in Sparta," said Agamemnon.

"This Trojan prince did not go to Sidon," Menelaus began. "No, this scoundrel led the ships to the Laconian Gulf and arrived in Gythium. By the will of some god, he missed me for several days and got the chance to carry out his insidious plan. Paris did not pull the ships ashore but left them afloat and, accompanied by several associates, headed for Sparta.

"He appeared before the king of Sparta, presented gifts, and told that he is the son of the ruler of Troy and is traveling in search of his father's sister. King Tyndareos invited Paris to dinner. There he met Castor, Polydeuces, and Helen. Paris said that Helen is the most beautiful woman, and even the gods should enjoy her beauty. That's what Helen likes to hear.

"Paris entertained the lord of Sparta with stories about the Trojan kingdom, Phrygia, and the Hittite empire. Tyndareos had heard before about the father of Paris, King Priam. Similar to King Tyndareos, Priam received his throne from Hercules himself. The king invited Paris to stay.

"A few days after the arrival of Paris, Castor and Polydeuces left the palace and went on a hunting trip to the mountains. A day later, at dinner, Paris announced to King Tyndareos that early the next morning, he was leaving for his ships to sail to the Phoenician Sidon. Having received goodbye gifts, he departed, and the king did not see him again. The next day, in the afternoon, the king was informed about the absence of Helen. With her disappeared two maids and many clothes and ornaments.

"You won't believe it, Agamemnon, but one of these maids was Theseus's mother, Aithra, the same one we talked about at Knossos. But that is not the end of the story. Soon, King Tyndareos discovered the loss in the treasury of the palace. Many gold items were missing. After that, the king had no doubt that the villain Paris kidnapped Helen and took along a significant part of his treasures.

"Tyndareos sent out three dozen warriors in pursuit, but they could not overtake Paris. Most likely, he left the night before and outstripped the chase by night and half a day. The ships of Paris left the harbor of Gythium in the morning, and the soldiers arrived only in the evening. No one knew in which direction he went, so the sea chase was not equipped. The king is furious and ready to send all Spartan troops on a campaign against Troy. That's what happened in Sparta."

After a long pause, Agamemnon turned to the lord of Ithaca.

"Worthy Odysseus, son of Laertes, now tell us your thoughts on how to return Helen."

"Lord of Mycenae, Agamemnon," Odysseus began, "and Achaean leaders and commanders, you know that a campaign against the Trojan kingdom will require enormous efforts. They say that the great Hercules, with a thousand fighters, took Ilion in one day. But about fifty years have passed since then.

"King Priam, who survived the attack of Hercules, had enough time to prepare the city for defense. He has at his disposal a large army and many allies in Phrygia, Thrace, Mysia, Caria, and Lycia. He is supported by the Hittite empire, whose forces are joined by many Trojans. No one can say how long the siege of the city will last and how many soldiers will be needed to take Ilion. Do you agree that it would be better to resolve this conflict through negotiations?

"Worthy Menelaus believes that Paris committed the abduction not by the command of King Priam but from his own personal motives. He was unable to fulfill the order of the king, but he wanted to preserve his chances for the throne. Paris thought that having abducted the beautiful Helen and a rich dowry in Peloponnese, he would be greeted at home as a hero who took revenge for Hercules's invasion. Furthermore, possessing Helen and the treasures of Tyndareos, he hoped to become a major rival in the contest with Hector. If that's the case, Hector is our best ally in negotiating Helen's return."

Odysseus looked around at those present and, after a short pause, continued.

"I propose to send an embassy to Troy. The Achaean envoy must convince King Priam to return Helen and the treasures if he does not want to see Achaean soldiers under the walls of Ilion and does not want a big war. The envoy will tell Priam that the Achaeans will not come in a few ships like Hercules did. No, the Achaean army will come in hundreds of ships that will cover the entire coast of the Hellespont.

"Having made such a journey, the Achaeans will not leave until they capture the city and take possession of all the treasures of Ilion. Most importantly, the envoy must meet with Hector and ask for his assistance. If Hector regards Paris as a real contender in the power struggle, he can take our side and advocate for the return of Helen. The embassy must be sent without delay. After all, if King Priam proclaims Paris the heir, the chance to rescue Helen peacefully will be next to nothing."

There was a long pause in the meeting.

Finally, Agamemnon, looking around those present and not finding those who wanted to speak, said, "Wise Odysseus, we'll think about what you said and meet tomorrow morning to make a decision. Chambers have been prepared for you and Menelaus. Eurymedon will guide you. I wish you all pleasant dreams."

Remaining in the hall with Menelaus, the king said, "If you are not too tired after a long journey, brother, I have few questions. First of all, how did the cunning Odysseus come to keep you company?"

"He arrived in Sparta the day before me," Menelaus replied. "The wife of Odysseus, Penelope, was relieved from the burden of a boy. The child was named Telemachus. Odysseus brought happy news to Penelope's father, Icarius, and received from him gifts for his daughter. Icarius, as you know, is brother and close adviser of Tyndareos. He told Odysseus about what had happened, and he came to me with an offer of help. We discussed the situation. His opinion seemed to me worthy of attention, and I invited him to follow me to Mycenae."

"You did the right thing," Agamemnon said. "I like what Odysseus proposed. But more on that later. First, tell me about the Dioscouroi. What do you hear from them?"

"I didn't want to talk about it in the meeting," Menelaus replied. "But it looks like what we discussed in Crete. King Tyndareos sent a messenger to them as soon as he learned that the pursuit had not overtaken Paris. However, the Dioscouroi did not return to Sparta. They conveyed through a messenger that caring for a wife is the responsibility of a husband. Polydeuces said that when Helen was captured by Theseus, the Dioscouroi gathered an army and freed her. Now Helen has been kidnapped by Paris. Thank the gods that she has now a husband who will take care of her salvation."

"I understand, brother," Agamemnon answered. "We do not know if they helped Paris or not, but the return of Helen to Sparta is not in their interests, so we can forget about Castor and Polydeuces."

"Unless they remind us of themselves," Menelaus replied. "I told you about the rivalry between the Dioscouroi and the sons of the Messenian lord Aphareus—Idas and Linceus. They have had many skirmishes over the years. But Aphareus and Tyndareos are half brothers and always contrive to resolve their quarrels peacefully. Now the Dioscouroi can escalate one of those disagreements to a military conflict and demand the support of the Spartan army. Then Tyndareos will have much less troops to send on Troy."

"You are right, brother," Agamemnon said after a moment's reflection, "every day of Helen's absence strengthens the positions of the Dioscouroi. Odysseus proposed to send an embassy to Troy as soon as possible. There is no point in waiting for a meeting of Achaean leaders. Instead, I will send messengers to the most influential leaders and inform them of Helen's abduction and our embassy to Troy.

"Tomorrow morning, I will send a messenger to Nafplion with an order to prepare a fifty-oared ship. Our envoy will sail the day after tomorrow. I think that no one can cope with this mission better than Odysseus. After all, this is his idea, and he is a master of negotiations. And if he refuses, let us remind him of the oath of the suitors, because as you said, he took it first.

"I know you want to go with Odysseus, but think of Paris's sneakiness. He may decide to get rid of you and settle the issue of Helen once and forever. However, Odysseus should not be sent alone. Talthybios will join him."

"I agree," said Menelaus. "We need to go immediately, and it's hard to find an envoy better than Odysseus. But Talthybios will not sail with him. I will. And don't argue, brother. After all, caring for a wife is the duty of a husband. King Priam will take our embassy seriously only if I will arrive in Ilion. Otherwise, he will think that we are just trying to intimidate him and get a ransom.

"After all, when Jason kidnapped Medea, the king of Colchis also sent heralds to seek her return. But Jason did not talk to them. I will demand that King Priam let me see my wife in the name of great Hera, the wife of Zeus the Thunderer. He can't refuse me. And don't worry about my safety. I am sure that the king of Troy does not want war and understands that if the envoy is killed, it cannot be avoided."

CHAPTER 8

TANTALUS'S KINGDOM
RECOVERY PLAN

The next morning, Odysseus listened to the proposal of Agamemnon and agreed to go to Troy. From the conversations with Menelaus, he realized that sons of Atreus had already decided to rescue Helen by force of arms.

Odysseus did not expect that the war of the Achaeans against Ilion would bring immediate success. Judging by the stories of merchants about the kingdom of Priam and its neighbors, the campaign promised to be difficult. The son of Laertes foresaw that Menelaus would demand his participation, and it would be impossible to evade. After all, he was the first to take the oath of the suitors, for which he did not get tired of scolding himself. Sons of Atreus recognized that if he refused, others might follow the example, and they could not allow this.

However, Odysseus did not want to leave Ithaca for a long time. His wife gave him a son a month ago. He had recently assumed the throne from his father and had not yet consolidated his dominion on the neighboring islands. Therefore, Odysseus decided to do everything in his power to convince King Priam to return Helen to her husband without confrontation.

At a meeting with the king of Mycenae, it was decided to notify Achaean leaders about the embassy to Priam and convene a council after the return. Envoys decided to leave the next morning.

Shortly after the conversation with the king of Mycenae, Odysseus appeared in the chambers of Menelaus.

"Valiant Menelaus," he said after the greeting, "what do you think about our embassy to King Priam? What should we do to get Helen to board our ship and return home?"

"I agree with you, wisest Odysseus," replied Menelaus. "We must get to Ilion as quickly as possible before King Priam proclaims Paris heir to the throne. The fastest ship loaded with supplies awaits us. The chariots must be ready by dawn. If we hasten on the road to the harbor, we will be out of the bay before noon and then all the time to sunrise, as helmsmen say. And in four or five days, we will see the shores—"

"Wait, Menelaus," interrupted Odysseus. "I'm not talking about the trip but about negotiations with the king of Troy and his sons."

"Wise Odysseus," answered Menelaus, "we will have time to talk about it on the way."

"There is something that needs to be discussed before leaving Mycenae," said Odysseus. "Neither you nor I know anyone in Ilion, and Phrygian lords are known for their arrogance. We demand that Helen be returned not from a simple citizen but from the beloved son of the powerful king Priam. In order for the king to receive us and listen in a favorable manner, we should enlist the patronage of an influential courtier, preferably a close adviser to the king. And there is no better way to get the support of the king's adviser than an expensive gift."

Odysseus waited for an answer, but Menelaus was silent, and he continued.

"You agreed in Sparta that we should try to talk with Hector himself. He is not interested in strengthening Paris and can persuade King Priam in our favor. But how to convince Hector to listen and support us? I do not know a better way than to give him a valuable gift. This is a sure way to get access to the king's ear. Do you agree that gold can increase our chances of success?"

"Come to your senses, Odysseus," exclaimed Menelaus. "That scoundrel Paris stole gold goblets and jewelry of significant value, captured several experienced maids and many expensive robes. And you suggest that I bring even more gold to Ilion."

"Listen, Menelaus," Odysseus answered. "If you want to return your wife and avoid war, it is better to forget about the stolen treasures. I think that it cannot be returned peacefully, because Trojans consider it the legitimate prey of Paris. In order for King Priam to pay attention to the words of strangers from a distant land, we need to show our power. In war, this is done with the help of bronze. And in peacetime, with the help of gold.

"You yourself told me about the ambassadors of the Colchis king to Jason. They arrived at Iolcus without gifts and returned without Medea. Jason refused to even talk to them. Think how great our chances will be if we come to Ilion empty-handed. I hope that King Tyndareos will agree to give ten talents of gold to save his daughter. It is better to wait a few days for the gold to be brought from Sparta than to sail tomorrow for Troy and return with nothing."

Menelaus considered the words of Odysseus for a long time. As much as he hated Paris, he knew that gold could be useful.

"The evening is still far away, wise Odysseus," he finally said. "I will go to my brother and talk to him. Then we will decide what to do."

*****

At dawn, the chariots of Menelaus and Odysseus left the Mycenaean citadel. They were accompanied by wagons loaded with two heavy chests. Agamemnon looked after the small caravan from the observation deck of the citadel. He thought that even if the gold in the chests was not enough to ransom Helen, it might be enough to pay for the life of Menelaus himself.

The night before, he told Clytemnestra about his suspicions of the Dioscouroi's role in the kidnapping of Helen and asked her opinion.

"Castor and Polydeuces are ready to use any means to eliminate a competitor in the struggle for their father's kingdom," answered Clytemnestra. "They were going to fight with their cousins Idas and Linceus for a small inheritance left from our grandmother. I cannot rule out that they decided to prevent the division of the kingdom, made a deal with Paris, and helped him kidnap Helen. But it seems more likely that Helen herself colluded with Paris and orchestrated the escape.

"From childhood, she had a strong passion for adventure, and our parents forgave all her pranks. And who besides her could show Paris the way to the king's treasury? How else could he have stolen the riches of Tyndareos? Castor and Polydeuces would never have taught him how to take possession of the gold, because it is their rightful inheritance."

"Do you think they could have given this gold to Paris as payment for the abduction of Helen?" asked Agamemnon. "After all, most likely, Paris had not heard of her before arriving in Sparta, and the Dioscouroi have been thinking for a long time how to clear their way to the Spartan throne. It is very important. If Paris kidnapped Helen for a reward, it would be easier for Menelaus to ransom her back."

"It's hard to believe," replied Clytemnestra. "After all, judging by your words, it was no less important for Paris to get Helen than for Castor and Polydeuces to get rid of her. If Paris told the Dioscouroi about his difficulties in the struggle for the throne and failure in finding Hesione, they could have figured out that Helen is for him a chance to return to Ilion with victory. It was then that they could offer him help in the kidnapping.

"If this was the case, they would not have rewarded Paris for what was already profitable for him. More likely, they would have asked for reward from Paris. Say what you like, but we do not know whether or not the Dioscouroi participated in the abduction of Helen. However, in any case, I believe that Helen herself helped Paris capture the treasures of Tyndareos—maybe under threat or maybe on her own. Menelaus, of course, can demand that the Trojan king return his kidnapped wife. But what will he do if she refuses to come back and decides to stay in Ilion with Paris?"

Agamemnon decided not to tell his brother about the conversation with Clytemnestra. He believed that Menelaus would not change his decision to go to Ilion and could take the words of Clytemnestra as another attempt to dissuade him.

However, days passed, and the king of Mycenae increasingly doubted the success of the embassy to the Trojan king. He was haunted by fears for the fate of Menelaus.

*****

When the second full moon came after the departure of Menelaus, Agamemnon sent for Calchas. The priest listened to the tale of the arrival of the Trojan prince, the abduction of Helen, and the voyage of Menelaus to Troy. In conclusion, the king lamented that Paris ended up in Sparta precisely when Menelaus was in Crete and managed to get away with Helen and the booty due to the help of some god.

"Tell me, wise Calchas, what do you think about these events?" Agamemnon asked, completing his story. "Almost two months have passed since the departure of the embassy. Winter is approaching. Maybe I should have talked Menelaus out of the trip. Should we make sacrifices? And to what god?"

"Lord Agamemnon," the priest answered after a short pause, "if you had called me few day ago, I would have doubted the answer. But the day before yesterday, after offering sacrifices in Heraion, I performed divination. I saw an omen of a long march. Not knowing the reason and purpose of this campaign, I did not notify you. However, after listening to your narrative, I will say that you have a trip to Phrygia ahead of you."

"You think that misfortune has happened to Menelaus!" exclaimed Agamemnon. "I warned him that Paris could be treacherous, but he still went to Ilion. However, if Menelaus is in trouble, what is the fate of Odysseus? He has no enemies in Troy and has gold to ransom. But Odysseus did not return either."

The priest was silent for a while and continued.

"King, why speculate when there are legends about the deeds of the past conveyed by the bards and prophecies about the future given by the gods? Many years ago, divine Atreus told me about the prediction of his father and your grandfather, which is now beginning to come true. According to Atreus, in ancient times, Pelops predicted that the gods would return Tantalus's kingdom to his heirs.

"This blessed country with its capital at Mount Sipylus has long belonged to your Phrygian ancestors. Your great-grandfather, the great Tantalus, fought for these lands with Tros, the great-grandfather of King Priam. After him, your grandfather, the divine Pelops, fought with Il, the grandfather of King Priam.

"Il was a mighty warrior. In his honor, the ancient city on the banks of the Scamander was renamed Ilion. He gathered allies from Phrygia and Paphlagonia and enlisted the support of the Hittite empire. Having a big numerical superiority, he defeated the army of Pelops and forced him to leave Phrygia. Il divided the possessions of Pelops, leaving for himself all the lands from Mount Ida to Kaikos and giving the territories south of Kaikos to his allies.

"Half a century after these events, Hercules went on a campaign against Troy. Then Eurystheus, who hated Hercules, reigned in Mycenae. Atreus was a young military leader in the service of Eurystheus. He wanted to but could not participate in the campaign. Hercules captured Ilion and destroyed King Laomedon, the son of Il, but he did not have troops to conquer and hold Phrygian lands.

"You have enough forces. You are supported by many Achaean leaders. You are right, King Agamemnon. By the will of the gods, the son of the ruler of Troy treacherously kidnapped the wife of Menelaus and gave you creditable reason to march on Phrygia. You can unite the forces of the Achaeans and return Helen to her husband and Phrygian lands to Tantalides."

Listening to the priest, Agamemnon felt that the events of recent days were taking new, deep meaning. He remembered his father's stories about the lost lands in Phrygia, about the beautiful, fertile valleys of the river Hermus, about the magnificent capital of the kingdom on the slopes of Mount Sipylus, and about the cruel wars waged by Tantalus and his son Pelops. Despite the fact that Atreus himself had never been to Phrygia, he knew the country from the stories of Pelops and his companions.

More than once over the past years, Agamemnon took in his hands the scepter of Pelops, the legendary gift of the gods, and wondered if it had retained his magical power and whether he would be able to see the lands of his ancestors.

"You are right, wise Calchas," said the king. "There will be no better opportunity for the return of the kingdom of Tantalus to his heirs. The Mycenaean army has no equal in Hellas. King Tyndareos promises to give Spartan warriors. I am confident in the support of the rulers of Argos and the king of Arcadia. We will conquer the Trojan kingdom, return Helen to her husband, and move south to Mysia. After all, most of Tantalus's dominion, conquered by Il, is now under the rule of Teuthras and is called Mysia."

"Yes, it is so," answered the priest. "Lord Teuthras, famous hunter and close ally of King Priam, until recently ruled in Mysia from his capital Pergamum on the river Kaikos. His domain is located opposite Lesbos and extends from Kaikos to the river Hermus. But I have heard from merchants from Lesbos that there is a new ruler in Mysia.

"They say that Teuthras, who has no descendants, adopted Telephus, son of Hercules, who came to him from Arcadia. Telephus defeated old enemies of Teuthras and consolidated his power in Mysia, and not so long ago, he got married to one of the daughters of King Priam. As a wedding gift, Teuthras gave him the throne of the Mysian ruler. Telephus is a mighty warrior, worthy of his father's memory. You will need experienced fighters to deal with him."

"I have heard about the exploits of Telephus," said Agamemnon. "I'm sure he will find worthy rivals among Achaeans, such as Ajax, son of Telamon, or Diomedes, son of Tydeus. I hope we will be able to enroll Achilles, son of Peleus. He is considered the best among young Achaean warriors."

The king was silent for a while and continued.

"Wise Calchas, you say that the grandfather's prediction is coming true. The future will show if this is the case. But what worries me now is the long absence of Menelaus. King Priam will pay dearly if trouble happens to him. The Achaeans will not leave such an insult unpunished. Tomorrow, I will send out messengers and call on the leaders to discuss the campaign against Troy and Mysia. I will assemble a council during the next full moon in Aegion, on the shores of the Gulf of Corinth. This place is easy to reach from all parts of Hellas, and it has a large and comfortable harbor."

"Lord of Mycenae," the priest said, turning to the king, "let me express my opinion, and do not get angry if I am wrong. I think it is not worth now to call on the leaders to march on the dominion of Teuthras. Achaeans may go to Troy to avenge the kidnapping of Helen. But they will not fight for the sake of the kingdom of Tantalus. Don't expect that Achaean leaders will agree to attack Mysia.

"You will be wise to call for war against Priam's kingdom in order to free Helen. But on the way to Troy, nothing prevents you from landing the ships for a breather on the Mysian coast. In fact, after a long sea passage, people will need a rest and replenishment of supplies. If you disembark your men south of the mouth of Kaikos, Telephus will not keep you waiting.

"According to the tales, Telephus is like his father. He does not need to be begged to start a battle. He will think that a band of pirates attacked Mysia and attack immediately. Hopefully, he will not wait to accumulate a strong army.

"If the gods grant good luck to the Achaeans, Telephus's detachment will be defeated. You will be able to subdue Mysia, reach Mount Sipylus, and reclaim the lands of Tantalus. If not, you can try to convince Achaean leaders that it is not wise to leave a strong enemy in the rear and continue the war until Telephus is defeated.

"In any case, you will weaken the ally of Priam, and he will not annoy you on the battlefield near Ilion. Having finished business in Mysia, you can go to Ilion either by land, bending around Mount Ida from the east, or by sea, bending around it from the west."

The king considered the words of the priest for a long time.

"Wisest Calchas," he said at last, "we will discuss later how to organize a march on Troy and Mysia. In the meantime, tell me, do you think that the embassy to King Priam is a mistake for which Menelaus risks his life? After all, if he returns with Helen, there will be no invasion to Phrygia. The prophecy of the return of Tantalus's kingdom will not come true."

"Lord of Mycenae," the priest answered after a long silence, "Pelop's prediction will come true by the will of gods. Your brother's trip to Ilion cannot change the divine providence, but it can reveal it. You will see the will of Zeus, the ruler of the sky, as an outcome of the embassy of Menelaus. If King Priam gives him Helen, then the time has not yet come for the march to Phrygian lands. If Helen does not return with her husband, you are destined to go to Mysia and restore the kingdom of Tantalus."

CHAPTER 9

EMBASSY OF MENELAUS IN ILION

A few days until the meeting of Achaean leaders were left when observers reported that the ship of Menelaus was approaching Nafplion. Agamemnon sent Eurymedon with three chariots to the harbor with an order to deliver the envoys to Mycenae without delay.

While waiting for their arrival, the king once again pondered the upcoming conversation. For several days, he had been tormented by suspicions that the priest Calchas had not foreseen all the possible outcomes of the embassy. The words of Clytemnestra that Helen might refuse to return to Sparta did not give the king peace. What would they do if Helen decided to stay with Paris?

The king remembered the lesson learned from his father in childhood. Then king Atreus was going with an army to the Isthmus to meet the Heraclids, and the priests were going to make fortune-telling about the outcome of the battle. Agamemnon asked his father if soothsayer could really predict the outcome of a battle.

Atreus replied that no one could predict how the battle would end. Even the gods might not know this. After all, the battles of people for the gods were a game, and gods were not interested in a game with a known result. Fortune-telling before the battle was needed to raise the spirit of the warriors. It was the duty of the commander to foresee all possible outcomes and plan his actions for each case, Atreus told his son.

What would they do if Helen refused to return to Sparta? Will Menelaus want to fight the kingdom of Priam in this case? After long doubts, Agamemnon decided to call Calchas and with his help convince Menelaus that Helen was bewitched by Trojan sorcerers and was not responsible for her words and deeds. After all, Calchas said that if Helen would not return, the kingdom of Tantalus would be returned to his descendants. The exact reason why she didn't come was not so important.

Finally, the guard reported that the chariots were approaching the citadel. The king went out to meet the envoys at the foot of the palace stairs. Seeing Menelaus, he was amazed at how thin he had become. Following Menelaus, the king recognized Odysseus and Eurymedon. There were no women among the arrivals. However, that didn't mean a lot. Helen could have been so exhausted from the trip that she had to stay overnight at Nafplion.

"I welcome you, illustrious warriors," Agamemnon said, greeting the envoys. "You are very tired after a long journey, so we will postpone the discussion until morning. Now you will be taken to bathe and offered a meal and quarters for a night's rest. Menelaus, one question. You're back with Helen?"

"No, brother," Menelaus answered quietly. "My wife is not with us. We were in Troy. We were in the walls of Ilion. But Helen is not there."

Having wished Menelaus and Odysseus light dreams, Agamemnon returned to his chambers. His thoughts were focused on the outcome of the embassy. Helen did not return, which meant, according to the priest, that an attack on Phrygia was pleasing to the gods. But if she was not in Ilion, how would they convince Achaean leaders to go ahead with the offensive without delay?

Agamemnon remembered the first abduction of Helen and the campaign of the Dioscouroi. When they came to Attica with an army, they did not find their sister. Athenians denied seeing Helen. It took the Dioscouroi a long time to trace where she was.

Perhaps the gods are using Helen for their own purposes, and we must follow their rules, the king thought. *When the Achaean army arrives in Troy, Helen will be found one way or another.*

He called the herald and ordered to inform Calchas that Menelaus and Odysseus had returned and to invite him to the palace tomorrow morning.

*****

The next morning, Agamemnon, in the company of the priest Calchas, met Menelaus and Odysseus in a small room adjoining the throne room. After the greetings, Menelaus took the floor.

"Lord of Mycenae, here is my tale about the embassy to King Priam. Thanks to a fast ship and an experienced helmsman, our voyage was not long. We arrived at the mouth of the Hellespont and landed at a ship's anchorage not far from Ilion. There is no good harbor near the city, and a strong current flows from the strait, so the ship had to be pulled ashore.

"Leaving the crew with the ship, Odysseus and I set out for the city, which is about twenty stadiums from the Hellespont. At the gate, we approached the guards, called ourselves, and said that we want to appear before King Priam. The guards replied that the king was not in the city. Then I said that we wished to see the king's son Hector. The guards replied that he was absent as well.

"The cunning Odysseus asked if the king's son Paris was in town. But here, too, the guards reported that Paris had been out of the city for a long time, and it is not known when he would return. We asked who is acting as the ruler. The guard said that one of the elders, Antenor, oversees the order in the absence of the king. We asked to be taken to Antenor.

"The guards dispatched a man, and soon, we found ourselves in the waiting room of a large house owned by this dignitary. After a short wait, Antenor himself appeared, a worthy, gray-haired warrior. He invited us to bathe after the road and dine at his table. After the end of the meal, Antenor invited us to tell who we are and what the purpose of our visit to Ilion is.

"Introducing myself and Odysseus, I said that we were the ambassadors of the Achaean leaders to King Priam. 'The purpose of our visit is to demand the return of my wife and daughter of the Spartan king Tyndareos, Helen. She was kidnapped by Paris, son of King Priam. He took her away from her home in Sparta in my absence. Paris left on ships from Peloponnese. We assume he has sailed to Ilion.'"

Menelaus was silent for a while and continued.

"I believe that before our visit, Antenor was not aware about the abduction of Helen. His face expressed extreme astonishment, and for a long time, he did not know what to answer. Seeing his confusion, I said that we were asking Antenor to help us meet King Priam. 'We want to talk to the king about Helen's return. This meeting may prevent a war between the Trojan kingdom and the Achaeans. If Helen and the treasures captured by Paris are returned, the Achaean leaders will not go against King Priam and will not destroy his kingdom.'

"Collecting his thoughts, Antenor replied that he had never heard before that Prince Paris was in Sparta and kidnapped the wife of the Achaean leader and the daughter of the Spartan king. He knows and it's no secret that a couple of months ago, Paris sailed across the sea to the Achaean lands. King Priam gave him ships and sent to search for the king's sister Hesione, taken as his wife by Telamon, son of Aeacus.

"'So far, there has been no news of Paris. As for King Priam himself, he is not in the city now. He left about ten days ago for Plakaean Thebe, which are located on the other side of Mount Ida, near its southern ridge, Plak. The king went to visit the ruler of that realm, King Eetion, for the wedding of his son Hector and Eetion's daughter Andromache. In Ilion, they expect the return of the king by the new moon.'

"Antenor further said that he was inviting us to stay with him, and in the meantime, he would send his eldest son, Kun, to King Priam. After consulting, we agreed. The next morning, Kun left with a message to King Priam, and we sent a courier to the ship and remained the guests of Antenor.

"Kun returned five days later and brought back an answer from the lord of Ilion. The king conveyed that he recognizes us as the messengers of Achaean leaders. He notifies us that he sent his son in search of Princess Hesione, his sister. He does not know where Prince Paris is now, but he does not believe that he has kidnapped the Spartan princess. He himself participates in the celebration on the occasion of his son Hector's wedding and sees no reason to interrupt it to discuss something that has not happened. He does not want war and wishes us a safe return to the lands of the Achaeans.

"Having heard the message of King Priam, which Kun communicated to us in the presence of his father and another Trojan elder, Ucalegon, I did not know what to answer. Odysseus took the floor. He said that Paris could show up any day. After all, the season of winter storms will soon come, and the helmsmen tend to return to their native harbor by this time. If Helen arrives with him, then our words will be confirmed.

"Odysseus said that the Achaeans would somehow find out that Helen was in Ilion. After all, she is not a simple townswoman but the daughter of a powerful Spartan king and the wife of the brother of the king of Mycenae. They are supported by most of the leaders both in Peloponnese and in Attica, Boeotia, and Thessaly. They are ready to march against Troy at the head of many thousands of warriors if Helen is not returned. Does the Trojan kingdom need a war because of the reckless act of Paris? Having finished his speech, Odysseus asked the Trojan elders to convince King Priam to promise to return Helen to her husband in order to avoid the war.

"Antenor replied that no one in the Trojan kingdom wants the war, but it was premature to talk about it. He thanked Odysseus and me for trying to keep the peace and said that he and Ucalegon were willing to make an effort to avoid the war. But not all elders are so peaceful. There are those who call the ambassadors liars and offer to expel them. They do not believe that the Achaean leaders would start a war for the sake of one woman.

"King Priam made it clear that until Paris returned, he would not negotiate. The envoys may, if they wish, return in the spring. If Paris and Helen are in Ilion by then, negotiations with the king will be possible. Antenor and Ucalegon are happy to be our hosts on the next visit.

"I thanked Antenor and Ucalegon for their hospitality and said that we want to wait until the new moon and meet the king. We hope that he will listen to us, and we will bring his answer to King Agamemnon and the Achaean leaders.

"Antenor replied that in the absence of Paris, King Priam would not speak with the ambassadors. This is what he said in his message. Meanwhile, the chances for a peaceful resolution may be lost. After all, there are people in the city who call to break the laws of hospitality and get rid of the Achaean ambassadors. One of them, Antimachus, is a wealthy merchant and close adviser to the king. At the gathering, he offered to kill the ambassadors, to burn their ship, and enslave the crew.

"Antenor said that he and other advisers managed to dissuade the Trojans from this venture. But Antimachus may try to bring his plan to life on his own in the hope of ingratiating himself with Paris. Therefore, Antenor advised us to depart without delay. He repeated that we could return in the spring in the hope that the situation would clear up one way or another. On this note, we said goodbye and went to the coast of the Hellespont to our ship.

"The helmsman said that while we were in Ilion, he spoke with local and visiting merchants. None of them saw the return of the ships of Paris. However, Paris could land south of Ilion without reaching the entrance to the Hellespont. There is a convenient harbor opposite the small island of Tenedos. The helmsman advised not to delay our return, as the weather begins to deteriorate, and the time of winter storms is coming. The next day, we went to sea."

Agamemnon was silent for a long time after his brother's story. Finally, he turned to Odysseus.

"Wise king of Ithaca, Odysseus, tell us what you think of your trip."

"Lord of Mycenae, I believe that Antenor does not know where Helen is," Odysseus replied. "But he is one of the confidants of King Priam. Other elders we met at his dinner table also denied knowing about her. The wise Ucalegon noticed that the ships of Paris could perish in the depths of the boundless sea, and we are discussing what is not existent. However, merchant ships sometimes return after a year or two of wandering through the vastness of the sea.

"Antenor and Ucalegon suggest that Paris sooner or later will appear in Ilion. They do not want the war. I believe that if Paris will return with Helen, they will try to convince King Priam to negotiate and persuade him to a peaceful resolution of the conflict. However, King Priam himself did not receive us. Maybe he did not want to overshadow the wedding of his son Hector, but I do not rule out that the king is more informed than he wants to show and is trying to play for time.

"Everyone knows how cunning cattle rustlers are. When you find a thief, he first denies that he saw your bulls. Then he says that these are not the same bulls, then that he bought these bulls elsewhere, and only then he starts bargaining how many bulls were there and when he will give them back.

"So did King Priam. Until we can prove that Helen dwells within Trojan boundaries, he will shy away from any negotiating. However, I believe he does not want war and will not risk losing his kingdom.

"I want to add," Odysseus continued, "that Menelaus wanted to wait for the king and seek a meeting with him or his son Hector, but I persuaded him to sail. The threats of Antimachus and his supporters seemed real to me. After all, having killed us and our companions, they could subsequently claim that we never set foot on Trojan coast, and they are unaware of the demands of the Achaean leaders.

"On the other hand, if Helen's husband succumbs to inevitable fate, then Paris does not have to worry about the revenge. So Antimachus hoped that having dealt with us, he would render a service to Priam and become a favorite of the future king, Paris. Therefore, we left for Peloponnese so that the Achaean embassy can return in the spring. Hopefully, they will find Helen in Ilion. Then the king will no longer be able to say that he knows nothing about Helen and avoid negotiations for her return."

"Wise Odysseus," said Menelaus, "the shepherds say that only at the gates of Hades the thief will voluntarily give up the stolen cattle. The kidnapper will return the prey only if he knows that you can take it by force. The great Hercules often took foreign bulls but never returned them to their owner.

"Perhaps next spring, King Priam will admit that Paris has arrived with Helen in Ilion. But will he let her go? Most likely not. Only when he sees a mighty army on the Trojan coast will he believe that Achaeans are ready to start a war. And without this, any negotiations will be in vain."

"Valiant Menelaus," answered Odysseus, "you want to go with an army to Trojan coast. In the eyes of Trojans, this already means starting a war. You saw the walls of Ilion. They are strong and high. As we have seen, there are considerable supplies inside the city. King Priam has many powerful fighters. I have heard how he marched with an army against the Amazons and defeated them. Even famous Theseus could hardly deal with the Amazons.

"Priam married off his many sons and daughters with the children of neighboring rulers. Even when we were in Troy, the king went to the wedding of his son Hector with the daughter of the lord of Plakaean Thebe. Troops from Phrygia, Mysia, Lycia will come to the aid of Priam, not to mention the towns subject to him along the Hellespont, on the Trojan plain, and around Mount Ida. Only a very powerful army can challenge Priam, and it will take time to assemble it.

"As a matter of fact, we do not know what happened to Paris and Helen since they left Peloponnese. Wouldn't it be better to wait until winter storms subside and send a new embassy to Troy? I suppose if Paris is alive, he should show up by then. We will send ships to the ports of the Hellespont, Lesbos, and Chios and find out what is heard about Paris. We must be sure that Helen is in Ilion before negotiating with Priam and demanding her return under the threat of the war."

Listening to Odysseus, Agamemnon thought that Calchas was right. Gods wanted the war. The peaceful words of the king of Ithaca sounded like an argument in favor of the crusade.

"Wise son of Laertes," said Menelaus, "you probably know that Helen is not the first time in the hands of kidnappers. About fifteen years ago, Theseus kidnapped Helen in Sparta and took her to Attica.

King Tyndareos sent many heralds, but they returned with the answer that Helen was not in Athens, and Athenians do not know where is she. However, when the Dioscouroi brought Spartan army to Attica, Helen was found pretty quickly.

"I believe this time, it will be same way. Helen will be found when King Priam sees an army of many thousands at the walls of Ilion and will realize that we do not intend to retreat. The king will realize that to protect his city from destruction, he must return Helen and the treasures. As you said yourself, Odysseus, the longer Helen stays in Troy, the harder it will be to get her back. If King Priam proclaims Paris heir to the throne, he will never agree to return Helen. You see, the only chance to avoid a big war is to march on Troy immediately."

"What will Priam do in the spring if we prove that Helen is in Ilion and demand her return?" said Agamemnon. "We all agree that Paris and Hector are competitors for the throne of Ilion. Is it feasible for a king to support one of them and cause harm to another? No, having married one of them, he will not take the wife from another. He will not interfere in the rivalry between Hector and Paris and take Hector's side. No negotiation will convince him.

"But if Priam sees a mighty Achaean army at the gates of Ilion, he will understand that the time of family troubles and court intrigues has passed. He will realize that the Trojan kingdom is on the verge of destruction. Only the fear of losing his kingdom can make him return Helen."

Soon after the return of Menelaus, Achaean leaders gathered on the shores of the Gulf of Corinth, in Aegion. They decided not to continue negotiations with King Priam but march on Troy after the end of the winter storms. The troops and ships ready for the campaign were to gather on the Boeotian coast of the Euboean strait, near the town of Aulis. The harbor there was well-protected from storms, rich in water sources, and capable of accommodating hundreds of ships.

The king of Mycenae, Agamemnon, was chosen as the leader of the campaign. During the remaining months of winter, it was necessary to recruit warriors and take care of the ships. Of the older generation, only Nestor, the lord of Pylos, decided to personally sail to Troy. The king of Sparta, Tyndareos, Helen's father, promised to put up to three thousand soldiers under the command of Menelaus and give additional ships to transport supplies.

The ruler of Phthia, Peleus, agreed to give soldiers, but he himself could not participate in the campaign due to the burden of age and illness. Peleus said that his son did not take the oath of suitors and was not obliged to march on Troy. Menelaus remarked that although Achilles was not bound by an oath, he could join the Achaean army at will. Peleus replied that he would talk to Achilles when his son returned from a sea voyage.

IPHIGENIA

CHAPTER 1

MENELAUS APPROVES THE CONQUER OF MYSIA

Achaean leaders convened in Aegion in the beginning of winter and agreed to march on Troy. A month later, Menelaus arrived in Mycenae to discuss the preparations for the campaign.

Refreshed after a long journey, he went to the throne room and joined the royal dinner. At the end of the meal, the king dismissed the courtiers and remained in the company of his brother and the priest Calchas.

"We've been waiting for you, Menelaus," Agamemnon said. "Winter will soon come to an end. The Achaeans will begin to gather in Aulis. It's time to assess what forces we can count on. Tell me how things are in Sparta. How many fighters can we expect from King Tyndareos? What have you heard about other leaders? You can speak freely in the presence of Calchas. He helps with his words and with his deeds. Then I will report on our progress."

"I have something to report, brother," Menelaus replied. "The king will fulfill what he has promised. Sparta will provide up to three thousand soldiers. The ships are gathering in the harbor of Gythium. Another month or two and we will be ready to carry out.

"But it seems that after my return from Ilion, Tyndareos began to doubt that he would ever see his daughter again. He told me that when Helen was abducted for the first time, the Spartans knew that she was in Attica. Now only the gods know where Paris could have gone. However, the king hopes that Helen will be found when the Achaean army comes to Troy.

"When Helen was abducted the first time, the king allowed the Dioscouroi to invade Attica only after making sure that Theseus was not there. After all, in the absence of Theseus, he did not fear for their lives. This time, as before, Tyndareos does not want to risk his sons.

"Recently, we discussed with him the preparation of Spartan troops and started talking about the participation of the Dioscouroi. I said that if such famous warriors as Castor and Polydeuces will come to Ilion, Priam most probably will return Helen without starting a war.

"Then I offered to share the command with the Dioscouroi so that each of us would lead a thousand fighters. The king replied that Castor and Polydeuces do not seek to participate in the campaign. They intend to stay in Sparta and guard the borders of their homeland. So I believe Castor and Polydeuces will not join us.

"However, this is only half the trouble. Ruler of Messenia, Aphareus, Tyndareos's half brother, also notified that his sons would not go to Troy. He will not give soldiers either. Tyndareos says that Aphareus fears an attack from the Aetolians, with whom he has a long-standing feud. But in my opinion, Idas and Linceus decided to stay at home because of the Dioscouroi. If the Dioscouroi had come out, the sons of Aphareus would have gone too.

"But that's not all. It seems to me that the Dioscouroi managed to sow doubts in the king of Arcadia. On the way to Mycenae, I visited Agapenor. He said that concerns were growing among the Arcadian leaders about the campaign, and one of them, Lord Phegeus, had already decided to stay home. Although the others are not refusing yet, many say that the Arcadian warriors are not trained in seamanship, and they do not have ships.

"I do not know what lord of Pylos, Nestor, will do. After all, his father, the famous Neleus, was promoted to the lordship by Aphareus. Aphareus is opposed to assault on Troy and could advise Nestor against it. And finally, I still haven't heard from Odysseus, and he promised to let me know how many warriors he has enlisted. If other leaders are in the same mood, I am afraid that only Spartans, Mycenaeans, and Argives will come to Aulis."

"I am sure, brother, the Achaean forces will be much more powerful," said Agamemnon. "The Mycenaean detachment will include warriors from all over the coast of the Gulf of Corinth, and these are thousands of fighters. Diomedes is proclaimed the head of Argos warriors. Sthenelus and Euryalus will go with him. They are preparing ships in Nafplion. I have received confirmations from Elide and Aetolia, as well as from Attica, Boeotia, Euboea, and Phocis. Everyone is ready to go.

"A messenger has recently arrived from Crete. King Idomeneus and his fleet will arrive in Aulis as soon as the winter storms are over. However, it is not yet clear what support we will receive from Thessaly. Only a few cities have declared their readiness. I believe the leaders of the north are waiting for the most influential ruler of this region, King Peleus. He's not talking yet."

"That's good news," Menelaus replied, "much better than I expected. But tell me, what do you think about Aphareus and Odysseus?"

"I was expecting that King Aphareus would not join the campaign," said Agamemnon. "And he could provide at least two thousand soldiers. The lord of Messene himself is already old, but his sons Idas and Linceus are mighty fighters. However, they did not take the oath of the suitors and also quarreled with the Dioscouroi and Arcadians. No, sons of Aphareus will not go to Troy.

"I have not heard from Odysseus either. Although I do not expect that the king of Ithaca would have many soldiers, Odysseus himself should arrive in Aulis. Otherwise, the leaders who gave the oath of suitors with him will have doubts. However, the most important thing is to ensure the participation of Nestor and his warriors. The invincible king of Pylos took part in many battles. In Aegion, he announced that he himself would lead his soldiers to Troy. However, like you said, the old lord of Messenia, Aphareus, can dissuade Nestor. If the king of Pylos will not come, many leaders will begin to hesitate."

"You are right, brother," Menelaus replied. "We must do everything possible to bring him to Aulis. Nestor has thousands of experienced warriors and good ships. I will go to Pylos myself and talk to Nestor's son Antilochus. He is a good friend of mine. We took the oath of suitors together. If Antilochus decides to join, Nestor will definitely go along with him.

"But what about the troops from Arcadia? King Agapenor has thousands of excellent warriors but has no ships. He suggested to go to Troy by land through Thessaly, Macedonia, and Thrace. Amazons once walked this way. Of course, they were moving in the opposite direction, from Thrace to Attica, where they were met and defeated by Theseus. Hercules also took this route.

"Guides can be hired in Macedonia. Agapenor says that the merchants there travel to Phrygia both by land and by sea. And the fleet will follow the army along the Macedonian coast and, passing off the coast of Thrace, will reach the Hellespont, the same way the Argonauts have sailed. I have seen the Hellespont separating Thrace from Phrygia. It is not that wide. They say in some places it narrows to five to ten stadiums. There the army can be transported by ships or rafts."

"The warriors of Agapenor will be needed at Ilion," Agamemnon replied. "But the way to Phrygia by land is long and treacherous. What Hercules was able to accomplish may not be within the power of an ordinary fighter. Moreover, we have in mind another route for the fleet. After the meeting of the leaders in Aegion, I have discussed more than once the campaign in Phrygia with the wise priest. Calchas, I think it's time to tell Menelaus about our plan."

"Valiant Menelaus," the priest began, entering the conversation, "as you said, the part of the Achaean army can go by land through Macedonia to Thrace and then cross the Hellespont. However, the Thracian rulers are mostly allies or relatives of Priam. They won't let the Achaean army through without a fight."

"Yes, we talked about this with Agapenor," Menelaus interrupted, "and decided that it would be easier to defeat the Thracian leaders one by one than to wait until they get together near Ilion and march against us with a united army of many thousands. Moreover, when Priam realizes that help from Thrace is not coming, he will become more inclined to negotiations."

The priest contemplated the answer for a long time.

"You are right, noble Menelaus," he finally said. "However, in this case, part of the army will be tied up in Thrace for a long time. This will interfere with the reason of the campaign. After all, the purpose of the war determines the strategy of the commander.

"Before deciding what to do with the warriors of Agapenor, let's discuss the purpose of the march on Ilion. We're going to Troy to free Helen. However, you must admit, even if Achaeans take Ilion, this does not guarantee the return of your wife. The will of gods and circumstances may be stronger than us. Odysseus hinted at this after your trip to Troy.

"This is probably what King Tyndareos was thinking when he decided to keep his sons home. Indeed, the ships of Paris could perish in the depths of the sea or be captured by pirates. Or maybe Paris and Helen have already left Ilion and got lost in the vast expanses of Asia or went to the Hittite empire.

"Remember, Paris told King Tyndareos that he was going to visit the Phoenician Sidon. What if he did and fell in battle with Phoenicians? What if the Achaean army takes Ilion, but they won't find Helen there? Do you remember how the Dioscouroi entered Athens, but Helen was not there?"

Menelaus wanted to interrupt, but Agamemnon raised his hand and held it toward the priest, inviting to let him speak.

"A worthy son of great Atreus," Calchas continued, "when entering a battle, a commander must be ready for any outcome, both defeat and victory. Even the great Hercules was defeated in his first battle with King Augeas. He managed to escape, they say, with the help of the beloved daughter of Zeus the Thunderer and, having healed his wounds, crushed Aegeus. Remember how Theseus went to Crete and defeated the Minotaur in single combat. He won the hand of Princess Ariadne and sailed home with her. But Ariadne never reached Athens.

"What if despite great efforts and sacrifices you fail to get your wife back? If there is no Helen, the lord of Sparta will most likely not recognize you as the heir. With this outcome, the king will give the Spartan kingdom to his sons, the Dioscouroi. But there is another kingdom, a rich kingdom, to which you have legitimate rights. This is the domain of your great-grandfather Tantalus in Phrygia, with its capital at Mount Sipylus.

"Your father said that the Phrygian kingdom would sooner or later return to the heirs of Tantalus. Listen, Menelaus, the march of Achaeans to Ilion can help fulfill this prophecy. The kingdom of Tantalus may belong to you. You will reign in the ancestral lands, become the ruler of a great state, but only with the right strategy of war."

Menelaus looked at the priest for a long time, trying to comprehend what he had said.

"Wise Calchas," he finally said, "the return of the ancient possessions is a worthy goal. But I doubt that King Tyndareos will send his warriors to fight for the lands at Mount Sipylus. And other Achaean leaders will not want to risk their lives for the sake of the kingdom of Tantalus. I believe that even our closest allies, the Argives, will not participate in this campaign. The Mycenaean army is big, but not big enough to conquer Phrygia."

Menelaus paused and continued.

"My brother and I have discussed the possibility of regaining the kingdom at Mount Sipylus many times, but we always agreed that Mycenae does not have enough power for this. Did you, Agamemnon, tell Calchas about this? If Theseus were alive, as he is Pelops's great-grandson by his mother, he might have come with us. But now we have no allies ready to fight for the lands of Tantalus in Phrygia."

"Yes, Menelaus, the Mycenaean army alone cannot cope with this task," Agamemnon replied. "But the combined forces of Achaeans should be enough to conquer Mysia. After all, that part of Phrygia where the kingdom of Tantalus lies is now called Mysia. Our great-grandfather Tantalus owned a huge kingdom situated between the rivers Kaikos and Hermus, reaching from Pergamum to Mount Tmolus. Its capital was located south of the river Hermus, at Mount Sipylus.

"There, according to legend, even the gods visited King Tantalus. There is Tantalus's grave. Fertile river valleys, wooded mountain slopes, and sea coast with convenient harbors protected from storms by Lesbos. They say that Lesbos was once subject to Tantalus as well. There was everything in his kingdom—beautiful vineyards, endless pastures, huge herds of bulls and horses, and even gold mines. It is time for his legitimate heirs to return to this fertile lands."

"I agree that the possessions of Tantalus are worth fighting for," Menelaus said. "But we cannot raise an army, even for the liberation of Helen. And this is after Achaean leaders confirmed in Aegion that they were ready to go to Troy. How do you intend to assemble an army to march on Mysia?"

"Listen to wise Calchas, brother," Agamemnon replied. "He has an interesting plan. But remember, everything that is said here must remain between us. The Achaean leaders are ready to go to Troy for the liberation of Helen and the spoils of war. But as you said, none of them will fight for Tantalus's kingdom. Even a hint that we are going to conquer Mysia will be detrimental to our cause."

"Sons of Atreus," Calchas began, "as you know, the lands that your great-grandfather Tantalus owned are now part of Mysia. Until recently, the ruler of Mysia was Teuthras, a close ally of Priam. Not long ago, Teuthras, who had no children, handed over the throne to Telephus, the son of Hercules himself. He is a talented commander and a mighty warrior worthy of his father's glory. Telephus arrived in Mysia many years ago and over time became a confidant of the ruler and his chief military commander. He fought several victorious wars and is married to one of Priam's daughters."

The priest paused for a moment and continued.

"In order to conquer Mysia, we must defeat the army of Telephus. His capital, Pergamum, lies in the upper Kaikos, and his sea harbor is located near the mouth of Kaikos. That's the target of our trip, where Achaean forces will need to come ashore. After leaving Aulis and having rounded Euboea from the south, our fleet will go to sunrise, pass Andros, Tenos, and Ikaria, then turn north to Chios.

"After leaving behind Chios, the ships will enter the strait between Lesbos and the mainland. There you will have to land on the south side of the mouth of Kaikos. We will announce that the soldiers need to rest before arriving at the Trojan shores, where they probably will have to disembark with the fight. It makes sense to first land a small detachment for reconnaissance.

"I assume that Telephus will be immediately notified of the arrival of the pirate ships and will head to the shore at the head of his armed forces. Judging by what they say about Telephus, he behaves like his father. Similar to Hercules, he attacks first and then negotiates. Our task is to draw him into battle, defeat him, and develop the offensive. After that, events can develop in three possible directions.

"Part of the Achaean army may head inland, up Kaikos, to the capital of Telephus, Pergamum. Telephus himself will most likely go there if he survives the battle. The city is located on a steep mountain and is very difficult to get to. Our troops will have to hold Pergamum under siege until we receive news from other fronts or until it surrenders.

"The other detachment led by King Agamemnon or Menelaus should march to the south. These troops will go across the plain, cross the river Hermus, reach Mount Sipylus, and seize the capital of the kingdom of Tantalus. This is how Atreus's prediction will come true. Finally, the third detachment will head north towards Troy. It should also be led by one of you. This detachment can go by ships and circumnavigate Mount Ida from the west or by land, bypassing it from the east.

"They will besiege Ilion and wait for the approach of all Achaean forces to storm the city. The rest of the troops will join the besiegers of Ilion as soon as they conquer the possessions of Telephus. When the whole Achaean army comes under the walls of Ilion, King Priam will have no allies in Mysia, and there will be no chance of victory for him. Such a campaign plan requires that the entire army arrive in Mysia from the south by the sea.

"Now you see, Menelaus, that we cannot send the warriors of Agapenor over land along the coast of Macedonia and Thrace. The army must cross the sea to reach Ikaria and, once near the shores of Asia, turn north. After passing Chios, the ships need to enter the strait between Lesbos and Mysia and land on the Mysian coast near the mouth of Kaikos."

"I think it's a good plan," said Agamemnon. "Unlike Priam, Telephus does not expect an attack and will not have time to gather his warriors. He will most likely take the landing of the Achaeans for a pirate raid and will come with a small detachment. If we manage to defeat Telephus on the shore, the whole country will be conquered within a month or so. We will tell Achaeans that it is better to deal with Telephus in Mysia than to let him escape, assemble forces, and come to help Priam."

Menelaus contemplated for a long time.

"I agree," he finally said, "the capture of Mysia will undoubtedly increase our chances of winning in Troy. Moreover, I think if Mysia falls, Priam will become more accommodating. After all, Teuthras is a longtime ally of Priam, and Telephus himself is married to the daughter of the king of Ilion. But you underestimate the strength of the enemy.

"Know that Telephus will not be left without help. While in Ilion, I heard from Antenor about the Phrygian king Mygdon, an old ally always ready to support Priam. The kingdom of Mygdon borders Troy and Mysia from the east. He is an experienced commander, victorious in many battles. Many years ago, he marched with Priam against the Amazons and defeated them. And as you know, that was not easy even for the famous Theseus.

"If we attack Mysia, Mygdon will come to help, just as he will come to help the Trojans. Thousands and thousands of warriors will be needed to defeat Telephus. Now you see that we cannot give up the fighters of Agapenor."

"You are right, Menelaus, we need the soldiers from Arcadia," Agamemnon replied. "Tell Agapenor that I will provide the ships and the helmsmen for his army. Tomorrow, I will send a messenger to Palamedes. He has a wealth of experience in sea voyages. Let him go with you to Agapenor and find out how many ships and what training will be needed for his warriors.

"From Arcadia, go straight to Pylos. There, try to secure the support of Nestor. Hopefully, he will give you a ship. Or even better, he himself will go with you to see Odysseus. The lord of Ithaca will not refuse to march on Troy in the face of glorious Nestor, especially when he learns that Agapenor and Nestor have decided to go.

"After leaving Ithaca, enter the Corinthian Gulf and sail down to Corinth. Try to arrive in Mycenae with Nestor and Odysseus no later than in a month. By that time, we will know how things are in Thessaly and will be able to assess what forces we can count on."

"All right," Menelaus said. "We'll leave as soon as Palamedes arrives. The warriors of Agapenor, Nestor, and Odysseus represent a powerful force. I will do my best to convince them to join the Achaean army. Tell me, brother, what are your plans about Peleus? If he refuses to go, many leaders of the north may follow his example. This is a great loss."

"Indeed," Agamemnon replied. "Most likely, Thessalian leaders are waiting to hear from Peleus. If he will not join the march to Troy, they will not move either. Maybe a small detachment of Helen's suitors will come, led by Philoctetes and Protesilaus. We need thousands of Thessalian warriors for the campaign planned in Mysia. To get them, we have to convince Peleus. He went to Ilion with Hercules and enjoys great authority in Thessaly.

"However, in Aegion, the king of Phthia said that he would not participate in the campaign, and his son did not take an oath and would do as he wishes. I think Achilles would like to lead the Phthian army, but Peleus is afraid of losing his only son and does not want him to go. Our best chance would be to persuade Achilles, and he himself will get the consent of his father. We need to talk to Achilles.

"But Peleus knows that Achilles may be easily influenced. I asked Peleus in Aegion when we would find out about Achilles's intentions. He replied that his son is not in Phthia and would make a decision when he returns. More than a month has passed since then. The time has come to send Talthybios to Phthia.

"He will deliver the gifts, find out what Peleus's intentions are, and if possible, talk to Achilles. Talthybios will leave immediately and return to Mycenae before you will be back. Then we'll decide what to do."

Agamemnon paused and added, "Remember, brother, only you, me, and Calchas know about the assault on the kingdom of Teuthras in Mysia. It is our duty to Atreus to keep this plan a secret and to carry it out in due time. For everyone else, it must be an unforeseen accident.

"If all goes as Calchas proposes, brave Telephus will attack us himself. Achaean troops will be forced into battle. Additional forces from the ships will join the fight, defeat Telephus, and restore the kingdom of Tantalus."

CHAPTER 2

THE LEADERS DECIDE TO INVITE ACHILLES

Two days later, Menelaus and Palamedes left Mycenae. The chariots carried them along the Argos road to Tegea, where King Agapenor resided. Shortly after, Talthybios went on his trip through Corinth and Boeotia to Thessaly to visit the lord of Phthia.

A few days passed, and Agamemnon received news from Menelaus. He reported that Agapenor had sworn to march on Troy. The king of Arcadia promised to bring the soldiers at the agreeable time to Nafplion, where Palamedes would teach them rowing and put them on the ships. Palamedes was of great help in negotiations with Agapenor, and Menelaus invited him to come visit King Nestor. Agamemnon was pleased with this course of events and sent a messenger after Menelaus to Pylos.

On the twentieth day, Talthybios returned from Phthia and reported that severe ailments did not allow King Peleus to go overseas. The lord of Phthia proposed to contribute a small detachment of soldiers. Achilles was not in Phthia at the time. Peleus said that he was on a sea voyage, and his participation in the war against Troy might be discussed when he returned. However, Talthybios learned from conversations with courtiers that Achilles had sailed for Skyros. He could be found over there at the court of King Lycomedes.

Agamemnon asked Calchas, who was present at Talthybios's report, "It looks like the king of Phthia is very resilient in getting his son involved in the campaign. Maybe we should seek help from the lord of Salamis, Telamon. He is the only brother of Peleus. Sons of Telamon, Ajax and Teucer, decided to join the march on Troy. Will Telamon help persuade the lord of Phthia?"

"King of Mycenae, don't count on Telamon's assistance in this matter," Calchas replied. "Peleus quarreled with Telamon many years ago. At that time, Telamon sought forgiveness from his father, Aeacus, for the assassination of an eldest son of Aeacus, Phocus. As they say, he went to Aegina, appeared before his father, and tried to convince him that Phocus had died at the hands of Peleus. Peleus did not forget about his brother's accusation. He also remembers that you have married your sister to the grandson of Phocus, Strophius, the lord of Phocis, with whom Peleus has an old hatred. It will not be easy to negotiate with Peleus."

In several days, Menelaus returned to Mycenae, accompanied by Palamedes, Nestor, and Odysseus. After exchanging greetings, the king of Mycenae invited them to wash, have dinner, and rest to be ready for the next day's meeting.

"Noble leaders," Agamemnon began his speech the next morning, "soon, the Achaean forces will begin to assemble in Aulis. I have received reports of readiness from most of the participants. Only the leaders of Thessaly have not yet responded to my messages. They are most likely waiting to see what the lords of Phthia will do.

"King Peleus is a famous warrior and influential leader in Thessaly. He took part in Hercules's raid on Ilion and performed many other feats. But until now, he has not shown support for the Achaean march to Troy. The herald, sent to him with gifts and an invitation to join the Achaean army, returned with nothing.

"Peleus answered the same way as in Aegion, where you all were. He himself, due to his old age, cannot go but offers to give a small detachment of warriors. He will not send his son either. But if Achilles will decide to go, Peleus will not interfere. When the herald expressed a wish to meet Achilles, Peleus replied that he had gone on a voyage. And when he returns, then it would be possible to talk to

ALEX KORNEYEV

him. However, Talthybios managed to find out that Achilles went to Skyros and, most likely, will stay there.

"To win the war, we need every warrior capable of carrying weapons. With that in mind, we should discuss how to convince Peleus and other Thessalian leaders to join the campaign."

Nestor took the floor.

"Lord of Mycenae, the famous Achaean leaders, you all know Peleus as a great warrior. When I talked with the king of Phthia in Aegion, I told him that I would join the march with my two eldest sons. Peleus replied that the gods had blessed me with numerous offspring. He has only one son, and he doesn't want to lose him. Peleus knows that if his army marches on Ilion, Achilles will want to lead it. The king of Phthia said that he does not want to risk the life of his only son and heir and does not intend to send his Myrmidons on a campaign to Troy.

"I then told Peleus a story from my youth. It was in hard times, after the assault of Hercules on Pylos. Many brave soldiers were lost in that war. All sons of the glorious Neleus, except me, perished. Yes, I remained the only son of the lord of Pylos, just as Achilles is the only son of Peleus.

"In those days, Augeas, the king of Elide, decided to take advantage of our weakness. He sent an army led by Moliones to the land of Pylos and besieged the fortress of Thryoessa. King Neleus gathered warriors to repel the raid but, fearing for my life, forbade me to join and even hid my chariot. Just like Peleus, the lord of Pylos did not want to lose his only son. But I was young, fearless, and eager to earn the fame. I disregarded my father's will and went on a campaign as a foot soldier.

"So will Achilles, I told Peleus. He is young, hot, and eager for military glory. Even if Peleus does not provide his army, Achilles can enroll as a regular warrior. But in that case, he will be at a much greater risk compared to a commander surrounded by devoted fighters.

"After much thought, glorious Peleus replied that a prophecy once given to his wife weighed on him. It says that Achilles will find the glory on the battlefield, but he is destined to perish there. Therefore, he will not change his mind. With that, we said goodbye."

284

"What you have told, wise Nestor, is right," replied Menelaus. "Peleus does not want his only son to go on a campaign and, therefore, will not commit his Myrmidons. Or else he hasn't forgotten that our sister Anaxibia married Strophius, with whom he has a long-standing feud. Their grudge started many years ago, when Strophius accused the lord of Phthia of the death of his grandfather, Phocus. This way or another, it's useless to talk to old Peleus.

"We need to meet with Achilles himself. Peleus sent his son to Skyros and, most likely, ordered the local lord, Lycomedes, to look after him. Everyone knows how insidious Lycomedes is. I have heard that Theseus's death on Skyros was not accidental, and his possessions there went to Lycomedes. If the ruler of Skyros made a deal with Peleus, he may hide Achilles and deny that he is on the island.

"We need to arrive there with a dozen warships to make Lycomedes more accommodating. Lycomedes himself can employ no more than two or three hundred fighters. Seeing half a thousand Achaean warriors at his door, he will not argue for long."

"If you come to Skyros on warships," Odysseus said, "you can face armed resistance. We islanders are always wary of pirates and keep our weapons close. Achilles, in this case, will join Lycomedes. Then we will not draw Achilles to our side but, on the contrary, will make him our enemy. Moreover, we will sow strife in the ranks of the Achaeans, even before the start of the campaign.

"We must persuade Lycomedes peacefully. A reputable envoy who knows Lycomedes well should go to Skyros. Palamedes has visited Skyros and met Lycomedes before. He will be treated with respect, especially if he brings gifts to soften Lycomedes's mood. There is no better candidate."

"You are right, worthy Odysseus," Agamemnon said. "But Palamedes cannot go to Skyros. He must leave for Nafplion as soon as possible and oversee the preparation of the ships for Agapenor's warriors. As you know, Arcadians have no boats. I promised Agapenor to supply ships for his troops, and Palamedes took over this matter.

"I propose to send the venerable Nestor. No one better than him will be able to set up Lycomedes in a peaceful manner. Moreover, Nestor is the only one of us who knew the grandfather of Achilles, the favorite of the gods, Aeacus. He can tell Achilles how Aeacus sailed to Troy even before Hercules."

"As I have heard," the priest Calchas interjected, entering the conversation, "the then ruler of Troy, King Laomedon, hired Aeacus and did not pay the promised reward for his labors. Before leaving Troy, Aeacus predicted that his descendants would come to the walls of Ilion to collect the unpaid debt. The gods listened to Aeacus's words. His sons went to Ilion and were victorious. Now it's time for his grandchildren. The sons of Telamon are ready to go. I think when Achilles finds out about his grandfather's prophecy, he will decide to participate in the campaign."

"Indeed, wise Calchas," Nestor said. "Moreover, the prophecy of Aeacus will help convince Lycomedes not to hinder the meeting with Achilles. The ruler of Skyros will not want to provoke the wrath of Achilles. And if Achilles finds out that Lycomedes acted contrary to the prophetic words of Aeacus, he will be very angry.

"With that in mind, I will go to Skyros and convince Lycomedes not to obstruct the chat with Achilles. But to talk to Achilles himself, we need a mighty warrior in the prime of his life, such as Odysseus. He has the gift of persuasion inherited from his grandfather, the unsurpassed Autolycus. Who better than Odysseus will convince Achilles that the campaign to Troy is an opportunity to perform great feats before the eyes of Achaean leaders and warriors and become famous throughout Hellas?"

"I agree," said Agamemnon. "No one can persuade Achilles better than Odysseus. And if Achilles marches at the head of the Myrmidons, other Phthian leaders will follow him. Then the rest of the Thessalian lords will also join. Seeing such an army at the gates of Ilion, Priam will be forced to agree to our demands. Or he will have to watch as the walls of his city fall, unable to withstand the Achaean might. There are no more suitable ambassadors than Nestor and Odysseus. Tell me, worthy Odysseus, if you agree to go to Skyros with Nestor and try to persuade Achilles."

"The more Achaean fighters come under the walls of Ilion, the sooner the war will end," Odysseus replied. "Achilles's participation is the best way to attract Peleus's supporters to the campaign. Yes, the lord of Mycenae can count on me."

"There are not many days left before the gathering in Aulis," said Agamemnon. "I think the fastest way to get to Euboea is by chariots. Today, I will send messengers to Thersander to have fresh horses waiting for you in Thebe and to Euboea to Elephenor with a request to have a ship waiting. With good rowers, Skyros can be reached from Euboea in one or two days. The gifts for Lycomedes will be ready for your departure. Calchas will take care of worthy sacrifices. Good luck will be on your side."

CHAPTER 3

PELEUS'S REQUIREMENT

Agamemnon looked once again at the panorama of the Euboean strait. He was pleased with the location on the hillside chosen for the royal tent. It had a wide view of the Aulis bay and the coast going north to Euripus. On the other side of the strait lay the city of the Euboean Abantes, Chalcis.

The ships of the Abantes and Boeotians, who were the first to arrive at the gathering place, occupied the coast closer to Euripus. Then the ships of the Argives and other participants of the campaign were located. Ships with the warriors of Sparta were still arriving from the southern side of the strait.

"You did a good job Talthybios," he said, turning to the herald, who had been sent in advance to prepare the royal residence in Aulis. "I see many detachments are already here. Go along the coast, greet the leaders, and invite them to dinner. Before leaving, send Eurybates to the Spartans' camp and let Menelaus know that I am waiting for him in my tent."

Menelaus, who had recently disembarked from the ship, soon arrived at the tent of the lord of Mycenae.

"Glad to see you, brother," Agamemnon greeted. "I hope the voyage went well and the time of winter storms has passed."

"Greetings to the leader of the Achaean army," Menelaus replied. "We have sailed with no incidents, without losing a single vessel. I see hundreds of ships off the coast of Aulis. We will have something to show King Priam.

"And that's not all. A messenger from Pylos arrived in Sparta recently. He reported that the fleet of King Nestor is ready and is waiting for the arrival of Odysseus to proceed together to Aulis. The lord of Pylos goes on a campaign with his two sons, Thrasymedes and Antilochus. If everything goes as expected, they will be here in a few days. The messenger also reported that the ships from Elide and Aetolia were on their way to Aulis. That's what I know.

"You were right, brother, we have gathered an impressive force. But tell me how things are with the troops of King Agapenor. What is heard about other leaders? When can we leave for Troy?"

"Old soldiers say that they don't recall so many Achaean warriors gathering in one place," answered Agamemnon. "We have assembled a great army. Agapenor's troops are on the way. A messenger from Palamedes arrived recently and reported that the ships carrying Arcadians are leaving Nafplion. We will sail when all the participants arrive.

"But there are also problems. I am most concerned about King Peleus. When Odysseus and Nestor arrived on Skyros, Lycomedes was very friendly. They managed to meet Achilles and convince him to go to Troy.

"According to Nestor, Achilles is in great shape and dreams of the glory of a warrior. He showed his father's armor and told stories about the exploits of Peleus. Achilles promised to come to Aulis and sailed on his ship to Phthia to prepare an army and a fleet. He left Skyros at the same time as Nestor and Odysseus."

"I know, brother. I got your message," Menelaus replied. "In fact, Nestor himself stopped in Sparta on his way back to Pylos and told me and King Tyndareos how he persuaded Achilles to join the campaign.

"After Nestor's departure, Tyndareos noticed that it was not difficult to persuade Peleus's son. Young warriors always want to gain fame on the battlefield, especially those who surpass their peers in exercises. There is truth in the words of Tyndareos, but this does not diminish the achievements of Odysseus and Nestor. I am very glad that Achilles and the Myrmidons will join us."

"Menelaus, you rejoice too early. This is not the end of the story," Agamemnon continued. "Soon after Nestor and Odysseus left Mycenae, Phoenix, son of Amyntor, arrived. He is Peleus's closest adviser and Achilles's teacher. He came to Calchas and asked for a meeting without witnesses.

"Phoenix reported that he had arrived with a message from the king of Phthia and told the following. Many years have passed since Peleus's wife disappeared into the vast expanses of the sea. Before leaving Phthia, she revealed to the king a prophecy about her son, which she received from the gods. Achilles is destined for a long, peaceful reign in the fertile Phthia. However, if he seeks glory on the battlefield, he will pay for it with his life.

"The king had faith in the words of his wife and does not want to lose his only son. Peleus believes that no one can demand such a sacrifice from him. The lord of Phthia is ready to commit a thousand Myrmidons under the leadership of Phoenix, as well as to support the campaign with provisions and supplies from all the lands and islands under his control, but only on the condition that Achilles stays in Phthia.

"If Achilles does go on a campaign, Peleus will announce at a meeting of warriors in Aulis that the far-reaching Artemis does not approve the assault on Troy and will deny the Achaeans good luck. The king has sworn on the altar of Artemis in all that has been said and is waiting for an answer. Phoenix left with the words that he was ready to stand at the head of the Myrmidons and go to Troy, not to bring Helen back but for the sake of the only son of the king of Phthia.

"You see, brother, that Peleus is ready to do anything to keep Achilles at home. I've been waiting for you to decide what we should do and how to respond to the lord of Phthia."

When the story was coming to an end, the priest Calchas entered the tent. After greeting the sons of Atreus, he announced that he had come at the call of the king of Mycenae.

"Glad to see you, wise Calchas," Menelaus said. "My brother told me about the demand of King Peleus. As I understand it, he could not persuade his son against going to Troy and asks for help from Agamemnon. Nestor was right when he told me that Achilles is eager to join the campaign.

"Peleus, of course, referred to the old prophecy, but he failed to convince his son. I have heard of this prophecy, but I think it looks more like the warning of a wise man than the prediction of a prophet. After all, what does it say? What message does it convey? Those who have devoted their lives to peaceful labors in the field and in the stable most likely will not perish in a bloody battle at the hands of the enemy. And if you choose the path of a warrior, put on armor, and join the battle, death lurks at every step.

"We must answer Peleus that he should not believe too deeply in predictions. Death can find a person both in war and in a peaceful life. The great Hercules spent his whole life in battles and fights. As they say, he even engaged in duels with the gods. However, the inevitable fate befell him in the time of peace. The same thing can happen to Achilles and to anyone else. Good armor and reliable companions, that's what can save a warrior's life in battle."

"I agree," Agamemnon replied. "Mortals cannot foresee whether he will fall in battle or stay alive. The covenant of Peleus's wife may not be a prophecy but a warning. However, Peleus says that he does not want to let Achilles join the campaign because of a prophecy received many years ago. We do not know the true motives of the king of Phthia. Maybe he uses the prophecy as an excuse to prevent his son from joining the campaign.

"But whether he believes this prophecy or not, Peleus seeks to protect his son from the dangers of war, which he knows firsthand. After all, King Tyndareos also does not want to send his sons to war, although it is about saving his daughter. The difference is that the Dioscouroi themselves do not want to participate in the campaign, whereas Achilles strives for the fight with all his soul.

"King Peleus is wise. He understands that a direct ban on participating in the campaign can cause an open quarrel. He knows that such quarrels do not end well. It was for good reason that Peleus sent to Mycenae no one else but Phoenix. I have heard that Phoenix's father, King Amyntor, had a conflict with his son over a concubine a long time ago and took this concubine away from him. Phoenix, the only son and heir of Amyntor, was so offended that he left his father's realm, never to return.

"Do you remember, Menelaus, when we were visiting Crete, Idomeneus told us that a similar story happened to King Catreus. The king argued with his son, the dispute escalated into a quarrel, and his son left Crete forever. Although the reason for the dispute eventually lost its significance, resentment and pride did not allow them to reconcile.

"Peleus is a wise and experienced man. He does not want to enter into an argument with his proud son, so he tries to achieve his goal in another way. No, it was not faith in the deceptive prediction but life experience and knowledge of Achilles's character that prompted Peleus to send Phoenix to Mycenae.

"Therefore, it makes no sense to convince the lord of Phthia that this was not a prophecy but only a warning. It doesn't matter to him. The more Achilles strives to go to Troy, the harder Peleus will struggle to ensure that this endeavor does not take place. Wise Calchas, you have heard the words of Phoenix with your own ears. Tell me what you think about Peleus's threats."

"You said it yourself, lord of Mycenae," the priest replied. "King Peleus chose Phoenix as his envoy for a reason. The lord of Phthia is well aware of Phoenix's quarrel with his father, King Amyntor. I will tell this story as I have heard it from Phoenix himself. He was born and raised in Ormenium, at his father's court. In the absence of Amyntor, he got together with one of the king's concubines, and she got pregnant.

"According to Phoenix, his mother was jealous of his father for this concubine and asked him to seduce her, hoping to turn his father away from her. But King Amyntor, upon learning of the betrayal, became so angry that he ordered the child to be exposed, and his only son was locked in the palace under guard.

"Phoenix, having learned about the death of his firstborn, escaped from the custody and left Ormenium. He wandered through the lands of Thessaly and in time found shelter at the court of King Peleus. Amyntor never saw his son again. Having unendingly quarreled with Phoenix, the king had to leave the throne to his nephew, the son of his younger brother, Eurypylus.

"I'm sure Peleus recalls this story every day. He does not want his son to perish in the war and does not want to lose him because of a quarrel. When Achilles lived on Mount Pelion with centaurs, he almost became involved in the war between centaurs and Dorians. Then Peleus barely managed to persuade his son to sail to Skyros, to King Lycomedes. He knows that he will not be able to convince Achilles to skip a war a second time.

"I would like to add that if Achilles suffers the inevitable fate, one of the sons of his brother Telamon or the descendants of his other brother, Phocus, may inherit the throne of Phthia. And this is the last thing Peleus wants, as he has been at odds with Telamon and at enmity with the grandchildren of Phocus for many years."

"However, what can the lord of Phthia do at this time," Menelaus asked, "when Achilles is getting his ships ready to set a course for Aulis? Peleus cannot forbid his son to participate in the campaign, and if he holds back his army, Achilles will not forgive the embarrassment. He will do his own thing and will join the campaign as a regular warrior. Remember how Nestor's father tried to keep him back from joining the fight with the army of Augeas. The only thing old Peleus is capable of is to discourage one or two Thessalian leaders. I don't see why we should be frightened of him."

The priest paused for a while and replied, "The lord of Mycenae reminded us about the quarrel of King Catreus with his son. I have heard that this quarrel not only deprived the king of Crete of his son and heir but also caused his death. Peleus probably knows about these events too. Let's not forget that Peleus himself quarreled with his father, Aeacus, and was forced to leave his homeland forever. It will never be erased from his memory.

"It is obvious that the king of Phthia is ready to do anything to keep Achilles at home without getting into a conflict with him. Peleus is the famous warrior and favorite of gods. He is said to be much loved by the daughter of Zeus the Thunderer, Artemis. Thanks to her, Peleus always struck without a miss, both on the hunt and in the battle. More than once, he got into a situation where everything was against him and emerged victorious.

"Peleus was capable of accomplishing the most daring deeds with the support of far-reaching Artemis. He can employ the help of the goddess to keep Achilles at home. King of Phthia expects that many leaders will obey the will of Artemis. He hopes that when they learn about Artemis's opposition, they will abandon the crusade. And if there is no crusade, then Achilles will stay home. I think this is his plan.

"And to say true, I suppose if Peleus announces at a gathering of the warriors that Artemis is against the campaign, many will doubt. And if some leaders refuse to go, others could follow them. We may lose half the troops or even more. Therefore, the message of the king of Phthia cannot be left unanswered."

"I agree with Calchas," Agamemnon said. "There has long been a rumor among Achaeans that Artemis is patronizing the lord of Phthia. Do you remember, Menelaus, what King Oeneus told us about Peleus? He said that Artemis always helps him deliver the decisive blow. Who could have expected that Peleus would be so strongly opposed to Achilles's participation in the campaign? If I had known this beforehand, I would have left Achilles to enjoy life on Skyros.

"But now there is no turning back. We won't be able to dissuade Achilles, and even if we could, it would sow doubt in the hearts of other warriors. After all, many already know that he is going to Troy. In a few days, all the warriors will gather. Achilles will arrive, and with him, Peleus. Imagine that the king of Phthia opposes the campaign at the meeting of warriors. He will certainly be supported by the Phthian leaders Protesilaus and Philoctetes. If other Thessalian leaders who have always gravitated towards Peleus listen to them, we can lose thousands of fighters."

"In that case, there is no need for Achilles to join the campaign," Menelaus said. "I suggest we wait for Nestor and Odysseus. They persuaded Achilles to join the Achaean army. They can talk him out as well."

"It is better if no one knows about Peleus's threats," Agamemnon replied, "most of all Odysseus. It seems that the cunning ruler of

Ithaca was opposed to the war with Priam even since you returned from Ilion. At present, he cannot refuse to participate in the campaign. But I am sure he will try to use the threats of King of Phthia and the wrath of Artemis to delay the departure and continue negotiations with Priam. We will seek the help of Odysseus only if there is no other way out."

Agamemnon paused for a while and continued.

"I see that Peleus is determined like the fisherman I heard about in childhood from King Eurystheus. This fisherman tried to catch one special fish in the pond, but it kept slipping out of his nets. Then the fisherman got angry and drained all the water from the pond. All the fish died, but he got what he wanted. If Peleus announces that the goddess is against the campaign, he will stop not only the Thessalian leaders. Even our loyal allies in Peloponnese will doubt.

"The glorious Diomedes will be troubled, because he remembers the fate of his uncle Meleager and other predicaments that his grandfather Oeneus suffered from Artemis. Even Nestor will fear for his sons. No, Peleus cannot be ignored. After all, we can lose the whole army this way. Wise Calchas, we seek your advice. How do we respond to the king of Phthia so that he does not obstruct the campaign?"

The priest thought for a long time, and finally, looking at the brothers, he spoke.

"Sons of Atreus, do not get angry at my words. For it was not I who invented what I am going to tell, but I learned it from the deeds of ancestors. It was a long time ago, about a hundred years ago, shortly after your illustrious grandfather, the beloved of the gods, Pelops, arrived from Phrygia to Peloponnese. Now is not the right time to recall all exploits that led him to the royal throne in Pisa.

"You may have heard from your father that at one time, Pelops experienced great difficulties. It seemed that the gods had turned away from him. Amphion, the ruler of Thebe, could help him but did not want to. To win the favor of Amphion, Pelops offered him his sister, the beautiful Niobe, as a wife. Amphion married Niobe and helped Pelops resolve his problems. So say the legends."

The priest paused and continued.

"Peleus does not want his son to participate in the campaign of Achaeans in Troy. One can only guess at his motives. Perhaps he believes in the prediction and is afraid of losing his son. Or he wants to take revenge on you, King, for marrying your sister Anaxibia to Phocus's grandson, Strophius. But if you act like Pelops and offer him a bride worthy of Achilles, I think he will be satisfied.

"King Agamemnon, you have a daughter, Iphigenia, who is about to enter the age of marriage. No one else is suitable. Menelaus's daughter, Hermione, is still a child. Offer Iphigenia to Achilles as a wife. Peleus's son can stay at home with his young wife or join the campaign later. But no matter what he does, it will not affect the mood of the warriors, and you will receive the troops and support of the king of Phthia, as Pelops once received help from the ruler of Thebe."

Agamemnon was silent, considering the priest's words.

After waiting a long time for the king's answer, Menelaus said, "You're right, Calchas. Father told me that Pelops married his sister Niobe to the lord of Thebe, Amphion, who supported him in difficult moment. I remember Father's words that Niobe's marriage to Amphion may have helped Pelops as much as his own marriage to Hippodamia. When Amphion and Niobe suffered the inevitable fate, Pelops was very upset. Laius became the king of Thebe. Father said that Pelops wanted to marry to Laius one of his daughters, but the king of Thebe had other plans."

"Our grandfather, the great Pelops, was a favorite of Zeus the Thunderer," said Agamemnon. "Not for nothing did he own the magical scepter of royal power. Father often recalled him. You propose to follow the example of Pelops, wise Calchas. You think that the marriage of Achilles to Iphigenia will solve our problems.

"Achilles can join the army later or stay at home, as Peleus wishes. But Achaean warriors will know that he does so because of a young wife and will not fear the wrath of Artemis. Peleus will be satisfied and will send Myrmidons to Troy under the leadership of Phoenix. Thessalian leaders will follow. Iphigenia will be glad that she is marrying one of the best Achaean warriors.

"I agree. That's what we have to do. I will send Talthybios to Clytemnestra with good news. You're going to Phthia tomorrow morning, Calchas. Talk to Peleus without other people's ears. Tell him that Achilles may not march with the Achaean army but stay in Phthia with his young wife. If it is his will, he will join the army later. But by then, the war will most likely be over. We will announce the wedding in Aulis at a gathering of warriors, and the wedding celebrations will take place before we sail. They will raise warriors' spirits."

"Lord of Mycenae," Menelaus replied, "why should we delay until tomorrow? Calchas's ship may miss the Phthian fleet. It will be much more difficult to negotiate if Peleus arrives in Aulis before he talks to Calchas, and it will be impossible to keep the negotiations secret.

"I have a ship ready to sail with rested rowers under the leadership of Phrontis, the son of Onetor. Phrontis is an experienced helmsman. He arrived in Aulis in advance to choose locations for the Spartan ships. He will bring the ship to Phthia in the shortest possible time. I will guide Calchas to the ship and give instructions to Phrontis. If the oarsmen work hard, tomorrow, Calchas will be at the gates of Peleus's palace."

CHAPTER 4

CALCHAS VISITS PHTHIA

Achaean commanders and helmsmen gathered at the tent of Agamemnon to discuss the route to the Trojan kingdom.

The king of Mycenae asked Elephenor, son of Chalcodon, how Euboeans usually traveled to Lesbos. The leader of Abantes replied that since ancient times, Poseidon had been pushing the water flowing from the Hellespont along the western Thracian coast. Helmsmen of King Chalcodon knew about these currents.

They sailed to Lesbos along the eastern shore of the Aegean Sea and returned along the western coast so as to not row against the current. Experienced helmsmen going to Lesbos from ports in the southern Euboea prefer to go to the sunrise.

If Poseidon was merciful, then passing by the northern shore of Andros and heading for sunrise, the sailors would see land in the north in a few days. This was the southern coast of Chios. However, many preferred to sail, staying in view of the land. They traveled along the northern shores of Andros, Tinos, and Mykonos and, when Mykonos began to disappear behind the horizon, set a course for sunrise. With good oarsmen, the ship would soon approach the coast of Ikaria.

After spending the night on Ikaria, the helmsman would take a course straight north the next day and could arrive at the shores of Chios on the same day or the next depending on the wind. Sailing from Chios to Lesbos was not difficult, and having rounded Lesbos, the ship would arrive at Trojan shores.

Elephenor was supported by Palamedes. He said that the helmsmen of Nafplion preferred to go along the southern shores of Andros and Tinos, where one could find more convenient harbors. Approaching Mykonos and rounding it from the north, it was necessary to set a course for sunrise so the ship would come to Ikaria. If you sailed from Ikaria farther to sunrise, you would come to Samos. And if you turned north, you would arrive at Chios. Circling Chios from sunrise and heading north, you would come to Lesbos, and behind it lay the Trojan kingdom.

After the discussion, the helmsmen agreed to sail from Euboea to Mykonos and farther to Ikaria and Chios. Agamemnon proposed to circumnavigate Chios, enter the strait between Lesbos and the mainland, and make a stop south of the mouth of Kaikos so that the warriors could take a rest before landing in Troy. The king of Mycenae was supported by Nestor. He said that Priam, apparently, was expecting the arrival of the Achaeans, and the landing at the Trojan shores would not go without a fight. A long voyage would exhaust the warriors, and good rest was necessary before the battle.

After making sure that the route he had planned was accepted and instructing the helmsmen to coordinate the details, the king of Mycenae invited everyone present to dinner and dismissed the meeting. Commanders had begun to disperse when Agamemnon noticed Menelaus slowly climbing to the tent from the shore of the bay. He was followed at some distance by a man whom the king recognized as Calchas.

He moved toward them and, having caught up with Menelaus, asked, "Tell me, brother, if Calchas had the meeting with Peleus. Did he accept our offer?"

"Calchas's ship has just arrived," Menelaus replied. "It has docked on the north side of Euripus. I met him on the shore, and we went straight to you. The priest said that Peleus has agreed to exchange the life of Achilles for the life of Iphigenia and that he would explain all the details to the king of Mycenae."

"I greet you, Calchas," Agamemnon said to the priest, who had come up. "Can you tell us about the meeting with Peleus now, or do you need rest?"

"Long live, lord of Mycenae, great Agamemnon," replied Calchas. "Rest would not hurt, because we have sailed from Phthia all night. But I think you should listen to me now and without any extra ears."

"Let's climb the nearest hill," Menelaus suggested. "There are convenient boulders there, and no one will bother us."

Having reached the top, the king and his companions settled down on the boulders warmed by the spring sun.

"Tell us, Calchas, what was the answer of the lord of Phthia?" asked Agamemnon.

"King Agamemnon," said Calchas, "do not be angry with me for the news I have brought from Phthia. I delivered your message to Peleus. The king replied that his son could not marry Iphigenia. Achilles already has a wife, and she bore him an heir. But the king of Phthia accepts the offer to give away Iphigenia. He's taking your daughter's life in exchange for his son's life.

"Lord Peleus demands that Iphigenia be sacrificed to the goddess of the quick arrows, Artemis. This sacrifice, according to Peleus, can avert the death of Achilles, predicted by a long-standing prophecy. If you agree, Peleus will not stop the Achaean fleet from leaving Aulis. Otherwise, Peleus will do everything in his power to prevent the Achaeans from marching to Troy. That's how Peleus answered."

Agamemnon was silent for a long time, pondering the priest's words.

After a pause, Menelaus said, "Old Peleus must have completely lost his mind. He was always thirsty for blood and never missed an opportunity to stain his sword, but to demand the life of a royal daughter is unheard of."

"It has been done before, and not once," Agamemnon said quietly. "You may not remember, but the daughter of Hercules, Macaria, was sacrificed before the Heraclids left Athens to fight with the army of King Eurystheus. It is known that the Heraclids received an oracle that in order to win, a descendant of Hercules must sacrifice himself.

Our father said once that Macaria's death helped them defeat the Mycenaean army.

"The Heraclids believed that after such a sacrifice, they could not be beaten, and faith in victory is the key to success. I have heard that a similar episode has happened during Adrastus's campaign against Thebe. But I didn't anticipate this from Peleus. Does he expect that I will accept his demand or that I will refuse? Calchas, tell us all the details of your visit to Phthia. Tell us exactly what the king said."

"Lord of Mycenae, I did everything I possibly could," the priest began. "But far-reaching Artemis and the treacherous ruler of Skyros, Lycomedes, did not allow our plan to come true. Under the skillful supervision of the helmsman Phrontis, our ship reached the realm of King Peleus in less than a day and a night. When I got ashore, I went straight to the town.

"It didn't take long to find Phoenix's house. He was home and invited me for a private conversation. After greetings, I said that the king of Mycenae had sent me to negotiate with the lord of Phthia. Phoenix replied that he was glad to see me and hoped that the message of the king of Mycenae had not arrived too late. Then he told me how merchants from Phocis had recently arrived in Phthia and reported that the Phocian ruler Strophius is not going to march with Achaeans to Troy.

"Peleus has long been at odds with the Phocian lord, and as soon as he learned that Strophius is not joining the campaign but is sending his nephew Schedius to lead the Phocian detachment, he became very angry. The king of Phthia was indignant that Strophius was spared the hardships of war because he was the husband of Anaxibia, the sister of the lord of Mycenae.

"Peleus said that Agamemnon gives indulgences to his relatives but does not want to do anything for Achilles. He threatened to announce in Aulis that Artemis, who throws fast arrows, and her brother, the bearer of the silver bow, Apollo, do not approve the campaign against Troy. Therefore, Phoenix concluded, he wants to discuss the message of the lord of Mycenae and decide how to report it to King Peleus.

"I replied that Agamemnon highly valued good relations with the mighty king of Phthia. Indeed, lord of Phocis, Strophius, will not come to the Achaean army gathering in Aulis, but the reason for this is the pregnancy of his wife. He can join the army after the birth of an heir. Moreover, not only Schedius will come forward instead of him, but all other nephews of Strophius—Epistrophus, son of Iphitus, and Epeus, son of Panopeus. They follow the prophecy of their ancestor, the god-equal Aeacus, for his descendants to return to Ilion.

"After responding to his accusations, I assured Phoenix that the lord of Mycenae understood how dear the only son is to the king of Phthia. Lord Agamemnon is ready to do everything in his power for the famous Peleus. He offers his daughter, the beautiful Iphigenia, in marriage to the king's son. The wedding will be held in Aulis before the departure of the Achaean fleet.

"After the wedding, Achilles can stay with his young wife in Phthia or, if he wishes, join the campaign at a later date. But by then, the war most likely will be over. Thus, the desire of King Peleus will be fulfilled. The king of Mycenae expects in response that the Phthian army, led by Phoenix, will join the campaign, and King Peleus will call on all Thessalian leaders to march on Troy.

"Phoenix considered my words for a long time. Finally, he said that he himself would meet with King Peleus and convey Agamemnon's proposal. Until an agreement is reached, this matter is best kept secret. He invited me to wait for his return at his house.

"The sun barely had time to set when Phoenix returned from the royal halls. He said that King Peleus wanted the envoy of King Agamemnon to appear before him tomorrow. Phoenix also said that the king intended to discuss the proposal of the Mycenaean ruler with his son. He invited me to spend the night at his house, and after dinner, I went to bed.

"In the morning, Phoenix went to the palace, saying that he would send a servant for me. His messenger came in late afternoon. I arrived at the palace and was shown into a small room next to the throne hall. Peleus and Phoenix were waiting for me. After listening to my greeting, the king was silent for a long time. Finally, he spoke. His voice was quiet and calm.

"'Worthy Calchas,' said the king, 'I am thankful to the lord of Mycenae for his proposal. To marry the daughter of King Agamemnon is a great honor. But by the will of the gods, my son already has a wife. He found her on Skyros. This is the daughter of King Lycomedes, Deidamia. Not so long ago, Deidamia gave birth to Achilles's son. He was named Pyrrhus.

"'I'm sorry, but the wedding will not take place. But most of all, I suffer because my son is about to sail to Aulis and join the Achaean campaign against Troy. You know about the prophecy given to Achilles. My wife believed in it, and so do I. I am ready to do everything to avert this prophecy. By my request, priests asked the oracle whether it was possible to change the fate of Achilles. An answer was given that Artemis could delay or prevent his death. To achieve this, a descendant of the king should be sacrificed to the goddess.

"'Tell King Agamemnon that he must make sure that Achilles will not participate in the campaign, or he should sacrifice his daughter to farsighted Artemis. Listen carefully, priest. You yourself must announce to Achaeans that Iphigenia must be sacrificed to Artemis for the victory in the campaign against Troy. Achilles and the Myrmidon army will arrive in Aulis after the sacrifice. Otherwise, I will declare that the march to Troy is against to the will of Artemis.

"'You should tell King Agamemnon that there are other gods who do not favor his campaign. After all, Prince Paris would never have kidnapped Helen if he had not been indulged by some god or goddess. Let the king of Mycenae know that detachments of Protesilaus and Philoctetes will not act against the will of Artemis and will not come to Aulis. And after them, the warriors from all over Thessaly will abandon the campaign. I will also address the Locrians, Aetolians, and Boeotians. Tell King Agamemnon that if he doesn't want to lose half of his army before the beginning of the war, he must listen to my words.'

"With these words, King Peleus got up and left the room. After the king left, I asked Phoenix why he did not tell me that Achilles had a wife and a son. 'May the gods punish me if I'm lying,' he replied, 'but to this day, neither the king nor I knew that Achilles has a wife. There were rumors that he has a girlfriend on Skyros, but we did not know that Achilles married the daughter of Lycomedes, and she had already given birth to a son. Achilles himself had never spoken of this before, and for the king, this was a great surprise.

"'Believe me, Calchas, King Peleus reacted well to the proposal of the lord of Mycenae. He wanted to convince Achilles to marry Iphigenia. This morning, he called his son to talk. Peleus suggested that before going to Ilion, Achilles should marry and leave a descendant, the heir to the Phthian throne. Then Achilles told that he already has a wife.

"'This is Deidamia, the daughter of King Lycomedes, and she recently gave birth to his son and legitimate heir, Pyrrhus. He told the king that the child was growing strong and healthy. Achilles promised to bring him to see his grandfather as soon as he returns from Troy.

"'Believe me, worthy Calchas, to this day, King Peleus did not know that Achilles had married the daughter of Lycomedes. The king said to his son that he approves his marriage and wishes to see Achilles's wife and son as soon as possible. After Achilles left, the king noticed that the lord of Skyros has managed to benefit from any situation, but what's done is done. Achilles has a wife and a son. Phoenix added that the king of Phthia intends to wait for news of the sacrifice. Only then will Achilles's fleet sail to Aulis. At the same time, the king will send messengers to the Thessalian leaders and will announce his attitude to the march on Troy.'

"Saying goodbye to Phoenix, I went to the harbor and boarded Phrontis's ship. We put out to sea immediately."

Calchas was silent for a while, but seeing that the king did not respond, he continued.

"I believe that Peleus did not know about the marriage until he began to persuade his son to take a wife. Perhaps Achilles's marriage has been arranged with the participation of some god. Artemis herself might have listened to the prayers of Peleus and sent him a grandson."

"Are you saying that Artemis gave Peleus a grandson and demands a sacrifice for it?" Menelaus interrupted. "Yet I believe that this is not Artemis. Bastard Lycomedes brought Achilles together with his daughter in order to intermarry with the mighty Phthian ruler. How else could he count on such a great game? And of course, he was in no hurry to inform Peleus about this marriage until the heir appeared.

"Now I understand why he did not try to obstruct when Nestor and Odysseus came to see Achilles. After all, it is preferable for him that Achilles himself updates Peleus about his new family. However, Achilles was in no hurry to tell his father. Apparently, he was afraid of his anger. Only a direct marriage proposal forced him to reveal his secret. He wanted to convince his father that he already has an heir and can go on a campaign. But instead, he convinced Peleus that the campaign must be stopped at any cost."

Agamemnon remained silent. Menelaus fell silent too, not knowing what to say. He couldn't talk about sacrificing Agamemnon's daughter. But it seemed impossible to him to agree to the loss of half of the Achaean army, if not more. If the Thessalian and Locrians leaders refuse to march, who else can follow their steps? Such a start did not promise success.

The pause was interrupted by the priest.

"Do not blame me, lord of Mycenae. No one could have foreseen the secret marriage of Achilles. But I believe that the gods approve the march on Troy no matter what the king of Phthia is saying. The situation with the threats of Peleus will be resolved by the will of the almighty Zeus.

"We mistakenly tried to help Peleus and keep Achilles out of the fight. But Zeus's providence prevailed. The prophecy of Aeacus is coming true, and his descendants will come to Ilion for the second time. They will come along with the mighty Achaean army, and the city of Priam will fall."

Agamemnon broke his long silence.

"I do not hold you responsible for the actions of Peleus, but how could you fail to see the will of gods? Although Father used to say that it is not given to a mortal to comprehend divine providence. One may say that your advice expressed the will of the deity. After all, nothing can prevent Achilles now from participating in the campaign.

"Even if Peleus does not give his Myrmidons, Achilles will join as a regular warrior. However, I think Peleus will not allow his son to go to Troy without an army. But what do we do now? Your previous advice to marry Iphigenia to Achilles did not go well, and meanwhile, the courier arrived and reported that Iphigenia had already set off from Mycenae and would be in Aulis in two days. She hopes to marry the best Achaean warrior, and instead, she may be sacrificed to the goddess-huntress, the same Artemis who took the lives of all of Pelops's nieces.

"Go, Calchas. Rest after the trip, and then make sacrifices to the gods. Pray to the lord of mortals and immortals, Zeus, to help us as he helped our grandfather, the great Pelops."

CHAPTER 5

DISCUSSION OF PELEUS'S TERMS

The next morning, Menelaus was awakened by a messenger who brought an invitation from the lord of Mycenae. The sun had barely risen over Euboea when Menelaus approached the royal tent. Calchas was waiting for him at the entrance.

"I called you to tell about the vision that appeared to me in the morning," Agamemnon said instead of a greeting. "In the dream, I saw Nestor. He leaned towards me and said the following: I will go to Phthia so that Peleus, son of Aeacus, will hear what he wants to hear and Agamemnon, son of Atreus, will see what he wants to see. After these words, the vision dissipated, and I woke up. Leaving the tent, I met a messenger who reported that the ships of Nestor and Odysseus had arrived in Aulis the previous evening. Wise Calchas, tell me how to understand my dream."

After listening to the king, the priest plunged into thought.

Without waiting for his answer, Menelaus said, "I also thought this night how to respond to the lord of Phthia. The arrival of Nestor and Odysseus is a good sign. No wonder the vision appeared to you. We must convince Nestor to go to Phthia. I am sure that together, Nestor and Peleus will be able to dissuade Achilles from participating in the campaign. They will tell him that there will be no fight with the Trojans, and therefore, there is no need for him to sail back and forth in vain.

"King Priam is a wise ruler. He will not put in danger his city and destroy his subjects. When the lord of Troy sees how huge the Achaean army is, he will give up both Helen and the treasures without a war. Peleus is personally acquainted with Priam and knows that the king of Troy is more inclined to negotiations than to battle, especially when the risk of losing his kingdom is so great. And in order to make Achilles more cooperative, Peleus can give up the Phthian throne.

"After all, Achilles already has a wife and an heir. He will go to Skyros for his family, and upon return, he will ascend the throne. Having reigned in Phthia, Achilles will be so busy that he will forget about Ilion. And finally, Nestor and Phoenix can promise the new lord of Phthia to send a messenger for him if King Priam will choose the war, and Trojans will begin to fight Achaeans. Surely two famous commanders will be able to convince one young warrior."

"Your plan is excellent, Menelaus," replied Agamemnon. "But I'm not sure whether the king of Pylos will agree to it. Do you remember, he told how his father, King Neleus, tried to forbid him to join the battle with the army of King Augeas? Neleus even hid his chariot, but this did not stop Nestor. And now Nestor, a renowned and highly experienced warrior, goes on a campaign with his two sons.

"It will not be easy to explain to him why, having first convinced Achilles to join the campaign, he must now persuade him to stay at home. Even if the lord of Pylos will agree, would he act with the same zeal as before? Even more doubtful is the very possibility of dissuading Achilles. I am sure the king of Phthia has already tried and used all possible arguments. Peleus could offer the throne to Achilles, but this did not deter him from the intention to participate in the campaign."

"Lord of Mycenae," Calchas said, entering the conversation, "warrior-goddess Athena undoubtedly appeared to you in the form of Nestor and announced that King Peleus should hear what he wants to hear. I will try to interpret the will of the goddess.

"As Menelaus said, the illustrious Nestor was undoubtedly chosen by the daughter of the lord of heaven to be your messenger. We should announce to Nestor and all Achaean leaders that for a successful voyage to Ilion and victory over Priam, it is necessary to sacrifice to Artemis the daughter of the leader of the campaign. The sacrifice must take place in the presence of all participants in the campaign.

"Let Nestor go to Phthia and inform Peleus, his son, and other Thessalian leaders that the daughter of King Agamemnon must be sacrificed to Artemis before the fleet leaves Aulis. The leader of the Achaean army is waiting for Achilles and the rest of the Thessalian leaders so that they can participate in the sacrifice.

"Lord Agamemnon, ask Nestor not to depart from Phthia until the ships of Achilles and his troops leave for Aulis. Let him make sure that King Peleus will not send his Myrmidons without his son, and the brave Achilles will not set out on his own without an army. As soon as Achilles goes to sea, King Peleus will do his best so that all Thessalian leaders will follow him. Then you will see the Thessalian fleet in Aulis, and the army will have enough power to conquer both Troy and Mysia.

"In the meantime, send Talthybios to Delphi to ask the oracle what kind of sacrifice will persuade the goddess of fast arrows, Artemis, to grant to Achaeans fair wind on the way to Troy."

The conversation with Nestor was brief. Having learned about the sacrifice, the lord of Pylos agreed to go to Phthia, taking Odysseus as a companion. He would notify Peleus, Achilles, and the other Thessalian leaders about the sacrifice to Artemis and the goddess's demand that all participants in the campaign be present at the ritual. The ship with the embassy to Phthia left the next morning.

CHAPTER 6

REPLY OF ODYSSEUS

After five days, Nestor and Odysseus returned to Aulis. Agamemnon, Menelaus, and Calchas were waiting in the tent for the envoys. After greetings, the lord of Mycenae invited Nestor to tell about the negotiations with King Peleus.

"Noble leaders of the Achaeans, I will tell everything as it is about the meeting with King Peleus and his son Achilles," Nestor began. "Having disembarked at Phthia, we reached the palace of Peleus and stopped at the gate to inspect the vast courtyard where the preparations for the sacrifice were taking place. Achilles spotted us first. He rushed to us, greeted us, invited us inside, and seated us in places of honor for the guests.

"Associates of the lord of Phthia had gathered in the courtyard. There were Menoetius, son of Actor, his son Patroclus, Phoenix, son of Amyntor, Bor, the son-in-law of Peleus, and other leaders. Also, we saw Automedon, the charioteer of Achilles, whom we met on Skyros. King Peleus sacrificed the thighs of an ox to the lord of mortals and immortals, Zeus. After the sacrifice, everyone was invited to eat.

"When the feast was coming to an end, Odysseus and I approached Peleus and informed him that we had arrived from Aulis with a message from the leader of the Achaeans, Agamemnon. The king replied that he was ready to listen to us.

"I told the king that the Achaean army was ready to march on Troy. The gods indicated to King Agamemnon that for the success of the campaign, he must sacrifice his daughter to the farsighted Artemis. The sacrifice must take place in the presence of all participants in the campaign. Only then will the march be successful.

"God-equal Achilles expressed a desire to join the Achaean army when we visited him on Skyros. Now his arrival in Aulis cannot be delayed. Odysseus and I are sent to notify the Thessalian leaders who are participating in the campaign that they must arrive at Aulis without delay. King Agamemnon asked us to visit the lord of Phthia first of all, as the most famous and influential Thessalian leader. Then we must notify Protesilaus, Philoctetes, and others.

"The lord of Phthia listened to me and, after long silence, turned to Odysseus. 'Wise Odysseus, son of Laertes, they say that you are similar in the strength of mind to your grandfather, Autolycus, and even to famous Sisyphus himself. I want to hear your advice.

"'A prophecy was given to my wife long ago that Achilles was destined to gain great glory on the battlefield, but his inevitable fate would also overtake him there. I do not want to lose my son. Achilles is young and ardent. He wholeheartedly strives to go to Troy with King Agamemnon. You recently had your first child. Swear on his life to tell the truth. What would you do in my place?'

"Worthy Odysseus answered the lord of Phthia in the following way: 'God-equal Peleus, I swear by the life of my only son, everything I will tell is true. You say that Achilles is destined to die on the battlefield. But joining the march on Troy does not mean taking part in the battle. The goal of the Achaean campaign is not war with the Trojan state but the return of Helen and stolen treasures.

"'King Agamemnon said that if we bring an army of incomparable power under the walls of Ilion, King Priam will recognize that Trojans cannot withstand the Achaean might and will not start a war. If Trojans will see the power of the Achaean army, they will return Helen and the trophies to avoid the fight. Wise Nestor and myself agree that the bloodshed can be avoided.

"'You know the king of Ilion better than anyone. He has always been a peaceful ruler. Moreover, he is not too young. They say that the king is over seventy. Seeing the great power of the Achaean army, Priam more likely will start negotiations and will return Helen and a rich ransom in exchange for the safety of his kingdom. With such an outcome, valiant Achilles will not have to take part in the battles, and the prophecy will not come true, because there will be no battlefield. Isn't that what you want?'

"'I want to preserve the life of my only son,' replied King Peleus. 'Tell me if I should believe in the prophecy.' Odysseus paused and continued. 'Lord of Phthia, let me tell you about my attitude to the prophecies. I was born and raised on Ithaca. Everyone on Ithaca knows the venerable Halitherses, son of Mastor. He is skilled in divination by the flight of birds and prophesies the future. My father, Laertes, son of Arcesius, trusts his predictions like you trust the prophecy given to your wife.

"'One day, I asked if there is a reason in his confidence in Halitherses. Father told me this story. Many years ago, Laertes was considering a campaign against Nericum, a well-fortified, wealthy city on the Thesprotian coast. He had already tried to take the city before, although without success. However, at this time, Halitherses predicted to my father that if he attacks Nericum again, the campaign would be successful, and the city would be taken.

"'Following the prophecy, Father equipped ships, gathered soldiers from Ithaca, Cephallenia, and other islands, and set out. Halitherses's prediction came true. Father returned with huge booty. Since then, he said that Halitherses knew the future as the past.

"'But wise Mentor, my father's adviser, told me that Halitherses had been to Thesprotia before and visited Nericum. He knew that although the fortress walls could protect against pirates, the city did not have sufficient supplies and was not equipped for a long defense. Therefore, Halitherses advised my father to take Nericum under siege from the land and from the sea and wait until the defenders surrendered or lost the ability to resist. Father did so and captured the city.

"'Few days ago, before sailing to Aulis, I asked Halitherses whether the campaign would be victorious. Instead of answering, he inquired what I considered a success. I replied that the campaign would be successful if we managed to free Helen and return home with rich trophies. After listening to me, the seer asked when

I expected to return. I said that by autumn or, if the war dragged on, next summer.

"'And would you, son of Laertes, consider the campaign successful if you return no earlier than twenty years? You will arrive at your homeland all by yourself, and after landing, you will meet no one who would recognize you.' This is word for word how Halitherses answered me. This was his prophecy. Tell me, lord of Phthia, would I leave my native Ithaca, my father and mother, would I leave my young wife and newborn son if I believed in prophecies?"

ABOUT THE AUTHOR

Alexander Korneyev was educated and employed as a health care professional and research scientist. His curiosity in ancient history, which initiated with *Iliad*, led to his participation in an archaeological excavation, visiting the sites of Bronze Age civilizations in Greece and Turkey and literature studies.